Anne Bennett was born in a back-to-back house in the Horsefair district of Birmingham. The daughter of Roman Catholic, Irish immigrants, she grew up in a tight-knit community where she was taught to be proud of her heritage.

She considers herself to be an Irish Brummie and feels therefore that she has a foot in both cultures. She has four children and four grandchildren. For many years she taught in schools to the north of Birmingham.

An accident put paid to her teaching career and, after moving to North Wales, Anne turned to the other great love of her life and began to write seriously. *Mother's Only Child* is her ninth novel. In 2006, after sixteen years in a wheelchair, Anne began to walk again.

Visit www.AuthorTracker.co.uk for exclusive updates on Anne Bennett.

By the same author

ANNE BENNETT

Mother's Only Child

HARPER

This novel is a work of fiction. The names, characters and incidents described in it are the work of the author's imagination. Any resemblance to actual persons, living or dead, events or localities is entirely coincidental.

HarperCollins*Publishers*
77–85 Fulham Palace Road,
Hammersmith, London W6 8JB

www.harpercollins.co.uk

A Paperback Original 2006
1

A catalogue record for this book
is available from the British Library

ISBN 978 0 00 780596 9

Typeset in Sabon by Palimpsest Book Production Limited,
Polmont, Stirlingshire

Printed and bound in Great Britain by
Clays Ltd, St Ives plc

To my youngest daughter Tamsin, with all my love

ACKNOWLEDGEMENTS

This book was written in memory of my uncle Willie MacDonald who actually did own a boatyard in Greencastle at the time in which this is set, though the family lived in Moville, the next village. He also worked for the military in a self-employed capacity in the docks in Derry once the war began and did have a accident such as I describe and the search, when it was realised he was missing, was hampered by the blackout, possibly increasing the severity of his injuries. He was paralysed from the waist down ever after and received no compensation, just like Sam Foley, but there the similarity ended.

My cousin, Maura MacDonald–Reynolds, who filled me in on parts of the story on which I was hazy, was just a child when these things happened, not sixteen as my Maria. Years later, a teacher spotted Maura's talent in dressmaking and wanted her to try for a scholarship in Dress and Fabric Design to the prestigious Grafton Academy in Dublin and though she was sure Maura would gain a place, there was no money to enable her even to try. I am indebted to my cousin for giving me the nub of this story. The rest is completely fabricated.

For the rest of the research, I used the internet extensively and the Palmer family of Moville run a wonderful website of 'Moville. Then and Now' with many photographs. The Londonderry and Lough Swilley Railway Company supplied old timetables, maps and general information, although a gentleman called Charles Friel also helped with transport links. Thank you, Charles.

However, reference books too are often invaluable. For example, Evelyn Ruddy wrote a book about the remoteness of life on Innishowen, calling it *Rekindling a Dying Heritage*, and a man known as John McLaughlin wrote *Carrowmenagh*, which is a village not that far away from Greencastle and Moville. Then there was the book *Our Town* by Naoi nGiallach about Letterkenny and the hinterland, and another, *Atlantic Memorial. The Foyle and Western Approaches 1939–1945*, was written as a souvenir catalogue by a team of people, and, as you might imagine, documents the story of Derry through the war years. I am so grateful to all these people.

For the Birmingham links, I used the *Golden Years Of Brum*, which is part of the 'Memories' series published by True North, as well as, of course, the works of Carl Chinn, who wrote, among many others, *Best of Brum* and *Our Brum*, and the newspaper extracts he compiles detailing people's memories, together with *The Story of Erdington* by Douglas V. Jones, helped me enormously.

Altogether, though the war is well-documented, the years that followed are not and to write about this accurately, I bought *London in the Post-War Years*.

I couldn't find anything similar relating to Birmingham, so maybe that is another one that Carl could do when he has the time. I also bought *The 50s and 60s. The Best of Times* to help my readers relate to and possibly remember that era.

Erdington was easier, for I remember myself how it was, though Erdington Historical Society were very helpful with specific points. Maria's house on the Pype Hayes Estate was the one allocated to our family when we were re-housed from our back-to-back in 1956; I went to the Abbey School, shopped in Erdington Village, swam in the swimming pool and borrowed books from the library. Nock's Brickyard on Holly Lane really did exist and so did Hollyfield's Sports Ground which the gardens on one side of Westmead Crescent used to run right up to.

My family are often at the forefront of my mind when I write. First and foremost is my husband Denis, who I love very much, his grey hair evidence of the hard life I give him. Then there are our three daughters and one son, son- and daughter-in-law, and my four adorable grandchildren, who are all so special to me. However, I cannot talk of the family without including Denis's mother Nancy, who died on 29 January 2005. She has often been mentioned in the acknowledgements for the help she has given me. She was a lovely woman, full of fun, and usually had a smile on her face. I feel it was a privilege to know her, and she is and will be missed for some time.

My very good friend Judith Kendall has a special place in my life and my heart. Thanks, Judith, for all you do.

However, without the tremendous team at HarperCollins, I doubt my books would ever reach bookshelves anywhere. I hope you realise how much I appreciate all you do and immense thanks must go first to my wonderful editor, Susan Opie. Maxine Hitchcock no longer does my books, but I still consider her very important and not least for the fact that she is an excellent champagne cocktail drinking partner. Hey! A person could do worse. It's a very important job. Ingrid Gegner, my marvellous publicist, is in a class of her own. She works incredibly hard and added to that, she is so lovely as well. Thanks, Ingrid, and thanks also to Peter Hawtin, who started the ball rolling and Judith Evans, now at Birmingham Airport bookshops, who was, and still is, so complimentary about my books.

Special thanks too must go to my superb and intrepid agent, Judith Murdoch, another whom I appreciate so much, who also always works so hard for me.

Last, but by no means least, extra and heartfelt thanks must go to you, the readers, the fantastic members of the public who not only buy and read the books but often take the time to write or e-mail to tell me how much you enjoy them. Without all of you, there would be no point to any of it.

So, thanks, thanks and once again thanks to each and every one of you.

CHAPTER ONE

Maria Foley almost ran across The Square that day in late July 1941. The faint summer breeze riffled through her long wavy hair, tied back loosely with a ribbon the same green as her eyes. Bella McFee, catching sight of the girl, stepped out of the post office-cum-grocery shop when she saw the envelope in Maria's hand.

'It's come then?'

'Aye,' Maria said. She tried to keep the elation out of her voice. 'I've passed.'

She saw Bella's lips purse in disapproval and, for a moment, Maria was resentful. She'd worked for Bella in the shop for two years. Couldn't she just say she was the tiniest bit pleased? Congratulate her even?

Her mother, Sarah, had said the right words – 'Congratulations. You've done well' – but in a flat, expressionless and totally insincere tone. However, what Bella did say was, 'I'm away to see your mother. She'll likely be feeling low after this. Mammy will mind the shop. And where are you off to in such a tear? You're not due in till nine.'

'The boatyard,' Maria said. 'I want to see Willie.'

1

'Oh, he'd like to know right enough,' Bella said. 'But you, Maria, aren't you the tiniest bit ashamed, wanting to go to some fancy academy in Dublin just now, when you could be a help and support to your mother? Have you no thought for her, and you an only one too?'

Immediately, guilt settled between Maria's shoulder blades. It isn't my fault I'm the only one, she wanted to cry. That was the main problem, of course. If her mother had had a houseful of children, she could have taken pride in the fact that her eldest daughter had won a scholarship to the Grafton Academy in Dublin to study Dress and Fabric Design for two years.

But Sarah's fall down the stairs when Maria had been just eighteen months old had killed the child she was carrying and assured there would be no more either. It had also, so it was said, given her 'bad nerves'. Maria hadn't known what 'bad nerves' were then, of course, although she knew her father was never willing to upset her mother and strongly discouraged Maria from saying or doing anything that might disturb her at all. She was well aware that the news that morning would have disturbed her greatly, and yet she couldn't help being pleased and, yes, proud of herself. She knew Willie would congratulate her warmly and, oh God, how she needed someone on her side for once.

'Mammy should never have let me go in for the exam if she can't take any joy in the fact that I have passed it,' Maria said.

'You don't understand anything yet, girl,' Bella said sharply.

Maria flushed at the sharp tone and then tossed her

2

head a little defiantly and said, 'I have to go, or I'll be late getting to the shop.'

Before Bella could say another word, Maria gave her a desultory wave and ran over the green to the coastal path, which ran to Greencastle, the next village up Inishowen Peninsular. It was the path her father used to take every day bar Sunday, when he'd owned a boatyard in the small village. Now he worked at the Derry docks, and Willie Brannigan was put in charge of the Greencastle boatyard. He'd known Maria since the day of her birth and she knew he'd wish her well.

She paused on the banks of Lough Foyle, the sun, warm on her back from a cloudless sky, glittering on the water. Well, what could be seen of the water. The lough was so filled with naval craft, she could barely see Milligan's Point on the further side, the side the British still owned. She couldn't see the airports at Limavady and Eglinton either, but she knew they were there. It was a fine sight to see the aircraft flying above the flotilla of naval vessels on convoy duty. Her father said they were more effective at sinking German U-boats than the ships. The British-owned six counties had been dragged into the war along with Britain, but the Free State, Maria's side of the border, had declared itself neutral and Maria knew there were soldiers from the Irish Army stationed at Buncrana, which was the other side of the peninsular, to try to ensure the Germans respected that neutrality

She gave a sigh and made her way to the boatyard. For a moment she wished Greg Hopkins was just a couple of miles away on his father's farm and she could rush to him with her news, for he was another one who believed she was doing the right thing. He was in the army now and, though she was proud of him, she missed him sorely. Letters couldn't make up for his absence.

It was strange how she and Greg had always been such friends, because Greg hadn't been born in Inishowen at all, but in Birmingham, England, where his father came from, though his mother was from Moville.

The whole family had arrived in 1934 when Greg's mother inherited a farm from an uncle. Maria had only been nine, and Greg thirteen, but she remembered the lost and unhappy boy he was then, who made no effort to make friends. He was like a fish out of water, her mother would say.

'But, why come here?' Maria had asked him one day, when he had been there more than a year and was ready to leave school. 'It seems such an odd thing to do, when you were not born and bred for it.'

Greg had shrugged. 'Dad hadn't worked for two years when we came here. He wasn't the only one, or owt. Many like him were hit by the slump. We were on our beam ends, nearly starving, and when we got the news about the farm out of blue, Dad said it was like a miracle. He's pulled the farm round and it's doing all right. At least we all get enough to eat.'

'Do you like farm work?'

'I hate it,' Greg had said fiercely. 'And I hate this little village – in fact, the whole of Inishowen – and one day I'll go back to Birmingham. I know I'll have to wait a while; Phil is only just ten, Billy two years younger still – the girls don't count – and they wouldn't be able to be much of a hand to our dad. Anyway, there's no work for anyone much in Birmingham at the moment, but I don't intend to stop here all the days of my life.'

But, while Greg had waited, he found Maria to be a fine distraction, especially as she grew and began attending the socials held for the young people at the church. There he danced with her many times, often walked her home and sought her company after Mass.

'You have an admirer,' Sarah said. She knew nothing of Greg's restlessness. All she saw was that Greg was the eldest son and set to inherit the farm, and the family were respectable and God-fearing. If her daughter was to marry Greg Hopkins, Maria would live not far from her parents at all, and that would fulfil Sarah's dream.

Maria wasn't ready for any sort of relationship. 'Don't be silly, Mammy, he's just being kind,' she said. 'He's the same with everyone.'

That morning, though, she so wished he was there to tell her news to.

There was another person she wished was still in Moville. Philomena Clarke had been the tutor at the evening classes for dressmaking who had recognised Maria's quite exceptional talent and knew that she had the chance of winning a scholarship to the Academy. They had gone together to the college in Derry for Maria to take the exam in May, and she had even promised she would travel down to Dublin with her and settle her in.

However, life had a hammer blow waiting to hit Philomena, for the day after the exam she had a telegram from New York from the husband of her twin sister, who had been badly injured in a car accident and was asking for her. Philomena was gone within days and a little after she had left, Maria had a letter from her.

Her sister had died, leaving the husband distraught, and she had decided to stay to help him rear his three small children, who were devastated and traumatised by the tragedy.

Maria was touched that even in the middle of that appalling upheaval and upset, while still grieving for her sister, she still had a thought in her head for Maria.

'*Please write and tell me as soon as you get news from the college,*' she had pleaded in her first letter to Maria. '*I will be on tenterhooks until I hear from you.*'

Maria would write to both Greg and Philomena that very night, she decided, and she walked on, composing the letters in her head as she went.

Bella found Sarah in the scullery, washing the breakfast dishes, her red-rimmed eyes betraying the tears she'd shed. Visibly she tried to take a grip on herself when she saw Bella.

'Shall I make a cup of tea?' she said. 'Have you time?'

'Aye, Mammy's seeing to the place and Maria will be there at nine.'

'Maria!' Sarah said plaintively. 'What will I do when she leaves, Bella? I'll be destroyed.'

'No, you won't!' Bella said emphatically. 'I'll see you're not.'

Bella remembered the time Sam Foley had brought his young wife back into the village to live. She'd been only young herself then, and, though married for eight years, she was still childless. Her frustrated maternal instinct was stirred by Sarah, who was only seventeen and looked such a frail and delicate wee thing, with her blonde hair and big blue eyes. The two became good friends.

'Tom Tall and Butter Ball,' Bella used to call the two of them, for though Sarah wasn't that tall, her slenderness made her appear so. Bella was, like her mother, under five foot and 'as wide and she was high', she was fond of saying. That wasn't strictly speaking true, but she was plump and her mother, Dora Carmody, stouter still. Everything about them was round, but their faces were open and friendly and their brown eyes kindly looking. Bella had once had dark blonde hair, but now it was as grey as her mother's and, like hers, fastened into a bun.

Sam Foley, being the third son, had never thought to inherit the boatyard in Greencastle, nor the family house in nearby Moville. Knowing there would be no opening for him in the family business, his father had apprenticed him to a carpenter friend, who ran his business from a small town called Belleek, in the neighbouring county of Fermanagh, when Sam had been twelve years old.

Sarah Tierney's family lived not far from the village, on a thriving farm in Derrygonnelly on the banks of the huge Lough Erne, and Sarah often shopped in Belleek with her sisters, Peggy and Mary.

There she met and fell in love with Sam, and he with her. No obstacles were put in the way of her marrying him, for everyone liked the man and knew he was set to inherit the carpentry business, so it was generally thought that Sarah had done well for herself.

Sam's family had come down for the wedding, and there Sam's two brothers sought him out and told him they were off to seek their fortune in America as soon as it could be arranged. The boatyard was all his if he wanted it.

Sam wasn't keen to go back and knew Sarah would be unhappy living so far away from her people, but he also knew his father couldn't run the place alone. His only option was to return.

The only sweetener to that very bitter pill for Sarah was the house Sam inherited along with the boatyard. It was a fine, solid house just off The Square in Moville. It had two storeys, three bedrooms, and was built of stone with a slate roof. 'A family house,' Sam's father had said. 'Me and your mother will be fine and dandy in the wee cottage in Greencastle by the boatyard.'

'I mind the day Sam's brothers left as if it were yesterday,' Sarah said to Bella as they drank their tea. 'We hadn't been in Moville more than a day or so and we went down to the pier to see them off. Sam had told me that the liners crossing the Atlantic had to be moored out in the deeper waters of Lough Foyle. Passengers were taken out to the ships in small tenders from Moville Pier. There was always a collection of people waiting and that day was no different.

'Sam's brothers seemed sorrowful yet, for all their sadness at the parting, they still left. When they climbed into that boat, Sam's mother's eyes were so bleak and bereft, I could hardly bear to look at her. The father was holding her fast, or I think she may have thrown herself into the boat after her sons. We waited at the pier side until we saw the small boat bump alongside the liner. The boys gave one last wave and we turned for home. Sam's mother was crying gulping sobs of such sadness I felt my heart turn over. I thought I understood how she was feeling; I remember thinking I'd die if one of mine was to go such a distance away.'

She sighed and went on, 'I tell you, Bella, children would tear the very heart out of you.'

However, more tragedy was to hit Sarah. She'd been married just six months when her mother and sisters, Peggy and Mary, took sick with TB. They were all dead before October drew to a close, before Sarah had been able to arrange to go and see them. She'd not even had the chance to bid them goodbye and she spoke of this now to Bella.

'D'you mind that time?'

Bella remembered it well. Sarah's grief had been so deep and profound, Sam had worried for her sanity. They travelled down for the funerals. Seeing everyone there so mournful and sorrow-laden had made Sarah worse.

'Daddy was so sad it near broke my heart to see him,' Sarah said to Bella. 'He didn't seem to see anything around him and it was up to my brother Sean to keep the farm ticking over.'

It was arranged that a widowed aunt called Agatha, whose children were grown and married, would see to things in the house and Sam and Sarah returned to Moville.

'I never thought I'd be happy again in the whole of my life,' Maria reminded Bella. 'And then I found I was expecting. A little life would be dependent on me, something to go on for.' She grasped Bella's hand and went on, 'You showed what a true friend you were then, for you showed not a trace of envy and yet I know how you had always longed for a child of your own.'

That brought the tears to Bella's own eyes, for it was a burden she carried with her always.

'When Maria was born, in 1925, I thought her the most beautiful baby in all the world,' Sarah said, 'and for sixteen years she has been at the forefront of my mind all the time. I love her so much, Bella, and I really can't bear the pain of losing her. Once Maria leaves this village I know she will never come back to live.'

'You will get through this, you know,' Bella said. 'It will take time, but it will get easier. I thought when my man died I'd never recover from it.'

'That was a tragic time, right enough,' Sarah agreed. It had been a tragic time for both of them. Sarah had just has the disastrous fall that rendered her sterile and was in the hospital. Bella was looking after the toddling Maria, when her husband, a fine, strapping man, who'd never had a day's illness in his life, suddenly keeled over as he was getting up from his dinner, and was dead before he reached the floor.

'We supported each other then,' Bella said.

'Aye, and wasn't it wee Maria who was the salvation of us both?'

'She was indeed,' Bella agreed. 'Then Mammy said she couldn't manage the shop on her own and asked me in with her. I don't know whether she really couldn't manage, or did it for me, but I know the occupation of it was a good thing.'

'I know it,' Sarah said. 'But what occupation could I take up that will chase the heartache from me?'

Bella had no answer to this and Sarah went on, 'I knew that Maria was good at sewing and all. I mean, I taught her to sew, darn, embroider, that sort of thing, and in time she was better than me – far neater, and faster too. I knew she had an eye for colour, the things that go together. Whenever we went in the draper's shops in Derry, she'd be fascinated by the array of fabrics. She'd feel them between her fingers and be amazed by the different things you could sew on to decorate clothes. She'd prowl around the haberdashery counter like another child might do around a cake shop.

'I took it as a good, wifely attribute, especially when she mastered that old treadle machine. I told her she'd be a catch for any man, for you know she could make something out of nothing, and I encouraged her to go to evening classes for dressmaking. People say you can't make a silk purse out of sow's ear – well, I think Maria probably could.

'She's a tidy cook too – we all know the way to a man's heart is through his stomach – and she's helped me with the laundry this past year or so. She can poss the clothes, starch and iron with the best of them.'

She looked at Bella with mournful eyes and said, 'She'll make a good wife for someone in a year or two, when she is fully grown. That's what I want for her – to marry a boy here so I can still see her and help her rear any children she might have. It's all I've wanted since the first moment I held her in my arms, and if it hadn't been for this damned war it would have happened like that. Whatever Philomena Clarke wanted, without the war, Maria going to the Academy would have been impossible.'

Bella knew that was true. By the time Maria finally left school at Easter 1939, everyone knew Britain, and therefore Derry and the other counties across the Foyle, was perched on the brink of war, despite Chamberlain's claim that there'd be 'peace for our time', the previous September.

As soon as Easter was over, Maria had got a job in the shop with Bella and her mother, Dora, and began at her evening classes, but wasn't in the house when Philomena went to see her mother and told her about the Grafton Academy in Dublin where the gifted Maria could learn Dress and Fabric Design, which would fit her for a fine and well-paid job in a Dublin fashion house later. 'I am sure she will win a scholarship,' she'd said. 'The girl has an amazing talent. I've never seen or taught someone so good before.'

'But she's so young,' Sarah had said. 'Little more than a child.'

'We're not talking about now,' Miss Clarke said gently. 'But of two years' time. Maria will be sixteen then.'

'But where would she stay?'

'Well,' Philomena said, 'I have been making enquiries and the college has a hostel nearby. I believe the rates are very reasonable.'

And there the discussion had ended, for times had been hard for years. Often Sam had repaired a boat for a neighbour, knowing that if he insisted on payment the man and his wife and children would not eat. How could he do that? Sometimes he took his payment in fish, sometimes in instalments, and sometimes he'd get nothing at all. He was glad his parents, who'd died within a month of one another in 1935, were no longer there to provide for from a yard that paid so little. In those lean pre-war years Sam often thanked God that he had just the one child to rear, though he would have loved a son.

When England finally made the declaration of war with Germany in the autumn of 1939, life became harder still. There was no longer any fishing at all, for Lough Foyle was commandeered by the navy, and so were the docks in Derry, which were renamed HMS *Ferret*. Lough Foyle was quickly filled with naval warships, destroyers, frigates, corvettes and converted trawlers.

The open sea, full of mines and German submarines, was no place for fishermen either, so they hung up their nets and many younger men enlisted in the armed forces, despite the neutrality pact.

Sam too had little work, although there was a small fishing fleet still operating in Lough Swilly on the other side of the peninsular. There he was able to pick up a bit of repair and maintenance work. Sometimes, though, he had so little to bring home at the end of the week, he was ashamed.

Many of the women took themselves off to Derry to work in the shirt factories, most now converted to making uniforms for the armed forces. In a good few homes it was the women who put the food on the table. Sam knew himself how it cut into a man's pride to see his wife provide for the family while he was idle. He was embarrassed that he was often dependent on the money that Maria would tip up on the table every Friday evening and the big bag of groceries that Bella would pack for her. They got by, like many others, but there was no money to spare and certainly none to send a daughter off to Dublin to train in some fancy academy. Sarah told Philomena Clarke that firmly. Maria never knew of her visit.

*　　*　　*

In June 1940, the rescue of the British from the beaches of Dunkirk was heroic, but while the operation was a magnificent achievement, it was still a defeat, a fact that couldn't be disguised. Most of mainland Europe was under Nazi control and only a small strip of water separated Britain from the German Armies, massing ready for invasion on the French coast.

A smartly dressed man called in to see Sam in the boatyard just a few days after the fall of France. He was so unlike Sam's usual customers that he was intrigued. 'Can I help you, sir?'

'Yes, I hope so,' the man said. 'My name is Robert Dawlish and I work for the Government in London. Word has it that you are the best around here at repairing boats.'

'I do all right.'

The man stood gazing at the very few boats bobbing in the small harbour. He knew the navy commandeering Lough Foyle had sounded the death knell for the fishermen that had operated from here and, because of that, this man's business too. But winning the war held precedent and everyone had to be expected to make sacrifices. He asked the question he already knew the answer to. 'Is the boatyard profitable?'

'Is that any of your business?' Sam snapped.

'It could be and I have a reason for asking.'

'I have no reason to reply.'

'Don't be so pig-headed, man.' Dawlish snapped. 'You haven't even heard what I have to say yet. I may be able to offer you something more lucrative.'

Then Sam knew he probably couldn't afford to be too rude. 'All right,' he said. 'State your business.'

'I'll come straight to the point,' Dawlish said. 'With Ireland determined to be neutral in this war, Derry is Britain's most westerly point. It will be needed as an escort base, to try and protect the merchant ships. We intend to establish a large repair workshop on Strand Road, alongside the present graving dock, and use Derry as a refuelling depot too.'

Sam nodded. He could see the sense of it. 'How do I come in?'

'I'd like you to be part of the repair team,' the man said.

'Working for the British Government?' Sam said, bristling.

'Indirectly, but if that offends you, think of it as working for a freer Europe,' the man said, adding more harshly, 'Do you think for one moment your neutrality will matter a jot to the Germans if they invade Britain? Norway tried that, to no avail. If Britain is invaded, Ireland will fall too. Mark my words.'

Sam was no fool and he knew the few men the Irish Government had stationed at Buncrana would be no match for the highly disciplined German Army if they were intent on invasion and so he said to the man, 'All right then, say I agree to this, how is it to be arranged?'

The man sighed inwardly in relief. He hadn't been sure he'd get this Sam Foley to agree. The word was he could be stiff-necked, and he was no lover of the English. Dawlish went on, choosing his words with care, 'You would work for the Admiralty, but in a civilian capacity, and as the foreman you could choose your own team, men you know and can trust.'

Sam knew he was being given a chance, certainly

while the war lasted, to lift the standard of living for all the men involved. Pride was a fine thing to have, when you had enough to eat, warm clothes to wear and a good fire to sit beside. 'When would you want us to start?' he asked.

'Time is of an essence,' Dawlish said. 'We have a war to win. Shall we say Monday week? Is that time enough to get people together?'

'Plenty of time, but how are we to get to the docks? The first bus from Moville doesn't get to Derry till eight twenty. Presumably you'd want us to start work before then.'

'Don't worry about that. We'll send a military truck to pick you up at half-past seven. How many men can you round up?'

Sam did a swift calculation. 'Sixteen, maybe seventeen at the outside. Would that be all right?'

'Splendid.'

'And wages. They'll need to know. I'll need to know.'

'This will have to be agreed upon officially,' the civil servant said, 'but it will be in the region of twelve pounds ten shillings for yourself as foreman, and ten pounds for the men you bring with you.'

Twelve pounds ten shillings – the figure floated in Sam's mind. It was riches. It would be riches for them all. He extended his hand to Dawlish and they shook warmly.

'It's a deal.'

Sam went out visiting the neighbours he wanted in his new team that night, even routing a few from Rafferty's pub. Eventually he had his chosen men around him.

His special mate, Conrad Milligan, was to be his second in command.

The men all went back to Rafferty's to seal their future in pints of Guinness. There they met Barney McPhearson, who listened to the talk of the men and then approached Sam and asked if he could be part of the team.

Sam had little time for Barney. The McPhearsons had always been known as a bad lot and Barney's brother was the worst of all. He had never had a real job of work, though he didn't seem short of money. Sam didn't want the responsibility of taking Barney on. Every man was hand-picked and he could vouch for their diligence and honesty. He could not do that with Barney McPhearson.

'I have all the men I need,' he said shortly.

Barney's face fell. 'I'm real sorry about that, Mr Foley,' he said respectfully enough. 'There's sod all doing in Moville just now.'

Sam suddenly felt sorry for the lad. Maybe Barney could be turned around yet, he thought. After all, he was just twenty. Maybe all he needed was a helping hand.

'I think you're right,' Sarah said that evening, when Sam discussed it with her. 'If you don't want the man on your team, why not give him a job at the boatyard? He can do the work you've picked up in Buncrana from the Lough Swilly fishing boats. Willie is too old to make the journey to Buncrana more that a time of two, but he'll be there to keep him in line.'

Sam offered this position to Barney, though he knew Willie, who'd been in the boatyard since he'd been a lad, working for his late father, wouldn't be able to keep anyone in line. He'd never been that sort and now the old man's mind had begun to slip. Sam kept him on only out of kindness. He didn't even pick up a wage any more, for he said he was fine with his pension and he just loved being around and dealing with boats.

Sam said none of this to Sarah, but what he did say was, 'Tell that teacher our Maria can go to that Academy place now. I'll be earning enough soon to pay for her accommodation.'

'The girl knows nothing about any academy, sure,' Sarah said to Sam.

'Surely she should have this chance?'

'Not at all,' Sarah said. 'She's not that type of child.'

'I wonder what Sean would think about it,' Sam mused.

Sean was the only sibling Sarah had left. She loved him dearly and thought a lot of his opinion. He'd been delighted when Maria was born and took great joy in her, seeing in his niece the child he might never have. Despite the confines of the farm, he saw the family as often as he could. Maria in turn adored her uncle.

Sean had often regretted that his beloved niece would be brought up on her own, but accepted it as the will of God, like he'd accepted the idea that she wouldn't be able to go to Grafton Academy, despite her gift, when Sarah had told him of the teacher's visit. Now, the opportunity was there again as Sarah explained when Sean next visited her. He fastened his wise brown eyes upon Sarah and said, 'It would be wrong to deny her the chance at least of trying for the scholarship.'

'Ah, Sean, how can you say that? You know I only have Maria.'

'You cannot chain her to your side,' Sean said. 'God knows, I'm well aware what that feels like.'

'You don't like the farm, do you?'

Sean sighed. 'It isn't me we're talking of. If Maria ever found out that you denied her this chance, she might hold it against you.'

Sarah couldn't bear the thought of that. Later, reluctantly, she said to Sam, 'I'll contact Philomena and see what Maria has to do.'

Maria, who hadn't any idea of the things being planned for her, was ecstatic when she was told. The light of excitement danced in her eyes at the thought of being given the chance of such a glittering and wonderful future, doing something she enjoyed above all else. She had no problem with the work Philomena set for her, either. The teacher explained that the academic standard was high too, and Maria would have to work hard if she wanted to secure a scholarship.

Maria told Greg all about the plans for her future as soon as she could, and though he was sincerely pleased for her and said so, other worries had been pressing on his mind after Dunkirk. One of these was the thought that it was wrong to sit out the war in Ireland, when Britain was in such dire straits. While he was milking the cows, hoeing the ground for planting and feeding the pigs, many like him were away fighting the enemy.

He turned this over and over in his mind. Phil, the brother nearest to him in age, was fifteen now and had left school, Billy was thirteen, and both of them were now well able to help their father. The girls, still at school, already helped their mother.

That same night Maria told Greg about the Academy, he told his father he wanted to enlist. Greg's father wasn't surprised, for he knew how the lad felt about farming. He respected him for the fact he had never shown any resentment and worked alongside him as hard as the next man. He knew too that Greg was worried about the war, the more so since Dunkirk.

'You've never taken to this life, have you, Greg?' he asked.

'No, Dad,' Greg said. 'I know why you took the place on and that if we were to make a go of it we had to work hard. Phil and Billy were too young to be of any use, but now . . .'

'Now they are,' his father finished the sentence for him. 'You must do as you feel fit. What outfit were you thinking of joining – the Fusiliers, the Inniskillings?'

'No, Dad,' Greg said. 'There is only one regiment for me. I want to go back to Birmingham and join the Royal Warwickshires.'

His father clapped him on the back. 'Good on you, son.'

'There's just Mom,' Greg said. 'She's bound to be upset.'

'Leave your mother to me.'

However, Greg's mother wailed and cried, and held her son tight as if she'd never let him go. When all this failed she said, 'And what of Maria in all this? I know you are sweet on her.'

'She is set for two years yet in the Academy in Dublin next year if she passes the scholarship,' Greg said. 'There is no understanding between us, although I will ask her to write. She will understand I must follow my heart, as she is doing.'

Greg's mother said no more. She knew she had lost.

Maria was sad to see Greg leave, but soon she was

too busy to miss anyone. She had little time for a social life – for going around the village arm in arm with giggling girlfriends, or having a day in Derry. She wrote to Greg, though they were letters only of one friend to another. Now, in her next letter, she could tell him all the extra work and worry was over and her future was set.

When Maria reached the boatyard to tell Willie Brannigan her news, the first people she saw were Barney McPhearson taking his ease outside, talking to his brother, Seamus. She knew her father wouldn't like Seamus hanging about the boatyard, for he always said he was a bad influence on his younger brother, but what could he do, away in Derry everyday, even if she were to tell him? And what could she tell him? Only that Barney was talking to his brother. She had no idea if Seamus was a regular visitor to the boatyard. Maybe he'd just popped in today with a message. Surely Willie would mention it if he were worried?

Barney's eyes lit up when he caught sight of Maria approaching, for he had a great fancy for the girl. 'Now isn't this a sight for sore eyes, or any eyes at all, for that matter,' he addressed Seamus. The older man looked her all over, his leering eyes raking her body in a way that made Maria feel uncomfortable.

She had no time for it, and none at all for Seamus, so she gave neither a greeting and asked instead, 'Where's Willie?'

'In the boathouse,' Barney said. 'What's up?'

'Nothing,' Maria said. 'It's not that important. Well,

I mean it is to me. I got this today,' and she handed Barney the letter.

Barney had known about Maria taking the exam for the Academy and hadn't been pleased. He was a handsome, well-set-up young man, and most girls and young women were falling over themselves to be noticed by him. But Maria, the one he wanted, seemed not a bit impressed by him. He had no desire for her to be spirited away to Dublin and snapped up by another, but he sensed that to say so wasn't the way to play this and so he congratulated her warmly.

'Why, that's tremendous, so it is, Maria,' he said, taking the paper from her hand. 'D'you see this?' he said to Seamus, pointing at it. 'Our Maria here has won a scholarship to a fancy academy, in Dublin no less.'

Seamus murmured his congratulations. Barney knew his brother thought him mad to hanker after the unattainable. Their parents had died when Barney was ten, but his father hadn't worked for years before that. The family had lived on charity. Barney was left in the doubtful care of his elder brother, who'd then been twenty-one. He had often gone hungry and Seamus was not averse to giving him the odd clout, or even a thrashing a time or two. The priest had been called out once by worried neighbours and yet Barney perversely loved his brother.

'Plenty more fish in the sea,' Seamus had said, when he first saw the lustful glances Barney was giving Maria Foley. 'She's not for the likes of you and guarded well. Anyway, you know what you are like. If you got her you'd likely not want her, because it's how you are with everything.'

'This,' maintained Barney, 'is different.'

And now here she was before him. Greatly daring, Barney put his two arms around Maria's waist, and drew her close.

Maria submitted to the embrace willingly, though usually would not have allowed such familiarity. She put it down to the man being so pleased for her. Certainly she found the kiss he planted on her full lips very pleasant indeed.

Seamus shook his head over his young brother. Willie, watching from the doorway, felt prickles of alarm down his spine. He could have told many a tale about the young man, like the fact Barney was too fond of drinking the afternoon away while he played a hand or two of cards with his brother and like-minded fellows and took little notice of Willie if he tried to take him to task about it.

Willie had said nothing to Sam because he could do little, away in Derry all the day. He'd never worry Sarah about such things. It wasn't as if they were over-burdened with work now that the fishing fleet had had to be disbanded.

Maria broke away from Barney's embrace, and ran over to tell Willie the news. He was as delighted for her as Maria had known he would be. His lined face beamed and his blue eyes became moist with the emotion of it all.

As he put his arms around her, his words of con-gratulations held a note of relief, though Maria wasn't aware of it. A new life beckoned Maria, Willie thought, and quite right too, well away from the clutches of people like Barney McPhearson. Really, he thought, it couldn't come soon enough.

CHAPTER TWO

All who came in the shop that day were told of Maria's success. Though they all congratulated her, Maria knew by their faces that many thought it a disgraceful thing for her to leave her mother. Some actually said this.

'I mean,' said one woman. 'It's hard right enough when you have just the one. Have you thought this through, Maria? Your mother will undoubtedly miss you.' and then added, 'Especially the way she is.'

'The way she is?' Maria asked. 'What do you mean?'

'Well, she's not very strong, is she?' the woman went on. 'And nervy, like. Not been right since she lost the baby and that was years ago.'

'She's fine,' Maria protested. 'She's grand now.'

The woman's face was grave. 'Funny things, nerves. Never really recover, if you have a tendency to nerves.'

Maria, who had been brought up to have respect for her elders and betters, could hardly be rude to customers, but by the time she was ready to leave for the day she was worn down by the disapproval many had shown her.

*   *   *

Maria wanted to let her Uncle Sean know the result of the exam, but he was no longer able to visit them so often because in January, Maria's Granddad Tierney had been diagnosed with a tumour in his stomach. Since April he'd been needing round-the-clock nursing. Sean took it in turn with Agatha, while he also did the work on the farm and Agatha the work in the house.

Maria was so insistent that her uncle should be told her news that Sam went with her to visit him by bus and train on Saturday, 26 July. Bella gladly gave her the day off, knowing how much she loved her uncle. Sean's praise and congratulations were genuine, and the welcome they both got was warm. Only Sam read the weariness in Sean's eyes.

As Sean hugged the girl's slight frame and told her how proud he was, he realised how like her mother she was, though her hair was the colour of deep mahogany, and her eyes vivid green, with long black eyelashes. But Maria had Sarah's slight frame and elfin face. Sean saw that his niece was shedding her childhood and becoming a stunningly beautiful young lady. He wondered if she'd make the two years at the academy before some young Dublin swain claimed her.

But, he reminded himself, the girl was focused on a new life for herself and so far had never let her head be turned. He was saddened that now he'd see even less of her. He knew he'd done the right thing encouraging Sarah to let her daughter try for the scholarship, although all their lives would be poorer when Maria moved out of the village.

* * *

Sarah, who'd prayed earnestly for Maria to fail the exam, now redoubled her efforts to stop Maria leaving home. To this end she had a Mass said, lit numerous candles, began a novena and attended every service at the chapel. Always she pleaded the same thing; 'Please God, Jesus, the Holy Ghost and Mary who has tasted sorrow herself, stop this. Let something happen to prevent my girl from leaving home.' The same beseeching plea was made as she knelt before her bed at night, and in the morning as soon as she woke.

Maria was unaware of this, but she was fully aware of her mother's sighs and reproachful looks. Though she was a model daughter, as the summer wore on, it began to wear her down and she wished the days could speed by.

She was due to go up on 9 September, although the term didn't start until a few days after that. It was to give the girls time to get to know each other and familiarise themselves with a city that would be their home for two years. Even to think about it sent a thrill running all through Maria.

Sarah and Sam threw a party on the night of 7 September to mark Maria's departure. As people hugged her, patted her on the back and wished her Godspeed, she realised how she'd miss them. She'd known most of them all her life and she felt tears stinging her eyes.

'Don't start being homesick before you've even left the place,' Sam said suddenly at her elbow.

Maria flashed him a watery smile. 'I'll try not to,' she said.

Sam patted her on the arm. 'That's my girl.'

All the evening, Sam watched his daughter, already aching with the loss of her. He could easily have resented Philomena Clarke for putting such odd notions in a young girl's head, but he knew she'd had only Maria's best interests at heart when she'd had made the suggestion. What sort of a father would he be if he didn't allow his daughter the chance of a better future?

Sam had loved Sarah since the moment he'd seen her, and loved her still, though her once blonde hair now had streaks of grey in it. His was the same, of course, though it had once been as dark as Maria's. His eyes, though, were a indeterminate grey, not vibrant green like his daughter's. Maria had been the icing on the cake for the pair of them. He knew when she left, a lot of the joy would go out of his life.

Sam recognised that Sean felt the same, for his deep brown eyes were full of sadness. His father was too ill for him to be away from the farm for long and it was still light when he left. Sam watched the stooped, dejected stance of him as he strode towards The Square and the bus into Derry. He remembered how straight and upright Sean had once been.

Now he was tied to a farm he had no love for, tended by the dour, sour-faced Agatha, and watching his father sink daily. He'd had no chance of a life of his own, no loving wife to greet him and warm his bed at night, no child to climb onto his knee and gladden his heart. Sam knew Sean would feel the loss of Maria almost as keenly as her parents would.

Eventually, the party drew to a close. There would be more than one thick head in the village the following morning. Sam felt a little that way himself, if he was honest. He'd drank far more than was customary for him and he had work in the morning.

He followed his wife and daughter to bed, but once there, despite the tiredness stinging his eyes and the beer consumed, he lay wide-eyed and restless for hours before utter weariness claimed him.

The following evening the truck stood ready and waiting to take the men home. Yet Sam was loath to leave the docks, despite it being Maria's last evening in Moville for some time.

'How important is the frigate? he asked the lieutenant. 'There's still a fault in the engine room and it can't go out tomorrow the way it is.'

'It's part of the convoy scheduled to leave at dawn.'

'Well, I'll stay to finish it,' Sam said. 'Con will give me a hand. There's no need to keep the others. More than two will not fit in that small space anyway. But how will we get back home when we've finished? I don't fancy walking.'

'I'll see if I can rustle up a couple of bicycles,' the lieutenant said. 'You can pile them in the truck in the morning. Will that do?'

'Aye,' Sam said with a chuckle, 'though it's years since I was astride a bike. I'll more than likely have a sore backside in the morning.'

The lieutenant smiled. He liked both Sam and Con, and knew them to be first-rate workers, the sort who'd get on with the job in hand and not need the whip cracked over them.

'I'm grateful, Sam,' he said. He hesitated a moment

and then went on, 'There's something else. Keep your eyes peeled, will you? There's a rumour circulating the IRA are planning something.'

'They'll never get in here,' Sam said. 'Haven't you the place as tight as a drum?'

'They might, if they had help from inside.'

'Who'd do that?' Sam said and then as the man said nothing, burst out, 'It'll not be one of my men. I hope you're not suggesting—'

'No, no, I'm not. They came on your surety and that's good enough for me, but I'm convinced if the IRA break in here, they'll do it because someone from the inside will have helped them.'

'They could cause havoc,' Sam said. 'Buggering up the boats could leave the merchant ships unprotected. Don't they think of that?'

'Obviously not.'

'Well, I'll keep my eyes and ears to the ground, never fear. Mind you, you'd have to have eyes like a cat to see anything in this blackness. Nights are certainly drawing in.'

The lieutenant agreed and watched as Sam walked over to the truck. Sam knew Con wouldn't bat an eyelid at working over, but he told a couple in the truck to tell Sarah and Con's wife, Brenda, where they were. 'Don't give them a time that we'll be home,' he cautioned. 'I don't know how long it will take us and I don't want Sarah fretting.'

It was Andy Carmody, Bella's nephew, who called at the Foley door later and told Sarah and Maria about Sam. Sarah knew her man and she recognised that, as the gaffer, the responsibility would lie on his shoulders. She was glad, though, when Andy told her Con was there too.

'Pity,' she said to Maria. 'And on your last night too.'

'It's Daddy I feel sorry for,' Maria said. 'He's already been at it for hours. The job must be urgent for him to stay. But I'm no wean any more; I understand these things.

In the engine room of the frigate, Sam and Con toiled away. The job was not difficult but the parts were tricky to reach and it was taking much longer than Sam had anticipated.

More than two hours after the others had left, Sam and Con tightened up the last bolt, wiped their oily hands on rags and climbed off the ship onto the dockside, where the lieutenant had left the bikes standing against a wall.

It was as they were pushing them to the gates that Sam heard the hoot of an owl, followed by a thud, as if a person or persons had landed on the deck of one of the ships.

'What was that?' Con asked.

'I don't know, but if that was an owl hooting just now, then I'm a Dutchman,' Sam said. He recalled the conversation he'd had with the lieutenant that evening and knew he'd have to investigate the noise.

'We'll go together,' Con said when Sam told him what the lieutenant had said.

'No,' Sam said. 'Brenda will be waiting with your supper. You best go on home.'

'Why don't you call the dock police?'

'I will,' Sam said, 'soon as I'm certain. Don't worry, I'm not bursting in there myself like some unsung hero, but it's just maybe two young fellows having a lark and I can send them home with boxed ears and no harm done. If I think it's more serious, then I'll get help quick. Don't worry. Go on, I don't intend spending one minute longer than necessary. I am fair jiggered and then it's Maria's last night. I'll likely overtake you on the road.'

Con went. He knew Brenda would go for him when he reached home as it was. She had a fine temper on her when she wanted. But he was worried about Sam and told the policeman, as he let him out of the gates, what they'd heard.

'I'm being relieved in less than ten minutes,' the policeman reassured Con. 'I'll take a look for your mate before I go off, but he'll likely contact us before then . . .'

When Con left, Sam began walking stealthily to where he was sure the thudding noise had come from. He knew he had to be careful, especially when he left the quayside and boarded one of the ships moving gently in the water. His eyes strained to see in the darkness and he crept gingerly forward.

A pinprick of light alerted him first, a match and then the smell of cigarette smoke on the breeze and the soft murmur of voices. He couldn't hear the words, but he didn't need to. He knew whoever the people were just ahead of him, they were not a couple of kids, but grown men probably intent on destruction, and the sooner he got off the boat and got help the better.

In his haste to turn round, he stumbled. He didn't fall, but stood for a moment stock-still, wondering if the slight sound he'd made had alerted the men in any way.

There was no sound of pursuit, however, so Sam went on again. He crossed to a gunboat, which lay against the dockside wall. Thinking it a safer route, he was creeping round the deck of the boat, next to the wall, when his foot slipped and he fell with a thud onto the deck. He lay still for a moment, but he didn't appear to be hurt anywhere, just winded. He began struggling to his feet.

There was a sudden thump in the middle of his back and, unbalanced as he was, he couldn't save himself. He couldn't prevent the cry that escaped from him. His hands clawed desperately at the air as he tumbled from the boat and hit the water with a splash.

The shock and cold of it took his breath away at first and then he began to thresh about, trying to find the side of the boat, anything to pull himself up. Suddenly the boat, jostled by its neighbour, moved slightly, crushing Sam against the harbour wall.

Sam screamed against the agonising pain, but the boat pinned him effectively and what came out was just a groan. He knew he would die, there in the dockside. The pain of leaving Sarah and Maria, and the thought of what they'd do if he wasn't there to see to them caused him to close his eyes against encroaching death.

By the time the policeman went off duty, Sam was unconscious and the dockyard as silent as a grave, the only sound that of the lap of water as the boats moved against the swell. He called for Sam – more urgently when he found his bicycle still propped against the wall – but there was no answer. In the end he went into the barracks room and reported that Sam was missing.

The lieutenant who had spoken to him earlier that evening was more worried than anyone. He led the search for Sam Foley, but in the light of the shaded torches, all that the Government allowed in the blackout, to search for anyone was a miserable and probably pointless task.

Despite the message sent with one of his colleagues, Conrad's wife berated him soundly for the time he'd got home, hours after the others. 'There was a job to finish. I'm second in command,' he protested. 'Sam was there too. In fact, I intend going over in an hour or so to see he's made it back all right.'

'Why shouldn't he?'

'He was still at the docks when I left.'

'Why?'

'He heard a noise and went to have a closer look.'

'What sort of noise?'

'Any noise would be unusual in a dockyard that is supposed to be deserted.'

'On his own?'

'Aye,' Con said. 'The police and military are almost within calling distance and military police patrol the dock every hour or so.'

'Well, then, what harm could come to him? Isn't he surrounded by people?'

'I know. I'd just like to check.'

'You'll do no such thing,' Brenda said. 'Isn't Sam a grown man?'

'I know, but—'

I know, I know . . . Dear Christ, if Sam suggested you leap in the fire, you'd likely consider it,' Brenda said scathingly. She was jealous of the deep regard the two men had for one another and always had been. 'It's not Sam Foley you're married to, a fact you seem to forget at times. I see little enough of you. The only place you'll go this night is to your bed with me.'

Con, seeing the set of his wife's mouth, wondered what would happen if he was just to put on his coat and push past her to still the tug of anxiety he had for Sam. But Brenda's temper was such that he seldom defied her and he was too weary himself to start a fight, which he knew from experience could go on for hours. So he shrugged.

'As you like,' he said. 'But, it's not unusual to be concerned for a mate.'

The knot of worry stayed with Con, even after he'd climbed the stairs and into bed, where he lay wide awake.

By half-past ten, Sarah became concerned. Andy had told them Sam would be late, but did he mean as late as this? She hated Sam to be in Derry long after dark in case there was a raid.

Derry had been attacked only the once, and that had been on the previous Easter Tuesday. The sirens were plainly heard in Moville, but in the end there was just one bomber, which dropped two parachute mines. The newspapers reported that the pilot was trying to bomb the river, but he missed that and the mines landed in the Messine's Park area of the city, killing thirteen people and injuring thirty-three.

Yet the city had got away lightly, because that same night, Belfast had been blitzed, leaving over nine hundred people dead. Sarah was always worrying that it might be Derry's turn next.

She put down her knitting and sat with her hands in her lap, listening.

Maria put down the book she'd been reading and watched her mother with concern. She too was anxious about her father and yet she knew she had to shield her anxiety from her mother. It had always been that way. 'Shall I put the wireless on, Mammy?'

'No, child, I have no heart for it.'

'I'll make a cup of tea for us then, shall I?'

Sarah didn't answer. Instead, her brooding eyes met those of her daughter. 'I didn't think your daddy would be this late,' she said.

'Maybe he stopped off at Rafferty's for a drink?' Maria said, though she knew her father had never done such a thing before.

Sarah shook her head. 'He wouldn't. He'd know we'd be concerned. And particularly tonight, your last night. He'd come straight home.'

'Maybe the job was more difficult than he thought,' Maria said soothingly. 'Would you like me to go and look for him, maybe have a talk with some of the men?'

'What good will that do?'

'You never know.'

'Oh, go if you want to.'

Maria was glad to be out of the house and doing something. She went first to see Andy Carmody, only to find he'd gone to Rafferty's pub. She made her way there uncertainly. She'd never been in a pub in her life. It wasn't done; the bar was the prerogative of the men.

Maybe in Dublin it was customary for women to visit the pub, but it wasn't in Moville.

She was hovering outside the door when Barney McPhearson left the pub, on his way home.

'Why, Maria, what is it?' he said, knowing only a matter of importance would have brought Maria there, and at that time of night.

Maria told him of her father's absence. 'Andy Carmody came with news he would be late,' she went on, 'and I've been to the house, but his mother said he'd gone to Rafferty's. I just wondered if he knew anything more. We're worried.'

With reason, Barney thought, with the time going on for eleven. But he didn't say this. What he did say was, 'Well, we'll soon find out, Maria. Young Andy is in there and I'll bring him out to talk to you.'

But Andy knew no more, though he did tell Maria that Conrad had been with him. That thought comforted Maria. At least he wasn't alone.

'D'you want to go up to see if Con's wife has further news?' Barney said. Maria nodded. However, when they arrived the house was in darkness. She hesitated. Was it likely Brenda would go to bed if Con hadn't returned?

Some women might doze in the chair, but nearly all would be ready with a hot meal when their husbands did appear. So, full of trepidation, Maria knocked on the door.

Afterwards, Con was to say the knock barely surprised him. It was as if he'd been half expecting it. He was out of bed in seconds, taking time only to pull his trousers over his linings before he answered. He was aghast when he learnt that Sam hadn't come home. He told Maria what he knew.

'Wait, I'll get dressed properly,' he said. 'We need to go down there and find out what's happened.'

'You must go home and support your mother,' Barney said to Maria. 'We'll be away to Derry as soon as it can be organised. Try not to worry. We'll find your father.'

She went home slowly, dreading to face her mother, for a heavy apprehension had settled inside her. Even then, with worry for her father gnawing away inside, she thought of the Academy and was consumed with guilt for even giving a thought to herself. The Academy and her future didn't matter any more, she told herself firmly; the only thing that mattered was finding out what had happened to her father. She told Sarah what she knew, which was precious little. Sarah stared at her in shock and sudden petrifying fear, but she said not a word. Maria enfolded her mother's frozen hands in her own, sat her down in the chair and made her a strong cup of tea, putting lots of sugar in, for she had heard it was good for shock.

As the news about Sam Foley spread around the village, men left unfinished pints or clambered from the bed they'd just got into. Those who owned carts harnessed horses to them and a good contingent of the men of the village clattered away in three carts as the church clock struck midnight.

Maria would have preferred to go with them. She always thought waiting for news the hardest job of all, but she knew she couldn't leave her mother. They sat in silence, listening to the tick of the clock and the peat settling in the hearth, Maria feeling sick to her stomach as the time passed slowly.

CHAPTER THREE

It had been half-past two when, hampered by the blackout, they'd found Sam, and half-past three before Barney McPhearson pounded on the Foleys' door.

Sarah's face was ravaged with worry, the puffiness around her eyes evidence of the time she'd spent weeping, but when Maria got to her feet to answer the door, Sarah stopped her. This was something she had to do herself.

Barney almost fell in the door, snatching his cap off his head as he did so.

He could barely look at Sarah's face. He'd have preferred to talk to Maria, for all she was so young, but Sarah blocked his way and he had to tell her first. 'Your man, Sam, has been injured,' he said. 'He must have slipped into the water.'

'Is he dead?'

'No,' Barney said. He didn't add 'he might soon be', though he knew the man must have been in the water some six hours. He'd been unconscious when they hauled him out and only prevented from drowning by the boat rammed against him. 'He's been taken to the hospital in Derry,' Barney went on.

'I must go to him,' Sarah said.

Maria didn't argue and neither did Barney. 'I have the trap outside. Wrap up well, for the night air can be treacherous.'

Maria would always remember that journey, the crowd of people outside the house and Barney McPhearson's arms encircling her as she emerged. He helped first her mother into the trap and then Maria herself, tucking the blankets he'd brought around them solicitously. Then they were off, the clop of the pony's feet on the cobbles almost drowned by the encouraging shouts of the villagers.

Sarah was sunk in misery and Maria could do nothing but put her arm around her. It wasn't just grief tugging at Sarah, but guilt too. For weeks, she'd prayed for something to happen to prevent Maria leaving them, but hadn't given a thought to what that could possibly be. She had never envisaged anything happening to Sam.

Later, as she looked down at her unconscious husband in the hospital bed and listened to the doctor telling her that Sam's legs were crushed beyond repair and he would never walk again, she knew she had condemned him to this living death. Maria would never leave home now but that thought now gave her little joy.

It was by no means certain that Sam would even survive. 'He is,' the doctor said, 'a very sick man. The next twenty-four hours will be crucial.'

'We'll stay,' Sarah declared, and Maria agreed.

And they did stay, sitting on a hard bench in a hospital corridor, Barney between them. When Sarah's body sagged against him in a sleep of total exhaustion,

Barney put his arm about Maria. 'This is dreadful for you,' he said. 'I do understand.'

Maria was glad he was there, glad of his solid bulk beside her. He seemed, at that moment, the only one she could confide in, tell of her confused feelings. 'Daddy – he means the world to me,' she said. 'I love him so very, very much, but this course at the Academy . . . For a full year I've worked towards it and for weeks have known I was going. I've never felt so excited, so exhilarated as I did the day I received that letter offering me a scholarship place. But, really, I shouldn't be feeling any regret at all about it with Daddy so ill. Surely my thoughts and tears should be all for him.'

'They are really,' Barney assured her. 'But you can't just turn off hopes and dreams, kept alive this long while.'

'You seem to understand so much,' Maria said in surprise. She realised she'd never really taken much notice of Barney before.

'That's because I care a great deal about you,' Barney said. 'All of you.'

Maria was relieved to hear Barney say that, because she knew her mother would never deal with this. Maria herself would shoulder the burden of the house, with not even Sean on hand, with his own father so ill, and she wasn't sure she could cope with all that responsibility alone.

'What if Daddy doesn't survive, Barney?' Maria asked a few moments later.

'Every hour that passes is better news, I should think,' Barney said. 'He's in the best place and all we can do is hope and pray.'

*   *   *

As soon as Bella heard about the tragic events in the Foley family, and the women had returned home, she went down to see them. Sarah had already gone to bed, but Maria was still doing last-minute things. At the sadness in the girl's eyes, Bella put her arms around her trembling shoulders.

'Maria, there are no words to express what I feel. This is a terrible thing to happen.'

'I know.' Maria's voice was barely above a whisper. 'Daddy will live. We stayed, me and Mammy, until he was out of danger, but, oh God, Bella, if you could see him lying there so still, so white. He's never regained consciousness and so probably doesn't know we were there, for all I spoke to him, as the nurse advised. She raised her eyes to Bella's and said, 'He'll never walk, nor work again.'

'And the Academy?'

'That will never be now, of course, and it does no good fretting over it. I will have more to occupy my time, anyway.'

Bella saw the disappointment in the sag of Maria's body and the tone of her voice, yet she was right to try to put it from her mind. It would be like probing a sore tooth.

'You know where my door is if you or your mother need anything,' she said. 'And I do mean anything at all.'

'Aye, Bella, I do, and I thank you, but just now I am too weary to think about anything but my bed.'

'And I'll not keep you from it a moment longer,' Bella said. 'Go on up now. I'll let myself out.'

*   *   *

When Sam was in a position to know that he was paralysed from the waist down, he wished he had died. Inside his head he ranted and railed about his condition, though he wouldn't let his daughter see his anger and frustration nor his tears of self-pity.

He worried as to how they would all manage when he would be unable to work and was glad that they had the support of Barney McPhearson. He'd completely misjudged that young man.

He felt bad about Maria, who'd once held her future in the palm of her hand and not only had it dashed to the floor, but trampled on.

'I don't want to hear another word about it,' Maria said firmly when he'd said this. 'It was an accident and that's all there is to it. Everyone has helped and the villagers have been golden.'

She didn't go on to say that it was as well they had, because her mother seemed incapable of doing anything, including speaking. Since the night the doctor had told them Sam would live, but never work or walk again, she hadn't spoken one word. Maria didn't want to burden her daddy with news like that.

Anyway, she'd told herself over and over, it was probably just shock. Everyone knew that shock could do funny things to a body and Sarah would likely get over it in time. Even Bella and Dora had agreed with her over that.

When the word was first out about Sam, the men from the dockyard had rallied around him and had gone to the hospital in droves. Con was a regular, though he felt bad that he was now made gaffer in Sam's place. Sam told him not to be such a bloody fool and there was not a man alive that he'd rather have taking over from him, but Con couldn't help feeling guilty about it.

Maria was almost overwhelmed by the people's concern and their generosity, though she knew the family couldn't live on their neighbours for ever. Sam knew it too. It was Barney that he appealed to one day to find out the position he was in with regard to the Royal Navy and whether he was entitled to any sort of compensation or a pension.

But the news Barney brought him was not good. Because Sam had been self-employed and just contracted to the navy for the duration of the war, they were under no obligation to compensate him in any way.

'It's a bugger, that's what it is,' Barney said. 'Con told me about the noise you went to investigate and I bet it was them IRA bastards tipped you in the drink.'

'Aye,' Sam agreed. 'Someone punched me in the back, all right.'

'That's what I mean,' Barney said. 'You probably foiled an IRA plot, and certainly saved more that a few ships from being damaged. You should be hailed as a bloody hero, not thrown aside like so much rubbish.'

'They found no one, Barney,' Sam reminded him gently.

'Well, of course they bloody didn't,' Barney cried angrily. 'Those lot would have scarpered not long after you hit the water. What did they expect – that they'd hang about to shake hands?'

'Barney, we can do nothing about it,' Sam said. 'The

official line is that I slipped in the water. It was no one's fault but mine and there is no one to be held accountable for it and that's that. I suppose the boatyard at Greencastle—'

'Don't even ask,' Barney said. 'If the boatyard earns anything at all it's a pittance. Willie has left now, his mind almost gone completely, but in all honesty he had been going that way for some time. I'm going to have to look for something else for myself soon. We could put young Colm, Willie's grandson, in for now, if you like, to sort of mind the shop? He's just left school and his mother was asking. Apparently, he's as mad about boats as his old granddad and would jump at it.'

'He is,' Sam said, 'and he would.'

'And he'd not need much of a wage,' Barney said. 'I mean, he is only fourteen.'

'It's something to think about, certainly,' Sam said. 'I'd not like the boatyard to lie empty altogether, for it would soon go to rack and ruin, but I understand that you—'

'Don't worry about it now,' Barney told him soothingly, 'and don't fret about me. I have a few irons in the fire. You just concentrate on getting well enough to leave here.'

Sean had come over to see Sam as soon as he'd been told of the accident. 'When it's all over with my father – and, God knows, he's in such pain, I hope that's not long away – will you all come up to live at the house?'

'I don't think so, Uncle Sean,' Maria said. 'I don't think Mammy would like to leave here. And I'm worried enough about her as it is.'

Sean thought Maria had cause to worry, for he had been concerned by the vacant look in his sister's eyes and the way she didn't seem to hear when a person spoke to her, or even be aware of her surroundings. It was as though she was on the edge of normality and he knew it wouldn't take much to tip her over into true madness.

Maria knew it too. Somehow she'd have to make a living, but she didn't know how she could leave her mother day in, day out for hours on end. She wasn't fit to be left. Dora or Bella would come to sit with her the times Maria went to the hospital, knowing she was worried about leaving her alone. Maria knew that when her father came home, she'd be his main carer too, and she just didn't know how they were all to survive. The anxiety of this drove sleep from her each night and so her eyes stung with tiredness and there were smudges of blue beneath them.

Sam saw how his daughter suffered and, though his heart ached, he could nothing to ease any of it for her.

By the beginning of the third week, Sarah seemed to have retreated into a world of her own. 'It is shock, as you suspected,' Dr Shearer said, when a worried Maria asked him to call. 'Her mind has shut down because she can't bear what has happened.'

'Is it permanent?' Maria asked.

'It's impossible to say,' the doctor said. 'The mind is a strange thing. I could arrange for her to go to the psychiatric unit of the District Hospital in Letterkenny for assessment.'

'A mental hospital?' Maria said. 'An asylum?' Unconsciously she curled her lip.

'The psychiatric unit of the District Hospital,' the doctor repeated.

'She isn't that bad, is she?' Maria asked.

'It isn't a question of how bad she is, but whether she can be helped further,' the doctor said.

Maria had a horror of her mother going to such a place. She had a mental picture of what went on in an asylum – and it was an asylum, no matter what fancy name the doctor gave it. She was sure there would be raving lunatics, encased in strait-jackets, or incarcerated in cells, sometimes padded, to prevent them injuring themselves. She wanted her frail and gentle mother nowhere near that, not mixing with mad people.

'I think she'd be better at home for now, Doctor, but thank you anyway,' she said.

The doctor shrugged. 'As you wish, Maria, but remember everyone of us has a breaking point, even you. Don't allow yourself to go under, for you'll soon not only have your mother to see to, but your father too.'

Did he think she was unaware of that? Maria shut the door behind him with a bang. She caught her mother up by the hand and, stopping only to wrap a shawl around her, made for the shop.

'I must get a job,' she told Dora. 'But I can't leave Mammy, and when Daddy comes home it will be worse. What am I to do?'

'And will your father get nothing from the navy or the Government?' Dora asked.

'Barney says not.'

'And the boatyard?'

'Limping along just,' Maria said. 'Willie's finished. He's living with his daughter now.'

'Barney's been a grand help to you,' Dora said.

'He's been wonderful,' Maria agreed warmly. 'I don't know what I'd do without him, and that's the truth. Daddy has quite revised his opinion of him, but that doesn't help me find a solution to this problem of earning some money.'

Dora was thoughtful that evening and eventually Bella asked what was bothering her.

'I could see to Sam through the day once he's home, so that Maria could get a job, but there's still the problem of Sarah.'

Bella had been heartbroken to see her friend so ill, and hoped and prayed she might one day recover. She'd taken on a girl called Maggie to help in the shop when Maria left. She said, 'I could maybe have Sarah here during the day. I'm sure I could find her some occupation, weighing and bagging up or some such. Between myself and Maggie, we'll manage her. After all, Maria can't do it all.'

Maria was almost overcome by Bella and Dora's offer and set about finding a job straight away in one of the factories making military uniforms.

However, a few days before she started work, Greg Hopkins came home on leave and soon landed himself at Maria's door. She smiled, glad to see him and invited him inside.

'I can't tell you how heartsore I am,' he said, and his dark brown eyes were troubled. 'My mom wrote and told me.'

'Thank you, Greg,' Maria said. She saw that Greg's boyhood had been shed and he was now a man, fine and strapping. He had always been handsome, but his face had once had a sort of soft look about it. Now that was gone. He looked more determined somehow. He was broader shouldered than he'd ever been and carried himself with confidence and assurance. Maria felt a tremor pass down her body as she looked at him.

'I'm truly sorry that I won't be around to help you through this,' Greg said. 'Pardon me asking this, and please don't be offended, but how are you managing for money?'

'I'm not offended,' Maria said. 'I know you are asking only out of concern, but you needn't worry. Daddy had a little saved from his time in the yard and then the villagers have been marvellous. With Bella and Dora's help, I have been able to look for a job and I am starting at a shirt factory in Derry in a few days' time. Bella is taking charge of Mammy during the day and Dora will see to Daddy, once he is ready to come home.'

It was said so matter-of-factly, but Greg heard the sadness and weariness in Maria's voice and his heart turned over in pity for this lovely, young girl with such a heavy burden across her narrow shoulders.

He was certain now he loved and would always love her and wondered how Maria felt about him. He wouldn't press her, knowing such a lot had happened to her recently, and she was but sixteen yet.

'Do you ever get out, Maria?' he asked. 'Have time for yourself?'

'What do you think?' Maria said. 'Free time is something I don't have an abundance of.'

'I have but a few days before I report back,' Greg said, 'and you have less time before you start work. It would please me greatly if you let me take you to the pictures this evening. *Gone with the Wind* is showing in Derry.'

'Oh,' Maria said. The pictures! She'd never been and oh, how she'd longed to often. But she shook her head regretfully. 'I . . . I couldn't,' she said. 'I'm sorry, but . . . but I just couldn't.'

'Why not?'

'My mother, I couldn't leave her.'

'Could someone sit with her, just for the one evening?'

Maria's mind was racing. Maybe if she got her mother to bed, Dora or Bella could sit in the house until she came back. 'I don't know,' she said. 'I'll get word to you if I can work something out.'

A little later she said to Bella, 'D'you think me awful?'

'No. Why on earth should I?'

'You know, going out enjoying myself with Mammy how she is, and as for Daddy . . .'

Bella liked young Greg Hopkins, had always liked him, and far better than Barney McPhearson for all the great turnout Maria said he'd made of himself.

'What difference will it make to either of your parents whether you go out or stay in?'

'It's just that I feel guilty.'

'You think things will improve for your mammy if you are miserable?'

Maria smiled. 'Of course not.'

'Well then,' Bella said. 'You go with an easy conscience

and remember Greg will only have a few days before he is back in the battlefields. I'll be there if your mammy should need anything.'

Maria had never enjoyed herself so much. The film was wonderful, and when she cried, Greg's arm had gone around her gently in comfort, as he passed her his snow-white hanky. She'd leant against him and sighed. How good it would be, she thought, to have someone special just for herself, someone to lighten the load a little.

Greg's heart was singing as the two alighted from the bus in The Square. He'd held Maria's hand in the cinema at first and she took it again as they walked home, as if it was the most natural thing in the world. At the door, Greg kissed her tenderly on the lips.

'Will you see me tomorrow?'

'Oh, I don't know.'

'Please. We can take a walk out if the weather is kind to us.'

Maria looked into Greg's clear, brown eyes and knew that she wanted to see him again and yet still she said, 'No, not in the daytime. Bella and Dora are kind enough to mind Mammy in the evening so that we can have time together. I will not take advantage of that kindness, and before we do anything else tomorrow, I must see my father.'

Greg didn't argue further, both because he knew Maria had a point and because she had a way of talking, a certain tone that would brook no argument. But the next evening he turned up in his father's rattly old tip-up truck he'd had the loan of and so they travelled to

Derry in style and Maria took Greg's hand as they went into the hospital.

Sam liked Greg. He knew too how Sarah had felt about him, the hopes she'd had for him and Maria. Greg sat beside him and told Sam about the lighter side of army life and the high jinks they got up to, and Sam laughed till the tears ran down his weathered cheeks. Then he discussed the true war situation with Greg and found his regard for the man growing.

Sam knew he'd be no help to Maria the way he was, and he saw plainly the way Greg thought about the girl. It was portrayed in his eyes. Of course, Maria was young yet, but so much had happened to her in her brief life that her youth mattered less than getting support for her. Greg Hopkins came from a decent respectable family, whom, he knew, would rally round Maria, particularly if she was the one he wanted. Pity the lad had enlisted really.

And as they left the hospital that night, Greg too wished he'd never left Moville and then he'd be around to help Maria, but nothing could be done about that now. They just had to make the most of the time they had.

'Care for a drink before we go back?' he asked.

'Oh, I don't know,' Maria said. 'I've never been in a public house in my life.'

'That's because you've been born and bred in Moville,' Greg said. 'In other parts of the country, the cities in particular, it is a respectable enough place for women to go to.' Maria still looked doubtful and Greg tucked her arm in his. 'Trust your Uncle Greg in this,' he said, and Maria laughed as he ushered her through the door.

Mindful of Maria's age, Greg brought her just an orange and for himself a Guinness. As they sat at a small table Maria glanced around self-consciously and saw that there were other girls and women in the pub. She began to relax.

Greg hadn't wanted to press Maria yet, but when she had excused herself for a few minutes at the hospital, Sam had asked him bluntly how he felt about his daughter. When he admitted he loved her to distraction, Sam had advised him to tell her.

'I know that Maria is barely out of childhood,' he said. 'Had things been different, then I would not be advocating this at all, but in the situation she finds herself, her needs have changed. It would ease my mind if you and your family were there for her if she needed you.'

Greg had quite understood Sam's reasoning, but he guessed Maria didn't know how he felt about her. How would she know? He saw that she was indeed surprised when he suddenly said, 'This is a conversation I didn't intend to have yet, Maria – not for a few years, when you were older.'

Maria was intrigued. 'What are you talking about, Greg?'

'Can't you guess?' Greg reached across the table and caught up her hand. 'I love you, Maria, and have done for years. I didn't speak of it because you were set for a glittering future in Dublin.'

'Would you have just let me go then?'

'No,' Greg said. 'You'd already given me the name and address of the hostel where you would be staying in one of your letters. I intended going to see you a time or two, when I had leave, so that we had a chance to get to know each other. That can never be now, so I will ask you today. Maria, will you be my girl?'

Maria was taken aback and she stared at Greg open-mouthed for a minute or two.

'Are you shocked?' Greg asked. 'Repulsed?'

'Shocked, yes,' Maria admitted. 'But never repulsed. It's just I've never thought of you that way, Greg.'

'Could you?'

Maria regarded the man before her, his wide-open face, with eyes now full of trepidation, and a generous mouth. She imagined what it would be like to kiss those lips properly, to be held lovingly in Greg's arms, and at these thoughts a delicious shiver ran all through her. Greg felt it through the fingers he held and still he waited. 'I think I could, Greg,' Maria said at last. 'Yes, I really think I could.'

Greg leant across the table and gave Maria a gentle kiss on the lips. 'You've made me the happiest man in the world at this minute, and on my next leave maybe we can get engaged?'

'Aye,' said Maria. It wasn't how she'd imagined her future, but then none of it was how she'd imagined.

'I love you so much, Maria,' Greg said. 'There aren't enough words to tell you.'

Oh, how wonderful it felt, Maria thought, to be loved like that. She laid one of her hands on Greg's arm and the heat of desire for this beautiful girl filled his body. He knew, however, she'd be pure and innocent so any courtship would have to proceed slowly. He'd had a few dalliances with women since he joined the army; most girls seemed to like men in uniform.

None of them had meant anything, including the clingy Nancy Dempsey, who tried to stick to him like a limpet, even after he told her it was over.

Well, there was to be no more of that, he told himself. He would be true now to Maria.

As he left Maria at the door that night, Greg kissed her chastely and tentatively, then, as she responded to him, more passionately. Maria felt as if she was drowning in pleasure. The yearning urges in her body she didn't fully understand, but they caused her to moan softly. Greg tried to loosen the arms he'd had tight around her, lest she feel how aroused he was and be alarmed by it. But his kisses had left her wanting more, and it was Greg who pulled away first.

'See you tomorrow, darling.'

'You will?'

'Of course. Don't you start work the day after?'

'Aye.'

'And the following day, I'm back at camp, and then who knows? We must grab every minute we can.'

'I know,' Maria said miserably. 'I will miss you so much when you go back.'

'And I'll miss you, my love,' Greg said, kissing her again. 'But go in now, or Bella will give out to you for keeping her up so late.'

Maria knew Greg spoke good sense. It was neither sensible nor right to alienate Bella. However, when she went inside, it wasn't Bella sitting in the chair before the fire, but Barney.

He had heard with irritation about the young Greg Hopkins, home from the war and buzzing around Maria's door. His anger was fuelled that evening when he'd called to take Maria to the hospital and found out she had already gone, and with Greg Hopkins. 'She called to see you at the boatyard and tell you this,' Bella had said. 'And all she saw was young Colm Brannigan, who didn't seem to know where you were at all.'

'I had to go to Buncrana to see about a boat,' Barney said. 'I did tell the boy. He must have forgotten.'

In fact he had been nowhere near Buncrana, but away in the hills with Seamus, learning about a very lucrative business proposal that he preferred above baby-minding a boatyard. However, he wasn't sharing that with Bella. She was suspicious enough of him already. What he did say was, 'Well, I have the night to myself, for I had thought to be taking Maria to the hospital, so if you want to get off, I will listen out for her mother. I need to see Maria tonight about a spot of business.'

'At this time of night?'

Barney shrugged. 'I've been busy all day and the plan was to talk to her on the way into Derry. Now I am here it is pointless the two of us waiting.'

It was, and Bella was tired. 'Well, I'll be off then, if you are sure?'

'Quite sure,' Barney told her, and Bella made her way home.

Barney noted Maria's flushed face and dancing eyes just as she noted the glass beside the large bottle of poteen, which was half empty. She was annoyed to find Barney sitting there as if he owned the place, and even more annoyed when he said he'd sent Bella home.

'You had no right.'

'I had every right,' Barney said. 'She'd been on her feet all day and was tired, yawning like a good one. I sent her home as a kindness to her, and said I would wait for you. Fine consideration you had for the woman doing you a favour, for you are powerfully late.'

Maria flushed with embarrassment, because she knew Barney had a point. 'Yes, I didn't mean it to be such a long night. We went for a drink after we'd been in to see Daddy.'

Barney's innards were twisted with jealousy for Greg Hopkins, who'd had Maria's company all night, but he remembered Seamus telling him not to fret when he'd complained before. 'Your man will be back to soldiering soon,' he'd said, 'and the way clear for you.' So Barney swallowed the anger.

'What are you doing here, anyway?' Maria asked him.

'I needed to talk to you.'

'It's very late, as you pointed out,' Maria said. 'Couldn't it have waited?'

'I didn't think so,' Barney said. 'We need to discuss the boatyard.'

'Oh, yes,' Maria said. 'I didn't know you'd engaged Colm, Willie's grandson.'

'He's left school now and was for ever asking me if I could get him set on.'

'Even so,' Maria said, 'it should have been discussed.'

'I talked it over with your father,' Barney said. 'All right, perhaps I should have mentioned it to you as well, but the point is the boatyard barely makes enough to pay the boy, so I have got another job.'

'Oh.'

'It's delivering supplies over the border to the naval staff.'

'Oh,' Maria said again, surprised. 'Are you employed by the military then?'

'No, it's a private concern.'

Barney didn't elaborate further. He didn't say he was joining Seamus to smuggle poteen and rationed goods across the border, bringing back petrol, fertiliser and animal feed. All these things were transported under the cover of darkness, as was Seamus's setting-up of card schools, which now Barney would be involved in. They had special packs of cards and many tricks to fleece the sailors of their money, especially when the sailors' brains were addled with poteen.

But Maria wasn't suspicious. In her opinion the services had to have supplies and the job seemed a legitimate one.

'I've told Colm in the afternoons I'll still be around to deal with anything he can't handle,' Barney said.

'I appreciate that.'

'Least I can do,' Barney said, pouring himself another large glass of poteen. He proffered the bottle in Maria's direction. 'Want one?'

Maria shook her head. She was more than tired – shattered suddenly – and she really wanted to be rid of Barney so that she could lie in bed and think about the new future Greg had offered her.

Barney saw the dreamy look in Maria's eyes. Christ! For two pins he call that Greg out and pound him to pulp. And then what? said a little voice in his head. You would be the one up before the magistrate and Maria would never want anything to do with you ever again. Wait till he's away and you are not before you move in.

'I'll be off then,' he said to Maria. 'Will I see you tomorrow?'

'Probably.'

Probably, thought Barney. One time it would have been 'of course', but that was before lover boy's appearance. Well, he would have patience. It wasn't something he was noted for, but he imagined he could learn it as quick as the next man if he had to.

Early the next evening, Greg took Maria into Derry after she'd taken tea with his family. Maria hadn't wanted to go to tea, but Greg had insisted. Greg's parents and his two brothers and two sisters were welcoming, and when Maria left, she knew they would accept her into their family with little or no trouble.

They went again to a cinema in Derry to see *The Road to Singapore*, which starred Bing Crosby, Bob Hope and Dorothy Lamour. Maria had never heard of them, but Greg told her these were the names of big stars that were in the major films of the time. Maria enjoyed the film immensely.

At the door, Greg took Maria in his arms and kissed her neck and eyes before moving to her lips. This time his tongue parted her lips gently and sent sharp shafts of desire that she didn't fully understand shooting through her body. She gasped with the shock of it, the beginnings of sexual awareness.

'I love you, Greg!' She didn't know where the words came from. She knew she meant them – that with every fibre of her being she loved Greg Hopkins.

Greg was overjoyed. 'I love you, Maria Foley, with every bit of me. You mean everything to me.'

They kissed and kissed again. Greg kept his arms around Maria though his hands tingled to explore every inch of her luscious body.

As Maria donned the overall and hat that every vestige of hair had to be tucked beneath, and began to work on the coarse army garb on the heavy machines, she couldn't help contrasting her life now with the life she'd once had offered to her. This work was mind-blowingly boring. The heat in the factory was stifling, and the lint floating in the air stung her eyes and made her sneeze and cough.

But the other girls made it all worthwhile. They laughed and joked, seeming not to care for the inconveniences.

'All I care about is the money,' Joanne, the girl sitting next to Maria, said. 'Everything else is secondary to that. What do you say, Maria?'

'I feel the same,' Maria said.

'And we get a good whack for what we do when all is said and done,' Joanne said.

They did. It was piecework and if you were a fast worker, you could make as much as five or six pounds a week. If they can put up with it then so can I, Maria thought determinedly. She laughed and joked with the best of them and found it helped the day pass quicker.

Nevertheless, she was pleased and relieved when the factory's blast declared the end of that first day for she felt incredibly weary. 'Someone's going to be in the pink all right,' shouted a woman from the head of the queue shuffling towards the factory gate. 'There's a soldier boy waiting for someone.'

Maria's heart leapt. She shuffled forward eagerly. Soon she was through the gate and Greg was in front of her. Once she was in his arms, tiredness vanished as if it had never been and they were kissing hungrily despite the people passing along the road. No one seemed to mind. In fact it seemed to lighten the dismal late October day to see a couple so much in love.

Maria and Greg were oblivious to everyone but each other.

'I'm taking you for a meal tonight,' Greg said, and as Maria was about to protest, he put up his hand. 'No arguments,' he said. 'I have cleared it with Bella and Dora, and tonight, as it is my last night, they are seeing to your mother. Come on, we have a few precious hours together – let's not spend them any other way than enjoying ourselves.'

And they did enjoy themselves. Greg was good fun and well read. He had an opinion on most subjects, and by the end of the meal, Maria couldn't think how the hours had sped so fast.

She clung to him that night as he saw her home, knowing she'd not see him for weeks, even months. She could cope with that, but what she fretted about was that Greg would be in some battleground, being blown or shot to bits.

'Please, please be careful,' she begged him, as they cuddled together.

'I will, my darling,' Greg said between the little kisses he was planting on her lips and eyes. 'Now, I have something to come home to, someone I love so much it hurts, I will take extra care.'

Greg's kisses sent Maria's senses reeling. His hands gently caressing her body felt so right. She made no protest, but kissed him passionately – so passionately that once again Greg had to pull back and his voice was husky as he said, 'Go on now in, before I forget myself.'

'I wouldn't mind.'

'You don't know what you're saying,' Greg said with a smile. 'But don't worry, I'd never show such disrespect for the girl I want to be my wife.'

'Oh, Greg!'

Greg gave Maria one last, lingering kiss and then backed away from her with difficulty. He had to leave the next morning before dawn and Maria didn't try to delay him. She watched him walk away from her. When he reached The Square he stopped to wave, and she returned the wave before turning away and going inside.

CHAPTER FOUR

The next week, Sam was declared fit to come home. Barney organised the whole thing. He also brought Sam's bed downstairs, and accompanied Maria to the hospital to bring her father home in the ambulance.

Maria had high hopes that once her father was back, Sarah might take a grip on herself. However, when Sarah saw her crippled husband carried into the house and laid in the bed, the guilt that she'd put him there, that it was her prayers and supplications that had brought Sam to this state, threatened to overwhelm her. She began to rock herself backwards and forwards in the chair and the noise of her keening filled the house as tears steamed from her eyes.

Dora, who had been minding Sarah while Maria was at the hospital, wrapped Sarah in her arms. Sam's eyes went from his wife to Maria. Maria had said nothing about the mental state of her mother and had just explained her absence at the hospital by saying she wasn't well, though other visitors had hinted how Sarah was. It was one thing hearing about it, however, and quite another seeing it. He asked himself how he expected Maria to cope with the two of them – he a helpless cripple and Sarah the way she was. It was too much for anyone, least of all a young girl.

'Holy Mother of God, Maria, I'm so sorry to bring this trouble upon you,' he said sorrowfully.

'It's not of your making, Daddy,' Maria said. 'Don't fret yourself.'

'Child, dear, it would have been better if I had died in the dock that night.'

'Now, Daddy, we'll have none of that talk, and you too, Mammy,' she went on, turning to her mother, still crying and clasped in Dora's arms. 'Come on now, That's enough. Tears never did a bit of good anyway.'

Sarah did try. The gulping sobs changed to hiccups and then dried up altogether.

Into the silence, Barney said, 'You only have to ask if you need help. If there is anything, if I can do it for you, then I will.'

'Thank you, Barney,' Maria said. She was grateful, because a person never knew when she might have need of a big, strapping man.

In time, Maria got into the swing of caring for her parents. She'd wash and change her father and help Sarah to dress before dropping her off at Bella's. Then she'd make for the bus, while Dora would go next door to see to Sam. On Maria's return, she would collect her mother and take her home, then get a meal ready for them. With the meal eaten and the washing-up done, she would wash and change her father and get both him and Sarah ready for bed.

She managed, just, but it was exhausting. The job

was the saving of her sanity. She was incredibly grateful to Bella for taking on the care of her mother, not sure if she could do it day in, day out. She only knew she was glad to go into the factory and see the other girls, have a laugh and joke and forget her problems for a while.

She was particularly close to Joanne, with whom she worked side by side. Maria had never had a friend before, for she had lost all those she had made at school when she had been working so single-mindedly for the scholarship. Joanne was four years older than Maria, Derry born and bred, perky, full of fun and just what Maria needed. Joanne thought Maria looked vulnerable, which brought out a protective streak in her.

Besides Joanna, there plenty more willing to be friends with Maria. She had never told them at work about how her life was, but there were others from Moville who had. In fact, Sam's accident had been the talk of the place. News of an accident of such magnitude cannot be kept from people, though because it had happened in a military establishment, in a country at war, it had never made the papers.

'Let me get this right,' said one woman, exchanging news in the street with a neighbour, a few days after Sam's accident, 'the man's a cripple, the woman is off her head and there is only the one daughter to see to them all?'

'That's about the strength of it, all right,' said the other woman. 'And she is only sixteen and not big, you know – slight, like. She looks even younger than she is. And then before all this, she had a glittering future handed to her and then it was snatched away.' And she went on to explain about the scholarship.

'Ah, God help her,' said the first woman.

This was echoed by many others. By the time Maria started her job in the factory, most of her new colleagues knew all about her and were determined to make the girl welcome. Maria had felt their friendship wash over her from the first day, when she had boarded the bus with neighbours and friends she'd known all her life. They patted her on the back, smiled and wished her well. Then, in the factory, many greeted her as if they had known her for years.

When Joanne asked her out with a group of them one night, though, Maria shook her head. 'I couldn't, honestly.'

'I know how you are placed –' Joanne said – 'well, most of it anyway – but do you never have time off?'

'No, not really.'

'What about lover boy, who met you that time?' Joanne persisted. 'You weren't making for the bus that night, I bet'

'That was different,' Maria said. 'Greg had been home on leave and that was his last night. Dora, who runs the store and post office with her daughter, Bella, went in and sat with my parents for me. Bella already looks after Mammy in the day and Dora sees to my father so I really can't ask them to do more as a regular thing. It isn't easy, you see, because my mother can be awkward and difficult – like a child, you know – and my father is almost completely helpless.'

'You poor cow.'

The sympathy in Joanne's voice was nearly Maria's

undoing. She felt tears stinging the back of her throat. She blinked rapidly and willed them not to fall, and her voice was husky as she said, 'Oh, it's not so bad. I am getting used to it. And we have marvellous neighbours. A young man that used to work for Daddy in the boat-yard comes in almost every night, I suppose on his way to the pub, to see my father. Daddy looks forward to it so much. I think he misses the company of men, you know, and of course the day is a long one for him. But Barney chats to him and they have a few drinks and a game of cards before Barney is on his way again.'

'It is good to have people like that around you,' Joanne said. 'God knows, you need it,'

Maria could only agree and admit to herself that she had been astounded by Barney's thoughtfulness.

'Well, I won't press you to go out with us,' Joanne said, 'or keep asking, because there is nothing so annoying, but I want you to know that you would be welcome any time to come out with the crowd, if the opportunity should ever present itself. Or if things start to get on top of you and you need a night out, all you have to do is shout and I will drop everything to give you a good time, a bloody good time because you deserve it.'

Behind the ensuing laughter there was hint of tears because Maria had been so moved by the understanding in Joanne's voice. She knew she was lucky to work with such lovely people.

In mid-November, Maria's grandfather gave up his fight for life and slipped away at home and in his own bed as he'd wanted to.

'I can't possibly go,' Maria said, as she read the telegram.

'Of course you must go,' Bella said.

'How can I?' Maria demanded. 'I can't leave Mammy and Daddy overnight, and that's what it would mean. I can't and won't have you and your mother do more. You do enough already. Uncle Sean will understand and I'll send a telegram now and a Mass card later that I will put a letter inside.'

Bella said nothing. She was realising that Sarah was one body's work. It took her and Maggie all their time to watch her and run the shop and post office; she'd not like to take the responsibility of having her overnight.

Sean did understand what Maria was going through and as soon as he'd settled everything, he went up to visit them.

Maria was delighted to see him, glad he'd travelled on Friday to stay the weekend for she couldn't really afford to lose pay and maybe her job by taking time off. Sean was appalled by the whole set-up. Heartbroken though he was to see his only surviving sister so ill, and his brother-in-law crippled for life, his sympathies lay with Maria.

Sean caught Sam's eyes on Maria often that weekend as she busied about and Sean knew he felt bad about the things she had to do for him.

'What can I do to help?' he asked Maria.

'Talk to Daddy,' Maria said quietly. 'I'm sure he must get lonesome and frustrated, though he never complains. Barney comes most evenings and they have a jar, play cards sometimes, but for all that it's a long day for him, though Dora does her best.'

'You'll have to keep me abreast of things,' Sam said to Sean, 'for I have no news. One day for me is very like the one that went before and the ones yet to come. Barney tells me how things are now and again. Like he says, the Americans will be in the war soon.'

Sean nodded. 'Don't see how they're able to stay out of it now,' he said. 'They're ready anyway. Been that way for months.'

'What d'you mean?'

'Well, they have bases built already,' Sean said. 'There's one the other side of Lough Erne. I can see it plainly from the farm. And, what's more, they're dressed in the same uniform as the British, but they're American all right. You only have to hear them talk.'

'Would you believe it?'

'One of my neighbours, who works in Derry, said there's another one there too. Probably peppered all over, if the truth was told.'

'Aye,' Sam said. 'Oh, here's Barney, look.' As the man came in the door he added quietly, 'He's been golden, so he has. Hardly misses an evening.'

Barney approached the bed, glad to see Sam so animated by Sean's visit. Sean had already hauled Sam into a sitting position, supported by the pillows, and when Barney produced the bottle of poteen from his pocket Maria didn't say a word, but got the glasses from the cupboard.

The first time Barney had suggested letting Sam have a drink, she'd been against it. 'He's always been a moderate drinker,' she said. 'He could take it or leave it.' Not that he had the chance of much poteen, though she knew he liked a sip if he did.

'Maybe he could take it or leave it when he had a pair of legs that worked,' Barney said, 'or a job of work to occupy him and support his family. For God's sake, Maria, what has he now that you can deny him a bit of pleasure?'

There was nothing, absolutely nothing, that Maria could say to that and she didn't try. Nor did she ask where Barney got the bottles from. Sometimes it was better not to know those things. Anyway, with her father entertained, she could get her mother into bed, which wasn't always easy. Sometimes it took all Maria's powers of coaxing to get her to undress, put on her nightdress and get between the sheets. 'Come on, Mammy,' she'd say to her mother, who'd be standing resolute, arms folded over her chest and her mouth in a mutinous line. 'Come on, to please me.'

Sometimes, when she was tired and had a mountain of things waiting for her to attend to in the kitchen, she wasn't so patient. 'For God's sake, Mammy, will you stop this and get your clothes off.'

She always felt mean when she'd shouted at her mother. If her mother looked at her with eyes filled with reproach it was bad enough, but sometimes her bottom lip would tremble and she'd begin to cry. Maria would be consumed with shame and it would take longer than ever to settle Sarah for the night.

'Will you be off to England now that Granddaddy is dead?' Maria asked her uncle that first night as they sat before the fire with Barney long gone and Sam fast asleep.

Sean was a wee while answering. The situation in the house worried him. Maria seemed to be working

69

herself to death. How could he swan off to England as if it was no concern of his?

'Not yet awhile,' he said eventually. 'Not while you are doing everything here. Now Daddy is gone, I'll come up more at the weekends and share the load. While I'm here, you don't have to worry about Sam, I'll see to him.'

'You don't have to,' Maria said. 'Really you don't.'

'I do,' Sean said firmly.

'I'd hate to think of you putting your plans on hold again.'

'It won't be for ever,' Sean said firmly. 'Tell me about the young man Sam mentioned. Thinks a lot of him, he does.'

The faint blush that flooded Maria's face amused Sean, but there was no doubt in his mind that this was the one for her when she said, 'Greg – that's his name. He's wonderful, tremendous, so he is, but he is in the army.'

'And . . . ?' Sean prompted.

'He wants to get engaged the next leave he gets.'

'And you?'

'Oh, yes, I want it too,' Maria said. 'I know I'm young, though I hardly feel it, but I know in my heart that Greg is the one for me. Marriage will be difficult, I know, even after the war, with Mammy and Daddy still to see to, but he assures me it can be done. His family all seemed to like me, the one time I went to tea. In every letter Greg tells me to visit them, but,' Maria spread her hands helplessly, 'I haven't been able to.'

'You can now. I'll be here,' Sean said. 'And that is one thing I insist on.'

'I can't leave you with everything.'

'Maria, Sarah is my own dear wee sister,' Sean said. 'I will always think of her that way and though I am heartbroken to see her how she is, I still love her. She too is one of life's casualties. Sam is also a fine man, one I am proud to know and one I knew would take care of my sister. To the best of his ability he has, and helped rear you to the fine young woman you are. It would be no hardship to me to care for them for an hour or two while you visit your intended in-laws.'

'Ah, Uncle Sean, you're so good,' Maria said, her voice breaking.

Sean leant over and patted her knee. 'It's what uncles are for, dear child,' he said.

Maria did go to see the Hopkins family the next Sunday afternoon, full of trepidation going alone, although after Mass that morning she had asked Greg's mother if she might call up that afternoon. Once in the house she was soon put at her ease. The whole family welcomed her as warmly as they had done the last time. It was good to talk about Greg openly, with people who loved him and worried about him as much as she did.

'I doubt he'll be home for Christmas,' his mother, Ellie, said.

'No,' Maria said. 'He said the same to me in the last letter.'

'Some special training he's into,' his father explained. 'Not that he was able to say much about it.' He saw Maria's eyes widen. 'Reading between the lines, that's what I think. We have a sort of code going between us two and you can surmise a lot by that.'

'At least while he's at training for whatever it is, he's safe,' his mother said with satisfaction. 'That's one blessing, anyway.'

'Oh, aye,' Maria agreed fervently. 'For my money, he could stay for the duration.'

But he wouldn't, of course. What could he be training for? Wasn't he already trained? Dear God, what horrors were in store for him?

'Now stop it, Maria,' Sean said firmly when she said this to him on her return. 'You have enough to worry about without thinking up further things. It might be nothing, just some notion his father has in his head.'

But Maria knew it wasn't. Didn't he mention the code they had? But, she couldn't burden Sean further. He had to catch the bus to Derry soon after, anyway.

'Now listen,' he said to Maria as he prepared to leave. 'I shan't be over next week, but I will be able to the weekend after. Is that all right with you?'

'Anytime I can see you will be fine,' Maria said in thankfulness.

The following Friday Maria had to be sharp with her mother to get her to leave Bella and the shop. She even had to take her hand to prevent her running back to it once they were in the street.

'For God's sake, Mammy, will you stop it,' she said. 'I'm too tired, cold and hungry for this carry-on. I need to get into the warm, have a sit by the fire and a cup of tea to keep me going till the tea's cooked and you are not helping, not one bit.'

Some of what Maria had said seemed to penetrate

Sarah's brain and she stopped pulling at her hand and walked calmly enough by her side, but Sam saw his daughter's face bleached white with tiredness as she bade Dora goodnight, and he felt consumed by shame.

He was always glad of Barney's company and even more glad of the poteen he brought. He knew that he was drinking far too much of it at times, but he needed it to blur the edges of his God-awful life.

That Sunday, Maria like millions of others, learnt of the bombing of the American Fleet by the Japanese at a place called Pearl Harbor.

Sam recalled the conversation he'd had with Sean just the previous week. 'The American's will be in now, whether they like it or not,' he said to Maria.

'Many say it's about time.'

'Aye, but I'd rather fight a Jerry or a bloody Eyetie than a Nip any day,' Sam said. 'Not bloody human, those Nips.'

Maria couldn't agree more. She wondered if American involvement would affect those in Britain and how, and seriously hoped not. She knew Greg had been based in St George's Barracks, Sutton Coldfield, but did much of his training in Sutton Park and another place called Cannock Chase, because he'd told her this much. She hoped he was still there, still safe.

Maria wasn't looking forward to Christmas one bit. She remembered other years when she would help her mother bake the cakes and mince pies, and boil the puddings. The sweet, spicy smell would linger in the air for days and they would sing carols together as they decorated the house with home-made streamers.

This year there was nothing. She was in no mood for making streamers, never mind finding the time to drape them around the room. She'd had no time either to make up any of the usual goodies and it was hard not to feel depressed about it, especially as there was no news of Greg coming home.

Then, the Friday before Christmas, 19 December, the men came. Con had visited before quite a few times, but this was every man that Sam had engaged to work in the docks. Many brought things from their wives – mince pies, a Christmas cake. Another brought a pudding, one had a cherry cake, another sausage rolls, while two sent half a dozen fresh duck eggs. Each of the men had a bottle or two in his hand.

Maria was overwhelmed with the men's generosity, but just as delighted that they took time to talk with her father. She busied herself bringing out more chairs and getting glasses for them all. Soon a bluish fug of tobacco smoke hung in the air, mixed with the smell of whiskey and poteen. Maria tackled a pile of ironing and listened to the chatter in the room. The voices rose and fell, occasionally laughter bursting into the air. Maria saw how her father's face was animated and knew she had been right: it was the company of men he missed.

Maria had given up her lunch hour to search Derry for presents, though the shops were not well stocked at all. She'd posted Greg's presents early: socks, a scarf, a large bar of chocolate, twenty cigarettes and a packet of the bull's-eyes he liked so much.

She also managed to get a soft shawl for Dora, fleece-lined slippers for Bella, and socks and hankies for Barney. For her father she had a new pipe and tobacco and a large bottle of whiskey.

She expected nothing from Greg but a card, if he was able to get one, so she was intrigued to receive a parcel the day before Christmas Eve. She lifted it down from the mantelpiece where Dora had put it, aware of the woman hovering, as anxious as she was to find out what was in it.

When Maria exposed the ring box, she felt as if her heart had stopped beating and she slowly opened it up. The ring was a diamond solitaire and so beautiful it took her breath away.

My Darling, darling Maria,
  I can wait no longer to give you this. I know girls often like to choose their own rings, but I want you to wear this now so that everyone can see your heart belongs to me. I had to guess the size, so if it's wrong, wear it round your neck till I come home. My beloved Maria, there aren't enough words to tell you how much I love you and miss you, and how I lie in bed each night and go over and over the time we spent together. I may get leave in the spring – I don't know. They tell us nothing, but you may be sure I will be hot-footing down to you as soon as I ever can.

There was more, much more, but the tears seeped from Maria's eyes as she put the ring on, twisting her hand this way and that so the diamond sparkled as the lights caught it.

'Ah, God, will you look at that. D'you see, Sam?' Dora cried.

'Come nearer, child,' Sam said, taking Maria's hand as she drew closer.

Maria was hesitant with her father. Maybe he'd be hurt by this sign that Maria was leaving childhood behind; maybe he'd feel his permission should have been asked.

However, when she said this, her father smiled and squeezed her hand. 'He did ask me, child, the time he came into hospital, when you took yourself off to powder your nose. He told me he'd loved you from the first time he'd seen you, but knew you were too young for him to speak and wouldn't have done it just yet if things had gone to plan. Child, I want you to have a good, caring man by your side to share this burden you have taken on. Oh, I know Greg is in the army just now, but the war will not last for ever. He is a fine young man, one to be proud of, and he will make you a good husband.'

'Thank you, Daddy.'

Maria doubted her mother took in the significance of the ring, but Barney did and he was shocked. He hadn't been aware the relationship had gone so far in the short space of time they'd had together, for Maria had never mentioned to Barney that she was writing to Greg, nor that she'd taken to visiting Greg's family.

'Can you not be happy for me, Barney?' she asked, noting his sullen face.

Barney could hardly tell her the truth. 'You're too young, far too young,' he said.

'For marriage, maybe,' Maria said, 'but this is engagement only.'

But it was enough. Barney felt sick to the pit of his stomach. 'I have a present for you too,' he said grudgingly, 'though you'll hardly want it now.'

'Of course I will.'

Later, Maria looked at the dainty gold locket on the fine chain and thanked Barney with a peck on his cheek, though she wondered if she had been wise to accept it. It was like the gift a boy or man would give to his girlfriend. Surely Barney didn't think . . . he couldn't imagine . . . He came nearly every night to see her father and that was all, she told herself. He'd never given her more than a cursory glance. He had no one to advise him that the locket was an unsuitable gift, that was all it was. She dropped the locket in the drawer of her dressing table and threaded the ring on the chain, for it was rather large for her finger and she didn't want to wear it openly till Greg was home and the engagement announced properly.

There was great jollification on New Year's Eve at Maria's house. The men who'd come before Christmas were joined by several others carrying instruments – a fiddle, banjo, accordion and bodhrán. They played the polkas and jigs they'd learnt in childhood.

Maria joined her female neighbours at the dancing. Then suddenly, as she wheeled around the room, she was caught up around the waist by one of the men not playing. Other men took hold of women until the whole room was a mass of people dancing. Even Bella, Maria saw, was inveigled into getting on her feet.

Sarah seemed to be enjoying herself as she sat before the fire, a smile playing about her mouth, and Sam's face was one beam of delight. Eventually Maria stopped, a rosy hue to her face and gasping a little with the unaccustomed exertion.

'Phew, I need a drink,' she said to Dora, who was sitting by the table laid with goodies.

'Another one has need of a drink too,' Dora said grimly, indicating Con's wife, sour-faced Brenda. 'She has upset half the room and has watched every drop that has passed Con's lips. Will you give her some stiff glasses of poteen to maybe loosen her up a bit? Anyway, the face on her would turn the milk sour.'

Maria laughed. 'Oh, Dora, I couldn't, and maybe she'd be worse if she had the drink on her.'

'She couldn't be worse, and if you care about Con at all, do all in your power to get that woman totally bottled,' Dora said with an emphatic nod. 'I'll help you.'

Maria, Dora, and Bella – who joined in, seeing what they were at – plied the woman with drinks all night. In the end Con nearly had to carry her home. 'At least she went with a smile on her face,' Bella remarked.

'Aye, but I wouldn't have her head in the morning.'

'It is New Year's Eve,' Bella remarked. 'They'll be a fair few the same.'

'Aye, and one of them my father,' Maria remarked. 'Good job I've kept my wits about me for I have the feeling Mammy will be the very devil to settle tonight too.'

*　　*　　*

Cold and blustery weather heralded 1942. First, there was snow descending from the leaden skies like a blanket of white, the blustery winds causing drifts as high as the windowsills, and piling on the roads to freeze at night, turning the place into a skating rink. The thaw in February was followed by rain, peppering the roads like bullets, driven by powerful winds to hammer on the windows and soak any unfortunate caught out in it in seconds.

Maria was glad to reach the mugginess and doubtful heat of the workroom. Often her sodden coat, like many others, would steam over the gas fire in the staff room, especially lit for that purpose.

The girls all grumbled about the weather. 'It's every day the bloody same,' Joanne said morosely. 'And the constant grey skies would put years on a body.'

'I must admit, I am fed up constantly feeling damp,' Maria said. 'The spring can't come soon enough for me.'

But the weather ceased to matter the day Maria got the letter inside the birthday card from Greg, saying there was every likelihood he would get a spot of leave towards the end of the month. That day she had met the postman on the way to the bus stop and read the letter on the way to work.

'What's up with you?' Joanne asked as she took her place beside her in the workroom. 'You've got a dirty great smile plastered over your face.'

'I got a letter from Greg,' Maria said. 'He thinks he'll get leave soon.'

'Embarkation leave, is it?' another asked.

'I don't know,' Maria said. 'Probably. But I am not

going to think of that. All I am going to concentrate on is my Greg coming home.'

She almost told them then about the ring, but she made herself wait. No one but her parents, Bella, Dora, Barney and Greg's family had actually seen it yet. Maria wanted to have a bit of a 'do' when Greg came home and announce the engagement properly. When she had suggested this in a letter, he had been all for it, so she wasn't going to spoil it now by telling, or showing anyone. She knew it would be all around the factory by lunch time.

In St George's Army Barracks, Sutton Coldfield, Greg was lying on his bunk thinking of Maria and how wonderful she was, when the sergeant strode into the room. Greg leapt to his feet

'Commander wants to see you, Hopkins,' the sergeant said. 'What you been up to lad?'

'Nothing, Sarge.' Greg could think of nothing he had done wrong.

'Well, go and find out quick,' the sergeant said. 'Don't keep him waiting.'

Greg thought back over the last few days for anything he might have done or said that was bad enough to be summoned by his commanding officer, but he could still think of nothing. Before he announced his presence he checked his boots, cleaning the toecaps with spit and a hanky, pulled his belt in, straightened his tie and knocked on the door with some trepidation.

'Come in!'

As Greg opened the door and stepped in, the two people sitting in chairs across from the commanding officer turned. The big bullish man Greg had never seen before, but the girl beside him was Nancy Dempsey, a girl he hadn't clapped eyes on for five months. This wasn't the Nancy he knew, however. No mischievous light danced behind those black eyes, and there was no sulky pout to the lip. In fact her lip was split right open and her whole face was swollen and bruised. Greg stared at the man beside her with distaste. He had no time for men who raised their fists to women.

And when Nancy spoke her voice was thick and indistinct. 'I'm sorry, Greg, really I am.'

Then Greg noticed something else. Beneath Nancy's coat was a definite protruding small bump. His head was reeling, his mind screaming denial.

'Well, Hopkins,' the officer said in clipped tones. 'Have you any idea why Mr Dempsey and his daughter are here?'

'Yes, sir . . . I mean, no, sir.'

'What d'you mean, "No, sir"?' the man demanded. 'I'll tell you what, sir. You took my daughter down and now I want to know what you are going to do about it.'

'Are you sure it was Hopkins?' The question was directed at Nancy, but it was her father who answered.

'Oh, it were him, all right. All over her like a rash last summer and into the autumn too, so her friends said. Then he dumped her like, but not before he filled her belly. She wouldn't tell me straight off. I had to beat her near black and blue before she let on it were him, like.'

'All right, Mr Dempsey,' the commanding officer said sharply. He looked at Greg. 'Do you deny this?'

He couldn't deny it, nor say before this bully of a man that Nancy had been mad for it, begging him. He'd taken precautions every time till the time he'd gone to tell her it was really and truly over, and had taken nothing with him. 'Just one last time to remember you by,' she'd begged, and then stupidly, because he felt sorry for her, he had obliged.

He felt sick to the base of his stomach. Almighty Christ, what was he to do? But he knew what he had to do. There was no other course open to him. 'I'll marry her,' he said. Then, because that sounded churlish and unkind, he turned to Nancy. 'Don't worry, Nancy, I'll not let you down. I'll marry you.'

'The chaplain can do the honours,' the commanding officer said.

'I must go home first, sir,' Greg said, 'to tell my parents.' But it wasn't his parents he had to tell most urgently, it was Maria. Maria, that he loved with all his heart and soul and mind, that he had lost for ever. He knew he would be dealing her a terrific blow and he didn't think he could bear her pain too; his own was making it difficult for him to draw breath.

The commanding officer surmised a lot by the look in young Hopkins's eyes, for it wasn't the first time such a thing had happened. 'When does your leave start?'

'In two days' time, sir.'

'Take it from tonight,' the officer said. 'I'll square it, don't worry. Tell your parents, then come straight back here. It's best the matter is done as speedily as possible.'

'You won't lose by it, Greg,' Nancy said. She was

imploring him to look at her with eyes of love and not duty, but Greg was dying inside, shrivelling up. 'I'll be a good wife to you, Greg,' she went on in desperation, 'and our mom says I'm a tidy cook, like.'

Shut your mouth, you sodding stupid bitch! Greg gasped. For a moment he thought he'd spoken the words aloud.

'You are dismissed, Hopkins,' the officer said.

Tears were smarting in his eyes as Nancy grabbed his hand. 'It will be all right, won't it, Greg?'

He couldn't speak, not without bawling like a baby. He said nothing, but pulled his hand away and left the room. He went outside the barracks, banged his head against the brick wall and he cried his eyes out.

CHAPTER FIVE

Despite losing pay, and her anxiety to keep in favour at work, Maria had taken the day off. Greg had told her what time the bus would stop in The Square. He could see her jumping from one foot to the other in excitement as the bus pulled in. He had barely left the vehicle when she launched herself at him, nearly overbalancing him, as he had a case in one hand.

'Oh, Greg, I've missed you and I love you so much.'

Greg just stood and looked at Maria. She cried, 'Put your arms around me, for God's sake. It's what I've longed for, for weeks.'

His heart like lead, Greg put his arms around the girl he loved beyond all others. 'Maria, we must talk.'

'Of course we must,' Maria said. 'Shall we go back?'

'No, not home, somewhere quiet.'

'There's only Daddy. Bella has Mammy till I go back.'

Was there nowhere in this whole God-damned place that they could be alone so that Greg could tell the lovely, wonderful girl that he was casting her aside for another? 'Maria, I need a private place.'

So did Maria. She wanted to run her fingers through

his regulation short hair, to trace the lines of his face with her kisses, and kiss his delicious lips until she was dizzy. And she wanted him to kiss her eyes and her throat in the way that caused her to moan in ecstasy as the yearning excitement mounted in her. Then she wanted to feel his lips on hers, his tongue darting in and out of her mouth, his hands feeling every bit of her.

Suddenly, she knew the place. 'We'll go to the boatyard,' she cried.

'Is there no one there? Colm . . . ?'

'Colm has the flu. He hasn't been there the last two days. He sent word down. There's even a heater there.'

Greg sighed. 'That's the place then.'

'Do you want to leave your case in the house as we pass?'

'No,' Greg said. He wanted to go nowhere and make small talk with anyone till he'd told his girl what he'd come to tell her. 'No, it's OK, really.'

They didn't take the coastal path; the wind was so fierce they'd be in danger of being plucked off it and flung into the lough. Even through the town, the wind gusting around them made conversation difficult, but Greg was glad of it. Maria had linked arms with him and the case dragged from his other hand as they toiled up the slight hill to Greencastle.

The boatyard was, as Maria had said, deserted, and she lifted the large stone beside the door, extracted the key and let them in. Greg was glad to be out of the wind, but the workroom was icy.

'Wait,' Maria said, seeming to know her way around the dim room, the light of the day, such as it was, hardly penetrating through the one small window.

Maria lit both a paraffin lamp and a stove, and then she wrapped her arms around Greg. 'Keep your coat on for a while,' she advised, ''till the room warms up a bit. Then,' she added impishly, 'we can take off as much as you'd like.' She clapped her hand to her mouth in horror at the realisation of what she had said.

'Maria!'

'Oh, Greg, how dreadful to come out with something like that,' she cried. 'You must be shocked, think me brazen. I don't know what came over me.'

'It doesn't matter,' Greg cried, putting down his case thankfully against an upended boat. The ground was littered with coils of rope and the room smelt of engine oil.

Maria produced two chairs and passed one over to Greg. 'Sit down, darling, and tell me what's on your mind,' she said. 'I can tell there's something.'

Now they were here, in this ideal place, isolated and alone, Greg didn't know how to start. He'd rehearsed it enough times. He'd travelled through the night, on train and mail boat, more trains and the bus to get here in the least time possible, but while it was one thing to rehearse his story cold, as if the tale was of someone else entirely, it was quite another to sit and look into the eyes of his beloved and tell it.

'Shall I make some tea?' Maria said suddenly. 'There's always some things kept in the cupboard in the kitchen place and I could boil the kettle on the stove, though I'm not sure if there's milk?'

Did he want tea? He didn't know. Would tea help the cold, dead feeling inside him? 'That would be nice,' he found himself saying.

So Maria busied herself and found milk that the cold weather had kept fresh. She asked no questions till the tea was made and poured, biscuits laid on a plate. Then she said, 'Now, tell me?'

Scalding as it was, Greg took a gulp of the tea, hoping it might steady his nerves. It didn't and he swallowed deeply before saying, 'This is hard for me, Maria, so hard. Before I realised that you felt as I had felt for years, that we're as one, in love, I went out with another. A girl called Nancy Dempsey.'

So that was it. In seconds, Maria was out of her seat and on her knees before Greg. She held his hands in hers and said, 'Greg, darling, I don't care about your past. You could have had a hundred girls and I'd not be a whit interested in any one of them. What I care about is here and now, you and me and our future together.'

'But that's it!' Greg cried desperately. 'We have no future together.'

He watched as the realisation of his words took hold, sank into Maria's mind. He saw the blood drain from her face, leaving it as white as lint, her eyes two pools of confused pain. 'What . . . what do you mean, Greg? What . . . what are you saying? Please, please don't say these hurtful things.'

Greg knew Maria was having difficulty even breathing. And her eyes . . . Oh God. He closed his own, but it didn't help. He still saw her look of betrayal. 'Dear Christ,' he cried, 'do you think I want to say such things? Enjoy hurting you, hurting myself this way?'

'Then why . . . ?'

'Listen,' Greg said. Maria had snatched her hands

away and he took hold of them again, massaging her fingers with his own as he went on, 'I would willingly give my life in exchange for yours and think it an honour. You are the first and last person I will ever love, for I will never, ever feel this way again. And yet, Maria, I must marry another.'

Maria gave a cry and snatched her hands away. One hand was before her mouth, the other folded around her chest as she sat down in the chair. Pain such as she'd never experienced before filled her body and she felt her heart – the heart she'd given to Greg – shatter into a million pieces.

'I have no choice,' Greg cried helplessly. 'Nancy carries my child.'

Now she understood. Greg, her Greg, had to be given to another. 'She is already five months gone,' Greg said, anxious that Maria knew it had been over before they declared their love for one another, before that first leave in October. 'And she'd had to be beaten quite severely before she would tell her father my name.' Maria seemed incapable of speech, so Greg went on, 'It is mine, Maria. I cannot deny it and I cannot desert her. What life would she have if I did that?'

Maria knew everything Greg said was true. The facts were like little hammers battering inside her head.

'Do you hate me, Maria?'

'I feel nothing for you,' Maria said flatly. 'My heart is broken.'

'I know,' Greg said. 'And mine too. Saying I am sorry is so inadequate, but I am sorry. You'd not believe how sorry I am. And though I must stand by Nancy and give her and the child my name, she will never have my love, or my heart. That belongs to you.'

Maria looked at Greg and wondered if he thought that made a difference. There was no point in talking any more. The talking was over now; to prolong it was pointless.

'I think you should leave,' she said, amazed by the controlled way she could say that, when inside she felt she'd been turned to jelly.

'I can't just leave you here.'

'You can't not,' Maria said. 'What I do is no longer your concern and I want you to go, now.'

'Maria, please . . .'

Maria leapt to her feet. 'Get out!' she screamed. 'God damn you. Get out! I don't want you here, or to ever see your face again. Now get out!'

Greg stood up and lifted his case. He knew he had no option but to go. 'Goodbye, Maria.'

Maria tossed her head, but did not acknowledge him in any other way. She was holding on to herself with great difficulty and barely had the door shut on him that she gave a great sigh. Her limbs were shaking uncontrollably. She had the urge to throw things – anything, everything. She wanted to scream at the unfairness of life.

Twice a tantalising future had been held before her and twice it had been pulled away before she could sample it. She thought she'd grieved for the college place, her father's accident, her mother's collapse, but it wasn't grieving like this – this devastating hurt flowing through her, the feeling that she was bare, exposed, for all to see.

She sank onto the floor, unable any longer to stay upright, and cried out all the anguish and pain, cried as if she'd never, ever stop. Eventually, she was quiet. She lay for a few moments longer before pushing herself into a sitting position and then getting to her feet groggily. She felt light-headed and she held on to the chair till the room stopped spinning around her. The future was like a bad taste in her mouth and she was in despair.

But there were still her parents to see to. She knew she must go on. She'd already left her father unattended for far too long. She didn't know the time, had no idea how long she had been there, but the paraffin lamp was spluttering and the fire in the stove much lower than it had been.

It was time to go, time to face the world. Maria put the biscuits away and threw the tea down the sink. She could go and tell the people of Moville of Greg's betrayal, then take on board their pitying looks and sidelong glances. No, by God, she'd not, she vowed. Pride was all she had left now and she wasn't losing one vestige of it.

Who knew anything about her and Greg anyway? Maria pondered as she made her way home. She had worn his ring beneath her clothes and had made no announcement. A few of the girls at the factory had known about Greg and they'd understand if she was to say she'd talked it over and they'd decided to cool everything until the war was over and she was a little more mature. They'd swallow that, even approve of it. 'Don't want to be rushing into anything now,' one woman had already said the once.

'Aye, that's right,' Joanne had agreed. 'I'm having the time of my life at the moment and I'll not give it up for any man till I'm good and ready.'

Bella and Dora would have to be told the truth, of course, but they'd not spread the tale about if she asked them not to. Her father would be disappointed, she knew. He wanted to see her settled and so did Sean. This latest development would once more chain him down. She wasn't worried about Barney for he hadn't approved of the engagement in the first place and she had no doubt that he'd accept what she said.

So, her pride would be intact, but inside she felt dead, numb, like half a person. This was a grievous blow she wondered if she'd ever recover from.

Her father was thankfully asleep when she reached the house. The first thing she did was to fetch an envelope from the bureau in her room and drop the ring in it. Tomorrow she would post it to Greg's parents, where she assumed he would be staying. There was no need for any explanation.

In fact, Greg wasn't at his parent's, for they wouldn't have him. His mother could scarcely believe that her son had slept with a girl before marriage, before even an understanding, and the news had shocked her to the core. Even his father, knowing more of the world and the need and urges of young men, was censorious.

'If you couldn't control yourself, couldn't you at least use something?'

Greg's head jerked up. 'What d'you know about things like that?'

'Enough,' his father snapped. 'I wasn't born yesterday.

91

I know too it's against the Church's teaching – not that they'd approve of fornication either, of course.'

'I did use something, Dad,' Greg admitted. 'Except for one time, the last time. I didn't think . . . Anyway, just once we used nothing.'

'Well, that one slip-up has ruined young Maria's life. I suppose you know that?'

And mine, Greg might have said, but he didn't. This was no time to think of himself. He nodded and his voice was thick when he said, 'I know, Dad.'

'You've condemned her to a life of drudgery and likely broken her heart, for she loved you dearly. The times she'd come here and talk about you, it's obvious what she thinks, how she feels. God, Greg, I'm surprised you can live with yourself.'

'Dad, I'm not proud of this, any of it,' Greg said. 'But, for God's sake, what was I to do? I'd finished with Nancy long before I declared myself to Maria and since that moment I have been true to her. But Nancy is pregnant with my child, Dad. I can't desert her.'

'Aye, I see that. It's a dreadful thing you did to that girl too.'

'Her father's beaten her black and blue.'

Greg's father imagined how the man would feel, how he would react if one of his daughters came home with the news she was with child. God, it didn't bear thinking about.

But what of his son? Should he allow him to come here, flaunting his sin for all to see, showing a bad example to his siblings and further heartache for Maria?

'Your mother and me have talked this over, Greg,' he said. 'You are right, you must marry this Nancy, but we don't want to see either her or you ever again.'

'What are you saying, Dad?'

'I'm saying you are not welcome here. Go back to England, do your duty by this girl and sever connections with your home. As far as your mother and me are concerned, by your actions and for the grave hurt you have caused a great deal of people, you can no longer regard yourself as a son of ours.'

Greg almost staggered from the room. He could scarcely believe the words his father had spoken. He'd always thought whatever he did, or said, they'd always love him, forgive him and welcome him. He'd never envisaged a time when he might be estranged from his parents – disagree with them, certainly, but exiled from home, never.

For Christ's sake, he was their eldest son. He sought out his mother, but her eyes were cold, her face set as she looked at him. 'I thought your father had spoken to you.'

'He has, Mom.'

'Well then?'

'I thought—'

'You thought I would be different. Let me tell you, Greg, you have cut me to the quick and I am engulfed with shame for the wrong you have done Maria and also, to a lesser extent, the piece you are marrying. Do you think I want you here after that, your brothers emulating you and your sisters thinking this is the way to behave? No, Greg. You made your bed and now you must lie in it. You can have one day here to get over the travelling and tomorrow you go back, and I don't want to see, or hear from you again.'

'Mom—'

'It's my last word on the subject.'

The ring plopped through the letterbox, the day after Greg left. Greg's mother opened the envelope and held the ring in the palm of her hand. She cried for Maria and the dream that had come crashing down on her head.

Knowing none of this, Maria skulked about the house for the first few days after seeing Greg, terrified of bumping into him.

Each day she'd wake with a heavy heart after a fitful sleep. It was as if she'd fallen into a pit of sadness and it tainted everything she did and said. Food tasted like sawdust, though the lump in her throat prevented her eating anything much. Never was she more glad of work, glad of the chatter of the girls that covered her own silence, and glad of the weary feeling after work, though she knew weariness alone didn't necessarily signify a decent night's sleep

She was worried which Mass Greg would attend on Sunday and she slipped into the one at nine o'clock, and looked around surreptitiously, but she was seen by one of Greg's sisters. None of Greg's brothers or sisters had been told about Greg, but they all knew. By eavesdropping on the raised voices, they'd put two and two together and, if there should be any doubt, one of them found the ring in the envelope that their mother had stuck behind the clock on the mantelpiece.

Now, that same girl, Josephine, sidled up to Maria

as soon as the Mass was over, guessing why she was so edgy. 'Greg's gone,' she said, with any preamble.

'Gone! So soon?'

'Well, banished is more the word.'

'Banished!'

'There was a terrific row,' Josephine said. 'We all know that our Greg did the dirty on you and none of us were too pleased with him. But Daddy and Mammy were furious. They told him to go and not come back, and none of us now are allowed to speak his name.'

Maria wondered if she had it in her heart to feel sorry for Greg, for she knew he cared for his family, but she felt nothing, as if his sister was talking about some stranger she hardly knew. It didn't make her feel any better, but it meant she could stop looking over her shoulder every five minutes.

'Thank you,' she said. 'Please give your parents my regards.'

''S all right,' Josephine said. 'We all like you. You could still come. Mammy and Daddy would love to see you.'

But that time was linked to Greg, visiting the parents of the man Maria intended spending the rest of her life with. 'I don't think that's a good idea,' she said, 'but thanks anyway.'

The following day in the chapel of St George's Barracks, a sad little group gathered. Greg looked tall and handsome in his uniform, but Nancy was dishevelled, her face still discoloured and awash with tears, her eyes red-rimmed and her hair piled untidily on her head.

But in front of her, for all to see, that no dress could hide, was the swell of her pregnancy.

The priest – Greg had insisted on a priest so that their marriage would be recognised in the Catholic Church – was a bit nervous of Nancy's belligerent father, sitting glaring at his daughter in the front row. He wanted the marriage over speedily and was glad neither had plumped for nuptial Mass. In a matter of minutes, Nancy was Mrs Hopkins.

She thought it made little difference. Greg was going overseas, so she was going back to live at home with the father, who had terrorised them all since babyhood.

However, Greg wasn't frightened of the man. He rather despised him as he would any who would hit a woman, and now he intended to see to it that marriage to him would protect her.

'There's to be no more heavy stuff,' he told Nancy's father sternly. 'Never raise your hand to Nancy again, or you'll have me to deal with. She is my wife now and not your responsibility.'

'You young—'

'There is nothing to be gained by calling me names,' Greg snapped. 'As soon as we can, we'll get a place of our own, but until then, please treat Nancy with respect.'

There was a lot more Nancy's father could have said, but looking Greg up and down he changed his mind and instead made do with a glare before leading his wife away.

Nancy's eyes were shining. No one had ever stood up to her father before. 'Oh, Greg,' she breathed. 'Oh, I love you so. I know you don't feel the same and I'm sorry you've been pushed into this.'

Greg suddenly felt sorry for the girl for the shabby wedding with the reluctant bridegroom, and he drew Nancy into his arms. 'I can't say I love you,' he said, for he thought she deserved honesty. 'But I can say I like you, and like you a great deal. I knew what I was doing the last time I slept with you. Between us we have created a baby, part of you and part of me, and for that I could love you. I'm sure when we are a proper family and have some place to call our own, then we will be happy together.'

Nancy thought of her own parents' turbulent marriage. 'D'you think so?' she said. 'See, my mom and dad—'

'Your parents are different people to us,' Greg said. 'I promise you two things: I will never raise my hand to you, nor will I be unfaithful. I might not have entered into this wholeheartedly, but now we are married I want to be a good husband to you and a good father to the child.' He'd been avoiding Nancy's eyes as he spoke, but he now took her chin and turned her to face him. 'Will that do?'

'Oh, Greg . . .' Tears sparkled in Nancy's eyes again, but they were tears of joy. What more could any woman ask? Greg's kiss, mindful of Nancy's puffy lip, was tender, and it caused such a feeling of exhilaration in Nancy that she felt she could have floated to the ceiling.

CHAPTER SIX

'So the way's clear for you, dear brother, now lover boy Greg is out of the way,' Seamus said to Barney a month after he heard about the split.

'She doesn't know I exist,' Barney said gloomily. 'Not like that, anyway.'

'Prove you do.'

'How d'you propose I do that?'

'You could try wining and dining her.'

Barney shook his head. 'She's changed,' he said. 'She's sort of sad all the time. I don't think she's thinking about men at the moment.'

'Well, get at her through the old folks, then, so she starts to notice you.'

'Not the mother,' Barney said. 'She gives me the willies, the mother, but her father's all right. Fact is, I've thought for a while it's a bloody shame for him to be lying in bed with the sun shining outside. Now that spring's definitely here, I could push him about in a wheelchair on fine afternoons.'

'You got a wheelchair?'

'No, but I'm sure the doctor can get a loan of one from the hospital or some such place.'

Maria, when he broached the subject one day, after Sam had gone to sleep, was doubtful. 'What harm could it do?' Barney asked.

Maria couldn't think of any. 'Come on, Maria,' Barney went on. 'It would be just like him sitting up in bed, and he manages that, all right. Surely it's not right for him looking at four bare walls when there is an alternative, and it would free Dora in the afternoons.'

'All right,' Maria said. 'Speak to the doctor. If he's in agreement and can get a wheelchair then I don't mind at all. But what about your job?'

'Oh, I start early morning, so I'm finished by the afternoon,' Barney said.

In fact they finished long before that – in the early hours of the morning sometimes – and would go home to sleep until hunger drove them to find out if they had anything in the house at all edible. But that wasn't something he wanted to share with Maria just yet a while.

The doctor was so enthusiastic about the proposal to take Sam out that all Maria's worries about it floated away. She trusted Barney to care for him, of course she did, and Sam liked the young man. Still, she arranged for the first outing to be on a Saturday when she could see to her father and be on hand if there were problems.

It was Sam himself who was the most hesitant. Though he missed the fresh air and longed to go out, he was nervous.

'It's to be expected, Daddy,' Maria said. 'Even putting clothes on after all this time has got to be strange.'

The clothes Sam had once worn so comfortably now

hung on his sparse frame. The effort of getting dressed, together with the fresh air, meant that the first outing wore Sam out so much it lasted only fifteen minutes. A week later it had risen to half an hour.

By then, Sam was the most enthusiastic of them all. He liked the chance to get out and about around the town, to be pushed to the pier or on the green and to look across the Foyle at the activity on the water and the docks. Sometimes he could hear and see the planes taking off. He also liked the chance to talk to people, to hear the news and gossip.

'D'you know what I'd really like?' he said to Maria that night after the first half-hour outing as she helped him into bed. 'I'd like to go to the pub a time or two. D'you think Barney would take me with him some night?'

'I don't know that you would be able for that.'

'Of course I would.'

Maria wasn't at all keen and she couldn't analyse why not. She asked herself, why shouldn't her father go to the pub? It was a normal thing to do, for God's sake. All the same she was glad her uncle was coming up the Friday that Barney had agreed to take Sam to the pub.

'Keep an eye on him, Uncle Sean,' she said as they were about to leave.

'God, Maria, what d'you expect him to do? Dance naked up on the table?'

'No.'

'Well then, what is it?'

'It's silly, I know it is,' Maria said. 'It's just that . . . look, Uncle Sean, Daddy hardly drank much before. He drank virtually nothing at all after the war started and before he began at the Derry boatyard, because he couldn't afford it. But, well, he's different now.'

'A lot of things are different,' Sean said gently. 'Then he was a man, fit and well able to look after his family and put money on the table for anything needed – money to send his clever girl to college. What does he have now? I'm delighted Barney is taking him out each fine afternoon, but it's still not much of a life, not compared to what he had. If he takes a drop too much and it helps him cope, can we blame him?'

'No, no, of course not,' Maria said. 'I told you I was being silly.'

Despite the assurances Sean had given Maria, he'd been a little concerned to see the amount of hard stuff – whiskey and poteen – that Sam was drinking each night, certainly the weekends he'd been there. Sam had been a Guinness man, and that in moderation, but he supposed as Barney had begun to bring round the hard stuff there was nothing to do but drink it. He'd advise him to go easy tonight, though.

However, Sean was soon aware there were no words invented that could stop the drinks piled on Sam that night. It was his first foray into the pub since the accident and, as it was Friday, many of his old workmates were in there. Everyone wanted to clap him on the back and buy him a pint. Those workmates not there were sent for, and those passing in the street came into the pub on hearing Sam Foley was in there.

Rafferty's had never done such trade. The noise, laughter, cigarette smoke and Guinness gave Sam back some of his pride, and when people sat beside him at the table, he was the same height as everyone else.

In the end, Sean had to hold Sam upright in the wheelchair while Barney pushed him home at just turned ten o'clock, for the man was very nearly comatose.

'I couldn't help it,' Sean said to Maria when he saw her eyes flashing fire. 'None of us could.'

'It's because it was his first time out,' Barney said.

'I had little myself,' Sean said. 'I'll see to him, if you like. And I'm sure Barney here will stay for a cup of tea.'

'No, no, I won't, if you don't mind,' Barney said with a glance at the clock. 'I said I'd meet Seamus later.'

When Barney let himself out, he slunk away in the shadows, down the hill and out of the town to the dark entry where Seamus was waiting in the lorry.

'Where the hell have you been?'

'I had to take Sam home,' Barney said. 'You mind I said I was taking him to the pub? I couldn't leave him with Sean. He couldn't sit upright even. Talk about legless.'

'I'll give you legless if you don't get in this sodding lorry and quick,' Seamus said, revving the engine as Barney leapt in. 'Ten o'clock we're supposed to start from here. You know this all boils down to timing. Can't have them hanging about waiting for stuff.'

'OK, I know,' Barney said. 'And I am sorry. It was his first night, for Christ's sake.'

'Filled that full of booze, it might be his last,' Seamus said, and added callously, 'Get him home for half-nine in future. It's late enough for a cripple like him to be out anyway.'

'That's a bloody awful thing to say, Seamus.'

'Look, Sonny Jim,' Seamus snarled, 'we're not

running a charity. This is how we live and I don't see you complaining when you get your cut.'

'No . . .'

'Well, then. Do what you like with whoever you like, but be here on bloody time or else.'

Barney knew what the 'else' meant. He'd been on the receiving end of it enough times and even now, fully grown as he was, he was frightened of his brother. 'OK, OK. Keep your bloody hair on.'

'As long as we get it straight,' Seamus said grimly and he let out the throttle and the lorry roared through the back roads on its way to Derry.

'Haven't you sweetened up that girl enough to go out with you yet?' Seamus asked Barney towards the end of June. 'You've spent enough time with the father.'

'I don't take Sam out because of Maria,' Barney said. 'I did at first, but not now.' Sam's first trip to the pub was not his last and now he usually went once or twice a week. If Sean wasn't there to take Sam home, Barney would deliver him to the door no later than a quarter to ten. He would never come in, claiming he had business with his brother.

'Well, is she nicer to you because of it?

'She's pleasant enough, but then she's always been pleasant,' Barney said.

'She's had time and enough to get over lover boy, surely to God.'

Barney wondered if she'd ever get over him. The whole experience had changed her. There had used to be a gaiety about her, the liveliness of youth, but that was gone now. She was still incredibly thin and Barney often saw her looking pensive, her eyes glittering with unshed tears.

However, he thought Seamus was right. He should bite the bullet and ask her out. What had he to lose? Anyway, how could she hope to get over Greg when she had nothing and no one to put in his place? Derry had plenty of cinemas, and he was sure she'd love to see Springtown Camp, where many of the Americans were based.

Maria, in fact, knew all about it, for the girls at the factory had told her and she'd seen pictures and reports on it in the paper. The like of it had never been seen in Derry before. It was all landscaped, with circular areas of grass broken up with concrete roads leading to the centre circle, where on the flag pole the Stars and Stripes fluttered. There was also a library, barber's shop, laundry, theatre and canteen complex that doubled as a dance hall. Soda fountains and an ice-cream machine were installed inside.

'God, Maria, if you go nowhere else in your life, go and have a peep at that place,' Joanne had said to her one day. 'Jesus, it's like something out of the movies.'

'Have you been to any of the dances?' Maria asked. 'Just last week there was a big feature about them in the paper.'

Joanne made a face. 'I haven't, worse luck. I would bite the hand off anyone who offered to take me there, though.'

'What's stopping you just turning up?'

'Well, that's just it. You see, all girls have to be accompanied by a man,' Joanne said. 'And I haven't got one at the present moment, not anyone permanent.

I'm more like playing the field. Anyway, I think it is one of the stupidest rules in the world. Think of all those homesick Americans I could be such a comfort to, if I could just get past the bloody sentry.'

'You've tried, haven't you?' Maria cried, knowing Joanne well. 'You have actually tried to get in?'

Joanne grinned. 'Aye, I did,' she said. 'It was just the once and I didn't go on my own. I was with a couple of friends and we had fortified ourselves first with a few gin and tonics. Anyway, this beefy Yank sent us away with a flea in our ears. How we've laughed about it since.'

But, despite Joanne's endorsement, when Barney asked Maria she said she had no desire to see Springtown Camp either now or in the future, and no thank you she didn't want to go to the cinema either.

'You go nowhere,' he complained.

'I don't want to go anywhere.'

'Maria . . .'

'Leave me alone, Barney, please.' She laid a hand on his arm. 'You're a good man, Barney, kind and considerate to Daddy. Concentrate your efforts there – they'd be better received – because I am fit company for no one.'

'Shouldn't I be the judge of that?'

'No, really, Barney. I'm fine as I am.'

She wasn't. He knew it and so did Bella McFee. A month later she also had a go at Maria.

'Your father has a better social life than you.'

It was true. As well as going out to the pub on Friday and Saturday nights, where Sam would meet again with all his mates, Barney had started taking him for a few jars after their afternoon walk too. Maria wasn't aware of this straight away, and even when Barney mentioned it she said nothing. She knew her father was probably drinking far more than was good for him, but he was happier in himself and looked forward to his excursions.

'You're not still pining for that Greg boy?' Bella asked.

'What if I am?'

'It's madness, girl. It's been over four months now.'

'I know just how long it is, thank you.'

'Rumour is his wife had a little girl; calls her Annabel.'

That hurt. Hurt like a knife in the heart. That Nancy had her man for her own and now she had a child by him. She had to stop this, get a grip on herself.

'How do people get to know these things?' she forced herself to say.

'You mind me telling you Maureen Kelsey has a daughter lives in a place called Aston in Birmingham. She saw them first at Mass. Course, it was Greg she recognised and he introduced his wife. She saw at once she was carrying, like, and then she saw her at the grocer's getting her rations and she had the wee one in the pram.' She shook her head and went on, 'I thought him such a decent, honest man – I never dreamt he'd do that to you. Betray you that way.'

'He didn't,' Maria said, 'not really. That business with Nancy was long over.'

'So he says.'

'He was telling the truth, Bella. I'd have known if he was lying. And when the girl found herself pregnant, what could he do but marry her?'

'Well, she's having to cope without him now,' Bella

went on. 'because she was telling Maureen's daughter she thinks he's in North Africa. No one's absolutely clear. You must forget him, girl, and I know that's easier said than done, but if you were to go out a time or two, you might find it a little easier.'

'You sound like Barney.'

'Barney?'

'Yes. He's at me to go out too.'

'With him?'

'Aye,' Maria said, and added with a wry smile, 'Hardly on my own.'

Bella had her own views on Barney McPhearson and they were the same as her mother's, and yet, well, it wasn't as if Maria was overburdened with offers and in some cases it was better the devil you know. 'Why don't you go then?'

'I don't want to.'

'Maria, you really can't go on like this,' Bella said sternly. 'You'll make yourself ill and it's upsetting your daddy.'

Maria knew Bella was right about that. Her daddy was worried about her, convinced he was spoiling her life and wouldn't rest about it, however much she tried to reassure him.

'You think I should go out with Barney?'

'Well, it would do no harm,' Bella said. 'Do you like him?'

'Bella, I don't know what I feel,' Maria cried. 'It's like I'm dead and shrivelled up inside. But I suppose I like Barney well enough.'

'Good God, girl!' Bella exclaimed. 'You're too young to be shrivelled anywhere. And if you like Barney well enough, that's a start. Go out with him, for heaven's sake, before you crumple into a heap of dust.'

Barney had negotiated with his brother to have Friday and Saturday nights free and took Maria to see *Fantasia* the following Saturday evening. Though Barney had thought it in the nature of a proper date, he didn't think that Maria saw it that way at all. He told himself it was something that she had agreed to go over the doorstep with him at all and he knew he had to proceed with caution.

Before Maria left that evening, she'd sat down beside her father and held his hand. Once his face had been as ruddy as Sean's through being out in all weathers, but now Sam's face was pale and the skin slack so that it lay in folds. His eyes were rheumy, but still full of love for Maria. When he told her he was happy that she'd agreed to go out with Barney at last, she knew he meant it.

'You'll have to forgo the pub tonight.'

'Aye, it'll do me no harm.'

'No harm indeed,' Maria replied with asperity.

'Ah, Maria, forgive my little weakness,' Sam said. 'It's all the pleasure I have left now and it helps me cope.'

Maria immediately felt guilty. 'Shall I run over to Rafferty's for a couple of bottles of Guinness?' she said. 'I'll have time before the bus.'

'No,' Sam said. 'I have a bottle of better stuff,' and he drew a bottle of poteen from under the covers.

'Where did you get that?' Maria asked, surprised.

'Barney brought it in earlier.'

Maria sighed, but said not a word more. Instead, she gave him a glass and went up to get ready.

'You look a picture, Maria,' Sam said, when she came back into the room.

'You're biased,' she replied with a smile, 'and your brain's addled with poteen. Listen, now, Mammy is asleep and Dora will be in directly. I'll knock the door as I pass.'

'Yes, yes. I'll be all right. Don't fret. Get yourself away.'

'I will, in a minute.'

Just then there was a knock at the door. 'That'll be him,' Sam said. 'Don't keep him waiting.'

Maria was impressed by Barney's appearance. He was wearing the suit he wore to Mass. His shirt was pristine white and not creased. His shoes were highly polished and she smelt the Brylcreem and knew he'd tried to curb his unruly curls, but not terribly successfully.

However well Barney looked, though, Maria was convinced she was making a mistake in agreeing to go out with him at all. Her stiffness and stance told Barney quite clearly that she would reject any move towards greater intimacy and so he didn't even try to put an arm around her shoulder, or hold her hand as they made their way to the bus stop Then she'd sat beside him in the bus as if she was a lump of wood.

It was slightly better when they got to the cinema. Although Maria did hold her body away from him pointedly at first, she did relax more as she began to enjoy the film. It was by the American, Walt Disney, whom everyone seemed to be talking about. Maria thought that if her opinion had been asked before she had seen it she would have said she wouldn't be interested in it at all. With all the animation and such, it sounded like something for weans surely. However, she found herself fascinated by it. She was glad it was as unlike the films she'd seen when she was with Greg as it was possible to be.

When they arrived home, it was to find her father fast asleep and Dora dozing in the chair. Maria's conscience smote her. Dora and her daughter had been so supportive, she felt she'd never be able to repay the debt. Without them, not only would she not have got out tonight, but she'd not have been able to work and what would they have done then? No one can live on fresh air.

Gently, she shook Dora awake. 'Do you want a cup of tea, or do you want to go straight home?' she asked as Dora struggled to sit up straighter, her eyes still heavy with sleep.

'Tell you the truth, Maria, I need my bed more than a drink,' she said.

'I'll walk home with you,' Barney said.

'It's just down the street. What d'you think would happen me?'

'Well, I'm leaving anyway, aren't I?' Barney said, casting an eye in Maria's direction. She knew she should offer him a drink of some such, say it was no bother, insist even, but she was too weary to play those sort of games and so she said, 'If you don't mind, Barney. I'm tired too.'

The flash of disappointment was gone in an instant. 'Did you enjoy tonight?'

'I did very much,' Maria said sincerely. 'Thank you for taking me.'

'No problem,' Barney said. 'Maybe we can do it again, sometime?'

'Maybe.'

'Like next week?'

'Oh, I don't know,' Maria said. 'That doesn't just depend on me.'

'If it's me you are thinking of, Maria,' Dora said, 'then don't. I can doze by your fireside as easy as I can by my own and everyone has to get out now and again.'

In the end a pattern was established and over the next few weeks, until the summer was passed and the autumn's nip in the air, Maria and Barney saw *The Thief of Baghdad*, *The Philadelphia Story*, *Dumbo*, and *Mrs Miniver*. They'd also been out to dinner once, to a theatre in Derry to see *Fanny By Gaslight*, and once just to the pub, where they'd talked all evening and found out a lot about each other. After each date, unusually for her, Maria would tell Joanne all about it.

Joanne was delighted that Maria, at last, was beginning to live a little. She had been very concerned about that business with the other boy that Maria had once seemed crazy about. She had said they had decided to cool it till after the war, and that was all well and good, but then she never mentioned his name again, as if he had disappeared off the face of the earth. When once Joanne, intrigued, had asked about him, Maria's eyes filled with tears and so she never asked again. Maria also seemed to have lost any of the gaiety she once had and seemed instead to be engulfed in misery. Joanne felt you could almost reach out and touch the sadness wrapped around her like a cloak.

Joanne knew Maria had been hurt, and badly, and had sincerely hoped that the experience hadn't put her off men for life. That would be a tragedy altogether. But she was fine now. Here she was, going with another strapping chap, by all accounts, and one she had known for years. He had been once employed by her father too, and her father fully approved of him.

'Do you love him?' Joanne asked.

Maria hesitated. She didn't love Barney like she had Greg, when just to whisper his name would fill her with joy and cause her heart to stop beating for a second or two, when she'd long to feel his arms around her, his lips on hers and the rapturous feelings they induced in her, especially when Greg's hands had explored her body.

She had not wanted or invited such intimacy with Barney. 'I don't know,' she said at last. 'But I don't think so. We don't . . . you know.'

'Kiss? You don't kiss?'

'We don't do anything.'

'Nothing at all?'

'No. I don't really want to.'

'And he puts up with it?' exclaimed Joanne. 'God, I didn't think they made them like that any more. I've never met any. You've got yourself a gentleman, Maria. But be careful – even gentlemen have their limits of patience.'

Maria thought long and hard about what Joanne said. Even if she didn't love Barney, she didn't want the outings with him to stop. It was the only light relief she had. She now looked forward to their weekends and had begun to laugh again. She knew, though, that if she wanted to continue to go out with Barney she had to start being fairer towards him.

It was as they were leaving the cinema the following Saturday, after seeing *Pinocchio*, that Barney said, 'There's a dance next week at Springtown Camp.'

Maria couldn't help smiling. Joanne would give her eyeteeth to be in my shoes just now, she thought, because as yet she hadn't been to one of the dances there. But how could she, Maria, go to a dance? She hadn't the clothes, and even if she had, she didn't know how to dance properly. So she said, 'I haven't danced for years. Anyway, they'll hardly be playing the music for a jig or the odd hornpipe.'

'No, they won't,' Barney conceded.

'Well, I don't know how to do anything else, waltz, foxtrot and all,' Maria said.

'There isn't much of that either,' Barney said. 'By all accounts it's mainly jitterbugging.'

'Jitterbugging! What the hell is jitterbugging?'

'The new craze sweeping America, if you believe all you read in the papers,' Barney said. 'Do you want to go?'

'Oh, I don't know.'

'Just for a look,' Barney said. 'Go on, Maria, say you'll go. I haven't seen jitterbugging either. I'd like to know what the fuss is all about.'

Maria couldn't see Barney's face in the blackout, but she heard the pleading in his voice and she felt sorry for him. He turned up every week, regular as clockwork, to take her to the cinema, to see something she chose, and she never gave anything back. A few times, he'd tried to hold her hand and she'd pulled away. Each time he'd left her at the door and she'd gone inside, while he'd walked home with Dora. He'd never complained to her, though she'd seen the disappointment in his eyes. Surely she could do this one little thing for him? 'If you want then.'

'If you don't like it, we don't have to stay.'

'No, all right,' Maria said. 'I expect I will like it well enough when I get there.' She reached for his hand as she spoke and heard Barney's sharp intake of breath as their hands met. It was surprisingly how comforting it was to have her hand held by a strong man's, Maria thought, and as they made their way to the bus stop, Barney's heart was lighter than it had been for ages.

That night, Barney was asked in and Dora made her way home alone, waving away Barney's offer of help. 'Not in my dotage yet, and don't you forget it,' she said.

Barney's grin at Dora's words took Maria by surprise. Barney was a handsome man, she'd always thought, but she hadn't seen him as desirable. For all they'd been out together, she hadn't counted them as dates. She'd never had the slightest interest in Barney that way. After Greg she thought she'd never feel that way for anyone again. Now it was quite reassuring to find she wasn't dead inside, but had just been deeply asleep.

Barney too felt the easing of tension in Maria and accepted the tea she gave him. But he was careful not to push it, not to outstay his welcome. When he drew her into his arms to kiss her good night, she went willingly, and when his kisses became more ardent, she didn't pull away, but responded.

He felt as if he was walking on air that night as he made his way home.

CHAPTER SEVEN

Maria was quite shocked by jitterbugging at first. It seemed too vibrant, the movements, such as they were, done in an almost abandoned manner. The place was, of course, dripping with Americans. Maria had come across many in Derry, but as she dressed in workday clothes, usually with her hair covered by a turban, she'd never had more than a cursory glance.

However, that night the dress she had on was one she'd made herself from some shiny green satin she'd had for ages. She'd often designed her own clothes and the dress was spectacular – fitted across the bust, with long flowing sleeves, the waist was dropped and the skirts fuller from there with little pleats tucking into the waistband.

Barney was almost speechless when he'd come to pick her up that evening. Her eyes looked greener and larger than ever. He saw many people turn to stare at Maria as they made their way into the hall. Nor was Maria allowed to sit at a table to watch all evening. She refused many offers to dance, saying she didn't know how to do it, but eventually a couple approached.

'Don't say you don't know how to do it, lady,' said the man. 'It's easy. So, how will it be if I teach you, while my girl teaches your man?'

Maria felt she'd rather have crept away to the ladies', but she saw by Barney's face he'd like to do this and so she nodded her head and let the man lead her onto the dance floor. It was as easy as the soldier had prophesied, and the music great to dance to. Maria was only afraid when the man caught her around the waist and swung her around that she might show her knickers, for the skirt of her dress fanned out like a flower.

But, all in all, she enjoyed her first American dance. Barney was proud of her, proud to be seen with her, and though he had no objection to her dancing with others, he kept a weather eye on the situation. He'd almost lost Maria once to another by staying quiet; he had no intention of running that risk again so he made sure he danced with Maria more than any other.

Maria knew what Barney was afraid of – she could almost feel his unease – but he needn't have worried. She had no designs on any American. But it was nice to be admired, to be openly told how beautiful, charming, truly lovely she was. It gave Maria a boost, as it would any girl. It didn't matter if they said the same to everyone, it made her feel good about herself, which was something she hadn't felt in a long, long time.

That evening there was no question of Barney going straight home. As he followed Maria in, Dora began collecting her things together.

'Good night?'

'Oh, Dora, it was wonderful,' Maria said. 'Did you have any trouble?'

'No, your mother never stirred and your father has been asleep for about two hours,' Dora said.

Maria knew it would have been a poteen-induced sleep, but she wasn't going to worry about that any more.

She closed the door on Dora and said to Barney, 'Thank you, I've had a lovely evening.' She kissed him gently on the lips and when he put his arms around her, she held him tight and sighed. Barney released her, took her hand and led her to the settee, where he sat and pulled her down beside him.

There was no point, Barney thought, in beating about the bush. 'Do you like me, Maria?'

'Of course I like you.'

'Could you more than like me? Love me even?'

'I've never thought of you that way.'

'Do you still think of him that did the dirty on you?'

Greg? All the time, Maria might have said, but she didn't say that. Instead, she said. 'I did. He hurt me very much, that time.'

'Did you love him?'

Maria nodded. 'And I know I feel something for you, but I'm not sure what yet. I think I need a little time before I can be sure of my feelings.'

'And we'll continue seeing each other?'

'Of course,' Maria said. 'Anyway, we could hardly not with all you do for Daddy.'

'I like your father, Maria,' Barney said. 'I get on well with him and always have.'

'I know this,' Maria said. She knew that Barney hadn't taken to her mother – couldn't take to her – but then he wouldn't be the only person made nervous by mental illness.

'We'll leave it so for now then,' Barney said, getting to his feet. 'I'll press you no further tonight, but will await your answer.'

Monday morning, Joanne wanted to know all about the dance, what Maria wore, what it was like and was jitterbugging as much fun as everyone said it was. When all the questions had been asked, she said, 'I hoped you thanked your Barney properly for taking you out to somewhere so fabulous.'

'Well,' said Maria with a smile, 'let's say I didn't leave him at the door.'

'I should think not,' Joanne said indignantly. 'You can carry this chivalrous behaviour too far, you know.'

'Actually he asked me if I could love him?'

'Golly, that was quick. Could you?'

'Oh, I don't know. Sometimes I think yes and other times no. I don't want to go back to the way it was, the daily grind with work and my parents and nothing to look forward to at all, but then . . .'

'Don't tie yourself down because of something like that,' Joanne said. 'God, I wish I looked like you and had your figure. Lads must be queuing up to claim you.'

'They're not, Joanne,' Maria said. 'I have a bedridden father, fast turning into an alcoholic, and a mother who doesn't know what day of the week it is. That is enough to put off any but the most stalwart. Barney knows the situation and accepts it. He is good with Daddy and they get on together. He isn't so good with Mammy, but then that is the same as everyone else.'

Joanne said nothing, for she sensed that Maria hadn't

finished. After a while, she went on, 'I suppose what I am really saying, Joanne, is if I don't take Barney, I think in the end I will be left alone, and I have coped alone for long enough. There is something else as well. So many demands are made upon me, I seldom have time to think about myself. It would be wonderful to have someone who cared about me and my needs. I could do with that so much sometimes when I feel the burden is heavy.'

'I've heard and understood every word that you've said,' Joanne replied. 'And all I would advise is, take your time over making the decision.'

'Barney isn't pressing me,' Maria said. 'But on the other hand, he'll not wait for ever.'

Before she'd analysed how she felt about Barney, Bella came over one evening to talk about Sarah. She left it till she knew Sarah was in bed and then she confronted Maria and her father. 'It's not that I'm not sorry for her. God, it breaks my heart to see her this way, but . . . well, it's the aggression, d'you see? She nearly scratched the eyes out of Maggie and bit me on the arm.' At this, Bella rolled up her sleeve to show the ring of purple teeth marks sunk into the skin. 'And it was for nothing at all, you know,' she went on. 'Have you not noticed it yourself?'

Maria had noticed Sarah often slapped out at her and pushed her away roughly, but she hadn't started biting or scratching. There was no doubting the marks on Bella's arm, though. 'I'm sorry to the heart of me that you have had to cope with this,' said Sam.

Bella looked from Sam to Maria and back again.

Maria said. 'I've noticed Mammy being rougher than she used to be.'

'Have you?' Sam said.

'Aye,' Maria said. 'I think it's frustration. It's always when I'm doing things with her.'

'I'm sure you're right,' Sam said. He too had noticed the deterioration in his wife and so had Barney. He knew because they'd talked about it often, as Barney wheeled him about the town, or later in the pub, sinking a pint or two. Sam knew Barney had been nervous of Sarah from the first, but didn't blame him for that. He'd known and loved Sarah for years, but that girl and woman had ceased to exist. Sometimes her odd behaviour left him edgy.

'She's getting no better, Sam, but worse,' Barney had said just days before. 'And it's Maria bears the brunt of it.'

'God,' Sam said, 'd'you think I don't know that?'

'I know,' Barney said soothingly. 'And it's never an easy choice to make to put someone away, but have you thought of it from Sarah's point of view? You might in fact be doing her a disservice leaving her in the house.'

'How?'

Barney chose his words with care. If any sort of future lay with Maria, as he hoped, then that mad old woman could not be part of it, but he knew he mustn't betray how he was feeling. 'Well,' he said, 'she's getting no treatment while she stays at home.'

'Is there treatment for what ails her?' Sam asked. Hope, like a flickering candle flame, began to burn inside him.

'I don't know,' Barney said. 'But she hasn't had the chance to see if they can do something for her.'

'Maria wouldn't like her going anywhere.'

'This isn't just about Maria,' Barney said bluntly. 'It's about what's good for Sarah. Why don't you talk it over with Dr Shearer? He could call one afternoon when Maria's at work, and she'd need know nothing about it. I should be guided by him.'

Sam saw the sense of that. Dr Shearer called a couple of days later and Sam asked Barney to stay. The doctor was not a specialist in matters of the mind and didn't pretend he was. His main concern was for Maria, for he'd often glimpsed her at Mass and knew she looked worn out.

What he said was, 'I don't know much about the treatments that could be offered to your wife, Sam, but they have made great strides in mental health in the past five years.'

'So she might get a little better if we agree to her going away for specialist treatment?' Sam said.

'She may,' the doctor said, and gave a shrug. 'She may not, but one thing I can say categorically is she'll not improve being left to languish at home.'

'She'll be upset,' Sam said. 'We'll have to prepare her.'

'If she is as bad as you say, she'll hardly know anything about it,' Dr Shearer said. 'It's Maria—'

'It's all right,' Barney put in. 'I'll deal with Maria.'

The doctor's eyes narrowed. So, he thought, that's the way of it. He had little time for the McPhearsons and knew they didn't earn a living honestly, and yet even those who whispered about Barney agreed he was kindness itself to Sam. Maybe, the doctor thought, if he married Maria, he'd have a turn-around. He'd seen it before.

Anyway, it wasn't as if the path to Maria's door was beaten down with a host of other suitors. He'd glimpsed her a few times some months back with the Hopkins lad, but that had obviously come to nothing. She needed someone to shoulder the burden she had piling on top of her and maybe Barney was better than none at all.

'Very well then,' the doctor said. 'I'll make enquiries. There's nothing to be gained by dallying.'

So, armed with the doctor's recommendation, they were all waiting for Maria when she came in from work. Sam had even asked Bella to come in to lend weight to the argument. Maria was semi prepared, for when she had called in at the shop to collect her mother, Dora had met her at the door and said to leave her a while, her daddy wanted to talk to her about something.

She guessed what it was, and when she saw the deputation waiting for her, she felt her heart sink. 'What's this?' she said, though she knew full well.

'Come up here to me,' Sam urged.

Maria didn't even remove her coat before approaching the bed and perching on the side of it, where she looked straight into her father's face and asked again, 'What's this?'

Sam reached for Maria's hands and said gently, 'It's about your mother, pet. You know what is to be done. There is now only one course open to us.'

The roof of Maria's mouth was suddenly very dry. They were all ranged against her, even Barney, she thought. But Sarah was her mother. Surely, they could see that. 'I can't . . .' she almost whimpered. 'I can't have her put away.'

'Come, come,' Sam said. 'Don't think of it as putting her away. Think of it as going to the psychiatric unit for treatment.'

'Huh.'

'Look, Maria,' Barney said. 'If your mother had something physical – pneumonia, let's say – then you wouldn't hesitate to send her to hospital. Why is this different?'

Maria didn't know why; it just was.

'The doctor said she'll not know a thing about it,' Sam said. 'It'll not matter to her where she is.'

Maria's intake of breath was audible. 'You've had the doctor,' she said almost accusingly. 'Behind my back.'

'We wanted to know the facts,' Sam said.

'And they are?' Maria demanded icily.

'The doctor thinks we're doing her a disservice keeping her here,' Sam said. 'He's making enquiries at the hospital.'

'And I can't have her in the shop any more,' Bella put in. 'Really I can't. It isn't fair on anyone. She often won't stay in the back like she used to and wanders about the place, picking things up. It puts the customers off, and Maggie is scared stiff of her now.' She stood up and put a hand on Maria's shoulder. 'I'm sorry, cutie dear. Heartsore for you.'

Maria's head was reeling and inside she felt wretched. She knew the decisions had been made, and she bent her head, despairing and let the tears flow unchecked.

Bella looked uncertain and Sam distressed, but Barney moved to Maria's side immediately. He signed for Bella to go as he took Maria in his arms. She clung to him, feeling the roughness of his jacket, which smelt of tobacco, against her cheek, and the strong muscled arms holding her, as if he could protect her against anything.

Dr Shearer was wrong: Sarah might not have been aware where the ambulance men were taking her, but she knew well enough that she didn't want to go. Maria had tried to talk to her, make her understand, but vacant eyes stared back at her and she didn't know how much had gone in.

She'd taken the morning off that day in mid-October to be there with her mother, and Barney was there too, feeling Maria might need support, though he was longing for his bed. He'd not finished unloading the stuff till half-one. Then at two, Seamus had organised a card shop. Many of the sailors had got paid and the McPhearsons knew they could lift the money from their pockets just as if they'd put their hands in.

The game had gone on till six and then the brothers had had to bring the stuff back to this side and unload it. He'd drank whiskey as if it was water during the games of poker, and now, two and a half hours later, Barney felt decidedly the worse for wear. His bleary eyes had bags underneath them. Maria didn't see how he looked straight away. She was just glad he was there and more than glad he was able to restrain Sarah, who attacked both the ambulance men, drawing blood from one one as her nails raked his cheek.

She began to scream as they strapped her onto the stretcher, blood-curdling screams that Maria thought could maybe be heard in Derry. They certainly brought people out to stand in the doorways, to see which poor soul was being murdered.

Sarah stopped screaming long enough to gaze slowly around the room, her eyes lighting on everything in turn, as if she was saying goodbye. Then she stared across at Sam and he gazed back at her with shame-filled eyes. Then she turned to Maria, tears trickling down her cheeks, and the look she cast them both was filled with hate. Maria staggered under the weight of bitterness behind her mother's eyes, as if she'd suffered a blow. Again it was Barney's arms around her shoulders that comforted her and pressed her to him. Then the screams began again as the ambulance men lifted the stretcher.

The Square was full of people. Maria was mortified by it all, and though most people's eyes were sympathetic, it hardly helped. The only thing that helped really was Barney's arm. Then, as most of the people dispersed to their homes when the ambulance was out of sight, Bella and Dora came over and some of the customers from the shop followed them.

'You're not to blame yourself, Maria,' one of the women said. 'You did your level best.'

'Aye, nothing to reproach yourself for,' another put in. 'Daughter in a million.'

These were the very women vociferous in their condemnation of Maria even considering a new life for herself in Dublin, yet now they seemed all of a sudden on her side.

She hadn't time for them, couldn't even bring herself to acknowledge their words, and Barney, feeling the raw emotions running through Maria, said quietly to Dora, 'Will you go in to Sam? He's bound to feel it. I'm taking Maria out of this. We'll go for a walk.'

'You do right,' Dora said, just as quietly. 'She looks done in, poor girl, and she's as white as a sheet.'

Still with his arms protectively around Maria, Barney passed through the knot of remaining people and strode up the road towards Greencastle. Once the town was behind, however, he turned inland and didn't stop until they came to a little hilltop with a grass-covered knoll at the top, above a swift stream surging down the hillside across its rocky bed on its way to join Lough Foyle.

'This was always one of my favourite places,' Barney said, and they sat down together.

Maria said nothing. At least, he thought, she had stopped crying and he withdrew his hanky and mopped her face and then kissed her eyes.

Maria gasped. That action reminded her of Greg. Stop thinking about Greg, she admonished herself. He belonged to another life now, he was someone else's husband, some wee child's father and lost to her for ever. This is the here and now, with Barney beside her.

And a very careworn, exhausted Barney, she noticed for the first time. 'You look . . . you look . . .'

'Awful, I know.'

'I was going to say tired.'

'Aye,' Barney said, and added, 'I worked all night so I could be with you today.'

'Ah, Barney!'

The words, spoken so lovingly, sent the heat coursing through Barney. He felt himself harden. 'Maria,' he said, 'I think I love you.'

He kissed her then with all the passion in him. When he pressed her lips open gently and let his tongue dart in and out of her mouth, she resisted at first. Then she relaxed and gave herself up to the pleasure of it, and moaned softly.

Barney smiled to himself. He'd had many sexual encounters and was a skilled lover. He began to kiss her again. Her senses reeled and she tried to press him closer, but Barney was busy unbuttoning her cardigan and then her blouse. Maria hadn't taken the time to bring her coat for the day was mild.

Maria wondered why she wasn't protesting, but it was as if she hadn't the energy. She felt incredibly sad still and terribly guilty. There was no room left in her to feel shame at what she was allowing Barney to do to her. She wanted to forget the events of that morning, even for the briefest of time. She wanted, oh, how she wanted, someone to bring her gratification for a change and Barney was doing an excellent job. She had no desire to ask him to stop.

Barney couldn't believe he had got so far. Every minute he had expected his hands to be slapped down, but Maria sat before him in her brassiere and when he gently pushed her onto the grass, lay on top of her, and covered her mouth with his, she returned his kisses passionately.

Maria felt as if she was floating in bliss. She closed her eyes as Barney kissed her neck and throat and then he slipped the straps from Maria's shoulders, pulled the brassiere down to her waist and saw the ripe juiciness of Maria's breasts before his eyes.

When he began to lick her nipple gently, then suck

at it greedily, Maria moaned in ecstasy and felt desire stabbing at her, demanding to be satisfied. 'Oh, Barney . . . Oh God . . .'

'Maria, you are beautiful, wondrous,' Barney cried huskily, his breath coming in short pants. 'I love every inch of you.'

He knew he could take her if he wished and presumed all the emotion over the last few days, culminating in that awful scene that morning, had drained Maria. She definitely needed him, and wanted him as she never had before. If he was to make love to her, she'd be his. She was ripe for it now, like she might never ever be again. 'You know I'd never hurt you, Maria,' Barney said, kissing her between each word, as he fiddled with the waistband of her skirt.

This was when Maria knew she should put the brakes on, but Barney had worked her up so much, it would have been like stopping the tide. All she said was, 'Yes, Barney.'

She was caught up in desire that she never felt before. Her brief courtship with Greg had been chaste, very proper, but now her whole being cried out for fulfilment, satisfaction for the passion that was almost consuming her.

Barney's hand was between her legs, rubbing her and teasing her, until she cried out, 'Oh, please, please.' She didn't know what she was asking for, just something to still the ache burning inside her.

'Are you sure?' Barney asked.

'Oh, yes. Quick.'

And then, Maria knew the doctor wasn't the only one to lie. He'd said Sarah wouldn't know or care where they took her, and Barney said he wouldn't hurt her but he did.

Then it didn't matter. They clung together, every nerve pulsating and moving as if they were one person. Waves and waves of exquisite joy that went higher and higher, and ever more rapturous, ran through Maria until she thought she'd explode.

'Oh, Barney, I love you, love you, love you,' she cried as Barney clasped her even closer.

'And I you, you darling girl,' he said.

Maria was breathless when it was eventually over, but still she held Barney close. 'You have your answer,' she panted. 'I will be proud to love you and to be your girl.'

Barney rolled off Maria and lit a cigarette. She lay beside him, satiated, contented in a way she never had been before.

They wandered back to the village some time later, hand in hand, and Dora had only had to catch the one sight of them to know what they'd been at, for the delight and joy of it still played around Maria's mouth. Her flushed face, tousled hair and grass-covered clothes told their own tale.

Sam was too bowed down with shame and guilt to notice anything. God, he'd be glad when the day was over. That look Sarah had given him should have turned him to stone. But he couldn't, wouldn't let himself regret the decision to send Sarah away, for now Maria didn't have the responsibility of her. Best thing he could do was get out of the road to and give the girl back her life. It wasn't as if he was any bloody use.

'Have you any drink on you, Barney?' he asked desperately, almost as soon as the man was in the door.

'No, but I'll get you one, and gladly.'

'Daddy . . .' Maria chided.

'Don't nag me, child,' Sam pleaded. 'Not today of all days. I'll not get through it at all without a drink.'

'Leave him alone,' Barney advised Maria at the door. 'It's all the poor sod has. You have me. We have each other.'

'Oh, Barney,' she said, then gasped as he slipped a hand between her legs.

'See what he's missing? What's a drop of whiskey?'

What indeed? Maria was smiling as she closed the door.

In the cold light of the next day, Maria faced what she had done with Barney and her face flamed with embarrassment. She remembered her abandonment and how she'd given herself so freely that she had begged and pleaded like some sort of wanton. Oh dear Christ, what had she been thinking of? However would she face Barney after this? She'd be barely able to look him in the eye.

Mind, she told herself, as she got up and dressed, he'd probably not want to see her after the exhibition she'd made of herself. Everyone knew that men would take what was on offer, but if the woman was too easy, they'd throw her to one side when they were done with her. And what if there were consequences, she thought in horror, as she went downstairs. The gasp she gave was so audible, it brought Sam's rheumy eyes to rest on her.

She looked at his dear face and knew if she ever had to tell him she was with child and unmarried the shock would kill him. Barney had said he loved her, but hadn't mentioned marriage. She knew if she should be pregnant and remain unmarried, rather than display that scandal that would drag Sam through the mud as well, she would throw herself into the Foyle.

She forced herself to smile at her father. 'Hello, Daddy. How are you feeling?'

'Badly, child.'

'Badly?'

'Aye, inside myself,' Sam said.

Maria crossed the room and smoothed down the lines on her father's forehead. 'I'll make us some porridge directly,' she said. 'It's Saturday; I have no work today.'

'I want no porridge,' Sam said. 'Just a drop of tea.'

'Daddy, you must have something,' Maria admonished.

Sam shook his head. 'I want nothing, child,' he said. 'I couldn't eat it.'

'Maybe you'll feel better when you have the tea taken,' Maria said, but without much hope. However, she was dismayed when she took the tea over to her father to see his hands shaking so badly, she had to hold the cup steady to prevent it spilling all down him. 'Maybe you'd pour me a wee glass of whiskey after this,' he said.

'Daddy!'

'To steady myself just,' Sam said. 'Go on, be a good girl now. To please your daddy.'

Feeling anything like a good girl, and very much against her better judgement, Maria poured a sizeable measure of whiskey into a glass and gave it to her father. She hadn't the time or inclination to argue with him, for Saturday was a busy enough day. After breakfast, she'd have to wash and change her father and put all the soiled linen to boil with the rest she had soaking. She also had the remainder of the wash to see to, the house to clean from top to bottom and the shopping to get in. She set to with a will as soon as she'd eaten, intending to work so hard she would drive the incidents of the previous day from her mind.

Barney had an idea how Maria might be feeling. He knew she hadn't really been herself when she'd more than submitted to him. But today, he imagined, she'd probably have come to her senses.

He knew his assumption was right when he came upon her just before lunch time as she was pounding clothes in the poss tub in the wash house. Despite the nip in the autumn air, her face shone with sweat and then flushed with embarrassment when she saw Barney approach.

'Hello, Maria.'

'H-hello, Barney.'

He stood at the doorway and looked out. Curls of mist in the air lingered from the morning. He said, 'Today is not such a good day to be sitting on a grassy bank, I'm thinking.'

Maria stared at him, wondering if he was playing some sort of game with her. 'No,' she said.

'Maria, do you feel bad about what we shared yesterday?' Barney said, seeing her discomfort and knowing it was best to hit things head on.

'What d'you think?' Maria said. 'Of course I do.'

'But there is no need.'

'Oh, Barney. How can you say that?' Maria cried. 'I am so ashamed, I can barely raise my head. I'm not that sort of girl at all. I know what I did, what I wanted to do, but it isn't . . . I wouldn't want you to think . . .'

Barney strode across the room, removed the poss stick from Maria's hands and took her in his arms. 'I love you, darling girl,' he said, 'and what we did yesterday was just one expression of it. Yesterday you needed that comfort.'

'Oh, Barney.'

'You said you loved me,' Barney said. 'Was it passion driven, or did you mean it?'

Maria remembered that she'd said it – shouted it – and she'd meant it at the time. But whether she really and truly loved Barney she didn't know. What did it matter now anyway? She'd burnt her boats with anyone else. So she looked into Barney's face and said, 'No, Barney. It wasn't just passion. I do love you.'

Barney gave a whoop of joy and swung Maria around. She saw the light dancing in his eyes.

CHAPTER EIGHT

'You won't be able to take your young lady out tonight,' Seamus said to Barney the following Saturday.

'How come?' Barney said. 'We were going dancing. Maria was looking forward to it.'

'Well, she'll have to be disappointed then. I need you tonight.'

'What the hell for?'

'To drive a car.'

'Are you kidding me, Seamus? You know I can't drive a car.'

'You're going to learn fast, today,' Seamus said grimly.

'But why d'you want me to drive a car anyway?' Barney said. 'And where to, for God's sake?'

Prickles of alarm suddenly ran down his spine. He'd never met the other men concerned in the smuggling. Seamus said they were hard knocks from the North and he didn't need to meet them, know their names or any other damned thing about them. Somehow, he knew this car driving was connected to those people.

'We're raiding a post office,' Seamus said.

Barney's eyes were like saucers. 'Are you mad?'

'I don't think so.'

'But, Seamus—'

'I want money.'

'We have money,' Barney said.

'Not those piddling little bits, real money,' Seamus said. 'And don't tell me you don't want money to spend on your lady love.'

Seamus saw Barney was wavering and he went on, 'Yours is a doddle of a job. All you do is sit in the car with the engine running. If the guards are alerted at all, you just put your foot down and you'll be over the border in minutes.'

'Have you done this sort of thing before?'

'Aye, but we've never hit a post office before.'

'In Derry.'

'Aye. The blackout is our best friend.'

'So who drove the car before?'

'A man by the name of P. J. Connolly, but, he's been taken sick. Appendicitis, they think it is. He's in the County Hospital in Letterkenny. So you're up for it?'

Barney knew he'd do it, though every bone in his body was sending him alarm signals. He always did what Seamus wanted in the end. He nodded.

'Good man,' Seamus said. 'Now come on. I want to try you out in the car and we have to collect it from P. J.'s house first.'

'I'll have to call at Maria's,' Barney said, 'and explain.'

'Well, make it snappy. We haven't got all day.'

Maria wasn't in. She was away in Letterkenny, trying to see her mother. Bella had gone with her.

Dora had told Bella of seeing the state of Barney

and Maria the day Sarah was taken away and at first Bella had been rather shocked.

'Surely, Mammy, you don't think . . . Maria wouldn't do such a thing, she's a good girl.'

'Maria is a girl with normal needs and desires,' Dora said. 'A girl with youth stripped from her, made to grow up before she's ready, before she's really lived, and one who has a gruelling life ahead of her. The day her mother was taken away, she needed comfort. And don't we all sometimes? That poor child has been dealt one hell of a fist in life.'

'It's just that I'm not sure about Barney,' Bella said. 'Will he marry her?'

'It could be that he will have to marry her.'

'Aye, but will he?' Bella asked.

'Dear God, I certainly hope so, for if he refuses, the girl's life will be destroyed,' Dora said. 'And the shock of it will likely kill her father.'

Bella knew it would and Maria herself would be well aware of that. God Almighty, Maria had the sort of life she wouldn't wish on anyone, so who was she to judge her? So when the girl expressed a wish to see how her mother was, Bella offered to go with her.

'The post office is shut from half-twelve on Saturday,' she said, 'and Maggie can cope with the rest, especially with Mammy on hand, though she'll be over the road seeing to your father.'

'Oh, you're very good,' Maria said. 'I'd welcome the company.'

'There,' Bella said, patting Maria's hand. 'I would say it's a desperate place to visit on your own.'

Dora said none of this to Barney when he called at

the door, because she had a feeling he wouldn't like the thought of Maria going to the hospital, so she just said Maria and Bella were away in Letterkenny.

Barney was sorry not to see Maria herself, but there was no help for it, he had to ask Dora to explain to Maria that he wouldn't be able to take her out that evening as he had to do a job of work for his brother. He didn't say what the job was and Dora didn't ask, but privately she could bet it wasn't something totally legitimate.

The hospital was on High Road. It was a two-storeyed, low-pitched, pleasant-looking building of light honey-coloured brick. In front of it were lawns encircled with a stone wall. Visitors entered through a wrought-iron gate that opened on to the pavement, and up a path with a lawn on either side. Some of the windows were open, Maria noted with pleasure as she and Bella approached three steps leading up to an arched doorway.

Even inside the building was pleasant. The autumn sun shone through the window and the whole place was airy and clean. The nurse behind the desk seemed surprised, though, that they wanted to see a patient in the psychiatric unit.

'If you wait a moment,' she said coolly, 'I will get someone to speak to you.'

'Probably some poor souls are put in here and forgotten about,' Bella said, seeing Maria biting her bottom lip in agitation.

Maria nodded, but the nurse had looked at them in such an odd way – as if they each had two heads, or maybe needed places in the asylum themselves.

The man who came to see them, who introduced himself as Dr Thorndyke, a clinical psychiatrist, was little better. 'I'm afraid we don't encourage visitors,' he said. 'It upsets the patients.'

'Doesn't it upset them more, thinking they are forgotten?' Maria asked.

'Believe me, Miss . . . Mrs . . .'

'Miss Foley. Maria Foley. Sarah is my mother,' Maria said. 'She was so distressed when she was brought here.'

'Indeed she was. She had to be heavily sedated,' the doctor said. 'In fact, she is still on medication. Even if I approved of it, there would be little point in seeing her. She wouldn't know you.'

'But, surely she isn't going to stay like that all the time she's here, is she?' Maria asked.

'We will use whatever medication we feel necessary to deal with your mother,' Dr Thorndyke said stiffly. 'She is now in my care and it is not for you to question my methods.'

'Yes, but—'

'We must await results and see what is best for her,' the doctor said firmly. 'You can do no good for your mother at the moment.'

'Can I come again?'

'I wouldn't advise it,' the doctor said. 'Your mother's mental balance is precarious. Any undue excitement or upset could harm her. I'm sure you understand it is in your mother's best interest that you leave her care to the professionals.'

Maria was defeated. There was nothing more she could say. How could she insist of seeing her mother and risk causing her harm? Anyway, she knew, looking at Dr Thorndyke's implacable face, that she could insist all she would and he still wouldn't budge. And maybe he was right. What in God's name did she know what ailed her mother, let alone how to go about curing it? She shook her head helplessly and Bella took her arm and led her back outside.

Dr Thorndyke watched the two dejected figures walk back down the path. He sighed. It wouldn't have done neither of them any good to see the woman brought in just over a week ago, heavily sedated and in a strait-jacket to avoid her hurting herself or others. With her vacant eyes and drooling from her mouth, he very much doubted she would ever be right again. The daughter would probably come to that decision in time, but for now, nothing would be gained by that young girl witnessing the deterioration in her mother.

Maria was quiet most of the way back and all the words Bella thought of to cheer her died in her throat. This was no small thing that could be eased by a few words of comfort. Maria held herself to blame. It was no good people saying she could do no other – she had put her mother away and the guilt that had lodged in her heart after making that decision had been hammered into place by their visit to the hospital. But for her father's sake she put a bright smile on her face when she returned home.

Maria had been disappointed when she was told that Barney would be unable to meet her that night. She'd have liked to dance the night away and try to crush down the memories of that day. She wondered what job of work it had been and presumed he would tell her when she saw him at Mass in the morning.

Barney had never been so scared in the whole of his life. He was scared of everything, including another so-called friend of Seamus's, who went by the name of Eamonn Duffy. He'd shaken hands with the brown-haired, scowling man, who'd nearly crushed his fingers in his vicelike grip and who frowned at him so hard his bushy eyebrows met above a nose that looked as if it had been broken a number of times. And if he thought Seamus aggressive in his speech, he couldn't hold a candle to the belligerent way Eamonn spoke. Not that he spoke much at all. He issued staccato-like sentences and his replies to anything asked were brusque, rather than succinct.

All in all, Barney neither liked nor trusted him. One job and that was all, he'd made clear to Seamus.

He had no part in the raid, but it had apparently gone like clockwork, though he'd sat in a state of such agitation he'd badly wanted to pee. But he'd had his brief: he had to stay in the car, with the engine running and the doors open, and that's what he had done.

He'd waited for alarms to start ringing, police whistles to be blown and coppers' feet to pound across the cobblestones. But none of that happened. In the black night, the only figures that appeared were Seamus and Eamonn.

'Get going, Barney,' Seamus commanded and Barney got going, while in the back, Seamus and Eamonn congratulated each other.

'So easy, it was no challenge,' Seamus said.

'Aye, like taking candy from a baby.'

That night, after Eamonn had been dropped off, Seamus peeled off notes from the wad in his hand. 'One hundred and fifty pounds,' he said. 'All right?'

It was more, much more than all right, and yet Barney forced himself to say nonchalantly. 'It'll do, I suppose.'

'It had better do, you greedy young bastard.'

Next morning Barney was full of apologies. 'I could do none other,' he said to Maria. 'Seamus needed a driver and his was taken ill with appendicitis.'

Maria, thinking Barney was referring to the job she thought he was doing legitimately, patted his arm soothingly. 'Don't fret,' she said. 'Such things can't be helped.' She smiled at Barney and took his hand as they went inside the church.

Later, when the Mass was over and they were wandering back, still hand in hand, Maria said, 'Will you come and have a bit of breakfast with us, Barney? Maybe you can persuade Daddy to eat something. He's like skin and bone. I've pleaded with him but he will eat nothing for me. It upsets me when he goes on like this.'

'Leave him to me,' Barney said.

Barney was far less patient with Sam than Maria. 'Stop being such a selfish bastard,' he told him, when he'd again refused anything to eat.

'She doesn't deserve this sort of life,' Sam said.

'She doesn't deserve to be upset either.'

'I just don't feel like eating.'

'No, you're too full of whiskey and poteen,' Barney said. 'Look, Sam, I know it helps and, God alone knows, if I'd had the accident you had, I doubt I'd cope any better, but all I'm saying is go easy. We seldom go anywhere any more because you're usually too drunk. It would please Maria if you'd just swallow a few mouthfuls of something. God knows, it's not much to ask. She has one hell of a life, so stop thinking about yourself all the time.'

Sam did see the sense of what Barney said. So when Maria came into the room and her father said, 'I think I could take a few spoonfuls of porridge now, Maria,' she was delighted and knew she had Barney to thank.

After breakfast, he came up to her as she washed the dishes in the scullery, pinning her against the sink as his hands cupped her breasts.

'Barney!' she cried, as Barney pushed himself against her.

'Feel what you have done to me,' he said.

Maria dampened down the excitement she felt rising in her. It wasn't the time or the place. Dora, Bella, anyone could be in on them, and if she didn't nip this in the bud, she'd be so worked up herself she wouldn't be able to think straight.

'Barney, I—'

'Just looking at you, does this to me,' Barney said, thrusting himself against her.

'Stop, please. Daddy needs seeing to and anyone could just walk in.'

Barney took no notice and when he spun Maria around to face him and kissed her, she returned it just as eagerly because she wasn't able to stop herself.

Leaving Sam asleep after dinner, Barney and Maria went for a walk. They were some distance from the house when the rain began coming down in sheets so that they were drenched in minutes.

Barney took hold of Maria's hand. 'Let's run through the rain like weans.'

They ran madly up the village street to arrive at the door sopping wet and laughing like a couple of hyenas. They entered quietly enough, though, mindful of Sam, though he was still dead to the world.

'Is your dress wet too?' Barney asked as he towelled his hair dry with a lascivious look at her. 'You could always take it off and let me keep you warm.'

'My dress is fine, thanks,' Maria said primly. 'And it's staying put, but my hair's wringing. Can you pass me another towel?'

Later, they sat before the range, drinking cocoa, Maria on the rug, her feet touching the fender, while Barney teased the knots out of her tousled damp hair and brushed it smooth.

He put down the brush suddenly and began nuzzling Maria's neck.

'Stop, Barney.'

'Stop, Barney,' he mocked gently. 'That's like saying stop to the wave crashing on the seashore. Your hair is tangle free and gorgeous, and I am burning up inside. Let me take you upstairs and undress you and make love to you?'

'Barney, we can't,' Maria said. 'The day I did that, it was . . . I wouldn't like you to think I had ever done anything like that before. I'm not that sort of girl. Anyway,' she added, as Barney lifted her from the floor and onto his knee, 'it's the middle of the afternoon.'

'So what?'

'Please, Barney,' Maria said, 'it wouldn't be right.

Barney knew what Maria was angling for: a promise of marriage. His brother had told him that was what all woman wanted but he didn't want to go down that alleyway – not for some time, if ever at all. He loved Maria, desired her, lusted after her, wanted to make love to her often, but he wasn't the marrying sort. He knew he had to do something, though, or Maria would never let him make love to her again.

That night he confronted his brother with the problem.

'What shall I do about it, Seamus? I only have to stand near her and I'm so hard it hurts.'

'Buy her a ring.'

'I told you I don't—'

'Listen, you bloody little fool, I am talking engagement ring. You've got the money after that latest job. I've bought a few of those in the past if a girl is unwilling. You don't have to go on with it when you get fed up with them. She'll probably be scared of getting pregnant, of course, and if you have any sense you should be scared of that too, so use a bloody johnnie. They sell packets of them in every barber shop in Derry.'

Maria thought one of the worst things about the war was the blackout. It always seemed worse when she came out of the lighted factory to make her way home. It took a minute or two for her eyes to adjust, and so Maria nearly walked straight past Barney, who was lounging in an entry, waiting for her.

When she felt the tug on her arm, she shone her shielded torch into his face. 'Barney!' she said in surprise and then shock took over. 'Has anything happened?'

'Everything is fine,' Barney said. 'I came to meet you. I have something to show you.'

'What?'

'Not here, not in the black night. I thought we might go for a drink.'

'I can't,' Maria cried. 'I have to catch the bus at twenty-five past five for the next one only goes as far as Quigley's Point.'

'You won't need a bus,' Barney said. 'You mind the time I did that driving job for Seamus?' And at her nod went on. 'He gave me the loan of the car to fetch you.'

'Still . . .'

'Just one wee drink?'

Maria laughed. 'You sound like Daddy,' she said, and allowed Barney to lead her into a nearby café, as the pubs were not open yet, and order tea and scones.

'What is it, Barney?' Maria said when the waitress had laid the things on the table. 'I haven't time for this.'

'Oh, I think you can take a little time,' Barney said. He withdrew the ring box from his pocket and gave it to her. When she opened it, she was speechless, for she'd seldom seen anything so exquisite. It was nothing like Greg's solitaire. This ring had an emerald stone in its centre. 'The colour of your eyes,' Barney said. And this was encircled by diamonds that caught the lights of the café, which brought the waitress's attention on them.

'God, what a ring,' she breathed, and Maria extended her hands so that she could look more closer. The waitress looked straight at Barney and said, 'I know the cost of a ring like that. You must be a millionaire. Still, congratulations and all.'

When the girl moved away, Maria, knowing Barney

was far from being a millionaire, said, 'Barney, about the ring? You didn't pay too much for it, did you?'

'Come on, Maria. What I paid is my business. You don't ask the cost of an engagement ring.'

'Yes, but—'

'I had money enough for it,' Barney said. 'That's all you need to know.'

Maria still looked concerned and Barney, attempting to lighten the mood, said, 'And as I am not a man of unlimited funds, I hope you are not going to waste more money by leaving those scones and letting the tea go cold.'

Maria laughed. 'You are a fool, Barney, and I don't know how you were able to afford that ring, but it is the loveliest thing I have ever owned and I thank you from the bottom of my heart.'

The ring was gorgeous, no doubt about it, but she wasn't sure she was ready yet to get engaged. She thought they would have a longer courtship and she certainly didn't want marriage yet awhile, but she decided not to say anything now and spoil the moment.

'There are many ways to thank me,' Barney said, catching up Maria's fingers and kissing them one by one.

She felt a tremor run all through her. She knew she could allow him more liberties now she had the ring on her finger and their relationship was official. But not all the way – she couldn't do that again before marriage and hoped she hadn't made that stand too late?

It was Friday, and Sean was coming. Barney popped in at lunch time and Sam asked him if he'd help him get dressed. He hadn't got properly dressed or left his bed for a few weeks now and Barney was happy to oblige and even happier when Sam said he intended going to the pub that night.

He noticed the ring immediately. Barney told him they were in no rush to get married, which relieved Maria's mind. Sam was delighted and happy for them both.

That evening, Barney was back from the pub at nine o'clock, leaving Sam in Sean's care.

'We have no time alone, Maria,' he complained. It was true, she knew, and she pulled him inside, drew the bolt, pushed the basket of mending she was tackling under the table and put her arms out to Barney.

He'd taken in the significance of the bolt and they lay on the rug before the range. Barney kissed and caressed Maria till she was dizzy and disorientated, removing the top half of her clothes at the same time. She allowed him that far and moaned out her pleasure when he kissed her neck and throat. When he stroked and fondled her breasts, she couldn't help writhing beneath him and when he nuzzled and sucked at her nipples, she got very excited and yearned for fulfilment, but when he attempted to go below the waist, she stopped him using every vestige of willpower she still had left.

Barney could scarcely believe it. 'Please, Maria, for God's sake.'

'Don't ask me,' Maria cried. 'Don't look at me that way. Don't you think I want it as much as you?'

'Then why?'

'It wouldn't be right.'

Barney's frustration came out in anger. 'Fuck that!'

he cried. 'Leading a man on and then putting the brakes on. Fine way to show how much you love me and how much you like the ring I paid an arm and leg for. I got something for me to use as well, so it isn't even as if you'd get pregnant.'

That did put Maria's mind at rest a little although she was hurt and somewhat angry at the way Barney had spoken to her. 'I am pleased with the ring,' she maintained. 'I said so. I love it, Barney. It is the most beautiful thing I have ever owned, and I told you so already, but it's just—'

'Don't just tell me, show me,' Barney pleaded. 'Show me how pleased you are. Show me how you love me?'

He had the urge to throw her down and take her by force. But he didn't have to, for Maria heard the hurt behind the anger. He had bought her the ring, which was his public way of showing her how much he loved her, and also what his intentions towards her were. Now he asked her for something in return. Small wonder he was frustrated and upset when she pushed him away. Surely it was all right now that they were engaged? Well, whether it was or it wasn't, it was definitely what Barney wanted and expected, and it was Barney, the man she was promised to, that she had to please. So she drew him towards her and kissed him. That kiss told him plainly that she was willing to go as far as he wanted.

Barney had to meet his brother that night at ten o'clock. After he'd gone, Maria tidied up and prepared for bed, too agitated to return to her mending. Once in bed she went over the encounter with Barney in her head. It was obvious to her that Barney expected sex now they were officially engaged every time they had the opportunity. He was that type of man. At least, she told herself, he took the time to ensure she enjoyed it as much as he did, which few man did if she were to believe some of the women at work.

She knew whatever state her father was in when he came home, Sean would see to him. She could just go to bed and sleep the sleep of the just. She was bone weary. It was unfortunate, then, that the one night she could do just that, she lay wide-eyed, too keyed up to be able to drift off.

Maria's prediction was right and at every opportunity they could, Barney expected sex from Maria. She tried to explain how she felt about that, but he really didn't want to hear and so in the end she put up with it. She had to admit she often wanted it as much as he did.

Barney thought the ring worth every penny and told his brother so.

Work dictated it was three weeks before Sean could visit again, which would be 4 December. As Maria looked at the calendar that morning, as she washed her father before she left for work, she realised she'd not had a period for two months. Her mouth went uncommonly dry and she stiffened.

'What is it?' Sam asked.

'Nothing,' Maria forced herself to say.

She finished her father's ablutions in record time, galloped up the stairs and, tearing off her jumper and brassiere, stood before the mirror. She saw with a sinking heart the slight darkening of her nipples and the way the blue veins on her breasts were much more prominent than they had been. Those signs, together with the sickly feeling she had woken up with the last two mornings, only pointed to one thing. She'd learnt that much from some of the talk with the women in the factory. It had shocked Maria at first, the way they could discuss the most intimate of things, but now she was grateful for the information.

Almighty Christ, she was also scared – bloody terrified, in fact. She told herself she was engaged at least, and that Barney loved her. Hadn't he shown her often enough? He would stand by her, she was sure of it.

She was glad she had work to occupy her that day. That evening she decided she would pack Sean and her father off to the pub and ask Barney to stay behind a while. He'd be quite willing to do this, thinking she wanted sex, and he could have sex or any other damned thing he liked as long as he agreed to marry her

Her plan ran like clockwork. Minutes after the door closed behind Sean and Sam, Barney was ensconced on the settee, Maria cuddled in to him as he liked her to do. In his other hand he held a large glass of whiskey.

'Oh, Maria, you must be gasping for it tonight,' Barney said, kissing her neck. 'God, I can hardly wait myself.'

Maria leant forward and kissed Barney gently on the lips. 'I do want you, Barney, but I need to talk to you first.'

'Sod that, woman,' Barney said. 'We'll talk after.'

'No, please, Barney,' Maria protested, struggling out of his embrace.

'Oh, all right, but make it snappy,' he said irritably. Maria snuggled back into the crook of Barney's arm again and said gently, 'This will probably be a bit of a shock to you, Barney, but I think I am pregnant.'

Barney sprang to his feet as if he'd been shot, drained his glass with one swallow and poured himself another with hands that shook. It was the very worst news in the world. His senses were reeling.

Maria watched him pacing the floor in an agitated manner, waiting for the news to sink in and for him to reassure her it would be OK, that he would stand by her and they would be married sooner rather than later, that was all. But when the silence had stretched out between them uncomfortably, she pleaded, 'Say something, Barney?'

'What would you have me say, congratulations?' he asked sarcastically.

'No,' Maria said. 'Come on. Don't be like this.'

'Like what?' Barney demanded. 'You hit me with the worst news in the whole bloody world and expect me to be happy about it?'

Maria felt the first flickers of alarm. Surely to God he realised they had to marry? He couldn't let her be disgraced in this way! She would have said she was sure of Barney, had known him years and understood him perfectly. Yet this Barney seemed like a stranger, one Maria didn't know and was slightly nervous of. But she wasn't going to let him see that.

'What's up with you, anyway? she said. 'It isn't as if we hadn't intended to marry. I mean, we are engaged and all. That is really a prelude to marrying, isn't it? All this means is putting the marriage forward a bit, that's all.'

'That's all,' Barney mimicked. 'But I don't want to get married yet.'

'D'you think I do?'

'Well, it's what most women want.'

'Eventually, maybe,' Maria said. 'But not now, not yet. I didn't engineer this on my own, Barney. It does take two, you know?'

'Don't be so clever,' he snapped. 'As if I don't know that.'

Maria, hurt by Barney's reaction, began to cry. 'You must see that we have to marry. Please, Barney. Please, for pity's sake?'

She had no pride left. What price pride against the ultimate shame of bringing a bastard child into the world?

'I can't,' Barney said. 'Not just like that, anyway. I need time to think.'

'Surely to God there is nothing to think about?' Maria said, clutching at him,

'Leave me alone,' Barney snapped in panic, pushing her clawing hands away.

Maria sank to her knees, tears streaming down her face, and watched Barney snatch his jacket from the hook behind the door. When the door banged behind him, she lay face down on the mat and cried out in anguish and despair.

Barney tramped the roads, the tantalising word 'pregnancy' with him every step of the way. He thought how unfair life was because after that first time, the day that they took Maria's mother away, he had always used johnnies. And Maria could never claim he forced her either. She had been like a different person, more than ready, asking him – more begging him – to go on. She was like a bloody harlot who knew the score.

Only she didn't know, not really. Christ, this news must have knocked her for six too. He turned for the village, knowing he had to see his brother.

He routed him from Raffety's without been spotted by either Sam or Sean and they went to the green, deserted at that time of night. In a few minutes had told Seamus the news.

'You bloody little fool, I told you—'

'I did get johnnies, like you said,' Barney protested, adding bitterly, 'Little did I know it was too bloody late, because it must have happened the first time we did it, the day the mad woman was taken away. Maria was upset and I sort of comforted her and then . . . well, it was if she'd had a brainstorm. I mean we'd done no more than kiss before, but when I tried it on then, she didn't stop me. I kept expecting her to, but she didn't. It was incredible and she's felt bad about it ever since.'

'Well, it's proper cooked your goose.'

'I suppose I have got to marry her?'

'If you want to stay in Moville you do,' Seamus said. 'I reckon half the village would lynch you if you let her down and they got news of it, and that uncle of hers would beat you to pulp. It isn't as if you weren't crazy about her for years, anyway. If you have to go down this road it is surely better to go down it with someone you are halfway fond of.

'I suppose,' Barney said. 'And I do still fancy her like crazy.'

'Count yourself one lucky bloke then,' Seamus said. 'Many go down the aisle for the same reason, with a woman they are tired of, can't bear the sight of in some cases. Pity about the smuggling, the cards and that, though.'

'What do you mean?'

'Well, Maria isn't stupid. She isn't going to believe that you're going out on legitimate business at ten o'clock at night. What about the times we don't come home till the next morning? No, brother, you will have to get a proper job, slaving away in some factory, for soon you'll be a husband and a daddy.'

Barney felt sick. He had no wish to give up his easy way of life. He was going to marry the woman and that should be enough for her. There was no way that she was going to dictate to him. 'Maria,' he said, 'will do as she is told and keep her mouth shut when I tell her so.'

Seamus was very glad to hear that. He thought wives were an utter waste of time and he had no intention of taking up with one himself. He only had to remember his parents' marriage to realise what a hell on earth that had been. They had seemed to do all in their power to make each other miserable.

'Are you sure?' he asked.

'Aye,' Barney said resolutely, 'I am sure,'

'Well, start as you mean to go on, brother,' Seamus advised. 'And now, if I were you, I'd go and put the woman out of her misery.'

'I'll do that,' Barney said, 'and you get the first round in at Raffety's because tonight I am going to get rip roaring drunk.'

'And I'll help you,' Seamus promised.

Maria was awash with tears. She had cried until she could cry no more. Her face was wet and her eyes so puffed up she could barely see. She still lay face down on the mat, feeling desperation and panic seeping out of the very pores of her skin. Barney, letting himself in the door, felt immensely sorry for her and sorry for the way he had behaved earlier that had upset her so much. 'Get up out of that,' he said gently, drawing her to her feet and into his arms. 'Don't worry. I was shocked and panicked, that was all. I didn't know the things I was saying. I needed to think it all through. But surely you knew I would never let you down. Haven't I told you I love you and shown you often? I know we need to be married. As it had better be done speedily, we will see the priest in the morning.'

Sheer and utter blessed relief, caused Maria's legs to buckle under her. She would have fallen, but for Barney's arms encircling her. He sank back on to the settee, pulling Maria with him so that she sat on his knee. She put her arms around his neck and kissed him with all the passion she had in her.

'Thank you, Barney. Thank you,' she said fervently.

She was so grateful to him. The alternative, for a girl finding herself pregnant and single, was very grim indeed, not just for herself, but for the whole family.

'There are better ways than words for showing a man how full of gratitude you are,' Barney said.

Maria pulled the jumper from her head and said, 'Come on then. What are we waiting for?'

Father Flaherty was no fool. 'Is the any reason for such a rush?'

Barney met his glance levelly. 'None other than

Maria needs help sooner rather than later, and we have the house and all and see no reason to wait.'

It was the same reason they had given to Sam and Sean – and Bella and Dora too. If the two women thought there might be another reason for rushing into marriage they didn't give voice to it. The priest, however, wasn't satisfied.

'Maria is still very young.'

'Aye, Father, which is precisely why she needs the help now,' Barney said. 'I know there is not much to Sam, but he is still a weight for Maria to lift on her own. I do what I can, but could do more if I was in the house.'

The priest could not argue with Barney's logic. He'd called to see Sam many times and lately he had often found him drunk or very near it, even by mid-morning. He knew the man would be no measure of support or help to Maria, and in the state he was often in, he would be a dead weight to deal with.

'He has given his permission, your father?' the priest asked Maria.

'Oh, aye, Father. Daddy is all for it. He thinks the world of Barney here.'

'Well, we are all set then,' the priest said, drawing a calendar towards him. 'If I call the banns tomorrow then the earliest you can be married will be the second of January, if you want a Saturday, because I wouldn't marry anyone on Boxing Day.'

Maria quite understood that. 'The second of January sounds just grand, Father,' she said. 'It will be good to start the New Year together.'

She squeezed Barney's hand as she spoke. Barney

didn't squeeze back, for going through his mind was the realisation that he had just a few scant weeks of freedom left to him and, by God, he intended to make the most of them.

The following Saturday afternoon, with the post office shut, Bella said Maggie could manage the rest and went to Letterkenny with Maria to get patterns and materials to make her wedding dress.

For the first time, Bella saw the Maria that Sarah had described the day she'd got the news she'd won the scholarship. She watched the almost reverent way the girl stroked the material as the bales were laid before her.

She chose white, although she really had no right to wear it, but it would have caused comment and speculation if she had chosen any other colour. When she made her choice, she then scrutinised the lace for the petticoats, neckline and sleeves, and bought decorative buttons and tiny rosebuds and seed pearls She even took time to decide on the cotton thread to use and confessed to Bella, as the assistant wrapped it all up, that she itched to get home and get started on it.

This was what Philomena Clarke saw, Bella told herself. Sarah had acknowledged the gift but didn't see its significance. Maria had a love of material and making clothes, right enough, and had things been different it could have been developed further.

But there was no good thinking that way, Bella chided herself. Maria's life has gone on a different tack altogether. Regret and wishing that things were different was worse than useless.

CHAPTER NINE

On the morning of the wedding, Bella helped ease the wedding dress over Maria's slim frame and fixed the veil in place. Maria swung around in front of the mirror and studied it critically. The scalloped neck showed the merest hint of cleavage and was trimmed with lace, like the wide full sleeves, caught in at the elbow. The dress was fitted to just past the waist and from there it stood out with the starched lace petticoats and the skirt was caught up at intervals with blue and pink rosebuds to match the headdress.

Maria wished for a moment that she could have invited Joanne to the wedding, but she liked to keep her work life and home life separate. She would have hated Joanne to see the state her father would be in by the time this day was over. He had started, and with gusto, the night before. She had heard him shouting and swearing and singing snatches of rebel songs, Sean trying to quieten him. Her toes had curled in the bed with shame and she felt dread like a large stone filling her stomach.

She didn't want to show her friend that side of her

father. Yet when Joanne had said wistfully, 'I'd love to be there to see you in that fantastic dress that you have told us so much about,' Maria had had the urge to say, 'Come, why don't you? You can stay with me in the house. I have the room.' However, what she'd ended up saying was, 'I'd like you to be there too, Joanne, but it has to be a quiet wedding, you see, with Daddy so ill and all. But Bella has a camera and I imagine that she won't be the only one. I'll have plenty of pictures, don't worry.'

Joanne, who knew more about Maria's life than most, accepted that. She was the only one in the factory that knew the real reason for the rushed wedding. When Maria had displayed her engagement ring first, there had been exclamations of delight from the girls. It truly was a magnificent ring and more than one person had looked ruefully at the rings they had been bought. They all advised her, however, to take her time settling down and to remember it was for life. She had replied airily that neither of them was in a hurry to wed.

When she had to tell them how things had changed and that the wedding had to be sooner rather than later, she gave the same reason for haste as Barney had to the priest. Only later when they were alone did Joanne ask, 'Was that the real reason?'

The crimson flush gave Maria away. Joanne nodded. 'I thought as much.'

'It must have been the day they took Mammy away,' Maria said. 'I was so upset and Barney took me for a walk and comforted me and . . .'

'You don't have to justify yourself to me,' Joanne said. 'I know just how hard it can be saying "no" and you wouldn't be feeling yourself that day. You weren't right when you came to work, and I thought it strange then. I mean, I expected you to be full of tears all day, but instead you were odd. It's hard to explain it, but you didn't look too unhappy.'

'I wasn't. Isn't that awful, with Mammy and all? I couldn't help remembering it.'

'It was good then?'

'Joanne!' Maria said, shocked.

'What?' Joanne said. 'It must have been good if you had a smile on your face when you remembered it. Go on, tell me, did you enjoy it?'

'Yes,' Maria said in a whisper, 'and that's shocking too, isn't it, because most woman don't,'

'Aye, or say they don't,' Joanne commented wryly. 'All I know is that if I was looking forward to a lifetime of something, I would face it with greater enthusiasm if I could find any sort of pleasure in it. So you don't be worrying about that, or anything else either. At least your man is standing by you.'

'Aye,' Maria said. 'Though I did think at one point he wouldn't. He went mad when he heard.'

'Oh, lots do that,' Joanne said.

'Do they?'

'Oh, yes. See it as a loss of their freedom or some such rubbish. Still, your Barney came through in the end, and that's the main thing.'

Aye, Maria told herself the morning of her wedding, that was the main thing. In a few short hours now she would be Mrs McPhearson, and that night she and her legally wed husband would snuggle together in the double bed in the room that had once been her parents'.

Barney could have sex all night if he wanted it. She blushed at the thought though her insides fluttered in delicious anticipation and the light pink flush leant a bloom to her face, as she twirled anxiously in front of Bella and asked, 'Do I look all right?'

'All right?' Bella exclaimed. 'My darling girl, you look perfect, so you do. You have a rare and wondrous beauty and Barney can consider himself a lucky man. Shall we go down?'

Remembering the state of her father the previous night, Maria descended the stairs with more than a little trepidation, terrified her father would still be lying in some drunken heap.

But, she needn't have worried. Sean had been up since six o'clock, waking Sam, who'd had as little sleep as he had, and washing him all over, even the sparse hair on his head. He'd also given him plenty of water to drink before getting him into the clothes he wore for Mass.

When Maria arrived in the room, he was sitting in his wheelchair, looking more respectable than he had any right to look.

He was actually feeling like death, but when he caught sight of Maria, the breath almost stopped in his throat and he was almost floored that he was the father of such a beauty. 'Oh Jesus,' he said, catching hold of the hands that she had placed on his shoulders. 'There just aren't the words to describe you.'

'Oh, Daddy, give over,' Maria said. 'I'll be going up the aisle the colour of beetroot.'

Sean stepped into the room, looking very distinguished in a black pinstriped suit and brilliant white shirt, his tie matching the handkerchief in his top pocket. He was across the room in two strides when he saw Maria.

He put his hands on her shoulders, looked into her large green eyes and said, 'Maria, I think you're one of the loveliest women to walk God's earth.'

'Oh, Uncle Sean.'

'Don't "Oh, Uncle Sean" me, Maria,' he said in a mock reprimand. 'Get used to compliments and used to the fact you are very beautiful.'

Maria's face was the colour of a ripe tomato and Bella, now dressed in a smart blue costume, clicked her tongue in annoyance. 'Leave her be, Sean,' she said and dabbed at Maria's face with powder from her compact to try to reduce the blushing redness of it.

Sean had one niggling worry and it was that Barney wouldn't make it to the church, because he'd still been drinking hard when he'd eventually dragged Sam home and in fine fettle, as if set to go on to the next morning. He'd had one hell of a job with Sam that morning and he hoped that someone, Seamus maybe, had made the same effort with the bridegroom.

He needn't have worried. Seamus, who was Barney's best man, had kicked his brother awake that morning. Barney couldn't ever remember feeling so bad. He had no recollection of how he'd got home and who had undressed him and put him to bed. Once roused, he had spent half an hour or more vomiting, with his brother roaring at him to get ready. That didn't help the pounding in his head and, even dressed, he felt the nausea rising in his throat. When they had nearly reached the church, Seamus had to stop the car for Barney to vomit at the side of the road.

'All right?' he asked, as Barney wiped his mouth with his handkerchief. 'We're nearly there now and we can't risk being late.'

Barney felt far from all right. His head thumped so badly he felt dizzy with it, his stomach continued to churn and he tasted bile in the back of his throat. It took a great deal of effort for him to smile at his brother and say, 'None better.'

It satisfied Seamus, though. 'Good man!' he said. 'Come on then.'

When they drew up before the church, the two stood in front of it for a few minutes.

'This here is the end of your freedom,' Seamus said. 'From now on you'll be at someone else's beck and call, someone who will tell you what time you are to be home, how much to drink.'

'No, man,' Barney said. 'Maria isn't like that.'

'She isn't a wife yet,' Seamus said ominously. 'From what I've seen in marriages, most wives are like that.'

'I'll see to it Maria isn't,' Barney said. 'I'd not stand it.'

'We'll see,' Seamus said. 'You ready?'

Barney gave a brief nod, which set off the pounding in his head again. He followed his brother down the aisle, greeting Father Flaherty, and hoping he could get through the next hour or so without disgracing himself.

And then the Wedding March was heard. Maria was at the door. All of the friends and neighbours thronging the church thought Maria a truly beautiful bride and many were awed by the magnificent dress, the like of which had never been seen in Moville before, but few could not be moved by the poignant sight of Sam. He was being pushed by Sean and he held tight to his daughter's hand, a smile of absolute pride on his face.

Barney felt a wave of dizziness assail him as he got to his feet and he swayed and would have fallen, but Seamus caught his arm.

'Go steady, man,' he hissed and Barney fixed his eyes on the altar steps and concentrated on not falling on his face.

The back room of Rafferty's was full as Barney and Maria entered hand in hand. Maria was smiling and Barney was doing his best, but still feeling sluggish.

Seamus had invited two friends to the reception. He introduced them to Maria as P.J. Connelly, now minus his appendix, and Eamonn Duffy. Maria cared for them as little as she cared for Seamus, and thought it presumptuous of him to invite them. But she didn't want to mar her wedding day with an argument. So she smiled as politely as she could. Nor did she say anything when Seamus put a pint of Guinness in Barney's hand, though she had noticed Barney's pallor in the church, his hazy eyes trying to gaze into hers, his indistinct and slightly slurred voice making the responses and the way his hands shook when they were signing the register. She knew he wasn't completely sober from the night before and she had no wish to see him drink himself stupid again.

However, she could say nothing without making him look a fool and her a nag, and so was pleased when she heard Barney say, 'Better not, Seamus. I thought I was going to be sick as a dog a couple of times in the church.'

'Hair of the dog. Best thing for it,' Seamus said. 'Trust me.'

Barney gave a nervous laugh and glanced at Maria guiltily as he took the pint. 'Oh, well, if you say so.'

Maria sighed in irritation and marched to the other end of the room as Barney took another gulp of the Guinness.

'Let her go,' Seamus said when Barney made to follow her. 'You've run after her for bloody months. Now you've got her, let her know who's boss from the start or she'll lead you a dog's life.'

'Maria?'

'Any woman,' Seamus said decisively. 'And get that pint down you and you'll feel a whole lot better.'

Eamonn and P.J. each insisted on buying Barney a drink for his wedding day too. He told himself he could barely refuse and Seamus was right: it was making him feel a whole lot better. After the second pint, he couldn't imagine why he'd ever thought P.J. and Eamonn so bad, and after the third, he thought them the greatest fellows in the world altogether – better company, anyway, than Maria, who was glowering at him from the other side of the room.

By the time he lurched over to join her at the table, he was feeling very mellow and Maria watched him nervously. The pub had donated bottles of wine and both Sean and Seamus bought more. Many men stuck to pints of beer, but Barney declared he liked the wine. Used to pints of beer, he was drinking it at a prodigious rate.

'Go easy,' Maria pleaded quietly to Barney, but he

remembered his brother's words and regarded her coldly. 'Are you telling me how much I should drink?'

A little late for that, Maria might have said, seeing that Barney was already pretty far gone. However, she wanted no row, not now in front of everyone and with Sean's concerned eyes upon her. 'No, of course not,' she said to Barney. 'It's just that you'll be expected to say a few words when Seamus has finished.'

'I can do that, no problem,' Barney said.

Seamus's speech was surprisingly funny, although it was a general dig at women and marriage.

'And, now,' he said at the end, 'I'll leave it for my brother to say a few words, another good man to bite the dust.'

Barney staggered to his feet and Maria noticed he had to hold on to the table to steady himself. He stood swaying while he pontificated. Maria was in an agony of embarrassment, for he was speaking rubbish, and in the end she tugged on his jacket.

'The musicians are setting up,' she said. 'And we have to cut the cake yet.'

'I'll have to finish here,' Barney said. 'My good lady wife has told me that, and like all married men I know I must do what I'm told.'

There was a ripple of laughter. Some even called out, 'Hear, hear,' but most looked definitely relieved, and Maria was just glad she had got Barney to stop talking at long last. She stood up beside him to cut the cake and then, with the tables rapidly cleared, the musicians began to play. Barney stumbled out onto the dance floor with Maria, to lead them all in a four-hand reel.

It was a disaster. Barney forgot where he should be

going and who his partners were. He trod on more than a couple of ladies' toes and fell flat on his face the once when he got his feet in a tangle. Eventually, the music drew to an end, and Barney said. 'That's me done with the dancing. I'm away for better pursuits.'

Maria stood abandoned and watched Barney go back to Seamus and his cronies until Sean rescued her and led her out onto the floor again.

Barney never came near Maria again. A couple of times he'd suggested it, but one of the others would always dissuade him. 'Isn't she surrounded by friends and relations?' Eamonn said. 'You'll have a whole life together, sure.'

'Aye. Long enough for anyone,' P.J. said.

'Too long, many would say,' Seamus put in.

Barney had no desire to alienate or annoy his brother and his two friends. He knew by the looks Maria cast him that he was already in her bad books, though for the life of him he didn't know why. She seemed to be having the time of her life, laughing with this one and that and she'd not been off her feet all evening.

As the night wore on, Maria began to feel decidedly weary and when she saw Sean tried to hide his yawns, she decided to call it a day.

'Will you take Daddy home?' she asked Sean.

He nodded, but grimly. 'I'll try,' he said. 'But he'll likely not want to come.'

Maria looked to where her father was sitting with Con and a few of his mates from the docks. He was regaling them badly with songs while the band were having a break, but the others, as drunk as Sam, applauded each one and encouraged him to sing another.

She knew too her father would have no intention leaving yet. 'Good Luck!' she said.

'Will you tell Barney?'

Maria had no wish to go near Barney, but she knew she couldn't just go.

She sighed. 'Aye, for all the good it will do.'

She's coming, your missis,' P.J. told Barney, catching her approaching out of the corner of his eye.

'Coming to join us, darling girl?' Barney said mockingly as she drew nearer. 'I'll get you a drink. What'll you have?'

'Not for me, thanks,' Maria said. 'Sean and Daddy have had enough. We were thinking of going home now.'

'Doesn't look like your old man's had enough,' Seamus said, with a wide smile.

He spoke the truth. Sam was resisting going home with every bone in his body, lashing out at Sean and roaring with the injustice of it. Many were sympathetic, including, it seemed, Seamus's cronies.

'Shame it is, poor old sod,' Eamonn said. 'Making him go home when he's enjoying himself so much.'

Maria knew just how difficult her father could be once he was home, and he'd still have to be washed and changed and got ready for bed. She knew Sean must have been up early that morning to get her father looking as respectable as he did. She didn't reply to Eamonn, but said instead to Barney, 'Will you come?'

'Now?'

'Aye.'

'He's not ready yet, are you, Barney?' Seamus said, 'and I've just got another round in. Barney wants to party on, don't you?'

''S right,' Barney said. 'Party on.'

'Can't you see he's had enough?' Maria cried, rounding on Seamus.

'Are you going to stand that, mate?' P.J. said to Barney. 'A woman telling a man when he's had enough to drink and when to go home?'

No, by Christ, thought Barney. Making a holy show of him like that. 'I'll drink as much as I like and go home when I'm good and ready,' he told Maria.

'That's telling her,' said Seamus approvingly.

'Shut up!' Maria snapped, and then more coaxingly to Barney, 'Come on home, pet,' and she put a hand on his arm.

Barney shook it off. 'When I'm ready, I've told you.'

'That's it, mate. Start as you mean to go on,' Eamonn said.

Maria was furious with Barney – with them all – but she knew they were too drunk to take any notice, whatever she said. She shook her head helplessly. 'You'll not come then?'

'I'll come home when I decide to come home,' Barney said with an emphatic shake of the head. 'Sure I can't get you a wee drink?'

'No, you can't,' Maria rapped out. 'Unlike some, I know when I've had enough.'

Dismissive laughter followed her as she strode back to the others. Sam was still remonstrating with Sean. 'Stop it, Daddy,' she said sharply to Sam. 'Are you also determined to ruin the day?' Her sharp words cut through the fog in Sam's brain and he sagged in his chair. 'Oh, let's just get home out of this,' Maria said wearily.

'What about Barney?'

'What about him?' Maria said scornfully. 'He can go to hell for all I care.'

Sam heard the hurt and disappointment in Maria's voice. He was saddened, but he said nothing.

Bella and Dora had seen the altercation at the other side of the room and the two bright spots of colour in Maria's cheeks. 'Not that I blame her being angry and upset,' Bella said. 'God, that Barney wants clouting with a rolling pin.'

Maria, if she'd heard them, would have agreed, but she had bade them them good night and gone into the night after her uncle and father.

When they got in, Maria put on the kettle for her father's wash, raked up the range, and put a nightshirt to warm for him on the rail. Sean did the necessaries for her father and when he was washed and in the warmed nightshirt he fell into stupor-like sleep while Maria and her uncle sat before the fire with a bedtime cup of cocoa.

Maria had said nothing about the scene at Raffety's, but Sean knew she was still upset. He said, 'Barney will likely be sorry for his behaviour in the morning – that is, of course, if he remembers it at all.'

'Huh.'

'Don't be too hard on him,' Sean said, though he was furious himself with the man for causing Maria such distress and making her look stupid.

'Huh,' Maria said again.

'He's been drinking solid for two days,' Sean went on. 'He's not himself at all.'

'No, he isn't,' Maria agreed vehemently. 'He's like some stranger I married.'

'Shall I wait up?'

'Uncle Sean, he could be hours yet.'

'I'll doze in the chair, if I have to,' Sean said, and then as Maria still hesitated, he said, 'I'd like to do this.'

Then Maria realised she'd feel safer with Sean waiting downstairs. Safer? She thought that was a funny word to use about her errant husband. She'd never before felt threatened by Barney, but then she'd never seen him so drunk that he degenerated into some kind of uncaring monster. 'Thank you, Uncle Sean. I'd appreciate it.'

'Go on up to bed,' Sean told his niece. 'You look all in.'

Maria was tired. She mounted the stairs and went into her parents' old room for the first time. As she took off the wedding dress and petticoats, the sadness of it suddenly got to her. Instead of clasping a young, virile husband to her and making love over and over again, she was going to bed alone on her wedding night. She put on her nightdress of the softest cambric that she had made and embroidered, remembering that she had done it with a smile on her face as she'd imagined Barney near tearing it from her in a frenzy of lust. She slipped into the double bed, which seemed so big compared to the one she had been used to – so big and so lonely – and she muffled her tears in a pillow.

Maria felt Barney being lowered onto the bed some hours after she got into it, but she didn't open her eyes. So the first time she saw him was the next morning. Sean had not tried undressing him, possibly because she was asleep, and Barney lay clothed on top of the bed, with just his suit jacket, tie and boots

171

removed. His mouth lay open and he was snoring. Maria looked at him distastefully.

She began to dress for Mass and went downstairs to see Sean already up.

'Did I oversleep?'

'No,' Sean said, with a smile. 'But if you did, it is allowed. Yesterday was your wedding day.'

'Aye,' Maria replied with feeling. 'Don't I know it?'

Sean said nothing about that – there was little point – but what he did say was, 'Do you want me to wait on with Sam until you come back, and go to a later Mass?'

Maria looked across at her father. 'No, Uncle Sean,' she said. 'He won't wake for hours. Let's go together.'

She was congratulated warmly by most in the church, both before the Mass and after it, and she saw many thinking it odd that Barney wasn't with her. As well they might, she thought.

Barney didn't emerge from the room till almost noon. He looked dreadful, as if he'd aged twenty years. His red-rimmed and bleary eyes were pain-glazed, the skin sagging and grey. Even his walk was the shambling gait of an old man, and his hair stood an end as if he had had a shock.

Maria's eyes raked him. 'D'you want tea?' she asked in a brusque tone.

Barney looked sheepish. 'Aye, tea. Thanks, Maria, a cup of tea would be grand, and have you a couple of aspirins?'

Maria gave a brief nod and, after putting the kettle on the range, she went into the scullery where she kept all the medicines. As she turned with the bottle, she saw Barney had followed her in.

'I'm sorry, Maria.'

'What for?' Maria demanded. 'Just what bit of yesterday are you apologising for?'

'Oh God! I don't know,' Barney said. 'I remember the wedding and the meal afterwards, and having the first dance with you, but little else. I know I got stinking drunk, and I must have done more than that, for your eyes are full of disgust.'

Maria didn't want to throw up a list of grievances, but knew if she said nothing she would always feel resentful that he had spoilt the day. 'Yesterday, you were awful,' she said. 'It was like you were a different person, not the man I agreed to marry at all. I've put up with Daddy drinking himself stupid and all it does most times with him is make him sleep. But you turned into some kind of horrible, nasty fiend. You hardly came near me all night and made fun of me when I asked you to come home. I came home with my father and my uncle on the day I married you and I slept alone in the bed. How do you think that makes me feel? You have no excuse like Daddy has for drinking so much.'

'I don't as a rule,' Barney admitted. 'But it was a wedding, Maria.'

'Aye, yours and mine,' Maria snapped back.

'I know, I am sorry,' Barney said, stepping close at her. He would have crushed her to him, but she was holding him at arm's length. 'Barney, you stink of stale beer, whiskey and cigarettes,' she said. 'Take your tea and aspirins and go upstairs and take off your best clothes. You have them almost ruined as it is. I'll bring you a bowl to wash yourself.'

Shamefaced, Barney did as Maria bade him. He

emerged in his everyday clothes, clean and smelling much fresher, with the stubble removed from his face. He was still unable to eat, though, as his stomach continued to churn. He even refused the glass of whiskey Sam offered him.

Instead, he talked to Sean, as Maria began making the dinner, beginning with an apology for the state he'd been in the night before. Sean admired the man for the apology, conceding it took a big man to do such a thing. The anxiety he had that Barney wouldn't be the good and supportive husband Maria really needed receded a little.

Sean and Maria went for a walk after dinner, although the day was raw, but it was nice to be in the air, even for a short time. It also gave Sean the opportunity to speak with Maria and for her to unburden herself, if necessary, without anyone else listening. It was the only chance she had, for he was leaving in the morning.

However, Maria did none of that. She had long decided that if she and Barney had problems, then they were theirs alone. She had laid it on the line for her husband and now she'd see. For too long Sean had been held back from going to England, which he'd hankered after, and she wasn't going to hold him back any longer. He must have his chance before it was too late, for he was already forty-one years old, four years older than her mother. Though she'd miss him, Maria loved him too much to try to bind him to her.

So they walked together quickly, arm in arm, and talked of all manner of things. Sean felt himself relaxing. Surely, he reasoned, if Maria was worried, she'd have said so.

It wasn't until they were nearly at the house again that Maria said, 'You're free now, Uncle Sean. Will you sell up?'

'I don't like to leave you, Maria.'

'I'm grand now,' Maria said, forcing brightness into her voice. 'Haven't I Barney beside me?' She felt her uncle stiffen and said, 'Don't give a thought to how he was yesterday. He's ashamed of himself and he has apologised. To be honest, his brother is a desperate influence on him, and I'd like Barney to have as little to do with him as possible after that performance, though that is hopeless because they work together.

Obviously, Maria didn't see Barney's behaviour as a major problem, Sean thought. He said, 'I might see what the market is like, see what I'd get for the farm. It might look better in the spring and, who knows, by then you might be expecting a wee baby.'

'Aye, I could well be,' Maria said with a smile.

'There will be money when the farm is sold,' Sean told her.

'No, Uncle Sean. The farm is yours,' Maria said. 'We have enough, and you will need money if you go to England.'

'Maria, you must have your share,' Sean said. 'By rights I suppose it should go to Sam, but we both know what would happen to it then. Don't worry about me. I hear jobs are ten a penny in England now.'

'You won't be worried about bombs?'

'I think most of the raids are over and I don't want to leave it until after the war and fight with the returning servicemen for every job going.'

'And is there somewhere in mind in England that you'll be making for?'

'Well,' Sam said, 'I had a neighbour moved to Birmingham before the war began, and he said Dunlop's is a great place – you know, where they make tyres?' At Maria's nod, he went on, 'He says there are tons of Irishmen there already.'

'So, that's where you will make for?'

'Aye,' Sean said. 'To start with, at least. This man will put me up for a while, help me get digs and likely put in a word for me at the Dunlop factory. A helping hand like that is invaluable. But,' he added, 'all this can be put on hold, Maria, if you want me to stay on.'

And she did, so much, but she kissed her uncle's cheek and said, 'No, though I'll miss you. You need have no worries about me now. Let's go in before we freeze altogether. We'll both need a drink to thaw us out.'

'Where are you going to at this time of night?' Maria said to Barney, seeing him getting changed in the bedroom at almost ten o'clock the following night. With a sigh, she added, 'To the pub, I suppose?'

'No, not the pub. I have to see Seamus.'

'Seamus!'

'Don't look like that, Maria. We work together.'

'Aye, but it's not work now, is it? You won't be delivering anything at this time of night.'

Suddenly, at the look in Barney's eyes, Maria was filled with alarm. 'Barney,' she hissed urgently, 'what manner of work is it that you do?'

'Best you don't know.'

'Barney, I am your wife.'

'Aye,' Barney said. 'And you're just that, remember, not my bloody keeper.' Then he kissed her lightly on the cheek and added, 'Don't wait up. I'll likely be late.'

He was gone. And what can I do about it? Maria thought. Angry and hurt, she promised herself that she wouldn't rest until she had found out what Barney was up to.

Marie didn't hear Barney come in, but found him sleeping peacefully beside her next morning. She dressed, went downstairs and greeted her father before putting the kettle on.

After breakfast, Maria, who was taking a fortnight's holiday from work, went for a turn around the village, then as far as Greencastle to look in on Colm Brannigan. Working full time, Maria seldom had the opportunity to visit the boatyard. Although Barney called in every week, she knew the responsibility for it rested on the young boy's shoulders, though she had to admit he didn't seem at all bothered by it.

She remembered that Willie had taken him there since he'd been a little boy and her father would always worry that he might fall in the water and be dragged away, but Willie had always maintained that Colm had more sense than that. Like his grandfather, Colm was more at home on, in and around boats than away from them. He kept the whole place spick and span and was more than pleased to see Maria, offering her his congratulations.

Barney was up when Maria returned and in good humour. He apologised for his manner of the night before when he had snapped at her, and suggested a day in Derry.

'Dora has already said she will look in on Sam,' he said. 'I want every man there to be envious of the lovely wife I have.' He put his arm around Maria and gave her a squeeze. 'What do you say?'

Maria hesitated. Really, she wanted to have things out with Barney, and yet a day in Derry would be grand. It wasn't as if they were having any sort of honeymoon. She sensed also that any confrontation she would have with Barney wouldn't be a pleasant one. Maybe a day's delay for her to gather her thoughts was just what she needed. So she agreed, kissed Barney on the cheek and thanked him for thinking of it.

The Derry streets were packed with people, despite the slight icy drizzle that had begun. Maria and Barney wandered about arm in arm, feeling the buzz of the place, noticing the many men that spoke with an American drawl.

Later, they roared with laughter at Chaplin's antics in *The Great Dictator*, and then tucked into fish and chips. Maria had had a lovely day and, on the bus going home, she told Barney so and kissed him.

'I want more than that, Mrs McPhearson,' Barney whispered. Though Maria coloured a little with embarrassment, she whispered back, 'You can have anything you like, Mr McPhearson.'

Barney put his arm around Maria and she leant against him and sighed in contentment.

Later that night, when Barney took her in his arms and kissed her, Maria felt her insides turning to jelly.

'Oh, Barney, I've longed for you to make love to me,' she said, for since the wedding he hadn't touched her.

'Aye,' Barney said. 'I couldn't perform with Sean just the other side of the wall, and last night, of course, I had that job of work with my brother.'

Maria felt she should ask what job of work, but she didn't want to spoil the moment. Anyway, what Barney was doing to her made her not want to do anything but respond.

'I thought you'd gone off me,' she said dreamily.

'Never!' Barney declared. 'But you've had enough shitty few nights one way and another. Take off that nightdress and let's make up for lost time.'

Barney took Maria to the very pinnacle of desire, until she begged, pleaded for satisfaction, before he entered her. She climaxed so suddenly, and with such power that it completely overwhelmed her. However, Barney wasn't finished and brought her to such heights again and again. She cried out over and over, engulfed by the sheer joy of it all, and tried to stifle the sounds with a hand across her mouth.

She slept eventually, happier than she could remember feeling for a while. She cuddled against her husband contentedly and drifted off into a dreamless and wonderfully deep sleep.

CHAPTER TEN

The next day, loath as Maria was to rock the marital boat, which now seemed to be floating in calmer waters, she knew the things she had to discuss with Barney couldn't be put off any longer. She had to know what line of business he was in with Seamus. Carried out in the dead of night, it didn't smack to her of anything legal.

As soon as breakfast was over, she told Barney she wanted to talk to him, but not with Sam in the same room. He was lying quiet and still, with his eyes closed, but Maria had known him do that before and then be able to recount a conversation she had had with somebody. Most things it didn't hurt for him to know, but she wasn't sure the answers she might demand of Barney were for his ears yet. She put her finger to her lips, pointed to her father and then whispered, 'We'll go into the bedroom.'

At the speculative light that suddenly burnt behind Barney's eyes, she said firmly, 'To talk, just.'

'The bedroom is no place to linger,' Barney said, 'unless we do something first to generate heat.'

'Barney, stop it,' Maria said. 'Be serious a minute, because I am not joking.'

Barney's eyes narrowed slightly, because he could guess what was coming and hadn't any idea what to say. Seamus would tell him to say nothing, but while Seamus could wine, dine and bed women, he hadn't a clue how their minds worked or how they might react to things. He was under the impression all you had to do was woo a girl until you married her and then she would do as she was told. Barney knew Maria wasn't that sort a wife at all. In fact, he doubted if many wives were.

So when Maria demanded, 'I want to know all about this so-called delivery business you run with Seamus,' he hadn't any sort of answer ready.

'Look, Maria,' he said, trying to assume a conciliatory tone, 'it's probably better if you know nothing about it.'

Maria gave a howl of outrage. 'Barney, listen to me,' she said. 'A few days ago, we stood before the priest, and nearly the whole community and became man and wife. From that moment, anything you do will affect me and vice versa because we became a unit. So, what the hell are you up to that you have dragged me into?'

Barney gave up trying to side-step the issue. 'We do deliveries to the north,' he said. 'That much is true.'

'In the dead of night?'

'Aye, why not?' Barney said. 'Less traffic on the roads then.'

'Don't treat me like a fool, Barney,' Maria said. 'Answer me straight. Are you smuggling?'

There was no point in denying it. Barney just nodded.

'Jesus, Barney, are you mad?' Maria burst out. 'There were two men gaoled for that near Strabane only last week. It was in the papers. So the guards will be on the look out, surely, checking there aren't more people at it.'

'Maybe we're too clever for them.'

'And maybe you're not,' Maria said. 'Have you considered that?'

'Look, Maria, I know what I'm doing.'

'So do I. I also know it's against the law and morally wrong. It's sort of stealing.'

'It isn't,' Barney contradicted. 'We pay for what we smuggle and we bring things back here to the south. It's sort of like doing a public service.'

'Don't kid yourself, Barney,' Maria said. 'You're lining your own pockets.'

'There's nothing wrong with that.'

'There's everything wrong with it when it's against the law,' Maria snapped back. 'Is there any other moneymaking scheme I should know about?'

Barney hesitated to tell her about the card schools, but if he didn't she'd go for him big style if it ever did come out. He shrugged. 'We run card schools for the sailors,' he said, 'after the drops. Sometimes it can go on for hours. Poker, you know?'

That tugged a memory in Maria's brain. 'The day that Mammy was taken to hospital,' Maria said to Barney. 'You said you had been working all night.'

'Aye, we were at a poker game that night,' Barney admitted. 'Didn't finish until six and then we had to unload this side.'

'Who is this "we"?'

'Seamus and me, that's all.'

'What do the others do then?' Maria asked. 'The ones who came to the reception and said they were friends of Seamus's?'

'I don't know,' Barney said. 'And that's God's honest truth. I mean, I think they're involved with the smuggling, but I don't know where Seamus gets the stuff from that we deliver, or what happens to the things we bring back. It's really better not to know too much and these fellows don't like people asking questions.'

'Right,' Maria said. 'We've established the fact that you are smuggling goods back and forth over the border and that you run poker schools to fleece the sailors of their pay.'

'We don't force anyone to play cards, Maria. They come of their own free will.'

'All right,' Maria said. 'I know some men haven't got the sense they were born with and I suppose they have as much chance of winning as you do.'

Barney gave a smirk. 'They do,' he said, 'if they play with their own cards and don't use Seamus's.'

'You mean, Seamus even cheats at these poker schools?'

Barney shrugged. 'Let's just say we win plenty and often,' he said.

'OK,' Maria said. 'Let's leave the smuggling and a poker schools. Now, is there anything else?'

Barney wasn't going to admit to the raids. He wasn't altogether stupid. So when Maria suddenly turned the ring on her finger and said, 'This was bought with cash from those ventures, I suppose?' Barney nodded again.

'Is it a real emerald in my engagement ring? she asked suddenly.

'Aye.'

'God! Barney, how much are you making?'

'Enough,' Barney said. 'Enough to take you out nice places, buy you beautiful presents. Didn't hear you complaining then.'

'I didn't know how you earned your money then.'

'And didn't enquire too closely either.'

'Why should I have done that?' Maria asked. 'I accepted what you told me in all good faith.'

'Think the Garda will believe that?'

'They won't have to be told,' Maria said, 'for you must give it up.'

'No,' Barney said.

'You must see it's wrong,' Maria said. 'It can't go on.'

'Yes it can. As long as the war and rationing goes on, we can make a good living.'

'You could go to prison,' Maria said. 'What if I was to shop you?'

Barney wasn't worried by that idle threat 'You'd just be shopping yourself,' he told her. 'How d'you think I paid Rafferty for the room we had for the wedding, and the money I put behind the bar so that everyone could have a drink? I also bought a new suit, not to mention the ring. How did you think I did it? Pulled it out of the air? D'you think the guards will believe that you had no knowledge of all this? Fine kettle of fish it would be for your father if we were both locked up, don't you think?'

Maria sat on the bed, defeated. She knew the guards might well believe she knew all about the smuggling, even had a hand in it. Then it would be Sam who suffered too. She couldn't risk that. 'Can you not give it up for my sake, Barney?' she pleaded.

'No,' Barney said. 'No, I can't and I don't want to.'

'And what if you're caught?'

'I'll take care I'll not be.'

Maria might have argued further, but she heard her father call her. Anyway, what else was there to say? All the important words had been used up and the end result was that Barney would continue this lawless and dangerous practice and drag her into it more and more. There was damned all she could do about it.

The next morning, Maria was wakened early with backache. Though she tried to go back to sleep, it kept returning to tug at her and she couldn't seem to be able to get comfortable at all. She lay in bed, wondering if she had strained herself at all. As the hours passed, the pain seemed to move around to Maria's front and became strong enough to cause her to writhe in the bed. Barney, who'd not reached his bed till the early hours, stirred and muttered at Maria to 'lie still'.

She tried, but the pains intensified until they resembled the ones she had each month and she had to draw up her knees to give herself some relief. For the first time she wondered if it were something to do with the baby and, if so, what she should do about it. No one in the village knew she was pregnant.

The pains became more severe and Maria was very frightened. She tried to wake Barney, but he was deeply asleep and not that keen on being roused. Maria continued to shake him until he opened his bleary eyes.

'Give over! What the hell is the matter with you?' he said, his voice sluggish with sleep.

'I need Bella. You must fetch Bella,' Maria said urgently.

'What time is it?'

'Just turned half-seven

'Jesus, Maria! Don't be daft, woman! What do you want Bella for at this hour of the morning?' he said wearily, his eyes already closing.

'Barney, please. Don't go back to sleep. I need Bella. I'm in pain, Barney.'

Barney sighed and opened one eye. 'Where?'

'Oh, for God's sake, where the hell do you think?' Maria snapped in sudden impatience. 'It could be something happening to the baby, Barney.'

And then at last he understood. 'Holy Shit!' He swung himself out of bed and began pulling on his trousers.

By the time Bella arrived, leaving Barney downstairs, Maria was crouched beside the bed, holding a towel between her legs. The blood, which had already stained her nightdress, was dripping through her fingers and beginning to pool on the floor.

'I'll get more towels,' she said, and soon had Maria back in bed, packed with towels and with a clean nightgown on.

'Do you think me awful?' Maria asked. 'Are you shocked?'

'Nay, lass,' Bella said. 'Human nature what it is, I'm not shocked.'

'He didn't force me – Barney,' Maria said, anxious

186

to put the record straight. 'I mean, I wanted it as much as he did.'

'Hush, Maria,' Bella said. 'I don't need to know these things and I am not apportioning blame here. What matters is you, and the baby that I think you are losing.'

Maria felt a sudden, sharp sense of loss. She'd not wanted this child at first, seen it as a burden that would bring shame on her. But not now. Now she was married and respectable, everything was different.

'Can't you do anything?' she asked.

Bella shook her head. 'I doubt it very much. You are losing a lot of blood. Have lost plenty already. Maybe we should have the doctor?'

'Then everyone will know.'

'Doctors can't tell. They are like priests in that way.'

'People get to know, though,' Maria said. 'And I don't want the doctor looking at me with disgust.'

'Maria, he wouldn't . . .'

'Can't you stay?' Maria pleaded. 'I'm frightened on my own. I know I'm losing it – I knew when I saw the blood – and I am more upset than I can tell you.'

Maria sounded so sad and forlorn that Bella put her arms around her. 'I'll stay with you,' she said. 'Till it's over, I will stay with you.'

'And will you tell Barney what's happening?'

'Aye, don't worry, I'll tell him. I have left him downstairs. This is no place for a man.'

Bella couldn't help contrasting Maria's reaction with Barney's, which wasn't so much sorrow as regret that it hadn't happened a few weeks earlier. Then there would have been no need for a wedding. He would still be footloose and fancy free, and they could have gone on as before.

Dora, summoned in to help, made breakfast for the men, washed and changed Sam and suggested Barney take him out for a drink as soon as the pubs opened to get them both out of the way. Sam was very agreeable to that and Barney too was glad to get out of the house. Seamus was in the pub and, seeing Sam was talking to friends, Barney and Seamus sat at a quiet table in the corner. Barney told his brother the latest developments.

'Ah Jesus, Barney she's really potched you,' Seamus said, his voice sympathetic.

'What you on about?'

'Are you half-witted or what?' Seamus demanded. 'There *was* no baby, you bloody idiot.'

'Course there was.'

'How do you know?'

'She said she was in pain, man.'

'That don't mean nothing.'

'Yeah, but that's it, her monthlies stopped.'

'Are you sure?' Seamus asked. 'I mean, you are lucky if you get two nights off a week. Do you ever have sex with her when you come in after a job?'

'No, she is always tired and she does get up early.'

'Well, then . . .'

'Come on, Seamus,' Barney protested. 'When she told me, God, she was real upset and looked like she was scared. And now Bella is up at the house and everything.'

'Look,' Seamus said, 'all that proves is that Maria is a bloody good actress. And as for Bella, haven't the two of them always been as thick as thieves? She'd stick by her. I mean, did either of them mention calling in the doctor?'

'No,' Barney said, his voice uncertain for the first time. 'I asked Bella that. I ain't seen Maria and Bella said that they didn't think there was any need for a doctor.'

'Yeah, I bet that is just what they thought,' Seamus said. 'Still, cheer up, mate, you are not the first this has happened to and you'll probably not be the last either. At least you got yourself a looker. Mate of mine was done the same way and he beat his wife black and blue when he discovered he'd been duped. She pretended to have a miscarriage as well. I tell you, brother, you can't be up to the tricks a woman will get up to in order to hook a man. Same again?' he went on, picking up the glasses.

Barney just nodded. He couldn't come to terms with it, and yet he never doubted Seamus was right. Well, the die was cast now and he was hitched, and for life. While he had no wish to lay a hand on Maria, he knew he would never think of her in the same way again. She must have been laughing up her sleeve at him all the time and now, he thought, the marriage was tainted and spoilt . . .

Bella and Dora hadn't seen Barney so drunk since the wedding and Seamus had had to push Sam home, because Barney had trouble enough putting one foot before the other. Bella was glad that Maria was asleep and unaware of it.

The baby had come away just an hour or so after Barney left for the pub and been dealt with, and the

189

room cleaned up and tidied. The fact that Bella said the child had been disposed of fuelled Barney's suspicions still further. There was no baby and never had been. Now he was certain of it.

He never went near Maria, but ate the meal Bella had prepared and then slept off the beer in a chair in front of the range. When he woke, darkness had descended and a pot of something savoury was simmering on the range. There was no sound in the house other than Sam's breath rasping in his throat as he slept. Barney lit the lamp and saw the time was nearly six. The pubs would be open soon.

First, though, he took a few cupfuls of stew out of the pot, ripped a quarter of soda bread from the loaf and wolfed it down, before leaving the house without a word to anyone. Bella, returning, saw that Barney had been home and presumed he had gone out on some errand of Maria's. She was surprised when Maria said she hadn't seen him.

'I have just woken though,' she said. 'He must have looked in and found me asleep.'

'Well, I hope it isn't the pub he's making for this early,' Bella remarked, 'for he had a hell of a load on him at lunchtime.'

'Men deal with grief and disappointment in a different way from a woman,' Maria said. 'If he got drunk that was probably because he was more upset than he was letting on. He'll likely be back early tonight and we can talk about it.'

However, Barney did not put in an appearance. Eventually, Maria, though she was upset with Barney and intended to tell him so when he did arrive home, felt too tired to keep her eyes open any longer. When she woke the following morning, Barney wasn't in bed beside her and she struggled out of bed, still feeling weak and light-headed, to see if he had slept in one of the other bedrooms. But he wasn't in the house and she returned to bed concerned as to where he was.

She mentioned her anxieties to Bella when she came in and Bella told her not to mind about Barney. Wasn't he a full-grown man, well able to look after himself?

Barney didn't arrive home until the afternoon. Again he was so drunk he could barely stand and Maria's heart sank as she saw him swaying in the doorway.

'How much longer are you going to lounge in bed?' he demanded.

Maria was surprised at the question. Bella had said she had lost so much blood she wasn't to think of getting up for a few days at least, and said she would see to things. She attempted to explain this to Barney, but he cut across her.

'I know what little plan you and Bella have hatched up between you, but you are my wife and I expect you out of that bed and downstairs seeing to things.'

'I'm not feeling so good, Barney.'

'Stop making such a bloody fuss.'

'Barney, I had a miscarriage.'

'Hah, so you say.'

'What do you mean?'

'Never mind what I mean,' Barney snarled. 'I've already sent Bella and Dora packing, so you best get out of that bed.'

Barney drunk was nasty and unpredictable, and so

Maria got to her feet holding on to the bed post until the room had stopped spinning. She began to dress, puzzling over his words. What had he meant? Didn't he believe that she had had a miscarriage, that she'd told him she was pregnant just to trap him into marriage?

Mother of God, surely Barney didn't think she would do such a thing? But something had put him in a tear all right. She would have to talk to him, make him see. Not now – there was little point in talking to a drunk man – but certainly at the first opportunity.

However, Barney refused to discuss anything to do with the 'so-called miscarriage', as he put it and over the next few days he was seldom truly sober. Maria felt too weak to try to insist when he was so belligerent all the time. She did try to take him to task about his drinking, but that made him really wild, and it made no difference to what he did anyway.

In fact, Barney was in a quandary. In the past he had always believed what his brother had said and did what he wanted him to do, but those things Seamus had said about Maria had really upset Barney. Part of his mind wanted to reject them and say she'd do no such a thing, while the other part of his mind was harbouring doubts, disappointment and hurt that she had made a fool of him that way. It was this dilemma that was making him drink so heavily, because there was no one he felt he could discuss it with but his brother, and he always laid the blame firmly on Maria's shoulders.

Maria couldn't seem to shake off the tiredness and lethargy, and knew a lot of it was depression at the way her marriage was turning out. Sometimes she could barely recognise Barney as the man she had married just a short time ago. The closeness between them seemed to have vanished completely, but she never breathed a word of her discontent to a soul, least of all Bella or Dora.

In a way, she was glad to go back to work and be away from Barney's brooding presence and ill humour. At work the girls were anxious to hear all about the wedding and Maria told them only the nice things, particularly Joanne, and she showed them all the photographs.

She also told Joanne about the miscarriage when they were on their own. Joanne seemed to think the few tears she shed were quite normal and she held her tight until she was calmer.

Barney's appetite for sex became more voracious than ever because he needed to prove that Maria still loved him. Words, he thought, were cheap. Now, even if he came home in the early hours, he would often wake her and demand sex, despite the fact that she had to be up early for work. These times he was usually rough and unfeeling too, and wouldn't take the time to put her in the mood, but she would hide her discomfort and soreness and say not a word about it. It certainly wasn't something she could share with anyone. Anyway, she did so long for a child.

Maria wasn't the only one suspicious of what Barney did. Dora too was curious. She was grateful that he continued to look after Sam in the afternoons, freeing her, but she often complained to Bella that he slept all morning long.

'Maria said he has a job delivering to the military,' Dora said one day. 'Well, why isn't he up and at it then?'

'Aye,' Bella said. 'People in the shop hint at things, I know that. I mean, one thing you can't stop is people's tongues and, well, maybe it's just rumour, but they suggest that this delivery business is not strictly speaking legal. And if that is the case he could be up and at it at the dead of night, couldn't he?'

'Smuggling, you mean?'

Bella shrugged. 'I suppose. But we have no proof about it and it could just be hearsay.'

'Well, whether it is or whether it isn't, we can do nothing about it,' Dora said. 'Not unless we want to risk it rebounding on Maria.'

'I know,' Bella said. 'And he is all right with her in other ways, isn't he?'

'I suppose so,' Dora said. 'But I seldom see them together now. She doesn't complain, at any rate, and she always has plenty of money to spend.'

Maria took the money reluctantly now, knowing that, by taking it, she was implicating herself further. It did mean, however, that she was able to put nearly all of her wages in the post office and that gave her a measure of security.

In March 1943, Sean sold the farm to one of Agatha's sons. When he went to tell Maria, she knew she would miss him sorely.

'Should I go and see Sarah,' he asked Maria, 'and bid her farewell?'

Maria shook her head. 'They won't let you in, Uncle

194

Sean. They don't encourage visitors – say it upsets the patients. I went the one time with Bella, but they told us Mammy's mental balance was precarious, and I didn't try again.'

'So you haven't a clue how she is?'

'No.'

'Why don't you have a word with the doctor chap?' Sean suggested. 'He seemed a good sort the time or two I met him.'

'I never thought of that,' Maria said. 'I will, Uncle Sean, and maybe I'll be able to give the news before you leave. You've no idea when that will be?'

'No,' Sean said, 'although the formalities are all done, so it will be in the next few weeks.'

Maria asked Dr Shearer if he'd find out how her mother was and really wished afterwards she hadn't bothered.

'Your mother is not responding to treatment at all,' the doctor told her. 'They have tried a variety of methods to help her mental state, but she continues to deteriorate. If you were to see her now it would only upset you. She wouldn't know you at all and might try to attack you.'

'Attack? Mammy?'

'This is not the mammy you know, Maria, you must remember that,' the doctor said. 'She has already attacked the staff quite a number of times and often has to be restrained.' He didn't describe the strait-jacket. There were some things patients' families didn't need to be told.

'I brought her to this,' Sam said, when the doctor had gone.

'Daddy, we've been through this.'

'I've been through it too, over and over,' Sam said. 'I know I should never have gone to investigate that noise alone. Why in God's name didn't I take Con with me?'

'Because you knew Brenda would rip him to bits with her tongue,' Maria said. She sat up on the bed and picked up one of her father's wizened hands. 'It's easy, Daddy, to be wise after the event,' she said. 'Please don't blame yourself for this.'

'I know what I know,' Sam said. 'And where the blame lies. Fetch me a wee drink, Maria, there's a good girl.'

In May, about the time Sean was packing up ready to leave, Barney too got a shock. 'I told you that raid was the first and last,' he told his brother, Seamus, angrily.

'And I'm telling you,' Seamus said, 'the situation has changed. The guards are after P.J. and he has to lie low for a bit.'

'But if they have P.J. in their sights, surely they'll know the car as well?'

'That's been taken care of,' Seamus said. 'It has a completely new numberplate and a respray, so you'll be able to drive it in perfect safety, provided you keep your wits about you.'

'And if I refuse?'

'If you refuse, brother,' Seamus said, 'you better get yourself into Derry tomorrow and take a job.'

'What d'you mean? I can still do the runs with you, can't I?'

'No,' Seamus said, shaking his head. 'I'd need to draft someone else in to do both, so it's up to you, Barney.'

Barney knew Seamus meant every word he said. Smuggling and the card schools, from which he drew such a comfortable living, would be things of the past. Instead he'd be at some back-breaking job for which he earned only half the money. Yet every time he thought about taking part in any sort of raid, even just driving the car, he felt sick with fear. Seamus saw this reflected in his face. 'Jesus,' he said 'you're scared shitless, aren't you?'

Barney didn't bother to deny it. 'Aye,' he said. 'So what? Any normal person would be scared.'

'I'm not asking a normal person,' Seamus said. 'I'm asking you, and I need the answer now. Will you do it or not?'

'What's the alternative?'

'There isn't one.'

'Then the answer is obvious,' Barney said.

Sean came to see Maria just before he left and he pressed some pound notes into her hand. 'It's from the sale of the farm,' he said. 'You mind I said you would have your share. I'm not telling Barney about this and I don't want you to. It's good for a woman to have a wee bit of money of her own. You don't know when you may have need of it.'

Maria put the money into the same account that she put her wages in every week. She had never told Barney of this. Not once had he asked what she did with her wages, and she kept the book hidden under the mattress.

As the spring rolled into summer the only change was that Barney was out more often through the night, but now he had a regular night or nights off, two or three sometimes. Maria didn't ask why. Barney had told her from the first it was best not to know and she was beginning to realise he was right. She worried constantly that he'd be caught. If she knew he drove a getaway car in the raids that were now being reported in the press, she'd have been frantic.

Just after Maria and Barney's first anniversary, Maria received a letter from her uncle. It was waiting for her when she returned from work one evening.

Dear Maria,

I hope everyone is keeping well, as I am myself. I have some news to tell you. I have met a widow called Martha. She is Birmingham born and bred and her man never returned from Dunkirk.

You'd like Martha, Maria. She is as good and kind as you are yourself. You may have the chance to meet her yet, and before too long, for I have asked her to marry me and she has accepted. We have not known each other that long, but neither of us is in the first flush of youth.

She has three children. Patsy, the eldest, is thirteen next month and such a clever girl. From her primary school in Aston she passed something called the 11-plus. It's a very stiff exam, Martha told me, and Patsy has a scholarship to St Agnes' Convent School a little way away in a place known as Erdington. She goes up on the bus or tram every day.

There are two boys too. Tony will be eight in April, and wee Paul five in March and we all get along splendidly. They all need a father in their lives and Martha has struggled alone long enough.

'God!' Maria exclaimed. 'Sean is getting married.' She could hardly believe it.

'Another man led to the bloody slaughter,' Barney said gloomily.

Maria made no comment, because sometimes the slightest thing she said would throw Barney into a rage, but when she saw him lift his jacket from the hook behind the door she did ask, 'Are you away to see Seamus?'

'No, just to Rafferty's for a few pints,' Barney said. 'I'd take Sam, but he's too far gone already.'

'I know,' Maria said. Her father was already in a semi-stupor.

'I'll not be that late,' Barney said. 'You be ready for me when I come in.'

Barney, when he was kind to Maria and patient in working her up before sex, could still send tremors down her spine and turn her stomach upside down. He knew that full well. He knew too that when he had sunk a few jars, Maria would be waiting for him, ready and willing, and he whistled as he made his way to the pub.

Though they had been married over a year, there was still no sign of the child that Maria so longed for. The men at the pub had begun to tease Barney about it.

'No lead in his pencil,' said one wag.

'Aye,' another agreed. 'Must be firing blanks.' And there was a chorus of laughter.

Women were kinder, but more insistent. 'No sign of the patter of tiny feet?' the women in the factory would enquire now and again.

'No, nothing yet.'

'There's things they can do now, you know. You want to get yourself seen to.'

'Aye, you and your man,' said one of the older women. 'Could be him at fault and they never like to admit that.'

'Surely it's early days yet?' Maria said, but she began to feel something was wrong too and wonder whether the miscarriage had damaged her, which was preventing pregnancy. But she kept that worry to herself.

CHAPTER ELEVEN

In March 1944 Martha and Sean were to be married. Sean wrote to tell Maria all about it.

> Martha has a house for sale in Aston, and I had invested the money from the farm. We have bought a lovely house on Arthur Road, not far at all from Erdington village, which has a wide array of shops. A works bus runs the length of nearby Holly Lane and takes me straight to Dunlop's. The little children are only a stone's throw from the Abbey School and Patsy's convent is even closer.
>
> There seems no reason now to delay the wedding, and it is set for Saturday, 11 March. I know how you are placed with your job and Sam, but it would make the day for me if you could see your way to come over . . .

There were tears of joy in Maria's eyes as she folded the letter and put it behind the clock. Sean had achieved the very thing he craved, the thing he thought lost to him for ever: a wife and children, a family of his own. Maria's heart filled with love for that good, kind man, and she thanked God he'd been so well blessed.

'I can't go, of course,' she said to Barney.

'Of course you can,' Barney said. 'You must go. It will make Sean's day. He says so.'

'But—'

'Maria, you're the only family he has,' Barney pointed out. 'You can't let him down over this.'

'But—'

'Will you stop saying but?' Barney said. 'Arrange time off from work. Dora and me together will see to your father. Write back to Sean and say you'll be pleased to go.'

Bella and Dora agreed with Barney, but Bella commented, 'I don't envy them, getting married in wartime Britain. I hear rationing is crippling, even on clothes. God alone knows what this Martha is getting married in.'

That night, Maria looked at her wedding dress hanging in the wardrobe and remembered how unhappy she'd been the night after her wedding, when she'd hung it up. Now it was going to waste when it could be put to good use.

'But do you have her measurements?' Bella said, when Maria told her what she intended.

'Course I don't,' Maria said. 'But maybe she could adapt the material for something else, if it doesn't fit as it is. I shan't mind at all if she cuts it up.'

'Not everyone is as adept with a needle as you, Maria.'

'Needs must,' Maria said. 'If Britain is anything like Derry, posters will encourage them to "Make Do and

Mend". To be a "squander bug" is the worst thing in the world, apparently. And aren't I squandering my wedding dress, leaving it hanging in the wardrobe where it is neither use nor ornament to anyone? Anyway, I'll write tonight and see if Martha wants the dress.'

Martha was delighted with the offer. The problem of getting suitable clothes on the allocated points had been playing on her mind. Maria bundled up the dress and send it to her the very day she got Martha's letter. She began to look forward to the wedding.

She was to travel down on Wednesday night to catch the ferry at Dun Laoghaire early on Thursday morning, because Barney said it was best to sail in the daylight. Maria was already nervous enough, because she'd never been further than Derry all the days of her life and she was glad that Barney was going as far as Derry with her.

'My insides are jumping about all over the place,' she said to Barney on the train, as he put her case on the rack above her head.

'That's natural enough,' Barney said. 'But the break will do you good. And don't you be worrying about Sam. We'll see he's all right.'

'I'll try not to,' Maria said. She knew Sam was less trouble than ever, for he was out of it most of the time, but she never stopped worrying about him.

'They're slamming the doors,' Barney said. 'If I don't get off soon I'll be travelling with you.'

Maria wished he was, wished anyone was, but she didn't say this.

Barney gave her a peck on the cheek, a thing he seldom did any more, and waited on the platform until the train pulled out before making his way swiftly to the back room of the pub in Derry, where he knew Seamus and Eamonn would be waiting for him.

However, when he heard what the other two proposed, he couldn't believe his ears. 'A bank!' he cried. 'Ah, sweet Jesus, Seamus. We'll never be able to rob a bank, or anything like it.'

'We're not robbing the bank,' Seamus said. 'We're robbing the men carrying the money. We've had a couple of fellows tracking the van's route for some time and there's this quiet stretch of road with plenty of cover either side. That's where we'll strike.'

'What other fellows?' Barney demanded.

'What did you think?' Seamus asked. 'Did you think we could do this job by ourselves? We are talking big money here, brother. We'll need another car as well.'

'Why?'

'To block the road,' Seamus explained. 'The car will be stolen and they will drive it in front of the van. We jump in, wrench open the door, clout the guards over the head and Bob's your uncle. We'll all be thousands of pounds better off. Now, do you want in, or don't you?'

Barney was tempted by the thought of thousands of pounds, and the plan seemed to have been thought out well enough. 'What a daft question,' he said. 'Course I want to be in.'

'So,' Seamus said, 'all you've got to do is keep out of sight while we deal with the guards and then pull in behind the van with the engine running. We'll be in and out in no time and it'll be as easy as that.'

Barney felt the beginnings of excitement at the

thought of it. The sick feeling and the fear had been replaced by exhilaration as each raid was planned and executed perfectly. He thought it the easiest way in the world to make lots of cash. He knew Maria wouldn't see it like that at all, but she needn't ever hear one whisper about any of it.

'All right?' Seamus rapped out.

'You bet,' Barney replied. 'Jesus, I can hardly wait.'

Maria was so weary by the time the train pulled into the station at Dun Laoghaire that she could hardly think straight. Once out of it, she followed the mass of people, who seemed to know where they were going. The size of the ferry unnerved her, but not as much as the grey scummy water lapping against it, or the vast sea, stretching out in the distance, that the ferry would be travelling across. She boarded with great trepidation.

All her life she had been surrounded by boats – not boats such as these, of course, though now the Foyle was full of boats of all sizes and shapes – but she had never been on a boat before, either large or small. She had a more than healthy respect for the sea, bordering on fear, and she had never learnt to swim. She looked at the mass of passengers on board and wondered how the boat ever kept afloat.

Before the shores of Ireland had disappeared in the early morning mist, however, she was less concerned with these niggling worries than with her stomach, which was churning in quite an alarming way. She soon began to wish she hadn't eaten the sandwiches she'd packed for the train journey.

She wasn't the only one to be in such dire straits.

Many of the passengers had a greenish tinge to their faces. Others seemed to have stomachs of iron and swilled back their pints of Guinness, despite the early hour, until the saloons reeked with the smell of the black stuff. This, mingled with the stink of cigarette smoke, didn't help anyone feeling the slightest bit delicate.

When the boat docked, Maria left it thankfully and followed the swell of people streaming into the smallish station and onto the waiting train. She perked up considerably in the train and watched the rolling countryside outside the window with interest until the swaying movement, together with the stress of the journey and the fact she'd had little sleep the night before, eventually overtook her and she slept.

There were no names on any of the stations, and when Maria awoke, she was disorientated, sure she'd sailed past New Street Station. More seasoned passengers sharing her carriage put her right. They told her where to get off, but she was still mighty glad to see her uncle waiting for her as she alighted from the train.

His arms went around her immediately. 'Ah, Maria,' he said, his voice husky with emotion. 'God, but you are a sight for sore eyes.'

Maria leant against him with a sigh, so glad he was there, for the size and clamour of the place unnerved her totally. People thronged the platform, shouting, laughing and crying, while above the noise, porters with laden trolleys were cautioning people to 'Mind your backs'. A newspaper vendor screamed out his wares, though Maria couldn't understand a word he was saying. Sean, taking Maria's case in one hand and holding her arm with the other, steered her through this mayhem, past the ticket collector, to the taxi rank outside.

How much more alarming it would have been without her uncle beside her, she thought, leaning back in the taxi with a sigh.

'Bad journey?' Sean asked.

'Unnerving just,' Maria said. 'And then I felt horribly sick on the boat.'

Sean smiled. 'So was I when I came over. And I'm sorry you had to suffer it too, but I can't put into words what it means to have you here for my wedding day.'

'Ah, Uncle Sean, you know you mean the world to me,' Maria said. 'And the journey is already forgotten.' She turned her attention to the city centre, shocked to see what a decimated place it was. There were huge gaps where she imagined once stores had stood.

Sean, guessing at her thoughts from her face, said, 'Aye, the city took a pounding, right enough. Martha said it was terrifying. Thank God that's all over now.'

'Are you sure it is?'

'Oh, aye,' Sean said. 'The war is coming to an end. Mark my words.'

Maria hoped he was right. Her work might be at an end then too, but she'd have to leave work anyway if and when she was ever to have a child, though sometimes that possibility seemed so far away.

Stop thinking about it, she told herself firmly. It only saddens you, and you are here to celebrate a wedding.

So she turned her attention back to Sean, who was proudly pointing out his adopted city to her as she passed. He indicated the big green clock at a place called Aston Cross.

'I live not far from here,' he said. 'Until the wedding, that is. Martha, of course, lived here too until she moved into the house a month ago. Grand place for work is Aston,' he went on. 'I might have tried my luck in one of the factories here if Kenny O'Connor hadn't spoken up for me at Dunlop's. They used to turn out all manner of things here too, so Martha told me, though much of what they make now is war-related, of course.'

Maria smelt a vinegary smell in the air, which Sean told her was from HP Sauce, overlaid by another heavier, sweeter smell.

'Oh, that's the malt,' Sean said when Maria mentioned it, 'from Ansell's brewery here.' He pointed out the tall, solid building of light-coloured brick beside the road.

Minutes later they were at Salford Bridge and Maria saw the network of sludgy canals that met there. 'Birmingham has more canals than Venice,' Sean told Maria proudly. 'Now we go up the hill here, and I've told the driver to go the length of Erdington village so you can see the shops that are just a stone's throw from the house.'

The taxi driver took them down a wide street, tramlines running the length of it. On each side of the road was every shop imaginable. There were grocery shops, butchers and greengrocers, drapers and haberdashery shops, even a few cafés. About halfway down they passed a churchyard on the right-hand side, graves grouped all around it behind a stone wall.

'Is that the church you go to?' Maria asked.

'No,' Sean told her. 'That's Church of England, the parish church. We'll be going to the abbey on Sutton New Road, which is where the wedding will be. Now we'll be passing the cinema in a minute.'

That did impress Maria. 'The Palace Picture House,' she read, and was slightly envious. Fancy having a cinema on the doorstep like that!

'We're coming to Erdington village green now,' Sean said. 'Martha tells me most days she goes no further than this, for it has all the shops she needs. And, of course, these days you have to register with a shopkeeper to get your rations.'

'Of course,' Maria said, though the idea of rationing was an alien one to her. She looked with interest at the shops surrounding the grassed lawn ahead of them. It had obviously once had a fence around it, but all that were left were metal stumps in the ground.

Before she could query this strange sight, Sean pointed to the other side of the road and said, 'That imposing building there is a public library. You can take two books out for nothing and keep them for a fortnight.'

Maria could think of nothing nicer, for though she had little time to read now, as a child she'd always read the books her father had bought her for school from cover to cover before the term began. There had been precious little other reading material in the house, except perhaps a paper.

But before she had time to digest this properly, Sean said, 'And this is Mason Road and the public swimming baths.'

Maria was amazed. So much entertainment and all close at hand. 'How far away is the house now, Uncle Sean?'

'No distance at all,' Sean said as the taxi turned left at a little crossroads ahead of them. 'It's just at the end of this road, in fact.'

The road was wide and lined with trees. Behind them were imposing terraced houses with steps up to the front doors and the taxi driver drew to a halt in front of one of these. Two young boys almost leapt on Sean as he got out of the car. Maria saw an older girl, but she stood a short distance away, by the gate.

'Away out of that,' Sean said, turning his attention to the boys after paying the taxi driver. 'Where are your manners? Greet your cousin Maria properly.'

'Hello, Maria,' the two boys chorused, but the girl, Maria noticed, said nothing. 'This young rip here is Tony,' Sean said, pointing to the sandy-haired boy with the dark, mischievous eyes. 'And this here is Paul.' He was younger and quieter than his boisterous brother. His hair was blond, his eyes blue, and he was not so cheeky-looking. 'And this young lady, of course, is Patsy,' Sean said, drawing her close and putting an arm around her. Patsy, who had been regarding Maria with dislike, now had a look of triumph on her face as she leant against Sean.

She's jealous of me, Maria thought suddenly. That's what's the matter with her. She decided to take no notice. It was something the young girl had to get over and if she didn't, it hardly would matter for the few days she would be there. She followed her uncle through the wrought-iron gate, down the side of the little lawned garden. There were six steps leading up to the front door. As they mounted them, Maria saw the window of a cellar room peeping from below.

She'd been impressed by the road and she was equally impressed by the house. The front door opened on to a small lobby. Another door with stained-glass windows opened on to a hall covered with patterned tiles.

'You have a fine house, Uncle Sean,' Maria said. 'How many bedrooms have you?'

'Four and a bathroom up there,' Sean said, jerking his head towards the wide staircase to the left-hand side. 'And two large attic rooms above that.'

'Wow, a mansion of a house.'

Sean laughed. 'Not quite,' he said. 'Come on and meet Martha.'

To the right was a long corridor with two doors leading off it and another at the end, but Sean didn't open the first door. 'The parlour,' he said, by way of explanation. 'It's Martha's pride and joy. What's the betting it will seldom get used.' Maria thought he was probably right and it seemed an utter waste of a room to her, but it wasn't her place to comment and so she kept quiet.

Sean hadn't noticed, because he was opening the next door, saying as he did so, 'Now this is lived in.' Maria saw the newspapers on the table, some of the cushions from the comfy-looking settee on the floor and cigarette ends in the ashtray. 'I come in here some-times,' Sean said with a wry glance at the children, 'to try and get a bit of peace. It seldom works. You can only come here when the weather is mild,' he added, 'for we can only get coal enough to heat the one room, so we tend to all live in the breakfast room. Thank God there is plenty of space in it.'

He had his hand on the door at the end of the corridor as he spoke, when suddenly it opened from the other side. Maria didn't need Sean telling her who it was, for Martha was the spit of her daughter only smaller and plumper. Her hair was dark and so were her eyes, and her face, like Patsy's, was long. The difference was that Martha's wide mouth was caught up in a smile of welcome, while Patsy's wore a sulky pout.

Maria extended her hand. 'Pleased to meet you,' she said, but Martha brushed her hand aside and put her arms around Maria. 'We have all heard so much about you, my dear. I feel as if I know you already,' she said. 'Come in, come in. You must be worn out with the travelling.'

She ushered Maria into the room, saying as she did so, 'I'd have been outside to welcome you, along with the children, but I was trying to get everything ready.'

'Please don't concern yourself, or go to any trouble.' Maria said, putting her case on the table and beginning to unfasten it. 'Knowing of the food shortage here, I've brought some food over for you.'

There was a large cooked ham wrapped in muslin, a whole dozen eggs, a large piece of cheese, a round of soda bread and another of barnbrack, and even some butter in a covered dish.

'I don't know what to say,' Martha said.

Sean, with a wink at Maria said, 'God! That must be a first if you are stuck for words, woman.'

Martha flapped her hand at him. 'Don't mind him,'

she said. 'He is just as grateful as I am, even if he is too pig ignorant to say so.'

Sean let forth a gale of laughter, the laugh Maria remembered from her childhood that she hadn't heard for years as he cried, 'I'll give you pig ignorant when I catch hold of you.' Martha gave a squeal and tried to twist away, but Sean caught her easily and held her tight.

Maria, though she was glad her uncle had found such happiness, felt suddenly bereft and alone, for she knew there was not that warm, comfortable feeling between her and Barney any more.

'Won't you sit down for a minute?' Martha said. 'The meal will be on the table in a jiffy and Sean will take your case up.'

Maria was glad to sit on the settee, for she was weary. The fire blazing merrily in the hearth was very welcoming. As she sat, she looked around the comfortable room. A fluffy cream rug was pulled up before the gleaming brass fender, covering some of the lino, which was patterned with dainty little blue cornflowers. On either side of the fireplace were filled bookcases, a wireless to one side on a small table. But dominating the room was a large wooden table.

Sean said to Maria, 'That's done sterling service. It was one of the first items Martha bought with her first husband, and now the children do their homework at it, especially in the winter months when their bedrooms are like ice boxes.'

'Some of us do homework,' Patsy said disparagingly, with a glare at the elder of her two brothers. 'Some thickos don't seem to have homework at all.'

'Who you calling a thicko?' Tony said. 'Anyroad, I do homework if it's set.'

'Doesn't seem to be set much then,' Patsy said and added, 'I suppose they think there is little point.'

Tony glared at her. 'Like our mom says, if you can't say nowt nice, you should keep your gob shut.'

'Why should I? Just 'cos you say so?' Patsy said sneeringly. 'And you are stupid. Paul gets more homework than you, *and* he gets it done quicker.'

'That will do, Patsy,' Martha said, coming in from the kitchen. Though her voice was quiet, it was firm.

'But, Mom—'

'You heard what I said,' Martha said. 'Come and get the knives and forks and lay the table.'

'Bloody great know-all,' Tony said to Patsy's retreating back.

'Tony!' Sean rapped out. 'We'll have less of that. If your mother had heard that she would wash your mouth out with carbolic. Anyway, I'm surprised at you arguing with your sister on Maria's first night here.'

'She started it,' Tony protested.

'Anyway,' Paul put in, 'Maria will probably get used to it.' And he added in an aside to Maria, 'Tony and Patsy is always at it, like hammer and tongs.'

The laughter resulting from this comment covered any awkwardness.

After the meal Maria tried hard with Patsy, asking her questions about her life, but Patsy made it clear Maria was not her favourite person by any means. She was too clever to be downright rude, but she still was able to make Maria feel she had no right to ask her any questions at all and any she did deign to answer she did briefly and brusquely.

When Maria went up the bedroom allocated to her later, to unpack her case, Martha followed her.

'Can I have a word?'

'Of course,' Maria said. 'Is there some sort of problem?'

'Yeah, in a way.' Martha said. 'It's Patsy. I'm sorry about the way she's behaving in front of you.'

'Oh, it's all right,'

'No, it's not all right,' Martha said. 'I suppose you know it's jealousy, pure and simple.'

'I had worked that out,' Maria said. 'But soon I will be miles away.'

'I know that,' Martha said. 'The problem is Sean has so effectively taken the place of Ted, something I thought would never happen. She doesn't like sharing him, even with me sometimes. We have such few family you see, and I don't suppose that helps. My mother and father, two younger brothers and a younger sister were all killed in a raid on Birmingham in November 1940, when Patsy was just coming to terms with her father's death at Dunkirk. Then Ted's father took sick with bronchitis the winter of 1942 and when the bronchitis turned to pneumonia and he died, his wife just sort of faded away. Ted was an only one, you see, and with him gone, and her husband, I think she lost all will to live. Anyway, she was buried alongside her husband and then it was just me and the kids.'

'Oh, Martha, I am so sorry.'

'It was grim,' Martha admitted, 'and though I weren't the only one to lose my family by any means, knowing that didn't help, and I was so incredibly lonely and sad. But you have to get on with it, don't you?'

'Aye,' said Maria with feeling.

'The losses of all those close to her affected Patsy most of all,' Martha said. 'She told me once she wasn't going to love anyone any more, because whenever she did, they were taken from her. When I met your uncle, it took ages for her to drop her reserve with him and then, once he'd broken through that, she loved him unreservedly, just like she had her father, though she won't call him "Dad" like the boys do. She's terrified of losing the special place she has in his heart, but even recognising this, her attitude towards you can not be tolerated and I will speak to her.'

'Please don't say anything,' Maria said. 'Now I understand a little more. You mustn't let this put a damper on your wedding day. I will be home in a few days' time anyway, and she will have Sean all to herself again.'

However, despite Maria's spirited words to Martha, she did find it difficult to live in a house where someone actively disliked her. Patsy was either barely civil, or icily overpolite, but the scathing and disparaging looks were nearly as bad as the words.

On Friday morning, Sean went to collect his suit from the cleaners and Martha the dress Maria had sent her, which she'd had altered to fit. The children had taken the day off from school and Maria, finding herself alone with them, commented to the two boys how lucky they were to be living so close to the village with its cinema, library and public baths.

Before either of the boys were able to speak, Patsy said, 'It's not so great. Aston was just as good. But,' she added scornfully, 'I suppose you would think anything was great, coming from a little tin-pot village.'

Maria refused to rise to the bait and just said pleasantly, 'There is little in the village in the way of entertainment unless we make our own, but Derry is only fifteen miles away, where there are attractions galore. I just meant it's handy to have them all on the doorstep.'

'I bet Derry is nothing to Birmingham,' Patsy went on. 'After all. Birmingham is the second city.'

'Well, I don't know Birmingham,' said Maria, 'except for the little I saw as we passed through it in the taxi. I did see it has an awful lot of bomb damage and if you have not seen Derry you aren't in a position either to make a comparison.'

'Oh, aren't you Miss Clever Clogs?'

'That's you,' Tony said. 'Swanking it up at St Aggie's. Surprised you even talk to the likes of us.'

Patsy's eyes narrowed. Tony was fair game. She could vent her spleen on him and leave Maria alone, and not have her mother on her back or Sean looking at her with reproachful eyes. 'I wouldn't talk to you if I had a choice in the matter,' she said.

'Don't then,' Tony said. 'I would suit me. Be a bit quieter with you keeping your gob shut.'

Paul caught Maria's eye and cast his own to the ceiling as if to say, 'Here we go again.'

Maria had to nip on her lip to stop herself smiling as Patsy snapped. 'Why don't you crawl under the stone you came from?'

'Why don't you?'

'You're a grubby, stinking, horrible little monster,' Patsy said, irritated by Tony's calmness. 'And I hate you!'

Not sure whether it was a wise move or not, Maria felt she had to try to intervene. 'Come on, you two.'

The look Patsy gave her was venomous. 'Keep out of this, you. It's not your business and the sooner you go home the better I'd like it.'

And me, Maria thought. She felt she already had enough going on in her life without taking on board the problems of a teenager she hardly knew, and whom she wasn't particularly keen on getting to know either.

She rose and said to Patsy, 'I think I will go to my room until you are in a better temper.'

'Huh, that'll be the day,' Tony said, with a hoot of laughter.

'Shut your mouth!'

'Shan't, just 'cos you say so.'

Maria shut the door behind her. They were well used to arguing this fiercely, judging by Paul's reaction, and anyway, she didn't care any more. They could go ahead and kill each other and she would leave them to get on with it.

'What d'you think of the dress?' Martha said a little later, lifting it from the box,

'It's lovely,' Maria said sincerely, 'and very different from the way I wore it.'

'Well, I'm dumpier that you,' Martha said, 'and a dropped waist wouldn't have suited me at all, so I had the waist raised and the leftover material made into two panels either side of the zip to accommodate my larger waist and bust.'

'The woman has done a good job,' Maria had to admit, admiring the workmanship.

'She's run off her feet with all this make do and mend,' Martha said. 'She told me when I took this in she hardly ever gets her hands on such lovely material and would enjoy working on it so much it would be a pity to charge me.' Martha gave a rueful grin and said, 'She did though, and a pretty penny too.'

The two women laughed together and then Martha went on, 'Anyway, because of your generosity in giving me this dress I was able to go down the Rag Market and get enough material to make Patsy a bridesmaid's dress.' She drew the beautiful dress of royal-blue satin from the box too.

Maria admired the dress, intrigued by where Martha said she had got the fabric. 'The Rag Market?' she asked. 'Where's that?'

Martha laughed. 'Terrible name, I know,' she said. 'And they don't sell rags, though they do have a few second-hand stalls, but it is a place where the bargains are to be had. Next time, if you come on a longer visit, the two of us will go and have a butcher's. What do you say?'

'I don't know when that will be, with Daddy the way he is,' Maria said.

'I know,' Martha said gently. 'But your daddy won't always be there. But what am I saying? By then you'll probably have a houseful of children around you.' She raised her eyebrows speculatively.

'I don't think so,' Maria said. 'There's been no sign yet, anyway.'

'It's early days.'

'We've been married fourteen months and it isn't as

if we are not trying,' Maria said. 'But I'm not going to think of it either today or tomorrow. I'm here to see my uncle make an honest woman of you and I intend to enjoy the whole experience.'

'It's made the day for Sean, you being here,' Martha said. 'And don't worry, I love Sean very much and intend to make him happy.'

'Well,' said Maria, 'you are doing all right so far, anyway. I've not seen Uncle Sean like this for a very long time. He's like a dog with two tails, so he is.'

The wedding, at the abbey church, went without a hitch. Both Martha and Sean were short on relatives, but many old neighbours had travelled up from Aston. Some of Sean's workmates were also invited, including Kenny O'Connor, who'd helped him get a job in the Dunlop factory. Everyone seemed intent on making the day special for Sean and Martha. Maria thought back to her own wedding day with sadness.

Later, back at the house, Sean introduced Maria to Father Flynn, who'd taken the Mass, and explained she was over from Donegal for the wedding.

'I'm from Connemara myself,' he told Maria. 'I believe Donegal too is very beautiful.'

'It is, Father,' Maria said. 'My home is in a little village called Moville on the Inishowen Peninsular, and we can look over Lough Foyle and Derry and all. It was beautiful once and will be again, I suppose, but now the docks in Derry has been given over to the navy, and naval ships, rather than fishing boats, fill the waters.'

'Ah, this war has affected many lives,' the priest said, shaking his head. 'Terrible tragedies altogether.'

'My uncle thinks it will be over soon,' Maria said. 'Do you see an end in sight, Father?'

'Ah, if only I had a crystal ball, my dear,' he said. 'I don't know, but I hope your uncle is right. I see you have a ring on your finger,' he added, looking around the room. 'Is your husband with you?'

'No, Father.' Maria went on to explain about her father's accident and the effect on her mother's delicate nerves, and Barney staying behind to see to things.

The priest listened without a word. When she was finished, he patted her arm as he said, 'Bear up, my dear. You are young to have such affliction land on you, and though you are not the only one affected by tragedy, that hardly helps. I will remember you in my prayers and you can be grateful at least that you have a good and understanding husband who is able to share this burden.'

If you only knew, Maria thought, watching the priest walking around the room, talking to this one and that one, but she acknowledged that he was right in one way: Barney was very good with her father and had been adamant that she come to her uncle's wedding. If only she could get him away from his brother's influence, their marriage might still have a chance. She could only hope that this might happen before it was too late for the pair of them.

CHAPTER TWELVE

Barney was waiting for Maria at Derry Station with a car on loan from Seamus. He seemed pleased to see her back, though he gave her no hug or kiss.

'How is Daddy?' Maria asked, as she settled herself in the car.

'Just the same,' Barney said. 'We haven't let him fade away, but between us both, we haven't persuaded him yet to go on the wagon, I'm afraid.'

'Oh, Barney, you are silly at times.'

'I know it.' He sighed resignedly. 'How did it go?'

Maria described first the house in Erdington village, before she got to the wedding itself. She told him of Martha and how kindly she was – just the wife for Sean – and of the children. She didn't say anything of the antagonism Patsy had shown her, feeling it somewhat disloyal to do so.

Barney listened with half an ear, nodding and commenting in the right places, but inside, he was buzzing with excitement. After the success of the last raid, they were already planning the next one, further inside the six counties. He already had a thick wad of bank notes in his pocket and he intended at least to treble that. Added to that, the following night, Seamus had a poker school organised after they'd done their drop. Bottles of poteen and Seamus's special packs of cards virtually guaranteed the brothers winnings – certainly by the end of the evening. That thought also brought a smile, to his lips.

Maria thought the smile for her and she leant back in the car with a sigh of contentment. It was good to be home. Maybe the saying 'Absence makes the heart grow fonder' really was true.

She dozed until they reached The Square in Moville, where the ride over the cobblestones woke her. She looked around with bleary eyes.

'Hello, sleepyhead,' Barney said.

'Sorry.'

'You likely needed that sleep.'

'Aye, I did.'

'Well, then,' he said, as he drew up by the door, 'let's away in. Sam will be delighted to have you home.'

He was. He was at the drunken, maudlin stage, and he cried as he clutched at Maria. She hugged him back, but holding her breath she did so. The smell coming off him, which no washing could get rid of, could sometimes make her feel quite nauseous. Dora was still in the house, and she too was glad to see Maria.

'There's a meal for you, in the oven,' she said, 'and a round of soda bread to mop up the gravy.'

'Oh, Dora, you don't know how good that sounds.'

The thick beef casserole Maria shared with Barney – for Sam would have none of it – put new heart into her. Later, sitting beside Barney before the range with a cup of tea, watching the peat settle into the grate, she felt contentment seep all over her.

It was even better when Barney said, 'Shall we go up?' his voice husky with desire. Her weariness dropped from her and she followed him eagerly. Their lovemaking was better than ever.

The Monday after her return was Easter Monday so Maria was at home when the doctor called unexpectedly.

'Your mother has pneumonia,' he told. 'She's in a coma.'

'Can I see her?'

Dr Shearer nodded. 'I'll take you. I have the car in The Square.'

'Will she recover from this, Doctor?'

'No, I'm afraid not,' the doctor said. 'She reached the crisis at three o'clock this morning, so the doctor told me just now on the telephone, and she slipped into a coma afterwards. The priest is with her at the moment. She's already received the Last Rites.'

'Hear that, Daddy?' Maria said gently, crossing to her father.

'Blessed relief,' Sam said. Despite the fact it was morning, he already had a bottle of whiskey by his side. He waved this at the doctor and tears streamed down his face as he cried, 'Best if I follow her. Bloody millstones round Maria's neck, the pair of us.'

'Daddy, hush,' Maria said, but slightly impatiently for she'd heard and refuted that refrain often, and there were things to do.

'Can you wait while I ask Bella if she wants to come

with me?' she asked the doctor. 'She was a good friend of Mammy's.'

'Aye,' the doctor said. 'But what about leaving your father?'

'Barney will see to him,' Maria said. 'He's having a lie-in, but he'll get up if I ask him.' She didn't say he had not been in until the early hours, and the doctor didn't ask what kept a fit young man in his bed past mid-morning. It was not his concern.

Sarah's face was not serene, as Maria had expected, but creased up in a grimace. Deep scarred lines dragged at her mouth and nose, and met across her brow. Maria was glad her eyes were closed.

'She looks as if she's still suffering,' Bella whispered.

Maria nodded. 'The doctor said it won't be long,' she said, 'and I hope it isn't.' Bella agreed with her.

By two o'clock, the growling in Bella's stomach could be ignored no longer and she lay Sarah's hand back on the counterpane and stood up, stretching to ease her aching back. 'God, I feel as if I've sat here for hours,' Bella said. 'I am as stiff as a board and feel as if I could eat a horse.'

'And me,' Maria said. 'But it's a bank holiday. Nowhere will be open.'

'The nurses might know of some place,' Bella said. 'This won't be the first time this has happened.'

She found the nurses very accommodating indeed, and a tray of tea and sandwiches were sent up from their canteen. The food, but more importantly the tea, revived both women.

'People say your life passes before you when you

are about to die,' Bella said. 'How the hell do they know these things?'

'I don't know and it might not be true at all,' Maria said.

'Anyway, remembering would hardly bring solace to Sarah,' Bella pointed out, 'apart from the love she had for Sam and you, of course. Some people can only take so many knocks in life before their mind shuts down and I think that's what happened to your mother.'

'Aye, I think you're right,' Maria said. 'Poor Mammy. And yet, you know, when you go to an England that has been at war so long and see the people, you are staggered by the suffering and the tragedy of it. Sometimes they have lost everyone belonging to them, like Martha, or have had their houses bombed from under them, and are often injured or maimed in some way themselves. It's a wonder their asylums aren't bursting at the seams. From what I saw, they just seem to get on with it.'

'Different characters, see,' Bella said. 'People can cope with different levels of stress and calamity.'

'Aye,' Maria mused. 'I suppose. Now Mammy's ordeal is almost over I will be glad. She isn't a happy woman and no one in their right mind would want her to pull through this.'

Bella said nothing, for there was nothing to say. A moment later there was a guttural sound in Sarah's throat and Bella knew it was the death rattle. The chest stopped moving and there was a sudden silence in the room. 'She's gone, Maria,' Bella said gently.

'I know,' Maria said with a sigh, and she kissed her mother's paper-thin cheek.

*   *   *

'I'll not have her lie in a pauper's grave,' Maria told the hospital manager, who'd come to see her to discuss funeral arrangements. 'I want her body to brought back home to be buried in the churchyard in Moville. 'Don't think I can't pay for this,' she added at the look on the man's face. 'I have money put by.'

In the Post Office, a sizeable amount, which she added to each week, had accumulated, and some of that would be used to lay her mother to rest for the last time.

Barney was in total agreement with Sam that Sarah's demise was a blessed relief. He knew it mattered to Maria that her mother was buried in Moville, and he told her she could leave all the arrangements to him. In response to Maria's telegram, Sean said he was coming over, but he would be alone because Martha couldn't leave the children.

Maria was so glad to see her uncle alight from the bus the day before the funeral, for her father had gone to pieces altogether. Sean saw that himself. The smell that emanated from Sam he'd encountered before in alcoholics, and he doubted he'd live long after his wife. But, he told himself, at least Maria has Barney by her side now. Despite Maria's assurances to him after the wedding, he had been worried. He knew the poor start the boy had had – it had been spoken of many a time – and sometimes that kind of thing could scar a man for life. But he seemed to have made a turnaround and Sean was impressed with how he'd lifted the burden of the funeral totally from Maria shoulders, which was how it should be.

Both Barney and Sean worked on Sam the morning

of the funeral to see he was at least dressed respectably so that he'd not shame the family. They could do nothing about his yellowing skin and eyes, nor the way his hands shook, but Sean took the bottle of whiskey from him, despite his protests, and put it away until the funeral was over.

Sam knew what they were doing and had no desire to bring disgrace on anyone, least of all his dear daughter, so, though his innards craved a drink and the pains that began in his stomach spread throughout his body, he bore it bravely and said not a word about it.

There were not that many in the church for the Requiem Mass and that saddened Maria. She guessed it was the fact that Sarah's death was tainted with the slur of mental illness that kept people away. Also Sarah had been away, so it was a case of out of sight, out of mind. She was grateful for the faithful group that gathered about the grave to drop clods of earth on the coffin.

'I've not shed a tear for her,' she said later to Bella when they were back in the house. 'Isn't that a dreadful admission to make?'

'No,' Bella said. 'That body laid in the churchyard isn't your mother. That mother died the day they found Sam crushed in the docks.'

Maria knew Bella was right, her mother had died long ago. She'd missed her and needed her so much at the time. Now she was dead and buried, and she knew with a dread certainty that soon her father would be too.

Sean knew it too, and he said as much to Barney as he watched Sam drink one glassful of whiskey after

228

another. 'He'll drink himself to death,' he said. 'You don't think we should try to stop him?'

'Why should we even try? We're not the man's gaoler.'

'No, but—'

'Look,' Barney said. 'I know you mean well, but Sam knows what he is doing. He has made this decision, and isn't it really his to make? We tried at first and, God knows, I did my best, but he feels useless and has told me often. He feels like a parasite, not only living off us, but sucking the life out of Maria in the process. He thinks he would be better out of the way. God knows, I think highly of the man, but if I'd been left like him I'd have wanted to do away with myself before this. I don't think anyone could stop him now, anyway. It has gone too far.'

'Doesn't it upset Maria to see her father in this state?' Sean asked, troubled.

'It did,' Barney admitted. 'She takes it all in her stride now.'

'Maybe it's as well there's been so sign of weans yet.'

'Oh, we've plenty of time for weans,' Barney said, trying to hide a slight shudder. 'I'm in no hurry.' Maria becoming pregnant, or at least saying she was pregnant – he wasn't quite sure which – had forced him into a marriage he wasn't ready for and didn't want, and had tied him down enough. He had no desire for the responsibility of children; he had never had much time for them.

Sean saw these emotions pass through Barney and knew that Maria felt quite differently, but he said nothing. He excused Barney. He was young yet and he'd had no experience with youngesters. If and when he had his own, it would be different, Sean was sure.

He just about to go over to speak to Sam when he saw Con cross the room. From the malevolent look on his wife's face, Con's decision to have a few words with his old friend on the day his wife was buried did not meet with her approval, but then when did anything meet with Brenda's approval?

Sean made his way over to Maria instead.

'All right?'

'Aye, I'm grand.'

'We won't let this go on long,' Sean promised. 'Barney and I will head them all off to Raffety's before long.'

Maria nodded gratefully. The noise was getting to her and so was the smoke. She'd be glad to get the house to herself for a while. 'Will you take Daddy?'

'If he is in any fit state,' Sean said. 'If he isn't, I'll put him to bed before I leave.'

Sean didn't want Sam to come to the pub that night really, because he wanted to talk to Barney, so he was glad when Sam fell into a stupor and he was able to leave him in his bed. At the pub, he drew Barney to one side. 'I know I've spoken of this before, but what are your plans for the future? Both of us know Sam won't last long, and the war won't last for ever either.'

'People have been saying the war is coming to an end for years.'

'I'd say it's real this time, especially now that Italy has surrendered,' Sean said. 'Anyway, eventually the war will be over, and Sam will be lying beside Sarah in the churchyard. I wonder if you've ever thought of moving to Birmingham? The two of you could bide with us and welcome till you got your own place. I could probably get you set on at the Dunlop if I put in a word. The money's good.'

Barney managed to suppress the shudder that ran through him. Work like a black in some stinking rubber factory for a pittance of a wage? Not likely. Yet he knew once the war was over and Sam had died he wouldn't be staying in Moville. He'd already discussed it with Seamus. The two of them and Maria would be moving to Dublin where the pickings were richer altogether.

Sean, though, didn't need to know any of this yet and so Barney said, 'I'll certainly think of what you said, Sean, and thank you for the offer, but you understand I won't be able to give you a firm answer straight away?'

'I know that,' Sean said. 'It's just an idea to think about.'

'I appreciate it,' Barney said. 'Now shall we join the others?'

They moved to join the cluster of men around the bar, who seemed intent on drinking the pub dry in an attempt to give Sarah a good send-off.

Maria missed Sean greatly after he'd returned home and so did her father. She was glad of her job, which stopped her feeling sorry for herself. The girls at work had been full of sympathy, hearing of the death of Maria's mother, but she knew many of them would have thought it a relief, the best thing, and she didn't blame them. Hadn't she felt the same, and her father had actually expressed it, so she felt a bit of a fraud accepting their condolences. She hoped by the time spring really took hold and the days were lighter and warmer she would be able to shake off the slight depression that was making her feel so low and tired all the time.

Much to Maria's consternation she heard that two units of the Royal Warwickshires were camped near Ballykelly Airport. At first, she worried Greg might be among the men – and she didn't know whether to treat him as just a person she used to know – but she saw no sign of him. However, some girls went out with the British boys, and by the middle of May they could tell the others of the rumours abounding in Britain about what was happening on the South Coast.

'Something's up, all right,' one girl said. 'My chap went home on leave and he said everyone was on about it.'

'My feller said the whole of the South Coast is out of bounds to civilians,' put in another.

'Can only mean one thing, my chap says,' put in the first girl. 'Another bloody Dunkirk.'

'Surely not?'

'Well, what else?'

'Whatever it is, you shouldn't be discussing it,' rapped out the factory supervisor. 'We'll all know soon enough. Till then do as the posters advise and "Keep Mum". Careless talk really can cost lives. We can help the service men best by not rattling on and on about something we really know little about as yet.'

But, though the girls knew what the supervisor said was sensible, the rumours, which increased when many of the Warwickshires were shipped home before the end of May, continued to filter through the factory.

It was in early June when Maria and Barney, who were having a drink prior to going to bed, heard the drone of what seemed like hundreds of planes overhead. Maria had often heard and seen planes taking off from the airports across the Foyle to protect a convoy, but this thundering in the sky was more that that. She looked at Barney fearfully.

'Shall we go and see?' he asked.

Maria glanced immediately at her father, but he was spark out, so she nodded and slipped out into the summer's night.

They were not the only ones gathered in The Square, to watch wave after wave of planes flying above their heads. Then someone standing on the green shouted out that the ships were leaving too and Barney, dragging Maria after him, went to see. Many of the ships were heading out to sea.

'This is it then,' Barney said. 'Make or break, this is. Won't be no second chance.'

That night in bed their lovemaking had a sort of desperation about it, for they knew, despite their neutrality, their fate was inexorably joined to that of Britain: if Britain fell, so would Ireland.

At work next day, no supervisor could still the talk that ran riot through the factory.

'Tuesday, the sixth of June,' one girl said. 'We'll remember this date, all right.'

'Aye. It's either the beginning of the end, or one massive defeat.'

'I'll shoot myself if the Jerries come here,' one girl declared fiercely.

'Oh, very dramatic,' another asked. 'What with? A popgun?'

'That's defeatist talk, anyway,' one of the girls shouted from further down the line. 'I'll not kill myself. I'd rather stay and fight the buggers.'

'Oh, let's hope it doesn't come to that,' Maria said. There was a murmur of agreement.

However, there was a mood of expectancy that morning.

Then the supervisor came bustling into the workroom. 'There's been an newsflash on the wireless from Reuter's news agency,' she announced. 'It said Allied armies began landing on the coast of France this morning.'

There was a collective sigh around the workroom.

'So now we know,' said Joanne. 'But this is just the start of it.'

'Aye,' another put in, 'they were in France before and look what happened.'

'If they are routed this time, we've had it, the lot of us.'

'Huh, I'll say,' Joanne replied. 'I haven't terrific confidence in the Home Guard to protect us all.'

'Who would have?' said another. 'What are they but a bunch of the old, very young, infirm and totally bloody useless, standing guarding the coastline against those goose-stepping bastards that have overrun most of Europe and seemingly without much effort?'

'People say their guns are from the First World War. How efficient will they be?'

Joanne laughed. 'Likely more efficient than the broom handles they trained with at first.' The memory of oddly assorted men training with such serious faces with broom handles over their shoulders caused laughter to ripple around the workroom.

Feeling the chatter had gone on long enough, the supervisor said, 'Now come on, girls, the war is not over yet and uniforms will still be needed, so can we please get back to work?'

Some moaned and Joanne gave such a grimace at the supervisor behind her back; Maria bit on her lip and shook her head in mock disapproval. However, most knew that the supervisor had a point and they settled down industriously.

Knowing the importance of the invasion, which everyone knew now as D-Day or Operation Overlord, Maria began buying a paper on the way home from work each evening. She read almost in disbelief at what was found at the concentration camps of Treblinka and Maidanek in Poland, which were liberated by the Red Army as they drove the Germans back. There were pictures in the paper of the skeletal survivors and the mounds where hundreds, sometimes thousands, of bodies had been tipped into pits.

Those pictures, and what the survivors said about conditions at the camps, shocked the rest of the world, especially when the Red Army said they believed that those camps were just the tip of a very big iceberg.

Throughout Europe, the Allies' advance went on liberating towns and cities, while the Red Army was advancing from the north. At last, the Heavy Tank Regiment from Derry came home. They had been away for four years, serving in North Africa. Maria's factory, like many others, allowed the workers time off to cheer the lads as the ship came in to dock.

Many of the ships and factories were blowing their hooters, the place was thronged with people, and the town band was playing to welcome the boys home. As they disembarked, Maria saw their loved ones scanning the soldiers' faces for the one they were waiting for, and then the families would be reunited. They embraced and kissed, some laughing while others sobbed in relief. Maria felt a lump rise in her throat.

'This might be the last Christmas with the world at war,' she said to Bella later. 'Just think on that.'

'Won't that affect your job?'

Maria shrugged. 'Maybe, but, you know, there have been too many deaths, too much tragedy and destruction for me to wish the war to go on for one day, one hour longer than necessary.'

She knew the end of the war would affect Barney too. In fact she knew it must be affecting him already, as there were very few ships in the Derry docks now. The poker schools must be getting sparse, for Barney now was usually back home in the early hours, and she would often hear him get into bed. He wasn't as rough as he once had been and if he reached out for her, she would submit to him without protest, often enjoying it too.

However, afterwards she would frequently lie awake worrying about what sort of a job Barney could do once the war was over.

*   *   *

As Barney and Maria sat before the fire one evening the following March, Maria, nearly bursting with excitement, told Barney that she was pregnant at long last. After the last time, she had waited four months before saying anything, but guessing that Barney didn't long for a child as she did, she watched his face as he digested the news, trying to judge his reaction.

Barney didn't know how to react. His initial feeling was one of rejection. He didn't really want a child at all, but if one was on the way that was that. It would be a son, he was sure, and to have a son he could be proud of and who would carry on the family name wasn't a totally bad thing.

He said nothing to Maria, but instead crossed the room and said to Sam, 'Hear that, Sam. A proper reason to celebrate. Maria is pregnant and you are going to be a granddaddy.'

Maria released the breath she had been holding. It was going to be all right; he really sounded quite pleased.

Sam's rheumy eyes filled with tears as they sought his daughter's and Barney hauled him further up in the bed. 'Come on, you old sod,' he said. 'This isn't a time for tears, this is a time to celebrate.' He placed a full glass of whiskey in Sam's hand and poured another for himself before crossing back to the settee where Maria sat knitting.

'You'll need extra money,' he said. 'There will be things to buy.'

'Not yet awhile,' Maria protested.

'Doesn't hurt to be prepared,' Barney said. He pulled a wad of notes from his pocket and began peeling pounds off, which he offered to Maria.

She stared at the money, aghast, and made no move to take it. 'Where did you get that sort of money?' she hissed in a whisper lest her father should hear.

'You know what I do,' Barney said. 'But you always said you don't want any details,'

'I know, but there aren't many card schools now – there can't be. There's hardly any ships left. You mean to tell me you can earn that kind of money smuggling things back and forth across the border?'

'Smuggling is very lucrative,' Barney said, 'otherwise I wouldn't do it. And when we do get a poker school going it runs for hours. Go on, take it, and get some things for the child.'

Maria was loath to touch the money. She knew that if it had been earned honestly and legally she would have taken it with joy.

'What's the matter with you?' Barney demanded.

'I am pleased, Barney it's just . . .'

But then she thought, wasn't she being some kind of hypocrite? She did know what Barney did and took some of his ill-gained money every week to buy food at the shop and run the house. Why was this any different?

'I'm sorry, Barney,' she said. 'I am pleased really. I was being silly.'

'That's all right then,' he said. 'And don't stint. Nothing is too good for my son and heir.'

Maria didn't bother telling him it might be a girl. They'd know the sex of the child soon enough and, boy or girl, they'd have no choice – Barney like everyone else.

CHAPTER THIRTEEN

Suddenly, the war was over. Hitler's death had been announced on German radio on 1 May as one of the casualties of the bombing of Berlin. However, the Soviet Army, who entered Berlin on 2 May, were told that Hitler had shot himself in his private bunker on 30 April; as if anyone cared, the man was dead, that's all that mattered, that and the final surrender of Germany on the seventh.

The following day was a national holiday in Britain and the sounds of revelry from Derry and the surrounding district could be heard across Lough Foyle. Maria had seen the joy, mixed with relief, on the women's faces in the factory the day that the war was officially over. Many had loved ones in the thick of the fighting and she didn't blame them one bit for letting their hair down.

Barney, however, viewed the ending of the war with a stab of dismay for he could see his way of life crumbling before his eyes.

'What if rationing ends too now that the war is officially over?' he asked Seamus in late June.

'Oh, I think it will go on for a fair bit yet,' Seamus said.

'Aye, but even so, we won't make much of a living on just that alone.'

'You were glad enough of it at the beginning,' Seamus reminded him.

'Aye, but I'll have a son to provide for soon,' Barney said. 'I need real money. The last raids we have carried out haven't yielded that much cash.'

'Listen to yourself,' Seamus said. 'I had to nearly twist your arm off in the beginning for you to even drive the car. If you want real money, then we need to hightail it to Dublin. P.J. was telling me—'

'I can't leave the old man,' Barney said. 'You know that. Anyway, I could hardly drag Maria down to Dublin, the size she is now. We will have to bide here till the baby is born, at least. As for Sam, God know what's keeping him going, but he can't last much longer.'

'So that's that, then, for the time being,' Seamus said. 'You'll just have to be a patient man.'

Anxious though she was for the birth of the child, Maria left her job at the end of June with some regret, for she'd become good friends with many of the women there, particularly Joanne. She knew she would lose touch with many of them as the factory was running down anyway. It would probably revert to making shirts again, so there would be work for some of the women, but not for all that were employed now.

'Write to me?' Joanne urged, pressing her address into Maria's hand. 'Tell me about the baby and all.'

'I will,' Maria promised, glad that she would have something to write about.

Philomena would be pleased about the baby too. Maybe she would see the doubts that she expressed when Maria wrote and told her she was marrying Barney McPhearson were unfounded.

As the hot days of July rolled one into another Maria found everything an effort. She knew from the letters that Martha, who was also expecting a baby in early August, was feeling in a similar way, especially when the schools closed for the holidays and she had the three children home all day. Maria's due date was 20 August, and she found in the last few weeks that she didn't always have the patience to deal with her father, or Barney, who kept on about going to Dublin to live when her daddy should breath his last.

Once she had so longed to go to Dublin to take her place at the Grafton Academy, but now she had no desire to go to there or anywhere else that they would be in close proximity with Barney's brother.

'Well, what opportunities are there here?' Barney demanded. 'Tell me that?'

Maria hadn't an answer. Times were hard for everyone. The lough had been and still was too polluted for any fish to survive in it and the boats weren't strong enough to set out on the open sea.

'The bottom's dropped out of the market anyway for the small fisherman,' a man remarked in the shop one day, when Maria was in getting groceries.

'My man said you can't compete with the big trawlers,' a woman said in agreement.

'And he's right. But even if I wanted to return to it, the young don't want to know,' the man replied. 'My young Mikey is not the only one who skedaddled to England in the war. He's now on the building and has no wish to come back and break his back and risk his life for the pittance we'd get for any fish we might catch.'

Maria felt sorry for the man and knew he was right. When the war put paid to the fishing, many of the young men left the area, and those who didn't enlist headed for the Dublin or across the water to England. Precious few had returned.

Barney wasn't nearly as flush as Seamus, and so was delighted when he told Barney of a raid planned on a security van the other side of Derry.

'When?'

'August.'

'Maria's due about the twentieth.'

'This is towards the end of the first week,' Seamus said. 'You will be home and dry well before the child is due, with your pockets full of cash. You'll be able to take us all out and wet the baby's head good and proper.' It was an attractive prospect. 'I don't have to ask if you are up for it,' Seamus continued, 'do I?'

'No, you bloody don't,' Barney said. 'Count me in.'

On 5 August Maria received a telegram.

Martha had baby girl. Everything perfect. Calling her Deirdre Maria after Martha's mother and you my dear. Write later. Love Sean and Martha.

* * *

'Any reply?' the telegraph boy asked.

'Oh, yes,' said Maria and wrote,

*Congratulations to the pair of you. Couldn't be
more delighted. Love Maria and Barney.*

After the boy had left, she hugged the telegram to her
in delight. Soon, it would be her turn and she could
hardly wait.

The following day, she was in the shop when Dora
came through from their living quarters.

'Come quick and listen,' she said urgently to the
waiting shoppers, and Bella only waited to turn the sign to
'Closed' and put the snib on the door before following
the others into the room.

There they heard of the atomic bomb that had
landed on a city in Japan called Hiroshima. It had
annihilated the place and it was estimated seventy-
eight thousand people had died.

Maria was transfixed with horror. Seventy-eight
thousand people! It was hard even to visualise so
many. Even Derry, with its influx of servicemen, had
never had a quarter that number – and how on
God's earth could all those people be killed by one
bomb?

'God Almighty!' she heard Bella, standing beside
her, exclaim. 'In the blitz of Belfast, over nine hundred were killed in the one night and that was
dreadful enough. And they were killed by many
bombs falling from waves of planes, attacking them
again and again.'

'Well, d'you think it will do any good?' Dora asked.

'I mean, will it put an end to the war in Japan? That is the only justifiable reason for dropping such a powerful bomb on civilians.'

'It must,' Bella said emphatically. 'No country could stand by and see that destruction, with so many dead, and not surrender.'

Dora wasn't so sure. God knew, the Nazis were bad enough, but everyone knew the Japs . . . well, they weren't normal. Look at those pilots who'd dive straight at a target and seemingly not giving a minute's thought to the fact that they would blow themselves up too. How is a country supposed to fight another when its people have a mentality like that?

Maria went home to tell Barney of the latest developments because he'd been up at the boatyard when she'd left the house and would likely know nothing about it.

Later, with the meal over and her father tucked up for the night, Maria barely looked up from her darning when Barney lifted his jacket from behind the door.

'You all right?' Barney asked. 'You are very quiet.'

'With the news I heard today, I didn't feel much up to chattering,' Maria said, gazing up at him.

'Is it just that?' Barney asked. 'You're looking a bit peaky.'

'Barney, all women get weary and fed up in their last few weeks.'

'Shall I ask Bella to sit with you for a bit?'

'No, you will not,' Maria said. 'The woman has been on her feet all day and I do not need a nursemaid.'

'If you are sure?'

'I am. Get yourself away if you are going.'

'Aye,' Barney said. 'And I'll likely be late. Don't wait up.'

'Poker?' Maria said. 'There's not been much of that just lately.'

'Not so many sailors now,' Barney said with a shrug. 'But this is a big one. Could go on for hours.'

Maria sighed. 'All right,' she said. 'I'll likely see you in the morning.'

Maria decided she'd make a cup of cocoa and go to bed; an early night would do her the world of good. She glanced across at her father, but he was well away in the land of Nod. She poured milk into a small saucepan and set it on the heat.

It was as she poured the hot milk into the cup that she got a pain that was so severe, she had to feel for the chair and sit down.

God, that was sharp, she thought. The sooner I get to bed and rest, the better. Obviously tackling that big wash was too much and I've strained myself.

The second pain attacked her as she mounted the stairs and doubled her over. She told herself it couldn't be the baby, not yet, it was too early. The midwife had told her a woman sometimes had these pains. They were like the body practising.

She'd reached the bedroom before the third pain attacked her and it caused her to gasp out loud and then gave another gasp, this time with dismay as she felt the waters gush from her and she knew that however early it was, this child was struggling to be born and quickly too. She needed help.

She struggled as fast as she could down the stairs

and although another wave of pain hit her at the doorway, she made no sound, mindful of her sleeping father. Never had the short journey to The Square appeared so long. She pounded the door as another pain doubled her up.

Bella knew immediately from the pain reflected in Maria's eyes what was happening.

She put her coat around Maria's shoulders as she said, 'Here, girl, you are shivering like a leaf. Just bide a minute till I send Mammy for Gracie Begley and then I will help you back home and into bed.'

Gracie Begley had brought nearly all the children in that area into the world and Maria both liked and trusted her. But as they reached the kitchen door she said to Bella, 'Will you stay too?'

'I will surely,' Bella said. 'Barney needs to be informed as well. Where is he, Raffety's?'

'No,' Maria said. 'I know where he isn't, but I haven't a clue where he is, only that wherever it is, they are likely playing poker, for that is usually the one thing that keeps him out all night.'

Maria was frightened of giving birth, frightened of the pain, frightened of making a holy show of herself over something most woman went through, and she was glad to see the competent and experienced Grace. She tied a towel to the bed rails and told Maria to pull on it when the pain got bad and Maria was glad of it as the hours ticked by. She made not a sound, but the spasms caused her to writhe in the bed and the agony was etched on her face.

In the end, Maria began to think that there was something wrong for the pain just seemed to be almost constant, with little space between one spiral of pain and the next.

'Does it always go on so long?' she gasped out at last.

'Bless you,' Grace said. 'It's been no time yet, especially for the first. And when it's over and the child is laid in your arms, why then, you'll forget all this.'

Maria doubted that and it was hardly reassuring that it would be some time yet before the child would be born. In fact, Barney might be home before she gave birth. She gave a long, low moan as another pain gripped her and her hand tightened around Bella's so much she scored the older woman's palm, but Bella gave no sign of this and instead, with her free hand, wiped Maria's glistening face with the damp piece of cloth she had ready.

Barney wasn't home by six the next morning when Maria suddenly said to Grace, who'd sat in the rocking chair placidly knitting, 'I need the toilet.'

Swiftly, Grace got to her feet and pulled the bed-clothes back.

'I need the toilet,' Maria said again.

'No, you don't, cutie dear, that's the baby,' Grace said. 'And I am just going to have a look and see what's what . . . All right,' she said a few moments later. 'Now it is time for you to do some work and I want you to push through the next contraction.'

That, Maria felt, was the beginning of hell. Both women urged her to push when she hardly had the strength to do so and longed to rest. The pain was exhausting her.

'Let me be,' she pleaded.

But neither woman would let her rest and kept urging her to push again and again. Surely the baby's head was too big, she thought, and she wanted to ask them this, but hadn't the breath to do so. Jesus Christ, it felt like she was trying to give birth to a red-hot cannon ball.

Suddenly there was one enormous contraction and nothing on God's earth could have stopped Maria's scream as she feared her body was being rent in two. She almost crushed the bones in Bella's hand as she pushed with all her might. She felt the child slither from her and immediately newborn wails filled the room and Maria gave a sigh of relief.

'It's a wee daughter you have,' Grace said with a smile. 'And she is quite perfect, and with a good pair of lungs too.' She handed the baby to Maria.

Maria was unprepared for the almost overwhelming love she felt for that child as she gazed down at her. It was so powerful; she knew that she would go through any trial imaginable to keep this wee mite safe. Her breasts ached and she opened the front of her night-dress and let the baby's small, protesting mouth fasten around the nipple. Bella let tears of joy slide unchecked down her cheeks at the sight.

Maria wondered what Barney would make of the child and if he would be disappointed that Maria hadn't yet given him a son. That was when he arrived home, of course, and she felt a niggle of worry begin to eat at her. It was going on for seven o'clock and he had never been so late home before.

As if she could read her thoughts, Grace suddenly said, 'Where is the child's father?' She'd thought it odd before this that he wasn't there, pacing the floor below and smoking one cigarette after another, but surely the man should be here now, praising his wife and taking joy in the child that they had produced together?

She was totally unprepared for the reaction her question caused. Maria didn't answer at all, only lowered her head, but not before Grace caught her face flushed with embarrassment. When her eyebrows raised in a silent query to Bella, she didn't answer either, but shook her head vehemently.

Sam had been woken by the scream, but hadn't been aware what it was that had woken him and he'd wondered to see the lights on, and a large pan of something boiling on the stove, but no sign of Maria. Then he heard the unmistakable sound of a newborn child and guessed what had happened while he'd slept. He called out.

'Rest yourself,' Bella said, glad of an excuse to leave the room and the unnerving silence that Grace's question had evoked. 'I'll see to him.'

She went out of the room with the soiled linen to put in to soak and Grace, after making Maria comfortable, followed her, saying as she did so, 'I'll be back in a minute or two with something to eat. You have done a hard night's work and now you must feed yourself well.'

'I'll be glad of it,' Maria said, for, now she had time to think about it, she was starving.

Downstairs, Bella had told Sam he was a grandfather and that Maria had given birth to a wee daughter.

'Is she all right?' he asked huskily. 'Are they both all right?'

'They are both grand,' Bella said. 'And now, will you have a cup of tea?'

Sam wrinkled his nose. 'Not tea. I am a grandfather and that calls for a celebration. Can you get me a wee tot of whiskey?'

'Not at this hour in the morning I can't,' Bella said firmly.

'Where's Barney?' Sam said, knowing he could always wheedle a drink out of his son-in-law.

'Ah well, now, that's a question we would all like an answer to,' Bella told Sam, just as Grace stepped into the room. 'For your sainted son-in-law did not come home last night, so you'll have to make do with tea this morning.'

'Not come home,' Grace asked in an undertone as Bella busied herself at the range. 'But where is he?'

'Maria doesn't know,' Bella said. 'But the man is a gambler and he enjoys a game of poker. When he left last night he said he might not be home till the early hours, but this is hardly the early hours.'

'No, indeed,' Grace said. 'Should anyone be informed? Maybe the man's had an accident.'

'It's a bit early to start to fret yet,' Bella said. 'Besides which, I can't think of many occasions when Barney would welcome the attentions of the guards, even to ensure his safety.'

'Oh, like that is it?'

'Aye, just like that,' Bella said. 'I'd be obliged if you'd keep it to yourself, for Maria's sake.'

'Don't worry,' Grace said. 'It seems to me Maria has her hands full enough without becoming the subject of gossip and speculation as well.'

'Thank you, Grace,' Bella said, knowing the woman to be trustworthy. 'I'm grateful and I know Maria will be. We don't know that Barney will not come through that door, and before too long either, hale and hearty and wondering what all the fuss is about.'

'Aye, Grace agreed, 'and it isn't as if he knew about the baby.'

'No, the child wasn't due for nearly a fortnight yet.' Bella said.

With everything done, Grace returned home. Maria said she was tired out and would value a wee sleep, and Bella laid the sleeping child in the waiting cradle and went home herself to have a short nap, for she too was fair jiggered.

Morning turned into evening and still there was no sign of Barney. No one in the village was told of Maria's confinement either, because they would all understandably wonder where the father was and Maria, concerned though she was, didn't want anyone to alert the authorities yet awhile.

Another night passed and Maria was worried enough to send for Con, knowing the man to be reliable, dependable and one without a loose tongue. He admired the child while listening to Maria's concerns.

'What do you imagine has happened to him, Maria?'

'I don't know, that's the thing,' Maria said. 'But Barney told me that when they play poker, Seamus has a special pack, you know. I mean, what if the other players tumbled to what he was doing, beat the two of them up and left them in a ditch somewhere?'

Con thought it only too likely, but he didn't say so. 'And you are sure that is where he was that night – playing poker? He told you that?'

'Not in so many words,' Maria said. 'But that was what he was always doing when he was out till the early hours.'

'Well,' said Con, 'I think we should check out the hospitals. I'll do that, if you like.'

'But—'

'I'll be glad to do it,' Con said. 'As long as you could see your way clear to helping me out with the bus fares. Brenda gets proper mad with me under her feet all day, anyway.'

'Of course,' Maria said. 'But go and see Seamus first, before you travel the length and breadth of the country. It might save you a journey.'

However, there was no sign of Seamus in the little shanty that had served as a home for the McPhearsons, though one of the neighbours said he'd heard tell he was off to Dublin.

'Good riddance to bad rubbish, as far as I'm concerned,' he'd added.

But this didn't help Con in his search for Barney so he set off for the bus.

Some hours later, Con was able to tell Maria that Barney's brother had all but disappeared too, but there was no sign of either man in the hospitals in either Letterkenny, or Derry.

'Do you think Barney and his brother could have just upped sticks and gone to Dublin together?' he said.

'Not without sending word,' Maria said. 'That's the tale I'll put about, though, until I hear differently: that directly the child was born, Barney and his brother had to go and do some job in Dublin.'

'Won't Sam think it odd?' Con said. 'I mean, he'll know that isn't the truth.'

'Daddy's out of it most of the time now,' Maria said. 'And if I feed him the same tale as everyone else, he'll likely believe it and probably won't even remember that Barney wasn't here for the birth.'

Con knew that Maria spoke the truth. Sometimes Sam looked at him strangely as if he couldn't quite place who he was.

'You don't think you should inform the police?'

Maria faced Con squarely. 'Maybe I should,' she said. 'It really is what any reasonable person would do. If I haven't hear anything in a week, I will inform the authorities, I promise.'

'Well, I will support you in any decision you make, or any story you tell,' Con said. 'But now I must away home and, God knows, I've been so long away, I don't know if I shouldn't throw my cap in first.'

'Aye, you go on home, Con,' Maria said. 'You've done more than enough for one day and I can't tell you how grateful I am for your help.'

An atomic bomb was dropped on the Japanese city of Nagasaki that same day. Dora came over to tell Maria, but by then she was so concerned about Barney, it didn't affect her as news of the first one had.

'Where the hell could he be, Bella?'

Bella had no idea, but her suspicions of Barney had resurfaced. 'I can't imagine where he is, or why he hasn't got in touch,' Bella said. 'And it's no wonder you are worried. It's dreadful not knowing. Even bad news is better than no news.'

'Sometimes I wonder if it will ever be explained to me, if I will ever see Barney again,' Maria said. 'People disappear all the time – you know they do – and are never seen or heard of again. I look at the baby and wonder if she will ever see her father.'

Later Bella said to her mother, 'God, I could kill Barney for putting Maria through this. She doesn't deserve it.'

'You don't believe anything sinister has happened to him then?'

Bella gave a hoot of derision. 'Not him,' she said. 'Bad things only seem to happen to good people. Christ Almighty, I bet if that man fell into a dung heap, he'd come up smelling of roses.'

Her mother chuckled at the mental picture. 'I wouldn't be at all surprised,' she said.

CHAPTER FOURTEEN

Moville was such a small village that any stranger was spotted and speculated about almost before he had set foot inside it. So the news that a little dapper man, sporting a neat moustache and wearing a suit and a trilby hat, was seen knocking on Maria's door was soon known by everyone.

Of course there had been much head shaking already about the child. All the neighbours had been in to see the baby, many bearing gifts, and all had asked about Barney. They had got the same message: Barney had gone to Dublin with his brother to take up some job for a few weeks as there was nothing doing nearer at hand. No one believed it.

'A man wouldn't go hightailing it to Dublin when his wife had just given birth,' one said to another. 'It doesn't make sense.'

'Anyway,' another commented, 'since when have the McPhearsons been that keen on work of any description?'

'You're right there. Jesus, neither of them would

cross the street to do a job, never mind travelling all the way to Dublin.'

The priest thought it odd too. He called when the child was five days old to discuss the christening.

'I can't think about anything like that until her father is back home,' Maria told him.

'When is that?' the priest asked. 'These things have to be attended to.'

'I don't know, Father,' Maria admitted. 'When I know anything definite, you will be the first to be told.'

When Father Flaherty had taken his leave, Dora said, 'How long are you going to leave it before telling the authorities that Barney is missing?'

'I don't know,' Maria said. 'I am worried to death about him. What if something bad has happened to him and my delay in telling the police has made things worse? On the other hand, Dora, you know Barney as well as I do. He could be mixed up in something not quite within the law.'

'I know one thing,' Dora said. 'You'll be the one in trouble if you are not careful.'

'I know,' Maria said with a sigh. 'If only there was some word.'

'Surely if he intended sending word, he would have done so by now.'

'You're right,' Maria said. 'And I know I am not helping myself by shillyshallying. Send for the guards tomorrow and I'll let them deal with it.'

'What about your father?'

'What about him? I'll get up tomorrow and explain what I intend to do. And don't look at me like that, Dora, I know I'm not out of my lying-in period, but

I refuse to speak to the police in my bedroom and dressed in my nightdress. The priest was bad enough.'

'All right,' Dora said. 'I do see the sense of that, but you take it steady.'

The next morning Maria had just come down the stairs, the child in her arms, when there was a knock on the door. Dora's eyes met those of Maria as the older woman went to open it. Few people knocked doors in the village, except those on official business and Maria felt for a chair with her free hand and sank into it. Her legs had begun to wobble and the roof of her mouth felt suddenly unaccountably dry.

Fully expecting to find a Garda outside the door, Dora was surprised by the stranger. Though the man was respectably dressed, she noted his blue eyes were so hard it was like looking at two pieces of flint. His eyes were narrowed and there was a frown creasing his brow as he said, 'I would like to speak with Mrs Maria McPhearson.'

'And what is your business with her?'

The man shook his head. He knew that this woman wasn't the one he was told to speak to and he had his orders. 'My business is with Mrs Maria McPhearson and it's private, but you can tell her that it concerns her husband.'

Dora opened the door wider and the man removed his hat before following her inside. He took a swift look around.

Maria had heard what the man said and she stood up again, the child held tight against her shoulder as she said, 'I am Maria McPhearson. You wish to speak to me about my husband, Barney?'

The man nodded.

'So,' Maria demanded, 'where is he?'

The man whetted his lips and twisted the hat he held in his hand nervously. 'I need to speak to you privately.'

'Do you?' Maria snapped. 'Well, you will have to need. Dora is my very good friend and my father has a right to know too what has happened to his son-in-law, so state your business.'

The man shrugged. 'If that's how you want it,' he said. 'I can't tell you where Barney is, but that he is in a safe house in the hills of Donegal and he will write when he can. That's all you need to know.'

'What are you talking about, "safe house"?' Maria said, confused. 'What's so unsafe about his own fire-side?'

'The guards could be after him,' the man said. 'They've already shot him in the arm.'

Maria stared at the man incredulously. The guards just didn't go around shooting people. 'What happened? How did Barney come to get shot?'

When the man shrugged, Maria shrieked at him, 'God Almighty. Don't you come to my door and say that my husband and father of our baby daughter has been shot and will write when he has time, and expect me to be satisfied with it. Tell me what he was about for him to get shot or, by Christ, I will shake the words out of you.'

'Aye,' said Dora grimly. 'And I'll help her.'

The man hesitated. He'd been told to say as little as possible, but he saw the younger woman's angry eyes nearly standing out in her white face and the older woman bristling with temper, and thought he wouldn't put it past the two of them to attack him if he said nothing at all. So reluctantly he said. 'We were intending holding up a security van taking money to a bank.'

'What?' Maria couldn't believe that she was hearing right. This surely to God couldn't be happening to her. 'Have you . . . has Barney done this sort of thing before?' she asked.

Again, the man shrugged. He had already said too much. Not that he needed to say anything, for Maria knew with dread certainty that this wasn't the first time that Barney had done this kind of thing and that was where he had got the wads of money from. She felt sick.

'Barney wants to know if you've had the guards around asking questions?'

'No. Why should I have?'

'Barney was the only one not wearing a stocking,' the man said. 'He wasn't sure he hadn't been recognised. That's why he didn't come home, and then, of course, the bullet in his arm would have taken some explaining.'

'Wouldn't it take some explaining anywhere?'

'No, not where he was taken,' the man assured her. 'The bullet is out now and Barney near back to normal and intends following his brother to Dublin in the next few days.'

'Oh, does he?' Maria said. 'And what of his wife and child?'

'He'll write when he has an address,' the man said again, and added, 'He made no mention of a child.'

'No,' Maria said. 'That's because he didn't know

that she was born. That happened the night he disappeared. But tell him not to fret. We can live on fresh air. I wouldn't touch a penny piece he'd give me, in any case, for it would be tainted money.'

Suddenly she was tired of it all – tired of Barney and his lies and deceit, his lack of any sort of moral fibre – and mortified that through her marriage she was part of it all. She glared at the man. 'OK,' she said, 'you've had your say, so get out. I just don't want you here another minute.'

The man was glad to go, and Maria managed to hold back the tears until the door shut behind him. But then she totally gave way. Dora took the sleeping baby and laid her down in the pram before taking Maria into her arms. Maria felt as if she was drowning in the tears pouring from her eyes and filling her nose and her mouth. Her sobs shook her whole frame.

Dora didn't urge her to stop. Instead, she patted her back and said, 'That's it, Maria, cry it out. You let go, mavourneen. You'll feel better afterwards.'

Maria wondered if she'd ever feel better about anything ever again, but she was eventually quiet. She didn't wish to relinquish the comfort of Dora's arms around her so the two sat there entwined.

Sam had understood enough of what the man had said to be shocked and disappointed in Barney. He quite understood Maria's collapse and had watched Dora comfort her, feeling frustrated and helpless. He dealt with those feelings the way he dealt with anything he found uncomfortable. He lifted the bottle of whiskey, never far from him, and took a long, long swig of it.

*   *   *

After the revelations about Barney, Maria was in a state of shock. She wondered what manner of man she'd married at all. Smuggling and card games were bad enough, but holding up a security van and stealing from it was an entirely different kettle of fish.

What was she to do about it? What *could* she do? She was married to Barney for life. Was what she'd found out about him a justifiable reason for leaving him? How the hell could she know that? She felt totally alone.

Only Dora and her father knew the truth, and though Dora had probably told Bella, she never spoke of it.

Maria couldn't even bring herself to tell Con the whole of it, so she told him Barney had got word that the guards would be wanting to question him about his smuggling activities in the war and he'd fled to Dublin for a wee bit. Con accepted it. Whether he believed it or not was another matter, but she knew he would keep his own counsel. He came as often as he could to see them all and spend time with Sam. Maria was glad of that, for she knew her father missed Barney, despite everything the man had done.

The lying in period was officially over and Maria had taken up the reins again, doing everything like an automaton and desperately worried about money because all she had was her savings and she knew those wouldn't last for ever. Her father's whiskey put a huge drain on her finances, and now that many men were unemployed there were fewer presents given to him, though Raffety's sent round the odd bottle and so did Bella. It helped only a little, and Maria viewed the future with fear.

Then, at last, she got the awaited letter from Barney.

Dear Maria,

I am sorry I was unable to get news to you sooner about what had happened to me. I know you must have been worried, especially with the baby coming as well. Pity it was a girl. Better luck next time. I was sure you'd know better than to tip the wink to the coppers and I told Seamus the same. Anyway, there is plenty of work here and I thought to stay around for a while. I will send you some money shortly. I know we are stuck in Moville for the time being, but when Sam dies, I think we should move here lock, stock and barrel. It would make a better future for us all.

Barney.

There was no remorse for what he had done. No shame. Maria read the letter to her father and then took it round to show Dora.

'I'd like to know the nature of the "work" that Barney mentioned,' she said, as Dora finished reading the brief missive and handed it back. 'Then again, maybe I wouldn't like to know. The fact is, Barney has never had a proper job, unless you count the time he had in the boatyard, when he left most of the work, first to Willie and then to young Colm.'

'How do you feel about Barney, Maria?' Dora asked.

'I don't love him, I know that now,' Maria admitted. 'It's not a nice thing to say, but I clung to Barney in much the same way as a drowning man will clutch at any piece of debris to help keep him afloat. I felt totally unable to cope with all the responsibility, even with the help you and Bella were, and then, of course, Daddy was all for Barney.

'But just maybe I wouldn't have married the man at all if I hadn't given in to him the day Mammy was taken to the asylum, Then, when I ended up pregnant, there was no other alternative. I'll tell you one thing, though,' she went on, 'I had no idea of the smuggling and all, before I was married, though I found out soon after it and I was devastated. I begged him to stop and when he point-blank refused, I suppose I began to lose respect for him. It's impossible to have deep feelings for someone when you feel that way. This latest business has just blown me away completely and there is no possible chance I am going to join him and take my daughter to be brought up among thieves.'

She looked at the sleeping baby in her arms and said, 'Sally is the only good thing to come out of this union with Barney. She will be my consolation.'

Barney was having the time of his life in Dublin. As P.J. said, there were rich pickings for a bright fellow and the raids he was involved in were on a much bigger scale.

Barney never asked what happened to the stuff he helped steal. He knew from his time in Moville that asking questions was a bad move, and probably wouldn't be answered anyway. He was more than happy with the payout he received. He'd never had so much money in his life.

In Dublin, too, he found that girls would flock around a man with money in his pocket to give them a good time, and were very appreciative later in bed. He had worried about being unfaithful to Maria at first, but Seamus said she deserved no loyalty

'Didn't she pull the wool over your eyes right and proper, so that you were hoodwinked into marriage?' he said. 'A woman like that needs no consideration at all.'

Barney knew Seamus was right. Any doubts he might have that she really might have been pregnant that time fled when he was with his brother, who was adamant that Maria had duped Barney right and proper. He'd been mad to have Maria, but now he had achieved his goal, she didn't seem that great. Anyway the girls they went around with were crazy for sex – expected it, almost. It would take a better man than him to refuse them and he put off his return home day after day.

Each week, he wrote to Maria, but as she'd told him she wanted no money he hadn't earned legally, he sent her none.

'What's she living on then?' Seamus asked when Barney told him this.

Barney shrugged. 'She has savings from the time she was working before the child was born, so I suppose she is using those.'

Seamus laughed. 'And what will she do when that's all gone? High principles are all very well when you have a full belly. The sooner the old man dies, and you move down here for good and bring Maria with you, the better.'

'I don't know. I'm having a good enough time without her.'

'That needn't change,' Seamus said. 'At least not if you're master in your own house, like I'm always telling you. Maria is your wife, not your bloody gaoler. She is there to cook your meals, keep the house clean, have your clothes washed and ironed, and be ready to accommodate you in bed when you fancy it. She is not there to tell you what to do, or monitor your every move. You have given her too much of her own way and she has those two witches from the shop to support her. Here she would have no one, and she'd soon see what side her bread was buttered if it was a case of knuckling down to do as she was told, or eating.'

Barney shook his head. 'Maria isn't . . . you don't know her, Seamus.'

'I don't need to know her personally,' Seamus said. 'She is a woman like any other.'

Then one night Seamus said, as they left the house, 'There's a man I want you to meet tonight. He's our landlord, actually – name of Ned Richards. He owns this house – and not just this one. The man is rolling in money. I met up with him at the casino last week and was telling him about you. He was mighty interested in the boatyard.'

Barney looked at him open-mouthed. 'Don't be daft! No one would want that place, man. The fishing is finished.'

'He isn't interested in the fishing.'

'Then what . . . ?'

'At least listen to what the man has to say. That can't hurt, can it?'

And it didn't hurt. Barney found he got along fine with the man who had plans for developing the boatyard for the tourist industry now that the war was over.

Two days later Barney received a telegram from Maria.

Daddy much worse. He's asking for you. Please come home immediately. Maria.

There was a warehouse job planned for that night, but Barney knew if Sam died before he reached home he'd never forgive himself and made plans to return immediately.

Maria didn't really know how to greet Barney. He'd been gone almost three months and it was now the beginning of November. She knew he'd likely been up to all sorts in Dublin, but it couldn't really be gone into that night, at least not until they went to bed and had a little privacy. And so she had the house cleaned and tidy, the baby fed and asleep in the pram, her father washed and a casserole in the oven when Barney opened the door.

The day had turned blustery and cold, and the warmth of the room hit Barney like a wave. He sniffed the air appreciatively. 'Something smells good,' he said. 'Bloody marvellous, in fact.'

Maria had turned at his arrival, and Sam cried, 'Barney! Lad, it's good to see you.'

Maria knew whatever Barney did, Sam would forgive him, and she wondered if he even remembered what he had heard from the man who had brought them the news of Barney, or even had any idea of the time that had elapsed since he had last seen Barney. The drink had addled his brain to the extent that he was losing his grip on reality and seemed to live in a world of his own most of the time.

She didn't know how to behave herself. For better or worse he was her husband, the father of their child. So when Barney put down his bag and took Maria into his arms, she went without protest. At first, she merely submitted to the kiss. Then she felt her body betraying her as the kiss grew in intensity, and Barney's hands moved over her body, pressing her against him in a way that was barely decent.

When he released her he was smiling. 'Later,' he said. 'That is, if you can wait that long.'

Maria's whole body was tingling and his words caused a tremor to run through her. She busied herself laying the table, while Barney rooted in his bag for a minute before crossing the room to Sam. The mark of death was on the old man's face, but Barney's manner to him was the same as it had always been.

'Come on, you old codger,' he said. 'I've got you a present,' and he produced a bottle of single malt whiskey.

There were tears in Sam's rheumy eyes. 'Ah, lad . . .' he said. Barney noted how he was wheezing and how each word was punctuated by a gasp. He felt immense sympathy for the man. 'God Almighty, that looks good,' Sam went on. 'Now if you could just get me a glass . . . ?'

'Daddy, I said you could have another drink when you'd eaten something,' Maria chided.

'Don't fuss me, Maria,' Sam said. 'I have everything I need in this bottle.'

Barney hauled Sam up in the bed gently and then he fetched two glasses. He poured a generous measure into both and as he placed them on the table beside the bed, he said, 'There's plenty more where that came from.' He saw the look of gratitude on Sam's face.

'You don't help,' Maria grumbled, when Barney came back to the table and sat down

'God, Maria, nothing will help now,' Barney said quietly. 'He's on the way out and there is nothing either of us can do about it.'

'I know,' Maria said with a sigh. 'God knows, I will miss him when he goes, and yet I know he's ready – been ready for years.'

'I am fond of the man myself,' Barney said. 'I always have been, but we have to face the inevitable and decide what we will do when Sam eventually dies.'

'What do you mean?

'Well, I mentioned it in the letters. I want us all to move to Dublin.'

'To where?' Maria said scornfully. 'Some rat-infested slum. You want me to bring Sally up in a place like that and be surrounded by vagabonds and scoundrels? Sorry, Barney, but I have no desire to go to Dublin.'

Suddenly Seamus's word came back to Barney about being master in his own house and not allowing Maria to have her own way too much. He was irritated by her attitude and he hissed quietly, so Sam shouldn't hear, 'I don't give a tinker's cuss for your wishes. When Sam dies, I will inherit both this house and the boat-yard, and I will do with both as I see fit. You will have to put up with it and as my wife you will go where I say.'

Maria regarded Barney with alarm. She had few rights now and she knew on her father's death she'd have even fewer, but, by God, she'd make her position clear. 'Don't you dare try to bully me, Barney McPhearson. Whatever you say I am not going to Dublin – not now, not ever.'

'It's about time we got this clear,' Barney said icily. 'I am head of this household and as my wife—'

'Oh, I'm your wife, am I? Pity you didn't remember that I was your wife when you went swanning off and I didn't even know where you were.'

'You knew why that was.'

'Oh, aye, I knew all right, eventually,' Maria commented drily.

'I got word to you as soon as I could,' Barney said, his voice rising in anger. Maria looked across at her father, but he was slumped against the pillow. Barney seemed unaware of Sam as he thundered on, 'And didn't I come like the very devil when you said your father was worse?' He banged his fist on the table as he cried, 'And it wasn't my bloody fault you had the baby the same day I disappeared.'

Sam had stirred at the pounding of the fist, but the child jumped and began to grizzle.

'Leave her be!' Barney commanded, as Maria got to her feet with a little sigh. 'She has to learn you cannot be at her beck and call.'

'She is but a baby!' Maria hissed. 'Don't you dare take your bad humour out on her, and don't try telling me when I can tend to her. I will do as I see fit. Anyway, she probably needs a feed, but might have slept a little longer and given me chance to finish my dinner if you hadn't tried throwing your weight about.' She lifted the child as she spoke.

Barney growled, 'You gave me cause.'

'I did no such thing.' Maria sat down with the wailing child and pulled up her jumper to begin feeding her. Barney felt a strange jealousy assail him as he watched his child sucking, and her little hands kneading the breasts he considered his property.

He regarded the baby with distaste. He had no time for daughters. Other men's daughters, grown to luscious maturity, he could handle with no bother at all, but daughters of his own? No, definitely not. But he contented himself with saying, 'She'd better not be any trouble tonight, Maria, I'm warning you. I have been away a long time and I will want you tonight, and as far as I am concerned, she can cry her bloody head off. My needs come before a child's any day.'

Barney attacked his meal with relish and yet his face stayed morose. Maria wondered where the old Barney had gone, for this harsh, brusque man who'd returned from Dublin was like a stranger. Maybe it was the people he was mixing with that had changed him. He had always been swayed by his brother's influence.

Barney finished his dinner, scraped back his chair, went across to the Sam's bed and poured himself another generous glass of whiskey.

'Hurry up,' he said to Maria. 'And don't say you have a hundred and one things to do. Leave everything to the morning, for I want you in bed now.'

'I'll be up as soon as Sally has had her fill and has been changed,' Maria said firmly. 'She won't settle if she isn't full and neither would you if you went to bed hungry, so don't look at me like that. Why don't you put the kettle on? I could do with a drink and don't fancy whiskey, even if you had a mind to offer it.'

'You're a sarcastic bitch, Maria. You know that?'

'For God's sake, Barney, stop this griping and complaining.' Maria said wearily. 'Either put the kettle on, or hold the child for a minute while I do.'

'I'll do it,' Barney said, putting the kettle on the range. 'I'm not great with babies.'

Not even with your own, Maria might have said, but she didn't. Barney at that moment was like an unexploded bomb and anything she said might set him off. She was too tired tonight for any more argument and hoped he'd be in a better and easier frame of mind in the morning.

CHAPTER FIFTEEN

The following day, when Barney seemed in a better temper, Maria said to him, 'I think we should get the child christened as soon as possible, while Daddy is still with us.'

'Hasn't she already been christened?' Barney said in surprise. Most Catholic children were christened when they were days, not months old.

'I wouldn't let her be until you came home,' Maria said. 'I had to fight the priest about it.'

'I bet,' Barney said. 'But what is the rush now? Sam will hardly care or even be aware of it.'

'He won't be fit to go to the church, I know that,' Maria said. 'But he has mentioned it. He wants the baby to wear the christening gown and bonnet that I wore, and my mother, and my grandmother, way down the generations. Also, he wants to see Con as her god-father. He asks for so little in life, Barney, and always has. This might be the last thing we do for him.'

Barney knew Maria spoke the truth. He thought a great deal of Sam and would like to please him in this one thing. 'It'd better be done quickly then,' he said, for Sam was sinking fast. 'Who have you in mind for godmother?' he asked with a grin. 'Con's wife, Brenda?'

Maria shuddered. 'No fear,' she said. 'I am going to ask Dora and Bella. Father Flaherty will understand about speed. He knows how ill Daddy is. He pops in to see him most days.'

The priest did understand and the christening took place two days later in the afternoon. Few knew about it, so the only people in the church were those involved, and Con's wife, who sat in the pew and stared at them all malevolently, furious that she hadn't been asked to be godmother. Maria thought it a shabby affair altogether, and not the sort of christening she had imagined, but she knew it had pleased her father, so it had achieved some purpose.

The baby, affronted that some strange man was tipping water over her head, let out wails that filled the church as she was christened Sarah Mary, though Maria knew she would be known as Sally, at least while she was young. She smiled as she remembered some old woman telling her once that newly christened babies needed to cry to release the devil inside them, which Maria had always thought nonsense.

Sally was handed to Dora, who held her against her shoulder and rocked her soothingly until the sobs turned to hiccuping sniffles and then stopped altogether. Maria's eyes met those of Dora over the child's head and they exchanged smiles. Maria knew without her and Bella's help and unfailing support she'd never have coped as well as she had. If she lived to be a hundred, she'd never be able to repay the debt she owed them.

There was no party back at the house, for Sam was

273

too ill for such a thing, but Maria had prepared food and provided beer and whiskey for the men, and sherry for any of the women that wanted it. Barney and Con sat by Sam's side, drinking with him and talking together. Con even got Sam to eat a little food. Maria found it was hard to talk to Bella and Dora as she might have liked with Brenda sitting there, so conversation between them was stiff. Brenda, still angry with Maria, was barely polite anyway.

Maria was glad to draw the small gathering to a close when she saw Sam slumping back tiredly against the pillows.

'Not much of a christening, this,' Barney said to Con. He glanced at his watch. 'The pubs will just about be open now. Fancy sinking a few at Raffety's before we call it a day?'

Con looked towards his wife. Maria wondered what Con had ever seen in her. Brenda's mouth, as usual, was like a thin slash of disapproval, her cheeks pinched in, as if she'd sucked a lemon. Her eyes were glittering with malice, especially when she cast them in Maria's direction.

'You're going nowhere but home,' she snapped to Con. 'Get your coat.'

Con made a move as if to obey his wife and then stopped. He turned to Brenda and said, 'The only place I am going is Raffety's for another few beers, and you can like it or lump it.'

Brenda face was almost puce-coloured with temper. 'You'll come home now,' she said through gritted teeth, 'or the door will be locked and barred against you.'

Con smiled and said, 'Thank you, Brenda, for informing

me of that. I shan't bother my head coming home at all then if I won't be able to get in. I'm sure someone will put me up for the night when I am ready to leave.'

Maria had the desire to cheer to see Con at last sticking up for himself, for Brenda had made his life hell for years.

After the christening, Sam seemed to go steadily downhill and Maria suggested letting Sean know how bad Sam was.

Barney nodded. 'I wouldn't leave it any longer. After all, he might not be able to come straight away.' He paused, then went on, 'I know it's not maybe the best time for visitors right now, but there is a fellow will be arriving today, name of Ned Richards. He wants to look over the boatyard.'

'Look over the boatyard!' Maria repeated incredulously. 'Why in God's name would anyone want to look over that boatyard? Few are fishing now, and Colm only keeps body and soul together with the work he picks up from the fishing boats going out from Lough Swilly. You know that as well as me. To be honest, I saw it as a millstone around our neck and never thought to get a penny piece for it.'

'Aye, so did I,' Barney said. 'Ned is Seamus's landlord and Seamus got talking to him one day and mentioned the boatyard and he said he might be interested.'

'But what for?'

'Listen, the man is rolling in dosh and has his finger in many pies. He owns houses all over Dublin and now he want to invest in what he calls the leisure industry.'

'What's that?'

'How people spend their free time,' Barney said. 'Ned says the working man will be demanding more of this now that the war is over. Maybe not straight away, but certainly soon, and he thought of maybe giving people trips around the bay first, all the time encouraging those wealthy folk who have their own boats – he knows a fair few already – to bring them in for repair and maintenance, and a safe dock for the winter. He says it will be a growing industry, but he obviously wants to look at it. We arranged it before I left. You don't mind, do you?'

Much as Maria wanted rid of the boatyard she had no real desire to meet anyone from those dark days that Barney had spent in Dublin.

'I suppose,' she said, 'he's some kind of crook.'

'No,' Barney said. 'He's straight as a die, Ned is. Seamus got to know him first as his landlord and then it seems they use the same casino and met up there.'

'Are you sure about this man?' Maria said. 'I want no untrustworthy criminal getting their hands on my father's boatyard.'

'I tell you, he is all right and genuine,' Barney said. 'You'll like him.'

Maria decided she would give the man the benefit of the doubt. If he liked the boatyard and was actually was prepared to pay money for it, it would be legitimate money, money she would feel justified in spending, she thought.

'What about the fishermen?'

'What about them?'

'Well, I feel so sorry for them,' Maria said. 'They

just hang about in the street. Every time I see Con his shoulders seem to sag further. He's been to Derry many times seeking work like most of them have, but they got not a sniff of a job. The situation in Derry is desperate, so people say.'

'If this takes off as Ned hopes,' Barney replied, 'he might be able to find employment for some of the men. I mean, he can't promise or anything, but even a glimmer of hope is better than what they have now.'

It was, and Maria looked forward to meeting this man. She was pleasantly surprised by Ned Richards when he arrived. He was smart and well spoken. When she took his overcoat to hang it up, she saw that under it he wore a pin-striped suit with a pristine white shirt and the tie matching the handkerchief in the jacket top pocket. Even his black shoes gleamed. Everything about him said this was a well-set-up man with money.

He oozed charm too. He kissed Maria's hand and claimed he'd seen few women as beautiful. She shook her head at him in exasperation, but, that flirtatious behaviour apart, she warmed to him for the kindness with which he spoke to Sam, and especially for the way he was with Sally.

Since his return, Barney had taken no more notice of the baby than he had that first evening home. He seemed to resent Maria doing anything for her, and when she breastfed, it really upset and offended him. If Sally cried while they made love, as she had the previous night, he wouldn't let Maria see to her until he was finished and satisfied. She couldn't enjoy sex under those conditions and Barney's reaction to the child worried her.

Ned lifted Sally from Maria's arms, which Barney had never done, and declared she was one of the bonniest babies he'd ever seen.

'Have you a family yourself, Mr Richards?' Maria asked.

'Ned's the name,' the man said. 'And I have no family and no wife either, but now I see what Barney has here, I envy the man.'

He said things in a similar vein as the men shared a few pints after Ned's survey of the boatyard, which he declared himself well pleased with.

'Why you spent so long in Dublin when you had that luscious creature waiting for you at home beats me,' he said as he sipped at his pint. 'You have a wife and child to provide for and you should look to that.'

Barney didn't like the man telling him what to do. He was here to look at a boatyard, for heaven's sake, not issue a lecture. 'When it's all over, with Sam and all, we'll be moving to Dublin,' he said. 'My brother—'

'That's one avenue that will be closed anyway,' Ned said.

'What are you talking about?'

'Look,' Ned told him, 'when I let the house to your brother, he had references and credentials I know now were probably false. He told me he was a businessman and I had no reason to disbelieve him. I would not have let my house knowingly to a pack of hoodlums and I'll tell you that I was bloody annoyed with your brother hoodwinking me like that.

'The Garda didn't see it that way, of course. The fact that a known criminal gang was operating out of a house I own convinced them that I was involved in some way, possibly masterminding the whole thing or something. I'll tell you, I went through some gruelling hours of questioning before my solicitor was able to convince them that I was totally innocent.

'However, the line of questioning meant I got to know what they thought I had been involved in. I can tell you, Barney, you are one lucky sod. The very day you set off for here to see your father-in-law, your brother and the ruffians he hangs around with were picked up.'

Barney's jaw dropped open. 'Picked up? You mean . . . ?'

'I mean,' Ned went on, 'I should imagine about the time you were being welcomed into the bosom of your family, the whole lot of them were lifted.'

'Ah, Jesus Christ!' Barney said. 'They could come for me too.'

'Only if someone says you were part of anything illegal,' Ned said. 'I think if they had wind of you they would have been here before this. Now I have seen the set-up you have here, my advice to you – and you can take it or not – is to keep your head down for now and look for legitimate ways to keep your family. And you can bristle all you like,' Ned added, seeing Barney's reaction to his words, 'but think on this. All of the gang are looking at hefty prison sentences so the papers say. The Garda apparently have been seeking them for some time. They say they nearly half killed one of the security guards. The man will never be the same again.'

Barney was silent. He knew Ned was right about the violence, which had sickened him at first.

'The pickings might be better here,' Seamus had

said, 'but so is the security. I mean, they are hardly going to open the doors of wherever, if we ask them nicely, and wave us on our way after.'

'I know, but—'

'There isn't a but in this, brother,' Seamus had said fiercely. 'You are either with us or against us. Your choice, but if you're in, you abide by the rules and accept that these guards sometimes have to be put out of action for a while. You're not being asked to do it, for God's sake, so what are you bloody worried about?'

'Plenty,' Barney might have said, but he didn't. He could sense Seamus's impatience and Seamus, angered, was frightening.

Ned, seeing Barney's preoccupation, added, 'You have more to lose than any of those lifted. As far as I am aware, none is married, let alone are family men.'

'No, they're not.'

'Well, then,' Ned said. 'Does that pretty little wife of yours know all this?'

'She can't be sure what I was doing in Dublin, though she will have a good idea, because I went there when things got too hot for me here.'

'And I could bet she wouldn't approve?'

'Huh, you can say that again.'

'I'd say she wouldn't approve either of some of the trollops you've been hanging around with. I've seen them draped all over you, when just a few miles away you had a prize like your wife waiting for you. Man, you want your head examined. Cut your losses. Get out while you can and keep well away from Dublin just at the moment.'

'Not got much choice,' Barney said morosely.

'Anyway, I can go nowhere while Sam is so sick. Maria's uncle from England will be arriving the day after tomorrow. I'd better put Maria in the picture about Seamus and all before she reads it in the paper, or someone thinks it is the nation's interest for her to be told.'

'I think,' said Ned, 'that would be very wise.'

Ned stayed overnight and the next day, about mid-morning, Maria and Barney left him up at the bus in The Square, Maria pushing Sally in the pram. After the bus pulled out, Maria turned for home.

'Not just yet,' Barney said. 'I have something to tell you.'

'It's cold, Barney.'

'This is just for your ears. Do you want to hear it or don't you?'

Maria didn't know if she did, but she knew she needed to be told and so she turned the pram towards the green. The day was overcast, the sky gun-metal grey. A fresh wind was threatening to pull the scarf from her head and she hoped Barney wouldn't take too long over what he had to say.

After a while, though, she didn't even feel the cold, burning up as she was in humiliation. She listened open-mouthed to the words her husband was speaking. They were alien words – about theft and arrest and court and imprisonment. Her mouth was dry and a hard lump had seemed to lodge in her chest as she eventually said, 'Let me get this straight: your brother and his cronies were picked up at a job they were on the night you arrived home?'

281

'Aye.'

'And if you had delayed your arrival here for one day, you'd have been in on it too, and you would by now be in a prison cell? Did it never occur to you that this very thing was almost inevitable?' Maria raged.

'You don't think like that.'

'Well, I bet Seamus and his cronies wish they had thought like that and also thought up some legal way to earn cash.' She stopped to think for a minute, then said, 'If you were in on the other jobs, what if they tell on you? The guards could be coming for you this very minute.'

'They could,' Barney agreed. 'But Ned said they would have probably have lifted me by now if they were going to.'

'Is Ned involved as well?'

'No, I told you, Ned's clean as a whistle,' Barney assured her.

'So, Barney, where do we go from here?' Maria said. 'I'll tell you now, I will not stay married to a petty crook. When Daddy dies I would rather take Sally and strike out on my own than live a life like that.'

Shock at the realisation of what would happen to his brother and the others had just begun to eat at Barney. At that moment he didn't know what he was going to do. But Maria was his wife. It was her duty to stand by her man, not to run away at the first hurdle, and he told her as much as they turned for home.

'Don't lecture me about my duty,' Maria said hotly. 'You have no right on God's earth to tell me how to live my life, or that of your child that you have barely cast your eyes on.'

'Don't start on about that as well as everything else,' Barney snarled, losing patience. 'I told you I'm no good with babies. Lots of men aren't. I suppose I will like her well enough when she is older and I can do more with her.'

'I wouldn't take a bet on it,' Maria snapped. 'There is only one person you care about and that is Barney McPhearson. Have you a plan in your little head as to how we are going to live, because the savings I had are almost gone?'

'I have money, plenty of it.'

'I want no part in that money, Barney.'

'There are no jobs to be had around here. You only have to look at the crowds of unemployed to see that,' Barney said. 'You said yourself, Derry is worse.'

'Well, you wouldn't know, never having put your big toe in it to find out,' Maria said. 'I could probably get a job at the factory where I worked, but then who would care for Sally, your child that you have never held in your arms, never mind looked after?'

'Look, Maria, nothing can be decided until Sam . . . well, you know.'

'I know that,' Maria said. 'I just want you to have some plan of action, because fresh air isn't very filling.'

'What can I do about it if there are no jobs?' Barney demanded. 'And you won't touch any money I have.'

'Well,' Maria said, 'you must do as you please, but if you want us to stay together, then I suggest you find out about the Public Assistance Board that plenty are claiming money from.'

Barney had no intention of doing that. Those places asked the kind of questions he wouldn't be a bit keen on answering. His details just could attract the attention of the authorities and then the Garda, who might feel it was in the public's interest to take him back to Dublin for interrogation. Keeping his head down, as Ned had advised, meant just that. He was filling in no official forms. When Maria's money was all gone, she would have to start on his, or starve to death.

'There is no point going to places like that,' he said. 'I'd be given little more than a pittance, and risk alerting anyone interested in my whereabouts that I'm here.'

'Who would be interested?'

'Well, the Garda for one.' Barney said. 'I've been warned to keep out of Dublin and not even go down for the trial in case they are all set to arrest me.'

'What sort of a fool are you, Barney, to get sucked into all this?' Maria snapped at him in anger and fear.

'You are a carping bloody bugger, Maria, do you know that?' Barney shouted. He swung away from the house as they came to The Square. 'I'm not coming in just at the moment. I feel the need for more congenial company.'

Maria was left holding on to the pram, staring after him, longing to throw something at his retreating back, but she would never show herself up like that. Besides, she'd left Sam long enough, and Sally would be demanding a feed shortly. She had to prepare a room for her uncle too, who would be arriving the following day. As far as she was concerned, Barney could go and hang himself.

Maria was so glad to see her uncle alight from the bus in The Square that she clung to his coat and cried.

Sean thought she was crying for Sam and patted her back as if she was a baby.

'Come on, cutie dear,' he said soothingly. 'It's a day that had to come. You knew that.'

However, Maria wasn't crying for Sam, but for her husband, already very drunk and seemingly intent on getting drunker. He was so bad-tempered and nasty, she was unnerved by him. She knew that vestige of love they might have had was well gone, yet they had to share a life, a house and a bed until one of them should die. Divorce wasn't recognised and even separation was frowned upon.

Sean noticed the tension between Barney and Maria straight away, but put it down to the strain of Barney not having a job and the added pressure of looking after Sam. He knew from Maria's letters that the doctor had suggested he go to hospital, but she wouldn't hear of it. She'd looked after him this long and would carry on doing it to the end. However kind the hospital staff were, they were strangers, and she wanted Sam to die in his own bed with his loved ones around him. Sean agreed with her wholeheartedly.

He knew how hard that could be, though. Hadn't he done it with his own father? And then Maria had a baby to see to as well. With Barney out of work, it was little wonder they were tetchy together and that Barney was drinking more than was good for him.

Maria had never told her uncle about Barney's sojourn to Dublin when the baby was born – she'd been too mixed up and ashamed – so Sean was unaware of Barney's slide into the criminal world. When he was told about Seamus and the others over the meal Maria had ready for him, he assumed that Barney was completely innocent. He expressed both shock and horror, and sympathy for Barney at having a brother involved in such goings on.

He was also concerned for the job situation in Moville and wondered how they would manage now that the war was over.

'I've mentioned before coming to Birmingham to Barney, biding with us until you've got yourselves straight,' he said to Maria. 'But then, of course, you were sitting pretty and there was Sam to see to, but now . . . to be frank, I can't see the situation improving. If you want to get a job at the Dunlop, I can put a word in, no problem, but you'd have more chance if you came as soon as you could, before all the men are demobbed.'

Barney had no more desire to live under Sean's roof and work in a smelly rubber factory than he had the last time it was mentioned to him, but then he had had a lucrative alternative. Now he had none and, on his own, little chance of earning money on the side. He could see too that Maria was all for it. With Dublin out of bounds, as it were, maybe it wasn't a totally bad idea. He didn't have to stay at Dunlop's. Maybe he could get something better once he was over there. However, he would commit himself to nothing. All he agreed to do was think about it, but Sean and Maria were well satisfied with that.

Sam died two days later, 8 November. The doctor had been to see him earlier and said it was only a matter of hours. Sam had slipped into a coma the day before.

The priest had been and administered the Last Rites. Maria had sent for Con, knowing he would like to be there at the end. She sat by her father's side, listening to each laboured breath, held his hand and talked to him, glad that Dora had taken charge of the baby. Her father, she felt, needed all her attention.

Barney was the only one crying. Maria wondered why he was. It wasn't as if this moment hadn't been expected and she herself was dry-eyed. Her feeling of loss went too deep for mere tears. There was no dramatic end, no death rattle, just a silence as Sam gave his final last gasp. Knowing he was at last at peace, Maria leant over and kissed him.

'Goodbye, Daddy.'

She heard Con give a gulp and turned to see his eyes sparkling with unshed tears. 'Bless you, Con,' she said. 'You were a good friend to Daddy. I'll move so you can sit by him and say your goodbyes.'

She got to her feet as she spoke, moved over to the window and looked out. The landscape was bare and muddy. It wasn't raining, yet damp was rising in coils of mist from the soggy earth as the weak sun peeped from beneath the thick dark clouds.

'All right?' Sean said, putting a hand on her shoulder.

'Aye,' Maria answered. 'I feel sort of numb and, if I'm honest, glad that he is now out of pain and misery.'

'You are a grand girl, Maria,' Sean said. 'Now Sam is no more, I am concerned about your future. Do what you can to persuade Barney to come over to us. We'd love to have you. I know this has been your home for all of your life, but there is little work and now you have another wee life dependent on you.'

'Don't I know it, Uncle Sean,' Maria said. 'And though I love this village, I would leave it tomorrow to make a better life for us, to provide a home and security for Sally. But you may as well know, Uncle Sean, I have little or no influence on what Barney does. I can talk until I am blue in the face and he will go his own way, though I will do my level best to get him to think seriously about your offer.'

First, however, there was a funeral to arrange, things to do, people to notify. With Barney seemingly descended into a sodden heap of misery, it would be up to her to do some of these, the last tasks she would perform for her beloved father.

Sam's funeral the following Monday brought the whole village out. The church was packed for the Requiem Mass and there were so many at the graveside, people spilt onto the road outside. Afterwards, the house was filled with mourners.

Sean couldn't help noticing the amount Barney was drinking. He hadn't been sober since Sean had arrived, and he mentioned his concern to Maria at the reception after the funeral.

'I know full well Barney is drinking heavily,' she said. 'I can only hope he will stop when all this is over. At the moment it's almost as if he's taken over from Daddy, and he can be very nasty in drink.'

She looked across at him now, already so drunk he could barely stand. Sean, following her gaze, said. 'Work on Barney, will you, Maria?'

'I will do my best,' she promised. 'The minute he is sober I will have my say. Really, there is no other option and he knows it as well as I do. Don't worry, he will agree to go when he thinks about it. We have even got a potential buyer for the boatyard.' She told Sean of Ned Richards and went on, 'It will be a cash sale, he told Barney, so that if it goes through quickly we'll have a bit of money behind us. Then if Barney has a job too we'll be fine.'

'What of this house?'

'It might be difficult to sell.'

'It might indeed, for beautiful though Moville is, there is little here to attract people,' Sean said. 'I'll talk to Barney tomorrow about letting it out. He could put it in the hands of an agent in Derry. I'd like something sorted, as I go home the day after.'

'I know,' Maria said. 'And how I will miss you.'

'Not for long,' Sean replied. 'If all goes to plan, you'll be in Birmingham in time for Christmas.'

'I can't wait.' And Maria couldn't, for she was nervous of living alone with the stranger her husband had turned into without the buffer of her father between them.

CHAPTER SIXTEEN

Barney woke the morning after Sam's funeral with a raging headache, a mouth as dry as dust and a stomach churning so much he was feeling sick. None of this was helped by the wails of a hungry baby.

Groggily, he got to his feet and stood still for a minute until the room stopped tilting. Then shakily he made his way across the room and down the stairs.

Maria, covered by a shawl, was sitting feeding the baby opposite her uncle, who was reading the paper. She was glad none other was there to see the state of Barney, for he was barefoot, his hair stood on end, his face was grey, red bloodshot eyes were narrowed against the light and he was dressed in only a nightshirt that barely reached his knees.

'A drink,' he croaked, as Sean turned to look at him. Without a word, Sean went into the scullery, reached into the bucket of water he'd got just that morning from the pump and filled a cup with it.

Barney drained the ice-cold water down in a couple of swallows, then passed the cup back for a refill. He drank three cups down before he felt moderately better and thought the nausea had been averted.

He ran his hand through his wild hair. 'Jesus, I must have had a skinful yesterday. Did you put me to bed, Sean?'

Sean nodded. 'Someone had to,' he said with a wry smile. 'You were in heap on the floor.'

'I owe you,' Barney said and Sean waved his hand dismissively.

Before Barney should disappear again, Maria put in, 'We do need to talk to you, if you are not going back to bed.'

Barney knew what was coming, and bed suddenly seemed a very delightful place to snuggle into, but he knew that was just putting off the inevitable. So he said, 'I suppose it will keep until I get my clothes on?'

'Away with you and make yourself more respectable-looking,' Sean said, 'and I'll put the kettle on for a sup of tea for us all. No sensible conversation can take place without a wee sup of tea.'

While Barney put on his clothes he searched his addled brain for a viable alternative to moving to Birmingham, but he knew there wasn't one.

Within a relatively short space of time, his objections and reluctance had been worn down by arguments he had no defence against. He found himself agreeing to contact Ned Richards and put the sale of the boatyard in motion. He also agreed to contact an estate agent about letting or attempting to sell the house, and preparing to leave Moville to start a new life in Birmingham, England before Christmas.

* * *

That afternoon, Dora came round and asked Sean if she could speak to him about a personal matter. Maria was intrigued, but Dora said she'd tell her all in good time and Sean followed Dora back to the shop and into the comfortable living quarters where Bella was also waiting. Bella had the kettle on and she bade Sean sit before the fire and had given him a cup of tea before Dora spoke again.

'Would it be possible to delay your departure a day or two?'

'I suppose,' Sean said, 'if I had to. I took over a fortnight from work and am not due in until the fifteenth, but why should I want to do that?'

'Because,' Dora said, 'we think you should take Maria back with you.'

'Why?'

'Look, Sean, we know you know all about Barney's brother and all,' Bella said. 'Soon, it will be all over the papers. People here won't believe Barney totally blameless. They know that, in the past, whenever Seamus was involved in something, his brother wasn't far behind. The whole family would carry the stigma of it. Maria is the helpless victim here, as far as all this is concerned, and we don't want her caught in the fallout.'

'You must see the strain she is under already,' Dora put in.

Sean had seen it. Maria looked ill. She'd had a tough time coping with a new baby, a bedridden father, and his recent death, and an unemployed husband with a great love of the drink that could make him difficult and aggressive. Shaming news about her brother-in-law would hit her hard. It would be far better that she was well clear of the place before the details became common knowledge.

'I see what you say,' Sean said, 'but I must ask one thing. You said Barney is usually dragged into anything his brother is up to. Do I take it that Barney could be implicated in any of this?'

'We know nothing about anything he did in Dublin,' Bella said.

'When was Barney in Dublin?' Sean asked.

Too late Bella remembered that Maria hadn't told her uncle about that time.

Sean noticed her discomfort and said, 'Come now, if I am to offer them a home with me and my family, isn't it fair that I should know it all?'

Bella looked across at her mother, who shrugged and said, 'The man has a right to know.'

'Do you want me to start at the beginning?'

'It's usually as good a place as any,' Sean said with a wry grin.

So Sean heard that Barney had been involved in smuggling and poker schools during the war. But then there was the birth of Sally and the disappearance of her father. Dora broke in to speak of the man that had come to the house telling of Barney being shot in a raid he had taken part in, and of his sojourn in Dublin.

'Maria said not one word about any of this,' Sean said, shaking his head. 'What the poor child has had to put up with.' He gazed from one woman to the other and added, 'I know what a help the two of you have been to Maria and how you will miss her.'

Bella swallowed the lump in her throat threatening

to choke her, and said brokenly, 'I've known and loved Maria since the day she was born and took pleasure in watching her grow up. That took a little of the ache from my own heart at never having a child of my own. When Maria gave birth to Sally I thought I'd take the same pleasure in watching her being reared. However, it isn't going to be that way. I'm not so selfish a woman as to want Maria to stay here in poverty when a better life awaits her in England, where she has an uncle to look out for her.'

'You are a very special person,' Sean said sincerly. 'But answer me this if you can. Surely if Barney had been involved, as you think he might have been, wouldn't he have been picked up with the others?'

Bella looked at her mother and then said, 'We know nothing concrete. I mean, Maria hasn't sat down and given it to us chapter and verse or anything, but from what she has let slip, and from the letters that Barney sent from Dublin that she'd often let us read, I'd say he was as involved as any of them. I think what saved Barney's skin was coming home in response to the telegram Maria sent to him when Sam took a turn for the worse. Altogether, he was away nearly three months.'

'Dear God!'

After these revelations Sean had no desire to have the man set a foot over the threshold of his house, but if he didn't, what of Maria? The man was her husband and the father of wee Sally, and therefore had rights. Sean would rather have Maria near him than not, but, by Christ, he'd put it straight down the line to Barney. He'd have no immoral or illegal dealings when he was under his roof, and he'd definitely take Maria back with him. After what he had heard that day, he had no intention of leaving her behind.

After the meal that evening, Sean suggested going for a pint and Maria was surprised because her uncle never went out the night before he left. When she commented on that, Sean said, 'I'm not leaving tomorrow after all, if that's all right with you. I sent a telegram to Martha while I was at the shop, telling her of the change of plan.'

Maria was pleased. 'Uncle Sean, you can stay as long as you like.'

Barney said nothing. He hadn't liked the way Sean had been looking at him, or the brusque way he had spoken to him all through the meal, though Maria appeared to notice nothing amiss. Now to suggest a drink and say he didn't intend leaving when he'd planned – the whole thing looked fishy to Barney.

And he was right to be suspicious. As soon as Sean had set the pint in front of him on a table in a quiet corner of the pub, he let him have it. He told him in a low but very firm voice that he knew all about his illegal dealings in Moville and of the time he spent in Dublin, and he was shocked and disgusted with him.

'I wouldn't give you house room at all if it wasn't for Maria,' he said. 'But there will be no second chance if you go to the bad again. You have put my niece through the mill one way and another. When I return to Birmingham, she is coming with me, for I am not leaving Maria here a minute longer than necessary. And if you know what is good for you, you'll put no obstacles in our way.'

Barney knew exactly what he meant and he also knew who had put Sean wise: the two witches from the shop had really stirred the shit. He knew Maria would have told Sean nothing, being too ashamed. Sean had the upper hand for the moment.

That night in bed, with the unaccustomed beer causing his head to spin, Sean hoped he wasn't taking Maria from the frying pan into the fire. He wondered what reaction there had been to the telegram he'd sent to Martha. He remembered the scene a few days earlier when he'd told the children he had offered Barney and Maria a home when Sam should breathe his last.

Patsy had clearly felt betrayed by her parents – Sean in particular.

She stood up, leaning her hands heavily on the table. 'Tell me that's not true.'

'It is true. Don't be so silly,' Sean admonished. 'Am I likely to say it if it isn't true?'

'How could you think of inviting her here?'

'Patsy!' Martha said. 'What on earth has got into you?'

'Nothing has got into me,' Patsy screamed. 'It's her. I hate her.' She pushed her face close to Sean's and sneered, 'Hear that? Your poor, precious Maria – I hate her.'

'That will do!' Martha snapped. 'Go to your room!'

Patsy was clearly too angry to stay. She gave her mother and Sean one glare before storming out of the room, slamming the door so hard it shook, and pounded up the stairs.

Tony glanced from his mother to Sean and then Paul, before saying, 'Phew! Thank God she's gone.'

'That sort of thing doesn't help.'

'Nothing helps,' Tony said. 'She's a mental case, a complete fruitcake.'

'Tony!'

'It's all those brains, gone to mush in her head,' Tony went on, unabashed. 'Don't do you no good anyroad, I don't think, brains.'

'Tony, I shan't speak to you again. Haven't you any homework?'

'Just reading.'

'Well, go and do it, for heaven's sake, and give us some peace. What about you, Paul?'

Paul pulled a face. 'I've got to find out all about St Paul. Miss has given me a book about him.'

'Off you go then,' Martha said. 'That will keep you busy. St Paul was quite a character.'

Paul slid from the chair and went upstairs.

The baby, who'd been lying asleep in the pram, had been disturbed by Patsy's slam of the door. She began to cry.

'Oh God,' Martha said, exasperated, getting to her feet, 'I honestly don't know what's the matter with our Patsy. She's been difficult for weeks, but that performance tonight beats the lot and now Deirdre is awake and might take ages to settle.'

'What has she against Maria anyway?' Sean asked, puzzled, as Martha hauled the baby from the pram and held her against her shoulder. 'She hardly knows her.'

'It's not just Maria, it could be anyone,' Martha said. 'I told you before the wedding, it's anyone that takes your attention away from her. She's jealous and she's been worse than ever since I've had Deirdre.'

297

'Well, going on like this is not going to make me love her more,' Sean said. 'In fact, the opposite is the more likely. And as for spending time with her, I think I'd rather share the room with a sabre-toothed tiger.'

'Me too.'

'The blokes at work say all teenage girls are like this today.'

'God, if I'd have said half the things she gets away with to my mother, I'd not be here today,' Martha said. 'She'd have killed me stone dead.'

'Maybe that's where we went wrong,' Sean mused. 'Too keen to make allowances. But I can't write and tell Maria now that she's not welcome.'

'No,' Martha said. 'No, you can't, and it wouldn't be true anyway. I'm looking forward to her coming and the boys really like her. It will be a long time, Sean, before I refuse to help someone because of some whim of a selfish child.'

'What about Patsy?'

'What about her?' Martha said. 'She'll have to like it or lump it. Don't worry so much, Sean. Maria is a big girl now and well able, I'd say, to cope with a teenage girl and her fancies.'

'Aye,' Sean said, leaning across to give his wife a kiss on the cheek. 'You're right as usual, and I think Deirdre has dropped off again. You can put her back in the pram now.'

Although Maria was glad to be going with her uncle – which she now knew Dora and Bella had arranged – she was very sad to be leaving the village.

'It's no wonder,' Dora said consolingly. 'You're

leaving behind all you've ever known, and for a life so totally different that it is bound to feel strange at first.'

'Aye,' Bella agreed, 'and I'd say you are almost bound to feel homesick. But you won't be the only one to leave these shores for a better life.'

'I know,' Maria said. 'But oh, how I will miss the pair of you.'

Bella held Maria tight. She didn't have to speak, though she couldn't have spoken anyway, for she was choked with emotion.

Con was driving Sean and Maria to Derry in a car borrowed from a neighbour. They were to catch the night train from there. Maria was surprised and moved to see how many had braved the icy wind and raw night air to gather in The Square and wish them Godspeed.

'You shouldn't have come out, Dora,' Maria admonished the older lady, tucking the scarf inside her neck more snugly.

'Maria, you leaving . . . well, it's like losing one of our own,' Bella said. 'We had to come and see you off.'

'Ah, don't, Bella,' Maria said, as the tears slid down her cheeks.

Con said gently, 'It's better if we get going, Maria, before these good people stick to the ground altogether.' Maria saw the sense of what Con said and she climbed into the car beside Sean. Without another word they were on their way.

Maria found it was far nicer travelling with someone than alone, especially a lovely man like her uncle. It seemed no time at all before they reached Dun Laoghaire.

It was still dark when they boarded the boat so they couldn't see that the sea was like a raging torrent, but they felt the boat listing from side to side even before it had left the harbour. Maria felt her stomach tighten as she remembered how sick she had been last time. This journey was little different. The boat was pitched and tossed in the turbulent water, and she was glad she had her uncle there to mind the baby.

Later, when her stomach was emptied at last, Sean insisted Maria try to rest. Wearied by sickness and sheer tiredness, she didn't argue, but lay across the bench with her head on her uncle's lap, and slept until the boat docked at Holyhead.

It wasn't until they were in the train that Maria allowed herself to think of Patsy and her previous animosity towards her, but she dismissed her apprehensions. Patsy had been a little younger then and perhaps not so sure of Sean as she was now. It would be almost two years since they had met and she was sure – well, almost sure – that this time things would run much smoother.

This time, the whole family were out to welcome them, even Martha, standing on the steps and holding the baby. She came down to kiss Maria, and they compared and enthused over each other's babies, while the boys cavorted around Maria, catching up the bags and cases excitedly.

Once more Patsy stood apart and Maria saw she had emerged from the gawky child to a very well-developed and beautiful girl on the verge of womanhood. She was tall and slender, with a lovely figure. Her hair, as dark as Maria's, was wavy and fell just past her shoulders, held back from her face with decorated combs. Her eyes, though, were her best feature, so large and dark, and ringed with long black lashes. Maria felt sorry that they were at that moment filled with resentment. Her rosebud mouth, pulled into such a sulky pout, caused lines to form at the side of it and at each side of her nose, which was pinched in with open disapproval. Maria knew that, just like nearly two years previously, the girl begrudged her presence there.

She was at that moment too tired to care. Seldom could Maria remember being so tired – almost too tired to eat the meal Martha put in front of her. Later, as she fed the baby, Sean said, 'When you've done, why don't you go on up, Maria? The bed's all ready for you.'

'Oh, but the dishes—'

'I wouldn't let you help with the dishes anyway,' Martha said firmly. 'And Sean's right, you look proper washed out. I've made up a drawer for Sally to sleep in for now, but we will get something more suitable in a day or two.'

'A drawer is fine, honestly.'

'Well, she can't stay in it indefinitely,' Martha said. 'But don't worry, there is a notice board at the clinic and there's always baby equipment advertised.'

'Well, I'm sure Sally will be more than happy in a drawer tonight,' Maria said. 'And I am so tired I could sleep on a washing line.'

'Will Sally sleep all night?' Martha asked.

'I don't know. She's just begun to do that, but I've probably upset her whole system. Does Deirdre?'

'Like Sally, she's just started to,' Martha said. 'Not like the boys. Tony was waking at night until he was nine months old, and even Paul was well over six months. Greedy, see.'

'Yeah, and nothing's changed,' Patsy said disparagingly.

'Don't start,' Martha warned Patsy. 'If you have enough energy to fight, young lady, you have enough to give me a hand, so start collecting the plates up.'

Sean had gone to work and the children to school when Maria came down to the kitchen the next morning.

As she fed and changed the baby Martha said, 'You need to get an identity card and a ration book, and a special baby's one for Sally. It wouldn't hurt either to put your name down at Bush House, for a council house, you know.'

'Yes,' said Maria. 'But ration books. I thought—'

'You thought, with the war over, rationing would be out the window now?'

'Aye. Something like that.'

'Lots of people thought the same way,' Martha said. 'But what has changed since the war really?'

'What do you mean?'

'Well, I know there is no longer any blackout, no bombs, but the men are only being demobbed slowly, so they might avoid the problems they had last time when the "Land fit for heroes" had only poverty to offer their serving soldiers and their families,' Martha said. 'We still have an army of occupation in Germany – that might go on for years.

'Then, lots of factories making other things, even food stuffs, were turned over to manufacturing munitions – like Cadbury's, where they were putting cordite in rockets rather than soft centres into chocolate. And they slaughtered hundreds of hens at the beginning of the war to save on food stuffs, so rationing might go on for years yet. If you don't get a ration card pronto you won't be able to get any food. As today is Friday, we're daren't leave it because they won't be open again until Monday.'

'So where do we have to go?'

'The Council House in the town. We'll have to take the two babies with us.' Deirdre, upstairs in her cot, chose that moment to begin to cry, and Martha said, 'Will you listen to that? She's woken just in time for our little outing.'

Barney contacted Ned the day after Sean and Maria left. He wanted to speak to the man anyway – not just about the boatyard, but also to see if Ned had any news of his brother.

'They come up for trial two weeks before Christmas,' Ned told Barney, a couple of days later. 'I've been to see your brother and he said to tell you to keep away. No one has mentioned your name in connection with any of this – that was your brother's doing – but the Garda aren't daft altogether. They know you're involved somehow. Apparently, Seamus heard the screws talking and they were certain you'd turn up for the trial and were intending to arrest you then.'

Barney felt as if an icy finger was trailing down his spine. 'Arrest me? What for?'

'Do they have to have a reason?' Ned asked. 'It could just be because they don't like the look of you. Anyway, according to Seamus, if once they get you in there, with the endless questions they fire at you for hours, one taking over from another, you're ready to swear that black's white and will admit to anything just to get them to stop.'

'So, what am I to do?'

'Stay here.' Ned advised. 'Or better still, hightail it to Maria's uncle's place as soon as you can, and certainly well before the trial. It's unlikely they would follow you there. As for the boatyard, you know I want it and the price we agreed on. As it is a cash sale, we don't need solicitors and all to make money out of it.'

'So Seamus doesn't want me at the trial?'

'What he wants is to keep you out of prison,' Ned said. 'I'll go along, if you like, and tell you the outcome, though it will likely make the papers, which is one more reason to be well away from here by the time the news breaks. I know from experience that mud sticks, and in a little place like this . . . well, I don't have to spell it out for you, I'm sure.'

No, he didn't. Barney could imagine it all. He shook hands with Ned.

'I don't know why you are doing this,' he said, 'but I'm grateful.'

'If you want the truth,' Ned said, 'I am helping you because of that lovely wife and baby you have. They don't deserve this. Do you think Maria could have stood the shame of being married to a gaolbird, or your child growing up in the shadow of it? I hope you have learnt a lesson from this.'

Barney didn't answer and Ned narrowed his eyes. 'Don't be a bloody fool altogether. You have the chance of a new life in Birmingham. Grasp it with two hands, if you want to stay a free man. Accept the fact that your brother is lost to you for now, and unless you want to join him, you will do as he advises.'

Barney suddenly felt bereft as Ned's words sank in. He was missing Seamus already. How he would manage years without him he didn't know, because he had never had to do it before.

CHAPTER SEVENTEEN

Maria registered herself with the same butcher, grocer and greengrocer that Martha used and found it a bit of a headache to jiggle her rations to make them stretch.

Martha had already had nearly six years of it and she showed Maria how to make things like sardine fritters and Poor Man's Goose, which had never been anywhere near a goose and was made with liver. She had books of recipes she'd copied out from *The Kitchen Front*, which she said had been on the wireless every morning after the eight o'clock news all through the war. 'We were burdened down with advice and recipes,' she told Maria. 'Every magazine and some newspapers had a food fact page and there were even food flashes in the cinema, so I was told. I used to listen to the radio doctor as well, because he'd tell you which foods were good for you and I wanted to rear healthy children.'

Maria could agree wholeheartedly with that sentiment. She knew Martha would have done her level best, but she suspected that many of the names of the dishes were more appetising than the actual finished product, when she examined the list of ingredients. There were completely meatless dishes like Mock Hare Soup, Vitality Mould, Vegetable and Oatmeal Goulash and Lord Woolton Pie, and others like Boston Bake, which had a little meat in it. There were even tips on how to make things like mock clotted cream, using dried milk and vanilla essence, Raspberry Snow and mock marzipan.

At least, though, there was extra milk on the ration for babies. At the clinic they could have free orange juice and cod liver oil to help keep them healthy. Maria and Martha would take the babies every week to be weighed. Maria found Martha had been right about the notice board too. By the end of the first week she was the proud owner of a crib, cot, pram, highchair and even a pushchair for when the child was older. Sean gave her a loan for these and said he would get the money from Barney later. Maria only let him do this because she had so little money in her purse, it was scary.

Barney was due to join Maria on Monday, 10 December, by which time Maria had been in Birmingham nearly a month. Sean left work early that day so that he could pick Barney up at the station. As the weather was raw, with sleeting rain, the family didn't go out to meet him and so the first time Patsy saw him was when he walked into the family's breakfast room.

She looked up from the table where she was puzzling over a maths problem and the handsomeness of Barney nearly took her breath away. When he smiled at her it was as if her heart had stopped beating for a moment or two.

Maria was annoyed with Barney. He flirted with women and always had. It was his way and he had a special smile he reserved for them, but surely he could see that he couldn't begin flirting with Sean's stepdaughter.

Patsy, unaware of Maria's concern, smiled back. It transformed her whole face, as if a light was turned on. She was almost fifteen and, educated at a convent school, she had no knowledge of boys other than her brothers. The conversations in the school yard, though, revolved around boys and sex – what you should let a boy do to you, how far you could go. Those girls with older brothers were often very popular indeed.

But Barney was no spotty crass boy; he was a man, a very handsome one, and he was looking at her in a way that . . . well, like she was a woman. It made her feel funny inside and her face went all hot. And then, when he suddenly gave her a broad and suggestive wink, Patsy felt as if there were butterflies fluttering about in her stomach.

Maria was amazed that no one else seemed aware of anything wrong. She would have to talk to Barney about this. The girl was young and impressionable, and might read more into his flirting than there was.

This wasn't the time to go into it, though. The table had to be cleared because the evening meal was about to be served. Over dinner, Barney told them all about Moville, what was happening and how he'd had to camp out in the boatyard for a few days because the tenants for the house in Moville wanted to move in before he was ready to come to England.

'Never mind,' Sean said. 'You're here now and can start work on Wednesday.'

Barney, who'd thought he wouldn't start until after Christmas, was appalled. 'So soon?'

'Why not?' Sean said, fixing Barney with a glare. 'The devil makes work for idle hands, they say. And tomorrow you will have to go to the Council House and get yourself a ration book.'

Barney said nothing to this. At that moment Sally began to cry. Maria lifted her from the pram and sat down in an armchair with her.

Sean said, 'You'll likely see a difference in young Sally. A month is a long time at this age.'

'Barney wouldn't notice,' Maria said a trifle bitterly. 'He barely looks at the child.'

Barney, annoyed with Maria, said, 'I'm just not a baby person, that's all.'

Sean had noticed Barney's indifference to the child. 'Haven't you found it different with your own?' he asked.

'No,' Barney said. 'Not really. I've no time for babies. They bore the pants off me, to be truthful, and as far as I am concerned it's Maria's job to rear the children.'

'That's a hell of an old-fashioned view today,' Sean said.

Barney shrugged. 'It's how I feel. How I am.'

'I agree with him, anyway,' Patsy put in. 'Babies are boring and the fuss everyone makes of them is sickening. I mean, what does our Deirdre do except eat, be sick and wee and poo all over the place?'

'You don't have to do anything to be loved,' Sean said. 'And babies—'

'Don't make me laugh!' Patsy said scathingly. 'I sure as hell have to do something. How often do you ask what mark I got for this essay and that exam?'

'That's because we are interested.'

'Yeah, so you say,' Patsy sneered. 'What would you do if I just threw it all in the air? I get fed up enough to do just that sometimes.'

'Patsy, this is silly.'

'Yep, that's what I am. Silly.'

Maddened at last, Martha burst out, 'I'll tell you what you are, girl, and that is damned self-centred. All this came about because of one comment Sean made to Barney and you managed to not only turn it around to discuss yourself, but complain how hard done by you are. Change the record, Patsy, for I'm sick listening to it.'

Patsy's face flamed with embarrassment and she stood up, pushing back her chair so violently it tipped over. She took no heed of it, just glared at them all. 'I hate you,' she declared. 'I hate you all, so there.'

When she'd left the room, slamming the door behind her and making Sally jump, Martha sighed and Tony let out a relieved, 'Phew!'

'Tony, haven't I told you off about this before?'

'Yeah, you have, but I don't think you're being fair,' Tony complained. 'You said we had to be honest and that is honestly how I feel. You feel the same or you wouldn't have sighed.'

'I'm not having any argument.'

'You let Patsy argue plenty.'

'That will do, Tony,' Sean cut in. 'Apologise to your mother, and I will apologise to Barney and Maria for that display of bad manners.'

'No need,' Barney said. 'Isn't that right, Maria?'

'Of course,' Maria agreed. 'It's fine, Uncle Sean.'

Later, when Rosie and Martha were washing up in the kitchen, the boys around the table doing their homework and Sean had retired to the sitting room to listen to the news, Barney crept up the stairs and knocked quietly on Patsy's door.

'Go away!'

'It's me. Barney.'

He heard the drag of her feet and then the door was opened a fraction. He saw tear trails on her face, her eyes were brimming and her hair was tousled. The effect was very provocative, the more so because Patsy would be unaware of it.

Sean's stepdaughter reminded him of a little girl he'd had a dalliance with in Dublin. She was about the same age, but knew what it was all about. He'd like to bet Patsy could be a little goer too, with the right teacher.

'What do you want?' Even Patsy's voice, husky with tears, sounded incredibly sexy.

'Can I come in?'

Patsy shrugged, but opened the door wider.

'I just wanted to say I know how you feel. How angry you get inside,' Barney said as he sat uninvited on the bed and pulled Patsy down beside him.

'Why do you?'

'I used to feel the very same.'

'I say things because I am mad . . . I don't always mean them.'

'I hope you didn't mean what you said tonight,' Barney ventured. 'You said you hated everyone. Did that include me?'

'Oh, no, not you.' Patsy's eyes were shining with hero worship.

Barney allowed himself a small smile of triumph. This girl would be a pushover. He slipped his arm around her and said, 'I would like to be your friend, Patsy, would you like that?'

'Oh, yes, Barney.'

'We must keep it to ourselves. The others wouldn't understand.'

'No, of course they wouldn't.' Patsy said.

'Anyway, Sean has his own child now and he'd never feel the same for a stepdaughter as one of his own,' Barney said, feeding Patsy's fears.

'Do you really think that?'

'Stands to reason. Now they have Deirdre, they probably see you as a nuisance.'

Every slight and injustice flashed through Patsy's brain and she knew Barney spoke the truth. She leant against him, suddenly feeling lost and cold, and was very glad he was there. Cuddled into Barney, she remembered how special she had been to her daddy and how he had called her his princess.

When he died, she had wanted to die too. Her mother was so upset it had been her grandparents who had helped her get through that awful time until they were all blown up with a bomb. She decided then that no-one else would ever have a piece of her heart. And they hadn't for years, till her mother met Sean. As she got close to him she grew to hate the way he'd go on about Maria. Because he could remember her from when she was born, Patsy worried that he'd think more of Maria than her and had taken a dislike to her when she was over for the wedding.

But she went away again and life went on as before

for a while. Then Sean and her mother told her they were having a baby. She had been disgusted. Fancy old people like them doing things like that! God. She was too embarrassed even to tell her friend Chloë at first. Even before Deirdre had been born she had felt pushed out. The way they went on, you'd think that there had never been a baby born before.

And now this wonderful handsome man had come to comfort her and say he wanted to be her friend. It was incredible and she was overwhelmed with his understanding of just how she felt.

Barney could feel himself becoming aroused at the nearness of Patsy's young, nubile body. He stroked her hair as he said, 'Anyway, now you know they don't care about you, you haven't got to do as they say. But, this is the clever bit. You have to pretend that you do. To get more freedom, you have to convince them that you are a model daughter. What do we care what they say or do? We can laugh at them behind their backs and we have our little secret they can do nothing about.'

It sounded terribly exciting the way Barney described it. Then he suddenly kissed her lips and got to his feet, saying, 'I had better go before I am missed.'

She wanted to beg him to stay, but knew he was right.

Barney, smiling, was cautious as he went out of Patsy's room, but there was no one around. Downstairs, he was sitting before the fire reading the paper when the women came in from the kitchen. The boys were still bent over their homework and Sean hadn't emerged from the sitting room. So far, so good, thought Barney.

*   *   *

When Maria saw the state of Barney when he came in from work that first day, she felt sorry for him. He looked completely exhausted. He also stunk of rubber. Black dust was ingrained in his skin, coating the lines on his face, encrusting his hands, caked beneath his nails and to his scalp.

'Sean used to be the same,' Martha said to Maria as she heated water for Barney's wash. 'Now that he is maintaining the railway that runs alongside the road through the Dunlop, he still gets dirty, but it's like normal dirt, not like the muck from rubber. It's why they get decent wages, I expect.'

'I suppose,' Maria said. 'I've never seen Barney look so tired either.'

'He'll pick up the hang of it in no time, you'll see,' Martha said. 'He won't be so tired then.'

Maria wondered if Barney would ever stick at the Dunlop factory long enough to pick up the hang of it. Well, if he didn't, she thought, then he'd have to do some other line of work. She tolerated a lot of Barney's behaviour, but no way would she stand for him returning to a life of crime. She thought the longer they kept Seamus and the others in prison, the better she would like it.

The following Saturday morning, at Barney's suggestion, Patsy offered to mind both babies if Maria and Martha would like to go into town that afternoon. They were delighted, although neither could be away long as they were breastfeeding.

'We'll go down the Bull Ring,' Martha declared.

Maria was dying to see the place she had heard so

much about, although she thought Erdington marvellous, and especially the market.

'What about you?' Maria said to Barney that morning when he came into the bedroom as she was feeding Sally. 'Will you be going to the match with Sean and the lads?'

'No, not this week,' Barney said. 'I have to see a man in the Cross Keys pub.'

'Cross Keys, where's that?'

'Just down from the abbey.'

'Plays card, does he, this man?' Maria asked.

'You're surely not going to nag the life out of me over a few games of cards? You knew I always played cards.'

'I worry about the money you are spending.'

'When I ask for any from you, you'll have that right,' Barney said. 'Till then, what I do with my own money and in my own time is my business alone.'

Maria sighed. 'All right then, what have you done with the money for the boatyard? Surely that is half mine.'

The money was in the tin where Barney kept all the money from the raids in Dublin, but he had no intention of telling Maria that. 'All your property became mine on your father's death,' Barney said, 'unless he specifically willed anything to you – and he didn't do that. So for Christ's sake, will you stop bloody nagging me? You never let a man alone.'

Maria knew that once Barney shouted at her like that any reasonable discussion would be useless, so when he left the room, though she sighed in vexation, she didn't bother calling him back.

Barney went out for a few pints about mid-morning and hadn't returned by the time Sean came home from work. The lunch-time meal was eaten quickly so that Sean and the boys could head off to the match. Shortly after they had left, the two women fed and changed the babies. 'Are you sure about this?' Martha said to Patsy as she lay the drowsy Deirdre down in the pram.

'Course I am.'

'It's just if they wake up together,' Martha said. 'Maria is leaving Sally in the bedroom, but they could still disturb one another.'

'If they do, they do,' said Patsy. 'I'm a big girl and I will cope. Don't worry so much.'

Really, thought Martha, Patsy was like a changed girl. She said as much to Maria as they travelled into the town on the bus.

'It certainly was kind of her,' Maria agreed. 'I just hope the two of them won't give her a hard time.'

'Me too,' Martha said with a laugh. 'Then she might do it again a time or two. Maybe whatever ailed her has gone now.'

Maria could have told her that she knew what had influenced Patsy's behaviour and that was Barney. He had told her that himself when she had tackled him about flirting with her. 'God in heaven, woman, I can't do right for you whatever I do!' he'd exclaimed. 'All right, I gave the girl a wink, made her smile, took the sulky look off her face. Tell you the truth, that look reminded me of myself about the same age – all at sixes and sevens, and thinking everyone hates you and is getting at you. I wanted to get on her side, tell her I sort of understood.'

'Did she listen?'

'Aye, aye, she did,' Barney said. 'I told her if she wanted Sean and Martha to treat her in a more grown-up way, then she had to stop acting like a child, and a spoilt child at that. And you have got to admit it's working.'

'Aye, so far, anyway,' Maria had to concede. 'And I'm sorry, Barney, if I have made a big deal out of it.'

She didn't tell Martha about Barney's involvement, for she felt it not fair to do so. She was glad that she didn't really have anything to worry about. Married to a man like Barney, she was finding life was often a whole catalogue of worry.

If she had been able to glimpse into the house a little later, worry would have been on high alert. Barney, as arranged, had come home from the pub early and Patsy was waiting for him.

'Do you want a cup of tea?' she asked.

'No, bring a couple of glasses,' Barney said. 'I have brought a few bottles home with me.'

'I've never had beer.'

'Well, now is your chance to try it. Fetch the glasses, then come and sit here beside me on the settee.'

Patsy didn't like the beer, but she covered her distaste and said it was fine because she thought that would please him. She hadn't liked the odd puffs of the cigarettes he had given her a few days before either, but she thought she would probably get used to them and it did make her feel very grown up to light one. So when Barney proffered his packet, she took one without hesitation.

'What would Sean and your mother do it if they could see you now?' Barney asked. 'Knocking back beer with the best of them and smoking.'

'They'd have a fit.'

'Right,' Barney agreed. 'And for what? We're not hurting anyone, are we?'

'No, we're not,' Patsy declared. 'They'd like to keep me a child for ever.'

'Ah, well, that's where I differ,' Barney said. 'See, I wasn't brought up like you. In fact, I was dragged up. My parents were either too sick, or sometimes too drunk to care what I was doing. I was often hungry and was dressed in rags and ran about barefoot, winter and summer.

'They died when I was ten. I didn't really miss them as my brother took me over. He was strict. I mean, I had to do what he said when he said it or he would take his belt off to me. Funnily enough, I didn't mind that because at least he showed he cared. He always said it was daft to have ages when you can do this and that and he let me try everything – booze, fags, even sex.'

'Sex!'

'Aye, when he judged the time was right, and I was more than ready.'

'I thought . . .' Patsy said hesitantly, 'I mean we're taught, aren't we, that sex outside marriage is wrong?'

'That's what we're taught, right enough,' Barney said. 'What do you think?'

'I don't know. I mean, I've never thought about it.'

'I don't believe that for a minute,' Barney said. 'At your age it was all I thought about, and I bet girls are

318

no different to boys. I can see you blushing. I'm right, aren't I?'

Patsy nodded and Barney laughed. 'Have you ever been out with a boy, Patsy?'

Patsy shook her head vehemently.

'Let me guess. Sean and your mother wouldn't like it?'

'I suppose not,' Patsy said. 'They haven't said. I mean, it's just not come up. I don't get much chance to see boys at the convent, you know. Mom did say I can start going to the youth club at the school hall at the abbey when I am fifteen in February. My friend Chloë will be fifteen two weeks before me and I think the parents have worked it out between themselves. I'll probably see boys there.' But it was said tentatively.

'Course you will. What's up?'

'It's just . . . I don't know, really,' Patsy went on. 'I mean, I know girls who go and they say the boys play table tennis all night at one side of the hall and the girl all dance together. There's none of that jitterbugging allowed either, and they'd be scandalised by this,' she said, waving her glass aloft. 'Nothing stronger than orange juice is drunk. Father Clancy is there to keep an eye on everyone.'

'See you don't leap on each other in a fit of rampant lust?'

Patsy laughed. 'Something like that.'

'Doesn't sound the most exciting place in the universe,' Barney said.

Patsy sighed. 'No. It's just better than staying in night after night – not much better, mind.'

'Come on, Patsy, now that I am your friend, I bet

I can think up better places to go now and again, even if we have to hoodwink the parents to do it.'

Patsy felt warmed and comforted by Barney's words. When he put his arm around her, she nestled against him. 'I am so glad I have got you for a friend.'

'Likewise,' Barney said, placing a chaste kiss on the top of Patsy's head. 'Now sit up, drain that glass, and I'll get us a refill and teach you how to play poker. What d'you say?'

'I say yes, yes, yes,' Patsy cried, aware, even as she spoke, that she would say yes to most things Barney might suggest.

Maria was following behind Martha as she led the way from the High Street down the hill to the Bull Ring. She'd been impressed enough with the shops, though horrified by the gaping holes and mounds of rubble that she saw in the streets everywhere. She would have liked to have lingered, but Martha would have none of it. 'We can come again to see the city centre, what's left of it,' she said. 'But we haven't got long, and today I want you to experience the Bull Ring.'

It was soon apparent that the Bull Ring had not come through the war unscathed either. On the left-hand side of the incline leading down into it Martha indicated the sea of rubble. 'These used to be shops once, bespoke tailors that would make up a suit for thirty bob, and another shop selling sweets and news-papers, side by side with a shoe shop and next to that a café and right at the end was a pet shop. There were always kittens in the window, and a large parrot sat outside on a perch in good weather. I used to be quite nervous of him, despite the fact he was tethered so that he couldn't fly away.'

Maria shook her head at the destruction. She looked down into the sea of people where the cries of the vendors vied with the noise from the thronging masses as they went down the hill and into the mêlée.

Either side of a large statue on a podium and surrounded by iron railings, barrows lined the cobbled streets, many with canvas awnings above them. Fruit and veg, rabbit and fish were for sale side by side with junk, and stalls selling baskets of odd crockery and battered pans. The amalgamated smells lingered in the air.

'At least there's more fruit now,' Martha said, 'more variety and more vegetables.'

'Whale meat for sale' said a board above one stall.

'Whale meat – ugh!' Maria exclaimed.

'I still do that as a change now and again,' Martha said. 'I thought it quite expensive at two and six a pound, but the beauty of it was it was off ration. Believe me, when you are trying to fill up hungry children you'll try anything. Rabbit is lovely, and I've even bought horse meat. I didn't tell the children what it was, though. It tastes very like beef, except that it needs more cooking to make it tender. Whale meat has quite a strong flavour. I always find it better mixed with mashed potato and made into fish pie. It's something else to eat on Fridays, anyway.'

Suddenly, Maria was aware of one strident voice rising above the others and she strained her ears to catch the words.

'Carriers. Handy carriers.'

'Who's that?'

'The old lady in front of Woolworths,' Martha said. 'Been here since the year dot and in all weathers. Everyone knows her. And this here is Lord Nelson,' she went on, indicating the statue in front of them. 'Before the war, flowersellers used to congregate all around here. But so much of the country was carved up to plant foodstuffs, flowers are not that plentiful any more. I reckon a lot of folk will be reclaiming the land back now, so the flowersellers might well be back by the spring. Come on, Peacocks is over here.'

Martha stood before the window, looking in. 'When Mom used to bring me here when I was just a nipper, and even when I used to take Patsy before the war, this place would draw us like a magnet. The toys then – oh, they were wonderful: beautiful dolls of every size and shape; prams and cribs good enough to put a real baby in. There were train sets running around in the window, and inside the shop – not just going round and round, though, but winding through towns and villages and countryside. I could have stood for hours just looking. There were cars of every description and a large fort full of lead soldiers. Most of it was too expensive for my parents, though it was nice to see it all. But now . . .'

Martha didn't have to say any more. The shelves in the window were almost bare and Maria guessed there would be little in the shop to buy.

'This must be one of the saddest sights,' Maria said, 'to have a toyshop without any toys.'

'Aye,' Martha said, 'but I hope we can pick up some wee thing for Paul and Tony's stockings at least. Their wartime Christmases have been pretty lean. The only time they had anything worthwhile was when we had a parcel from America, delivered through the Churches.' She smiled at the memory. 'Poor little beggars were that excited, you'd think they had been given the Crown Jewels.'

'I'm sure we'll get them something,' Maria said. 'We'll make it our mission today.'

'OK,' Martha said. 'We can take a look in Woolworths as we are passing. We might be able to get a necklace or bangle for Patsy, or some ribbons for her hair.'

They did better than that. As well as the ribbons, Martha seized on a brush and comb set. The plywood model shop Hobbies was next door. Here again Martha told Maria how it used to be before the war when the window was full of yachts, trains and cars, with row upon row of kits inside so that people could make up their own.

She peered through the window into the near-empty shop and turned away sadly. 'Tony would have loved to have one,' she said with a sigh. 'But there is none to be had now. It won't matter so much if Sean can get them a ball. He has put in for one at the Dunlop shop, but then so have a lot of people and there are only so many to go around. I've no idea how they decide these things.'

Maria felt sorry for the children, who would wake up on Christmas morning to no presents, as presumably they had all through the war. 'There must be something,' she said, pointing to the other side of the street where she could see a building behind the barrows. 'What's that place?'

'That's the Market Hall,' Martha said. 'It has no roof now, courtesy of the Luftwaffe.'

It was a sorry sight. Maria could guess it must have been a fine building before it was stripped of its roof and had holes pounded into its sides. Arched windows were set on either side of stone steps and the whole building was supported by Gothic pillars. And once inside, such an array of things for sale.

'There used to be a magnificent wooden clock on the wall,' Martha told Maria. Carved figures – three knights and a lady – were on it, and they would all strike the bell on the hour. Burnt to a crisp now, of course. I always worried what happened to the animals. There were two pet places and probably the animals perished in the fire.'

'Oh, look,' Maria said, suddenly pouncing upon a yo-yo and a penny whistle.

'Dear Lord, they will have us deafened with that whistle,' Martha chided her gently, but she was glad she had found something to put in the children's stockings.

'We can't go home until you have a peep in the Rag Market,' Maria declared, leading the way down the steps of the Market Hall, across the cobbled street past the church, with a fringe of trees in front of it and, dodging the trams and dray horses, into the another large hall, which smelt a little of fish.

It was an eye-opener for Maria. She spent a long time at the second-hand clothes stalls – so long, in fact, that Martha left her when she spotted a man selling wind-up mechanical toys from a tray around his neck and bought two of them before joining Maria again.

'Look what I have!' she exclaimed in delight, and

then realised by Maria's pensive face as she fingered a soft wool dress in dark red that she hadn't even heard her speak. She nudged her. 'Whatever are you thinking about so hard, Maria?'

'I'm just thinking it's a pity that I haven't got a sewing machine,' Maria said. 'I could unpick some of these and make up something decent.'

'Could you really?'

'Aye, if only I had a sewing machine.'

'I might be able to help you there,' Maria said. 'The point is, Sean asked me if I wanted one for Christmas. Apparently, one of the men he worked with had bought the machine for his wife two years ago and she's never used it and so he's decided to sell it. I don't know anything about sewing. I mean, I can sew a button, hem a dress and turn a collar, but you don't need a machine for those types of jobs. Any other type of sewing is beyond me and so I told Sean it would be a waste of money buying it for me, but if it's still available then it would do you a treat.'

'Is it a treadle?'

'No,' Maria said, 'Sean said it was a modern one that you worked by turning a handle with your hand.'

'I'd love it,' Maria said. 'But there is no need for Sean to pay for it.'

'Oh, we can sort that out later,' Martha said dismissively 'All I know is I would pay for it myself, and gladly, if you could make me up a decent dress and keep the kids respectable. We've been making do and mending for so long, the material is wearing out. Tony's trousers are nearly indecent and his shirts are hard to fasten across his chest. For Patsy it's even

325

worse. She had developed quite a little bust on her. She hasn't anything that isn't too short or tight. Even her uniform is getting skimpy on her now and I bought that big to last.'

Maria had actually noticed the state of all the children's clothes and she hoped the sewing machine was still available. So in a mood of optimism, the two women left the Rag Market with as many clothes as they could carry.

By the time they arrived home, with Sean and the boys following on their heels and Tony declaring, 'They was robbed,' there was no indication of how Patsy and Barney had spent their afternoon. The glasses had been washed and put away and Patsy had sucked a peppermint Barney had given her to get rid of the smell of alcohol and cigarette smoke on her breath. Then for good measure she cleaned her teeth.

As she was coming out of the bathroom, she heard Deirdre beginning to cry down stairs and so when her mother came in she was nursing her. 'Oh God,' Martha said, taking the baby from her daughter's arms, 'has she been like this since I left?'

'No, she's just woken up,' Patsy said, adding, 'Oh, listen, now the other one's started.'

'I'll get her,' Maria said, galloping up the stairs to her complaining child, leaving Martha to explain about the clothes and the lack of a sewing machine.

All the talk around the table was about that and Sean said he would go to the fellow's house directly after the meal to see if it was still for sale.

Patsy was torn. Much as the thought of new clothes

excited her, she didn't want to feel beholden in any way to her step-cousin, particularly when she was engaging in a secret friendship with her husband. Just how good was she, anyway? What she turned out would probably be rubbish, which Patsy wouldn't be seen dead in.

And what excitement there was when Sean carried the machine home. The dinner things had been washed and put away by then and the clothes tipped out on the table. Maria ran her hands over the lovely shiny machine, the nicest sewing machine she had ever owned, and her hands itched to use it while her insides churned with excitement. Even Patsy decided to give the women a hand unpicking the clothes while the two men took themselves off to the pub.

CHAPTER EIGHTEEN

As she had been doing every Sunday since she had
arrived, the next day Maria went with Martha and
the children to the children's Mass at nine o'clock
at the abbey. Barney was still in bed after declaring
the night before he would be going to the one at
eleven o'clock, and when Sean, who usually went to
a much earlier Mass, said he'd go along with him,
Maria guessed they wouldn't be back until the pubs
closed.

At half-past twelve Martha began to wonder what
was keeping them, for the Mass was just an hour and
the abbey a mere ten minutes' walk away.

'They'll have gone for a pint,' Maria said.

Martha frowned. Neither of them had had anything to eat or drink since the night before, as they
intended to take Communion, and so Martha knew
any beer they took would go straight to their heads.
'I wanted dinner at one o'clock or thereabouts,' she
said. 'It can't be much later than that because Patsy
has choir practice at three.'

'Have the dinner when you want,' Maria said.

'Sometimes all Barney is fit for is sleeping off the beer when he does come home.'

'Don't you mind at all?'

'I've given up minding things I can't change,' Maria said. 'I could nag Barney till the cows come home and it would make not a ha'p'orth of difference. So what would it achieve? I would get upset and nothing would change. In fact, if I was to nag him, he'd probably act in a worse way.'

Martha shook her head sadly. 'Can't you talk to him, explain how you feel?' she asked. 'After all, marriage is a partnership.'

'Your marriage is,' Maria said. 'I can see how happy and close you are. With me and Barney, it's entirely different. Oh, don't worry,' she went on, seeing Martha's concerned face, 'I am well used to it now.'

She could have told Martha that the rot had begun in their marriage when Barney believed she had tricked him into it and hadn't been pregnant at all, an idea she could guess had been implanted by Seamus. But that would have meant admitting to Martha how she gave herself freely to Barney before they were married and she'd hate Martha to think badly of her. And what if she were to tell Sean? How disappointed he would be in the niece he so loved.

So she said, 'I came to the decision a long time ago that what can't be cured must be endured. That is the only way I can deal with it. Don't mention a word of this to Uncle Sean. He would feel he had to speak to Barney and that could only make things worse for me.'

Martha knew Maria was married to a totally selfish man, and so she said, 'I have no desire in the world to worsen things for you, so don't fret, Sean will not hear a word from me.'

Martha, Maria and the children ate the dinner at the normal time with Sean and Barney's left on plates over pans of water to heat for them when they came in. Afterwards Patsy washed up and Tony dried so that Maria could get on with the dressmaking. Despite herself, Patsy was surprised and quite impressed at her step-cousin's talent. She was making her a dress in a soft, dark red material and had measured her the previous night, then, using those measurements, had cut a pattern out of pages from the *Birmingham Evening Mail*. She had pinned the pattern to the material and carefully cut it out. Patsy could barely wait to see the finished article.

However, first she had the choir practice. She hadn't gone very far from the house on her way to the abbey when she met Sean and Barney making their way home. She'd seen few people drunk, and never her stepfather, and at first she was slightly repelled. But she saw Barney was not the slightest bit ashamed of the state he was in. As he caught sight of her, he exclaimed, 'Isn't this a sight for sore eyes, Sean? Isn't young Patsy here a true vision of loveliness? An angel from heaven, so she is.'

Sean could never remember feeling so drunk. The beer had reacted straight away on his empty stomach and he had no desire other than to reach home before he fell down and made a holy show of himself in the street, and no time at all for such talk with his stepdaughter.

'Come away, man,' he said, pulling at Barney's arm.

Patsy's face was bright red and she was flustered and

330

embarrassed at the way Barney was carrying on. She had to remind herself this was Barney, her special friend. 'I have to go,' she said. 'I'm due at choir practice at the abbey.'

'Would you mind if I walked along with you?'

'No, but—'

'We need to go home,' Sean said. 'Come on.'

'You go,' Barney said. 'I'll be along later. The walk will clear my head.'

'Don't be crazy,' Sean said. 'Martha will kill me as it is. As for Maria—'

'Maria will say not a word about it,' Barney said emphatically. 'But you go on home and say I went for a wee walk.'

'I need to go,' Patsy said. 'I'll be late.'

'Can't have that, princess, now can we?' Barney said, catching up her arm and tucking it into his. 'Be seeing you, Sean.'

Sean stood in the road, watching them go, Barney weaving ever so slightly and Patsy helping him walk straight. He wondered if should have made a stronger stand about letting Barney go off like that. But then what could he have done without making a scene? By God, he wasn't really in any fit state to argue the toss with anyone. He was a little concerned with the way Barney had spoken to Patsy, but he knew it was just his way. Patsy was little more than a child, and almost related. No harm would come to her with Barney. He pushed his concerns aside and went home to face Martha.

Patsy felt nothing like a child as she walked along arm in arm with Barney. 'Do you like choir practice?' he asked.

Patsy shrugged. 'It's all right.'

'If you didn't go one Sunday, what would happen?'

'Nothing. What do you mean?'

'If I took you somewhere more interesting,' Barney said. 'Like the cinema, say. No one would have to know. It would be our secret. How long is choir practice?'

Patsy thought of snuggling in the cinema beside Barney and it suddenly looked a far more attractive prospect that practising hour upon hour in a freezing cold church.

'It depends on the time of year,' she told him. 'Now, of course, we are practising for Christmas and all, and we may go on for two hours. Usually it's an hour and a half.'

'Not enough time to visit the pictures, though.'

'It might be,' Patsy said, 'because I don't go home afterwards – well, not till later. I have tea at my friend Chloë's house, and sometimes we do a bit of home-work together.'

'And wouldn't this Chloë wonder if you didn't turn up?'

'Well, I'd have to tell her,' Patsy said.

'And what if she mentions it to her mother?'

'She won't,' Patsy said confidently. 'But I couldn't miss choir before Christmas. I would be missed then because I have some solo parts.'

They had reached the church and Barney said, 'Then it will be something to look forward to in the New Year.'

'Oh, yes,' Patsy said, and felt her insides tingling with delicious excitement. Greatly daring, she stood on tiptoe and kissed Barney on the cheek.

He fought the longing to crush her to him and kiss her properly. Plenty of time, he told himself, and he waved as Patsy ran up the path.

On Thursday morning a letter with a Dublin postmark, addressed to Barney, arrived after he'd left for work. Knowing it was probably from Ned, when he got home he took it to the bedroom to read, just as he was, unwashed. When he didn't come down again, Maria crept upstairs to see what news that letter contained.

His head shot up as the door opened and Maria was shocked by his red-rimmed eyes. They were dry, but ravaged by pain. She approached the bed cautiously and said gently, 'What is it, Barney?'

'What is it, you ask?' Barney said sneeringly. 'I'll tell you what it is. They have given my brother ten sodding years.'

Ten years! The words resounded in Maria's head and she forgave Barney for the way he had spoken to her. He was hurting and lashing out, that was all, because if there was one person in the whole world Barney loved more than himself it was Seamus, a fact that she had realised long ago.

This news must have knocked him for six. Dear Christ, it had shocked her to the core. Ten years! She never imagined such a sentence, and she suddenly went cold. She'd read reports of other trials and often the defendant would ask for a number of similar cases to be taken into consideration. She wondered if Seamus had done that, how many he had cited and whether that had decided the hefty prison term. She broached this question to Barney and he growled that of course he'd done that – they'd all done a variety of previous jobs.

'But it wasn't that alone,' he said. 'It was the violence used, so Ned says.'

Maria's eyes opened in disbelief. 'Violence!'

'Don't look so bloody shocked, woman. We were stealing, weren't we?' Barney yelled. 'What do you think they were going to do, these people set to guard the stuff, stand at the door and hand it out? They had to be put out of action. I never had a hand in it so don't look at me like that. Maybe I should have done, because the man that dealt with most of the security men, P.J., seemed to take pleasure in laying them out and often went too far.'

'I can't believe that you are talking so calmly about this.'

'But you never did understand it, did you, Maria?' Barney said. Then, wanting to wound someone as he had been wounded, he added, 'I tell you, there were many women, even girls, in Dublin more appreciative of me and the money I had to splash about than you.'

'What do you mean?' Maria asked, though she knew full well what Barney meant and she was angry, suddenly furiously, blisteringly angry. But she was living in her uncle's house, and this was between her and Barney alone, so she hissed her heated reply in a whisper. 'Well, I suggest you go back to them. If you have slept with whores and prostitutes, you'll not get near me in bed again.'

The slap took her by surprise and she put a hand to her face and looked at Barney in sudden fear. He'd been rough with her at times in the past, but had never hit her. Now the violence seemed to emanate from him, could almost be felt coursing through his whole body, and his fists were balled at his side.

She knew if she said anything, anything at all, she could be at the receiving end of any further slap or punch. When he put his face close to hers, she would have recoiled if he hadn't held on to her. 'Now,' he said, 'I am going downstairs to have a wash and then I am going out to get very, very drunk. Oh,' he added, 'a word of warning. You mention one word of what has happened in this bedroom tonight and it will be the worse for you. Do I make myself clear?'

Abundantly, Maria could have said, but she was still too nervous to speak so she just nodded.

'Good girl,' Barney said mockingly. 'I knew you'd see sense.'

Maria was so shocked she just sat on in that freezing bedroom until she heard the front door slam and knew that Barney had gone. She examined her face in the dressing table mirror and applied a little powder over it before going downstairs herself, her head still reeling with the things she had heard that evening and her husband's reaction to them.

The dinner was on the table and though Maria knew that Sean and Martha would be curious about the contents of the letter, she also knew that they wouldn't appreciate her talking about in front of the children so it had to wait. In the end, Maria told Martha as she washed up in the kitchen.

'Ten years,' Martha repeated. 'No wonder Barney was so upset. I've never seen him in such a tear. Where has he gone now?'

'I'll give you one guess,' Maria said. 'It's the way many men deal with things.'

'He's going out to get drunk?'

'You've got it in one.'

'Look,' Martha said tentatively, 'you can tell me to mind my own business if you like, but has anything happened to your face?'

Maria looked at Martha levelly and said, 'For your own good and mine, mind your own business, Martha.'

'But, Maria . . .'

Maria sighed. 'At the moment Barney is wanting to lash out at anyone, or anything. He was shocked to the core at his brother's sentence, and I got in the way of it tonight, that's all,' Maria said. 'He has never laid a hand on me before. It will probably never happen again, and if it does, then I will deal with it.'

'You are sure there is nothing that Sean or I can do for you?'

'Nothing at all, honestly, but thank you for asking and for being concerned,' Maria said. She just hoped the reassurances she had given Martha so glibly would be the way it was from now on, for she would become no willing punch bag for any man.

Maria was awakened that night by Barney's drunken stumbles around the room as he attempted to get ready for bed. She had no idea of the time, but she knew it was late, very late, and she made no sign that she was awake, but still lay curled in a ball, although she stiffened as he slid in beside her and she realised he was naked.

And then his hands were upon her – big, brutal

336

hands, pawing at her. Mindful of the sleeping baby at the foot of the bed, Maria hissed, 'Leave me be, you drunken lout.'

'Leave you be,' Barney repeated in a thick, slurred voice. 'You are my wife, woman.'

'Aye, fool that I am,' Maria spat out. 'Did that slip your mind when you were in Dublin?'

'Enough of this,' Barney said impatiently. 'You promised to obey me, so let's have your legs open and,' he added, 'we'll have this off.' Taking hold of the neck of her nightdress, he ripped it right down the front.

Maria gasped, and then he was on top of her, pinning her arms to her sides with his knees, pummelling her breasts so roughly and painfully she bit on her bottom lip to stop herself crying out.

'Barney, for pity's sake,' she pleaded at last.

'Shut up!' Barney said. 'Seamus always said you had it your own way for far too long and now I am going to teach you what happens if you ever refuse me.'

He slid further down the bed as he spoke, forcing her legs wide open with his. His lips fastened on hers, and he pushed his thick tongue into her mouth till she felt she might choke. He twisted her hair painfully with one hand so that she was unable to move while the other powered a punch between her legs. The pain was excruciating, and when Barney punched her again she threshed so much in the bed, she was able to tear her lips from his. Oh, how she wanted to scream in pain at the outrage, the assault on her body, but all she would allow herself was a low moan.

Barney, however, seemed well satisfied. 'I'll bet you'll

337

never try refusing me again,' he said. 'For if you do, you'll get more of the same.'

She moaned again when Barney entered her. There didn't seem one bit of her body that didn't ache or throb and she just waited for him to be finished with her. When he eventually did, and rolled off, almost immediately falling into a semi-stupor, relief made Maria cry. She cried not only for the pain she was in, she also cried for the man she had married. He'd always been self-centred, work-shy and not totally honest, but the man who lay beside her in the bed was like a raging beast and she was frightened of him.

She was frightened of staying with him and yet frightened of leaving him, with nowhere to go if she did. She knew if she tried to do that Barney would likely take revenge on the wife who dared to shame him in such a way. Not even Uncle Sean could protect her totally day in and day out.

Anyway, how could she tell her uncle? How could she tell anyone, least of all a man, what Barney had done to her? She'd die of embarrassment. She knew too for a Catholic wife actually to leave her husband was a dreadful thing, a disgrace. The shame of it would impinge on Sean and Martha too, and the priests would take a very dim view of it altogether.

She had thought fiercely that she wouldn't stay around to be anyone's punch bag, but she was beginning to realise that there were few alternatives open to her.

Next morning Barney couldn't be roused. In the end Sean came into the room and threw cold water over him. He gave a yell that wakened Sally and she started to cry.

'Come on, you!' Sean shouted at Barney. 'Out of that bed! I spoke for you to get you this job and you are not making a monkey out of me by not turning in because you had a skinful last night.'

Barney looked dreadful. He got to his feet, but stood swaying, holding on to the bedpost. 'I don't think I can.'

Sean wasn't a big man, but he seemed to grow in stature as he said fiercely, 'You'll go, my lad, if you have the toe of my boot up your arse every step of the way.'

'I'm going to be sick.'

'Then be sick and be quick about it.'

As Barney rushed past them, Sean looked at Maria, who was now sitting nursing the child, and asked, 'Are you all right?'

She wanted to cry that she wasn't. She felt as if her hair had been pulled out by the roots and she knew that one of her lips was split for she'd felt it with her tongue and tasted the blood in her mouth. As for her breasts, they ached so much she wanted to fold her arms around them but she couldn't do that for her arms were bruised all down the length of them. She'd had to bite her lip against the pain in her arms as she lifted Sally, but the real throbbing, unrelenting pain was between her legs. She could barely walk and every step was agonising. She really didn't know how she was to get through the day.

And yet she was able to smile at her uncle and say, 'I'm fine.'

'You look white, strained.'

'I'm grand,' she assured him. 'It's the light. We only use the table lamp when Barney gets up, to avoid waking the baby.'

And how glad she was they devised that system. If Sean had seen the state of her clearly, he would demand answers to questions that would surely backfire on her with dire consequences. When her husband and uncle were gone, she would dress, thanking God that it was winter and her clothes long-sleeved, and she would try to repair the damage to her face before facing Martha.

She stayed in the bedroom till she heard the children leave for school, for she knew they would notice and comment. Martha wondered about her absence, for she was always up early, but she understood when she caught sight of her.

'God Almighty, I don't have to ask what happened to you.'

'Then don't.'

'Maria, you can't go on like this. Men can't get away with things these days. Sean will—'

'Sean mustn't know a thing about it.'

'Don't be silly!'

'I'm not being silly,' Maria cried. 'Do you think I like my husband behaving like a bullying brute, displaying the results of his handiwork for all to see. You haven't see the half of what he did to me in that room last night and, yes, I am bloody terrified of him now but I would be more scared of what he would do to me if Sean was to go for him. Would Sean be able to stand guard in my bedroom all night?'

'We can't just stand by and see it happen and do nothing.'

'That's exactly what you can and must do, because I am the victim in this,' Maria declared. 'And this is what I want because in the long run I think it would be the wisest course of action.'

'Isn't there anything I can do?'

'Just let me get on with the dress for Patsy,' Maria said. 'To tell you the truth, all movement is painful, but sewing always soothes me.'

'I have no problem with that,' Martha said. 'And before the children come home I will try and do something more with your face, but you'd better be ready with some reason why you look like you have done ten rounds in the boxing ring. Oh, that's better,' she said, seeing the ghost of a smile on Maria's battered face.

'Bless you, Martha,' Maria said.

She was incredibly nervous of seeing Barney that evening. She still could scarcely believe the way he had violated her and how cruel he had been, and she didn't know how she was going to be even civil to the man.

But when Barney arrived home from work that evening, he was so exhausted he hadn't more than a grunt for anyone and took himself to bed straight after he'd eaten. Maria was nervous when she joined him, but Barney was not even the slightest bit disturbed by her getting in beside him and lay so deeply asleep that, except for the rising and falling of his chest, he might have been dead.

Martha lay in her bed, wide awake, long after Sean had fallen asleep, and worried about Maria. Through the day, she'd noticed the stiff, slow way she moved and the odd grimace or wince when she thought no one was looking. At least Sean had noticed nothing amiss.

Over the next few days, as Maria's injuries got easier to bear, it became obvious to her that Barney was going to make no reference at all to that night. She began to wonder if he had any recollection of it at all. In the end, she decided to put the attack out of her mind. He had had distressing news that day, had got extremely drunk and really wasn't himself at all. That was that.

Patsy had her new dress, her first grown-up dress, and it fitted her like a glove. She tried it on in front of the mirror, admiring the way it fell over her budding bust. It had a dropped waistline and the skirt fell in soft folds. The material felt lovely against her skin.

She was so pleased with the dress that she examined her relationship with Barney and for a moment felt guilty. But then she thought, how is it hurting Maria, being friends with her husband? And decided it wasn't at all.

However, to make up somewhat as the Christmas holidays had begun, she offered to mind Sally as often as Maria wanted so that she could get on with making things for the others, knowing Maria wanted them all to have something new for Christmas.

Maria was grateful for the help and pleased the Patsy didn't seem to hate her so much. She set to with a will, going back to the Bull Ring one morning on her own to get more material, together with buttons, zips and hook-and-eye fastenings. She'd already made everyday things for the boys and a dress for Martha in Wedgwood blue trimmed with white. Martha was so overcome when she tried the dress on that she cried and declared it to be the prettiest dress she had ever had.

Sean wasn't surprised at what his niece could do, for he had seen evidence of her work before, but he was pleased she'd thought to make new clothes for everyone.

'I could book us all for the pantomime on Boxing Day,' Sean confided to Martha. 'The Hippodrome is showing *Aladdin* and it would be a way of saying thank you to Maria, but someone would have to baby-sit.'

'I bet Patsy wouldn't mind,' Martha said. 'She probably feels she's too old for pantomimes.'

'What are you talking about?' Sean said. 'You are never too old for pantomimes.'

'When you are nearly fifteen, you have all sorts of mad notions.' Martha said.

He laughed. 'When I was fifteen, I was working my fingers to the bone on the farm. I had neither time nor energy to have notions of any kind – mad or otherwise. But you are right: Patsy might not care for it at all. I'll ask her and see what she says. I can bet Barney won't come either. Not that he would be any good at looking after the babies, even if he was willing.'

'I'd hesitate to leave them with him if he was,' Martha said. 'On Boxing Day he will likely be in no fit state anyway.'

'You could be right there,' Sean said. 'God Almighty, the man can knock it back, all right, and the gambling fair takes my breath away. The money that is put on the table is often more that I earn in a week.'

'How does Barney afford it?'

Sean shrugged. 'I asked him that and he said he wins some and he loses some.' He looked at Martha and went on, 'It's Maria I feel for. I have met gamblers who would sell their own grandmother to get a stake. I know one man who lost the roof over his head, and that of his wife and family too, at the turn of the cards. Has Maria confided in you at all?'

Martha nearly told Sean then about the beating that Barney had given Maria. She wasn't used to keeping things from him, but she remembered Maria's frightened face and she had made a promise to her, so she said, 'No, she's not said a word to me.'

Patsy said it was no bother to baby-sit and she thought the pantomime rather babyish. Sean hid a smile and thought that Martha had read her daughter well. Barney had gone out for a drink before the family left, but Patsy knew he wouldn't stay there all night. By the time he returned, she had put both babies to bed, changed into her Christmas dress and dabbed the Californian Poppy perfume that Maria had given her for Christmas behind her ears and daringly between her breasts. Her friend Chloë said it was THE place to put it.

Barney was certainly appreciative and he pulled her into his arm as she opened the door. 'God, you smell delicious.' He kissed her gently on the mouth. 'Have I got a surprise for you,' he said, and he drew a bottle of port from his pocket. 'You mix it with lemonade, and most ladies prefer it to beer.'

Patsy found she too loved the taste of port and lemon, and downed the first two Barney gave her like pop. Barney told her to slow down. She didn't know there could be so much pleasure to be had from the feel of someone's arms tight around you, or snuggling together smoking and sipping away at a drink while listening to music on the wireless or talking together. It was such a grown-up thing to do, and the time seemed to slip by. She drank more and more of the port, having taken a real liking to it.

'It's a pity we can't go out in the evening properly,' Barney said eventually, his arm around Patsy.

'We can,' she said, wondering why the words seemed so hard to say. Her tongue seemed to have swollen to twice its size and her whole mouth seemed sort of wobbly, but she persevered. 'I'm allowed to go to the youth club after Christmas and I don't . . . don't have . . . don't . . .'

'Barney laughed. 'You, my dear girl, are drunk, very drunk. I told you not to knock back those drinks so fast. I know what you are trying to say, but just now you have to get to bed, and quick, before they come back and see you in this state.'

Barney pulled her to her feet, where she swayed and would have fallen if he hadn't held her. He very much wanted to carry her up the stairs and make love to her and he knew she would be in no fit state to stop him, but he hadn't any contraceptives and what would happen if she became pregnant and named him? Sean would kill him without thinking about it, he knew. So instead he sat Patsy down on a dining chair, brought her a big glass of water and forced her to drink it. It made her feel only moderately better but she was able to stagger and stumble her way up the stairs.

Barney washed and put away Patsy's glass, emptied the ashtray and hid the bottle of port in his wardrobe. He was only just in time. He heard them coming in the door as he was pouring himself a beer.

'Where's Patsy?' Martha asked.

'She's gone to bed,' Barney said. 'I told her to. She was yawning her head off and I was in early tonight and I said I'd wait until you came in.'

'That's not like her at all,' Martha said with a frown. 'I hope she's not sickening for something. I best look in. Would you put the kettle on, Sean, and I'll make a bit of supper for these tired boys?'

'I ain't tired,' complained Tony. 'It was Paul went to sleep on the bus.'

'I never.'

'Yes, you did.'

'No, I never.'

'You did so.'

'That will do, you two,' Sean said firmly. 'I don't care if you're tired or not. I am tired and that means you have to go to bed, because you both wear me out.'

'It ain't fair we have to go to bed because you are tired,' Tony declared.

'Tony, it's way past your bedtime anyway.'

'But I ain't sleepy yet.'

Martha came into the room then and said, 'You're overtired, that's what's the matter with you. Patsy has more sense. She is dead to the world up there, whereas you two are like a couple of weasels, so don't spoil a nice night. I am going to do you a slice of dripping toast each and a cup of cocoa and then you are going to go to bed with no argument.'

346

Tony looked across at Paul and he shrugged. They both knew to their cost that when their mother spoke in a certain way, the wisest course by far was just to agree.

Maria was tired too, but when Barney drained his glass and suggested going to bed, she said, 'I'm all for it, but I'll have to feed Sally first.'

'Well, let's go up, anyway,' Barney said. He felt as if he was on fire, and he barely let Maria in through the door before he was stripping her clothes off her.

'Barney, the baby,' Maria said, for Sally was beginning to stir, but Barney was far too worked up to wait any longer and he pushed Maria down on the bed.

She found it hard to get aroused, or enjoy the act itself, when in the background Sally had started to moan and grumble. Then began the ear-splitting wails that demanded attention. Maria lay under Barney and wondered what Sean and Martha would think of her, just leaving her baby to cry.

CHAPTER NINETEEN

Patsy woke next morning with a raging thirst, a feeling of nausea and the thought that ten thousand hammers were pounding inside her head. In fact, she felt ill, really ill. She could never recall feeling so bad.

Martha looking in on her daughter later, took in the flushed face and the way her eyes were screwed against the light, and suggested she have the day in bed. She took her up her breakfast with a couple of aspirins, convinced she was coming down with something. Patsy did have a pang of guilt at having her mother fuss around her, but she did feel far too ill to get up.

By lunch time she'd begun to feel a little bit better, but it was coming up to teatime before she felt able to get up.

'It must have been one of those twenty-four-hour things,' Martha said later, as the family sat eating the evening meal. 'I mean, Patsy is fine now, but this morning she looked like death warmed up. I really did think she was getting flu or something. Once that gets in the house, it goes round everyone like a dose of salts.'

Barney met Patsy's eye across the table. Both of them knew it was no flu she had, and they shared a special secretive smile. No one noticed it but Maria, and she told herself that she had imagined it.

'We always said we would go to the youth club together,' Chloë grumbled in the school yard that raw January day. 'We've talked about it for ages.'

'I know, but it's my only chance of getting out for the evening,' Patsy said. 'Go on, Chloë. I'd do it for you.'

'I really hope that you know what you are doing. This Barney must be an old man.'

'No, he's not,' Patsy said. 'But he is a man, not some pimply boy acting daft in front of his mates. He's really handsome too,' she added dreamily.

'And related.'

'No, he's not, not really. Only through marriage.'

'Yeah, and that's it, isn't it? The man is married.'

'I know that, but we're just friends,' Patsy maintained.

'Oh, yeah,' Chloë said sarcastically. 'Were you born yesterday? A man like that doesn't want a friend.'

'He does,' Patsy said. 'He treats me like I am really grown up. He gives me cigarettes and everything.'

'You smoke?' Chloë squealed. To her, smoking was the ultimate in sophistication and she couldn't wait till she could start herself. 'Does your mother know?'

'Don't talk daft. Course not, but as Barney says, he does and Sean does, but I bet Sean would throw a dickey fit if I just lit up.'

'What's it like?'

'Good,' Patsy said. 'I didn't like it much to start

with, but I stuck at it and it makes me feel great now. Calms you down and everything. Mind you, I don't row like I used to, and that was Barney too. He said if I offered to do things and stuff like that – model daughter, you know – then they would give me more freedom and he was right. As he said, they don't really care about me now they have Deirdre, especially Sean. I mean, he's bound to think more of his own daughter than someone else's. Before I had Barney as a friend that used to upset me and make me angry, but now I don't care that much and if I do get het up, I get out of the house and have a fag.'

'God, Patsy,' Chloë said enviously.

'I drink too when I am with Barney,' Patsy said, rubbing it in. 'He buys me port and lemon.' No need to tell Chloë she'd only had it the once. 'He's taking me to the pub tonight, as a matter of fact. He plays poker and they have a card school there. He's taught me to play poker, but he says I must only watch, no women play poker in the pubs. It would be frowned on.

'And I'll tell you one thing: Maria has never been to watch him play. Barney says she never has shown an interest in any of his pastimes and isn't that the very thing it tells you a woman should do in that *Woman's Weekly* magazine your mother has?'

Chloë nodded. She couldn't deny it. When her mother finished with the magazine, she would give it to Chloë. She'd often bring it to school and she and Patsy would read it avidly together. It had tips on a woman making the most of herself and many ways of making a man happy. Both Chloë and Patsy decided they wanted to be model wives when their turn came, and that article about taking an interest in your man's hobbies was in the issue just before Christmas.

'Why doesn't she?'

Patsy shrugged. 'Barney said she doesn't approve of cards. She's proper prissy about it. He doesn't have much of a life with her really. He says she's a terrible nag.'

'Well, you never took to her, did you?'

'No . . . ,' Patsy said. But she said it slowly for she was finding it hard to keep the animosity alive when Maria was so good about making her some decent clothes. She had made her a new navy skirt already, and was going to knock up a few blouses to go with it, she said, but Patsy didn't tell Chloë that.

The pub that night was everything that Patsy could have dreamt of in terms of excitement. Mindful of last time, Barney told Patsy to stick to orange, and that is what she told the first man who offered to buy her a drink, but unbeknownst to Patsy, the man had vodka added to it and any time after that, if a man said the drink was for the little lady the barman added a shot of vodka.

Barney was much too engrossed with the cards to notice, and Patsy, knowing the rudiments of the game, was almost as agitated as Barney. She was glad he had left his pack of cigarettes on the table so that she could just help herself without disturbing him. She sat so close their knees touched and she felt a thrill of exhilaration running through him, his face tight in concentration, his brow puckered so that his eyebrows met across the bridge of his nose. As the stakes were raised, and more money thrown into the pile, the excitement was at fever pitch.

Barney was lucky that night and he came away with a wodge of money. 'Come on,' he said to Patsy. 'It's nearly closing time anyway, and I have to get you home.'

Patsy obediently tried to get to her feet, but staggered and quickly sat back down again.

'How much have you had to drink?' Barney asked.

Patsy had no idea. Drinks had been pushed into her hand all night. 'Lots,' she said, starting to giggle, 'but only orange juice.'

'Like hell it was,' Barney said, fastening Patsy's coat around her. 'Let's hope the walk home sobers you up some, or we are for the high jump.'

Barney held her tight against him as they walked and when he felt her burrowing closer, he led her to an alleyway off Mason Road, took her in his arms and kissed her, teasing her mouth open. When his tongue began darting in and out of her mouth she felt strong urges begin in her body – so strong they frightened her and she pushed Barney away.

'What's up?' Barney said, puzzled.

'It's just . . . well, we are just friends, aren't we?'

'Of course.'

Patsy was embarrassed and she hoped Barney would not be cross, or think her silly, but she went on anyway, 'The thing is, I don't think that sort of kiss is for friends.'

'Well, you sure as damn don't give it to your enemies.'

'I know, but . . .' Patsy couldn't explain that that sort of kiss stirred up feelings in her that she could barely understand, but knew she shouldn't have for

Barney. She liked cuddling up tight or holding Barney's hand, and had no objection to a kiss on the cheek or lips, but she didn't want to go further than that.

Barney looked at her in exasperation. She was very young and totally inexperienced so he decided he would play it her way for now. 'Come on then,' he said. 'Let's make for home.'

'You aren't cross with me, are you?'

'No, I'm not cross with you.'

'It's just, well, it doesn't seem right.'

'I know, you said.'

'You are cross.'

'I'm not cross,' Barney said. 'It's just that you're so scared of things. How will it hurt Maria if you and I have a bit of fun together?'

'I suppose it won't, but . . .'

'There is always a but with you, Patsy. How do you feel about sex?'

'What do you mean?'

'Would you go all the way with someone?'

'Of course I would, when I was married.'

'Not before?'

'Oh, no,' Patsy said. 'I couldn't do anything like that.'

'Why is that?' Barney asked. 'Is it because the Church says so?'

'Partly, and there's the fear of getting pregnant,'

'Oh, there's things can be done to prevent pregnancy,' Barney said airily. 'As for the other, what do celibate priests know about desires of the body? If two people want to have sex together, what harm does it do?'

Patsy had never ever heard a viewpoint like this

expressed before. 'Have you done that,' she asked, 'had sex with other women?'

'Aye.'

'Lots of women?'

'A fair few, aye.'

Patsy wanted to ask him if he'd had sex with others since he'd married Maria and if they still had sex together, but felt those things were too personal to ask.

They'd nearly reached the house and Barney stopped and held out his arms. 'Come here.'

Patsy went willingly and Barney kissed her, but made no effort to do anything else and Patsy was able to relax.

He gave her a peppermint and said, 'Now listen, suck hard on that and, for God's sake, unless you want this to be the last time we do this, concentrate on walking in a straight line and talking without slurring your words. Now go in and tell them how marvellous the youth club was.'

'What about you?'

'Well, we can hardly go in together.'

'No,' Patsy said, and noted the fact that Barney didn't say what he was going to do. She had no right to ask either. She was so relieved when she got in that Sean and her mother had gone to bed for she felt decidedly odd and knew her mother would have cottoned on straight away. But there was no one about to see her staggering up the stairs.

Martha wasn't asleep. She called out as Patsy passed the door, 'That you, Patsy?'

Patsy concentrated on keeping any suggestion of

slur out of her voice as she answered, 'Yes, Mom. Tell you all about it in the morning.'

Chloë wanted a blow-by-blow account the next day, when she called round so that they could go to the library together. Patsy gave her an edited version of the evening, but it sounded terribly exciting to Chloë, who had had a fairly dull night at the youth club.

'I am seeing Barney on Sunday afternoon as well,' she said.

'What about choir practice?'

'What about it?' Patsy said. 'I'm not going. I am going to the pictures instead.'

'The nuns will go mad.'

'No they won't, not if I tell them I've given up choir to concentrate on my studies,' Patsy said. 'They'll want as many to matriculate as possible next year and I bet you they won't say a word about it.'

'Got it all thought out, haven't you?' Chloë said glumly. 'Where does all this leave me? We're supposed to be friends.'

'We are friends.'

'Yeah, seems to me you would rather be with that bloody Barney than me.'

'Don't be silly,' Patsy said, but she knew Chloë was right: she wanted to be near Barney at every opportunity and she really couldn't care less about anyone else.

When Patsy asked her mother a month or so later if it was all right for her to go to Chloë's house a couple of nights a week to get her homework done, Martha had no suspicions.

'It's obvious they will get more done there,' she told Sean. 'After all, Chloë just has the one sister and she is away at university most of the time.'

In late February, Barney had started visiting his brother in Mountjoy Prison at the weekend every few weeks. He'd been writing to Seamus every week as soon as he got his address, and Seamus had asked if Barney would come and see him now he considered it was safe for him to do so. Maria could hardly object, for the brothers only had each other, but Barney was always harder to handle when he got home from these visits on Sunday night. He was usually quite drunk and belligerent too. That alone made Maria nervous, but he didn't ever do anything remotely like he had the day he got the letter from Ned.

'Where did you stay?' Maria asked Barney the first time, for he would take the train late on Friday night, catch the early morning ferry and arrive in Dublin mid-morning. He would see his brother that afternoon, stay the night and return on Sunday.

Barney stared at Maria and said, 'You don't really want to know that, nor do you need to know it.'

Maria knew then he had been with some woman and she felt cheap and shoddy. What should she do – rant and rave, forbid him do such a thing and shame her in this way? Would it change Barney's behaviour at all? No, she knew it wouldn't and at least she could give herself the dignity of never asking that question again. Later, when Martha asked the same thing, Maria was able to meet her gaze steadily and in a controlled voice say his brother had had lots of contacts in the city and Barney lodged with one of those.

Barney felt guilty every time he saw his brother, knowing that if it hadn't been for Seamus, he could well be in an adjoining cell. There was a young girl, barely older than Patsy, who would be waiting for Barney after his prison visit, and who was only too willing to accommodate him and make him feel better about himself.

Every Sunday night of Barney's return, Maria would empty his bag and smell the cheap perfume on his clothes and sometimes see the mark of lipstick on his shirt collars. She would say not a word about it and hide them from Martha's eyes, knowing she would never understand.

Maria wasn't the only one to hate Barney going to see his brother. Patsy did too. She had neglected Chloë too much to seek her friendship the weekends that Barney was in Ireland. In case there was any doubt of this, Chloë told her straight: 'You can't just pick me up and drop me again like some old rubbing rag, and don't think you can. You don't want me when lover boy is around and I don't want you when he isn't. You made your choice.'

Patsy could hardly blame her, if she was honest, but it did make the weekends a bit of a lonely time. She did go to the youth club on Friday because her mother would have thought it odd if she didn't, and it was moderately better than walking up and down the length of Erdington High Street, where, anyway, she was bound to be spotted and notice brought to it at home.

However, she could hardy just turn up at choir practice and she had to skulk about until it was time to go home. She gave the excuse she had a test to revise for or an essay to write as the reason she hadn't gone back to Chloë's after choir. In actual fact she did get more done those weekends because there was little else to do. At least that was a good thing, for she gave scant regard to her studies when Barney was around

Spring gave way to early summer and when Patsy asked if she might go to the odd concert with Chloë in the city centre, neither Martha nor Sean could see anything wrong with it. As Sean said, 'The girl works hard enough' and he upped her pocket money so that she could pay for the things she wanted to do. Patsy felt a heel as she took the money each week.

She didn't really need it. Barney or his friends supplied her with cigarettes and booze, and she needed little else. While Barney had taken her to the cinema a few times and the theatre once, mainly he took her to pubs where he would play poker. She would share in the excitement and get happily tipsy, glad that when she got home late Sean and Martha had gone to bed.

In late June, Paul made his First Holy Communion and Maria made him a new white shirt and grey trousers for it. He was as proud as punch, being nearly the best dressed there, for not everyone had such a skilled dress-maker in their house. In August, she made matching dresses for Deirdre and Sally, but in different colours, for their shared first birthday party. The two looked as pretty as a picture.

Everyone was always grateful, but in many ways it also helped Maria. Barney, never an easy man, had got more difficult since they had come to Birmingham, and going to see his brother made him worse. Barney wanted and expected the water for his wash to be ready when he was in from work and then for the meal to be on the table. The clothes he dropped on the bedroom floor he wanted washed, ironed and put away so he could just put his hand on them, and he wanted his wife waiting to satisfy him when he rolled in from the pub.

Sean and Martha viewed all this with concern, but if they asked Maria if there were any problems, or whether she wanted to talk, she always said she was fine. She had often thought that if she could get Barney away from his brother, their marriage might have a chance, but that hadn't happened and she often felt a failure as a wife. Making something good out of someone else's cast-offs gave her back some of her self-esteem.

The good summer eventually drew to a close and autumn was heralded in with gusty winds and extreme cold, that ensured snow before Christmas. The children were ecstatic. That snow was to herald in the worst winter in living memory, but no one knew that then. The adults viewed the snow apprehensively but stoically, knowing that it never lay long in Birmingham, while the children at least had a great time.

There was crisp snow on the ground on Christmas morning, for the previous day's fall had frozen overnight. Both Martha and Maria thought it too cold to take the babies out. 'Anyway,' Martha said, 'the pram will be the very devil to push in this.'

'I'll stay here and go to a later Mass,' Sean said.

'No, I will,' said Patsy. 'You should be together at Christmas.'

'If you are sure . . .'

'Course I am.'

'Do me a favour then, Patsy, and give Barney a shout in about half an hour, will you?' Maria said. 'And I'll have another go when I come home. He must have one hell of a hangover from the state he was in last night, but if he doesn't get up, he will miss Mass altogether.'

Patsy decided she wouldn't just call him, but take him a cup of tea. She remembered how thirsty she had been the first and last time she'd had a hangover of any significance. She quite often felt delicate in the mornings now, and sometimes queasy, or might have a bit of a headache, but nothing like that first time. But before she could do this there were the babies to see to, and they were more of a handful now that they were both on the move. She gave them both a drink and a biscuit, threw a load of toys into the large playpen Sean had bought to keep them safe, and left them both in there while she took the cup of tea to Barney.

He took some time to rouse. When at last he opened his eyes he shut them tight against the light. 'Jesus, dammit, what are you at, shaking me like that?'

'Barney, it's me, Patsy.'

'I don't give a holy shit who it is.'

Barney had never spoken to Pasty in that way before and she was taken aback, but she remembered how she had felt and said, 'I've brought you some tea.'

That brought Barney's bleary eyes open again and slowly he pushed himself up in the bed. Patsy saw with a little consternation that, on his top half anyway, he was bare. He had a mass of black hair on his chest.

Barney saw her discomfort, but made no comment on it. Instead, he took the cup from her, drained the scalding liquid with a couple of good swallows, and wiped his mouth with the back of his hand as he put the cup on the table by the bed. 'God, that was a life saver.'

He patted the bed. 'Why don't you sit down?'

Maria was nervous and she ran her tongue over her lips. 'Better not.'

Before she could do a thing about it, Barney's arm shot out. He grasped her hand and gave a tug so that she fell onto the bed in a heap. Barney was becoming frustrated with Patsy. He'd been taking her out for almost a year and was no further forward with her, and he didn't intend to wait much longer. He had decided by the New Year he wanted to have shown Patsy what she had been missing all this time and this was a heaven-sent opportunity.

Still holding her hand, he began to massage it gently between his fingers. 'There,' he said huskily. 'That's better, isn't it?'

Patsy nearness was arousing him so much, he thought if she could see beneath the covers she would be scared to death. As it was, Patsy was realising it had been foolish to come into Barney's bedroom. The look in his eyes was frightening her a little.

'I have to go,' she said, trying to get up, but Barney didn't let go of her.

'Not yet awhile,' he said. 'Can't I have a kiss for Christmas?'

'Barney, I—'

'Just one little Christmas kiss?' Barney pleaded. 'It's

361

not much to ask, especially as I am feeling like death. Come on, I need cheering up.'

Thinking she would humour him, Patsy bent her head and when their lips touched it was as if an explosion happened in Barney. He grabbed Patsy and pulled her on top of him while he kissed her in a frenzy of desire, his tongue darting in and out of her mouth. She fought him at first and then she was kissing him back, hardly aware what she was doing, for strange yearnings were flooding Patsy's whole being. She didn't understand them fully, but knew she didn't want them to stop.

'Ah Patsy, Patsy,' Barney said, releasing her lips at last. 'I have wanted this so much, and for so long. I'll never hurt you, so don't worry.'

'What are you talking about?' Patsy asked, still breathless from the kiss.

'You just slip in here beside me.' Barney said, moving the covers over, 'and, God, I'll transport you to Paradise.'

Patsy was on her feet in an instant. 'Barney, I couldn't do that. How can you even suggest such a thing?'

'You want it as much as me, if you would only listen to your own body,' Barney snapped. 'The kiss said as much.'

'Yeah, well, the kiss was a mistake.'

'Some mistake.' Barney said, grabbing at her suddenly and yanking her into the bed beside him. He was totally naked – she soon realised that – and he pushed her hand down on to his stiff and throbbing penis, just as Sally let out one of her ear-splitting yells.

Patsy was feeling sick and dirty. She had never seen

a man's penis, let alone held one in her hand, but Barney's mouth was covering hers, one arm surrounding her so she was unable to pull away. His tongue was darting teasing her mouth. With a sense of horror she felt herself responding. Her hand was being pushed up and down Barney's penis and she heard him groaning.

She stiffened. What the hell was she doing, she thought, and the next moment she was fighting like a wild cat. She tore her mouth from Barney's and bit the hand that tried to restrain her.

He gave a yell. 'What the hell, you bloody little sod!' he cried, looking at the blood dripping on to the coverlet before sticking his injured hand in his mouth.

'Leave me alone,' Patsy demanded. 'Let me go.' Barney's attention was centred on his throbbing hand and he had relaxed his grip on Patsy. She pulled her hand away and brought her knee up sharp. He gave a moan of pain, but when Patsy tried to get out of the bed, her legs got tangled in the covers and Barney was able to grab her again as she struggled.

'By God, you'll pay for that, you little tiger,' he said, and slapped her hard across the face with the hand she had bitten. Patsy opened her mouth and screamed as loud as she possibly could.

'Shut up, for Christ's sake,' Barney shouted over the noise, knowing such sustained screaming would eventually arouse the notice of the neighbours. 'Give over. I've not touched you yet.'

Patsy continued to scream and then she suddenly yanked her hand. Taken unawares it slipped from Barney's grasp and then she was off the bed, out of the room and down the stairs with the speed of light.

She pulled Sally, awash with tears, red with temper and still crying, from the playpen. Sobbing herself in panic and fear, she went into the kitchen and picked up the carving knife, fully intending to let Barney have it if he came after her.

However, the skirmish with Patsy had taken it out of the hungover Barney and his hand was throbbing. He swung his legs out of bed and sat there for a minute or two, waiting for the tilting room to right itself and the dizziness in his head to ease, before making his groggy and shambling way to the bathroom where he vomited over and over. He was in no state to pursue anyone.

Maria felt herself soothed by the familiarity of the Mass that morning, the Latin words and responses that she had known from childhood, interspersed with beautiful carols. It had been just what she had needed after Barney's assault on her body the night before, when he had been so rough and unfeeling she knew she would be bruised in many places, and had been feeling depressed by the whole scenario.

Outside they were greeted by many, and were making for home when Martha was hailed by Chloë's mother.

'How is dear Patsy getting on?' she asked.

Martha laughed. 'I should think you could tell me that,' she said. 'She's at your house more than she is at her own.'

Chloë's mother looked a little stunned. 'At our house?' she repeated. 'You must be mistaken. Patsy hasn't been to our house in months.'

Now it was Maria's turn to look stunned. 'You

mean she doesn't come round to do her homework a couple of nights a week?'

'No, as I said . . .'

Maria, seeing that there were problems that were probably not for the boys' ears, began to walk on with then. They were just as anxious to get home, for laid out on their bedroom floor was the train set Santa had left. At least Paul knew it was Santa and though Tony had his doubts, a train set was still a train set and it was just begging to be played with.

Sean, beside Martha, watched them walk out of earshot before he said, 'Have they gone to concerts a time or two, or to the pictures?'

'Not together. Chloë is mixing with a completely different set these days.'

'Where is she?' Martha said. 'We will ask her.'

'She isn't here. She was in the choir at Midnight Mass, but your Patsy has given that up too, so Chloë was telling me. Said she needed time for her studies. Commendable, if a little sad. My dear, are you all right?' she said, seeing the colour suddenly drain from Martha's face.

'She's fine,' Sean said. 'It's the fasting and the cold.'

'Of course,' said Chloë's mother soothingly, but she knew that was not what had so upset Martha. It was because her daughter had been deceiving them. Why should a girl do that unless she was up to no good? She scurried home, anxious to regale her husband with this juicy snippet of gossip. She'd pump Chloë too, she decided, and find out just how much she knew.

Martha's mind was screaming denial and yet she knew that what Chloë's mother had said had been true.

So where had Patsy been all those times she was supposed to be with Chloe, and who with? These were the questions to be asked. As soon as Martha was in the door, she told Patsy she wanted to see her in her room.

The latest encounter with Barney had shaken Patsy and she had begun to realise that Chloë was right. Barney wanted more that mere friendship and she knew exactly what he would have done to her had she not fought him off. The realisation made her feel physically sick. And then her mother was home and attacking her like a raging virago.

Everything was exposed, all the lies and deceit, the very things that Martha came down hard on.

'Who were you with?' she demanded. 'That's what I want to know.'

Patsy knew to be truthful here would not help her case, but she didn't have a plausible lie to hand and so she shrugged. Martha grabbed her shoulders and shook her. 'Don't you shrug your shoulders at me, my girl, or I'll give you a good hiding, big as you are. It was some boy, no doubt?'

It was better she believed that, Patsy thought, and she nodded dumbly.

'Name?' Martha rapped out.

Patsy shook her head. 'Don't want to tell you.'

'By Christ, my father would have taken his belt off to me for less than half of what you have got up to.'

Patsy's head shot up. 'You don't know what I have got up to.'

'What I do know is a girl who says she is up at her friend's house, or going out with her when she isn't, is up to mischief of one kind or another. If a boy asked you out and he was a decent, honest boy that you could bring home and introduce properly, then I probably would have had no objection to you seeing him a time or two. But not like this – underhand and secretive. It points to the boy not being at all respectable. I just hope that you have respected yourself and not let this boy take liberties.'

'I have, I mean I haven't,' Patsy said flustered, but the memory of that morning and the kiss that she had responded too so eagerly pushed itself to the forefront of her mind. She blushed with embarrassment and gave a sudden shudder.

Martha saw the flush and the shudder and put a different interpretation on it altogether. She felt for the bed and sat down, for her legs threatened to give way on her. 'Holy Mother of God!' she cried brokenly. 'Have you forgotten everything I have ever taught you?'

Patsy stared at her mother. 'You don't think . . . you can't imagine . . .'

'Patsy, I will ask you this one question,' Martha said. 'Think before you speak and tell me the truth. Did you go with this boy?'

'I don't need to think,' Patsy cried. 'The answer is no! No! No!'

Martha sagged with relief. 'That is the absolute truth?'

Patsy nodded. 'The absolute truth.'

'And you still won't give me this boy's name?'

Patsy shook her head. 'No,' she said. 'But you may as well know I had already decided just today, while you were at Mass, to end it.'

'Good,' Martha said. 'And that would have happened anyway now, because after this performance, my girl, you'll be lucky if you are allowed to put your nose outside the door for some time. Now get ready for Mass and, much as I would love to sit down now to a lovely Christmas breakfast, I will walk with you to the abbey to make sure you get there.'

Patsy was glad her mother was going with her, because she had dreaded meeting up with Barney on the way. She fully intended to dodge him after Mass too, but Sean was waiting for her when she came out of the church.

'Is this how it is going to be from now on?' she asked.

''Fraid so,' Sean said. 'But you brought it on yourself, Patsy, and proper upset your mother. She doesn't deserve this, you know, because she loves you dearly. We both do and I don't know why you ever doubted that.'

Every word was like a hammer blow to Patsy's heart and she was engulfed with shame. She knew now Barney was wrong – wrong about many things – and she had been such a silly little fool to believe him. Both her mother and Sean cared about her, and loving Deirdre too had not changed that. She had let them down badly. She would make it up to them, she decided, and in time maybe they would learn to trust her again.

CHAPTER TWENTY

Barney was soon well aware that somehow Martha had found out that Patsy had been deceiving her, and though he knew Patsy couldn't have involved him, because Martha wasn't the sort to sit on that sort of information and do nothing about it, he still wanted to know exactly what she had said.

However, she was guarded too well and Patsy herself seemed to be steering well clear of any situations when they might be alone together. He supposed that he had really frightened her on Christmas Day.

Patsy actually felt burdened down with guilt and shame, and full of remorse. It was as if blinkers had been removed from her eyes and she saw Barney clearly for the first time. He was a drunk and a liar, not always kind to Maria, and took no notice of his own wee daughter. Patsy castigated herself for the fool she had been. She was very glad the relationship with him had gone no further and deeply regretted that one kiss when she had almost forgotten herself. She was aware that Barney was trying to have a word with her and she knew too that all he cared about was saving his own skin. Well, she thought, he can just sweat. It will do him good.

It was two days after Boxing Day and a Saturday when Martha asked Patsy to fetch the rations from Erdington as both she and Maria had very heavy colds. Patsy wrapped herself up well and had wellingtons on her feet, for the falling snow was being driven by the wind into drifts. It was bitingly cold.

It was as she turned for home that she saw Barney coming towards her and knew she would have to face him. She stepped back to where the overhang of the shop gave her some shelter and where she could put down the bags, which felt like a ton weight.

'You have been avoiding me,' Barney snapped as he drew near.

'What if I have?' Patsy retorted. 'And do you blame me after you attacked me on Christmas morning?'

'Don't give me that,' Barney snarled. 'You came into my bedroom. You knew what you were about and then you got cold feet and now you are turning the blame on me. Anyway, I heard Martha going for you afterwards. How much does she know?'

Patsy sighed. She knew that Barney was right about one thing. She had gone into the bedroom, knowing he was in the bed. Who would ever believe that all she intended giving him was a cup of tea? No one would think a person could be that naïve. So she didn't bother trying to defend herself, but instead said, 'Well, Mom knows nothing about you – and not for your sake alone either. If I had spoken about you, it would have hurt too many people. Mom thinks I went out with some boy and she knows no more than that. So you can rest easy in your bed,' she added mockingly, seeing the relief flood Barney's face.

'I should have known I could count on you,' he said.

'Count on me?' Patsy repeated. 'Yeah, once, bloody little fool that I was, you could have counted on me. What we did . . . I can hardly believe I was so stupid, but while I was wrong, you were worse, and all that stuff you said about Mom and Sean not caring for me was rubbish. I regret what I did with you, but I can't change that. There is to be no more of it though.'

Barney looked at Patsy disparagingly. 'You're a cocky little sod.'

'You can call me all the names you like,' Patsy said with a shrug, 'because your opinion doesn't matter a jot to me.'

'You cheeky bugger!' Barney said through gritted teeth. 'Don't worry yourself, for I wouldn't touch you with a barge pole.'

'Good. Suits us both then.'

Barney longed to give Patsy a good hiding, talking to him like that. She felt the suppressed violence and saw the balled fists, yet faced him unafraid. Barney looked away first.

'Go home to your mammy and daddy, little girl,' he said mockingly. 'I'm away for a pint.'

Patsy picked up the bags again as Barney walked away. A pint, that's a laugh, she thought. A great many pints is more like it.

The weather worsened. Each day brought more snow, blown, by the gusting, billowing winds, into drifts, some big enough to cover a man. Each night the snow froze, making the roads and pavements like sheets of ice, which were then covered by more snow the next day.

Anyone who ventured out was in danger of being swept into a drift by the relentless wind, or slipping and breaking a limb. The cold was bone chilling; water pipes burst all over the city and affected power supplies. Few went to the sales that year, but the *Evening Mail* had pictures of the intrepid souls who did, to shops often lit by candles and served by those shop assistants who could make it to work, still wearing their outdoor coats.

The schools opened, but the children were often sent home, for there was no power. Many roads became impassable and trains were either delayed or cancelled altogether. Supplies weren't getting through to the shops so even the rations couldn't be relied on, and there was further rationing on coal.

Few buses were running, including the one down to the Dunlop factory. Barney, by preference, would have stayed in bed, but Sean said they couldn't afford to lose money and so they walked, along with many others, wading their way through the drifts and trying to keep their feet on the icy roads.

Martha worried about them being in wet clothes all day, for when they returned at night, they were grey with fatigue and soaked to the skin. Patsy would often come in from school in the same state and soon the house smelt permanently of damp and steaming clothes. Some of the younger girls at the convent were sent home, but those studying for the matriculation or

Higher School Certificate were encouraged to continue to come to school. Patsy wouldn't have dreamt of having any time off, only too aware of how little she had given her studies the previous year.

She had plenty of time now to study, for most of the girls left her alone. This wasn't just to do with her neglect of them, but also because of the things Chloë had whispered to them of Patsy's exploits.

'. . . With a married man, and a relative into the bargain,' she'd said, aghast. 'Smoking and drinking, no less, and plenty of sex too, I imagine, for all she tried to say there wasn't.'

Chloë had envied Patsy's illicit carry-on while it had remained a secret, but the envy turned to outrage when it had all come to light, and it seemed suddenly sordid and wrong. 'My mother says I am not to have anything more to do with you,' she told Patsy.

Patsy was saddened, for they had been friends a long time, but she told herself she deserved no better. Patsy wasn't the only one grounded at that time. It was such an effort to go anywhere that most people were content to stay in if they had the choice. Even Barney had to forgo many of his evenings at the pub. Being unusually sober didn't improve his temper any, and he frequently took his bad humour out on Maria, snapping and shouting at her often, for little or nothing. Patsy saw Maria bore it with little complaint.

'Don't you mind?' she asked one day.

'Patsy, I mind so much about the things Barney does that I cannot change,' Maria said. 'Shouting at me doesn't even seem worth caring about.'

'Why don't you at least shout back?'

'That wouldn't help and it might frighten Sally,' Maria said. 'She's nervous enough of her father as it is.'

'I would say that's because he virtually ignores her.'

He did, and it hurt Maria. Sally had given up on her own father, but loved Sean. Both her and Deirdre would clamber all over him at every opportunity. He had immense patience, treated both children the same, and would play with them and read them stories endlessly.

The big freeze went on until mid-March and then the thaw began. Icicles disappeared and the snow began to drip from the gilded trees and run down the hedges from the crusted tops. The snow on the ground softened and turned slushy. Often there would be a roar like that of an express train and snow would slide from roofs to lie in sodden lumps in streets and gardens.

The drains were unable to cope with this amount of melted snow and there was much flooding. Martha and Sean were more fortunate than many, being halfway up a hill, but, even so, their cellar didn't escape and Martha and Maria had to attack the offending seepage with mops and buckets. Even the children were glad to see the back of the snow.

With the warmer weather, towards the end of March, spring felt only just around the corner, though Patsy couldn't really enjoy the spring that year. She was up to her eyes in revision and often looked strained and white with exhaustion. She really seemed to have taken almost a dislike to Barney, which Maria thought odd when she'd once thought him such a grand fellow. Maria wondered if Barney had done or said something to offend, but hesitated to ask. She was getting on better with Patsy now, but both were feeling their way and she didn't want to rock the boat.

Patsy had even said to her once, 'Why don't you hate me, Maria?'

'Why should I hate you?'

'I gave you such a hard time,' Patsy said candidly. 'And I more than hated you – I loathed you.'

'Why?'

'That's just it,' Patsy said. 'I don't know. I mean, you'd never done anything to me.'

'Your mother said you were jealous of Sean's affection for me.'

Patsy pondered this for a moment and then went on, 'Mom's probably right. I know I was angry about a lot of stuff then. That seems really stupid now.'

'That's called growing up,' Maria said with a smile.

'Yeah, I suppose,' Patsy said. 'I'm glad we are friends now, though.'

'Me too.' And she wasn't going to disturb that by asking if Barney had offended her in any way.

She'd never risk asking the man himself. During the big freeze, Barney had been unable to visit his brother, so in April he had gone over for a week. While their marriage had not been a bed of roses before he left, after he returned it was worse still. It was hard now to remember the man who was once so full of fun, or how gentle and understanding he had been with her father. There wasn't even the spark of gentleness in him now.

These days the most innocuous of remarks could result in a tirade. Many times she had wished Barney would give up the drink – or at least drink less, and less often – but when he couldn't go out some nights in the freeze, he was worse, and often lashed out at her when they were in the bedroom. This she kept hidden from everyone.

Deirdre and Sally turned two and as before the two girls shared a party, on Saturday, 9 August. The two of them, one so fair and one so dark, were the greatest of friends and a delight to all of the family.

For the life of her, Maria could not understand how Barney could be immune to the charms of his small daughter, but he was. That was why, when she told Barney the morning of the party that she was pregnant again, she expected no burst of enthusiasm, which was just as well. All he did was look at her with glowering eyes and say, 'Let's hope you get it right this time and give me a son.'

Maria had the urge to lie down and weep, she felt so demoralised by Barney's reaction. Martha and Sean more than made up for it, though. 'I thought there was something about you,' Martha said. 'A sort of bloom. When's it due?'

'In February,' Maria said. 'Sally will be two and a half,'

'A nice age,' Martha enthused. 'Won't she be delighted?'

'I hope so,' Maria said. 'But I'll say she won't be on her own. In fact, she might not get a look in at all with wee Deirdre, for I think she will be just as excited.'

'Oh, I'll say,' Martha agreed. 'Was Barney pleased?'

She saw the shadow of disappointment flit across

Maria's face before she said, 'He'll probably be satisfied if I give him a son this time.'

'Well, that's one thing no one has any control over,' Martha said grimly. 'Barney will have to be content with whatever God sends, like many more.'

Ten days after the girls' party, the results of the matriculation exams were sent to the convent. Patsy wished she had someone to walk up with her to get them, for it was lonely and a little scary on her own. She'd always imagined that she would go up arm in arm with Chloë, but she barely spoke to her any more.

She needn't have worried about the results, however. She had passed everything with flying colours, and Sean was like a dog with two tails.

In September, Patsy entered the sixth form at the convent and settled down to study for her Higher School Certificate. Tony went into the secondary school of the abbey that September. He'd point-blank refused to take the eleven-plus. 'I aint clever enough and I don't need no bits of paper to tell me that,' he'd said. 'I think all this book learning is flipping stupid anyroad, and I'm going down the Dunlop with Dad when I leave school.'

Theresa Margaret McPhearson was born in the afternoon of Thursday, 5 February 1948. While Maria was captivated with the tiny wee thing, she knew she'd have disappointed Barney once more and wondered if she'd suffer for it later. But she was immensely glad she'd had another child. She knew from experience the burden laid on an only child, and she would not wish that on any child of hers.

Patsy brought Deirdre and Sally in to introduce them to the new addition to the family. 'She's my sister,' Sally said possessively; this had been fully explained to her.

'And mine,' Deirdre said. The girls normally shared everything.

'No,' Sally said almost triumphantly. 'Just mine.'

'That will do, Sally,' Maria chided gently, for she had seen the wobble of Deirdre's bottom lip. 'She is your sister, but Deirdre's cousin, and both of you can help me care for her.'

'World War Three averted,' whispered Patsy, and Maria smiled.

Tony and Paul, when they came home from school, were delighted with Theresa too.

'Ain't she small?' Paul breathed. 'I can't ever remember our Deirdre being that little.' He touched the baby's hand delicately with one stubby finger and was delighted when Theresa grasped it tight and folded her fingers over it. 'She's holding my hand, Maria,' he cried. 'That means she likes me, don't it?'

'All babies do that, stupid,' Tony informed him.

'I ain't stupid, and how do you know that anyroad?'

''Cos our Deirdre did it to me when she was a nipper and our mom told me they all did.'

'But I'm sure she will like you,' Maria said. 'Why wouldn't she?'

'I can think of plenty of reasons.' Tony said with a grin.

Paul punched him on the arm with his free hand. 'Shurrup, you.'

Tony ignored him and instead asked, 'Can I hold her, Maria, just for a bit? I'll be real gentle.'

Later, Maria contrasted the boys' reaction to that of her husband when he came home from work. He barely looked into the cradle and only said, 'Another bloody girl.'

'Aye, a fine and healthy wee girl,' Maria snapped, hurt by his reaction. 'Can't you take joy in that? How can you not be moved by such a tiny thing?'

'I'm just not that way inclined,' Barney said. 'It seems like I'll have to wait for ever for my son.'

Theresa was three months old when Sean told Maria she should go up to the council offices and see where they were on the housing list. Maria had put her name down the day after she had arrived in Birmingham, the same day she had got her ration books.

'We are not that overcrowded, but with our own four children and your two as well, you might be in with a chance.'

Maria knew she should feel pleased. Everyone surely wanted their own front door, their own place, but she was wary of moving away and living just with Barney. She seldom complained about her husband, and though he did give her the odd slap now and then, she guessed it was the proximity of Sean that made him go no further than that. But the arrangement to stay with Sean and Martha was never meant to be a permanent one.

'I'll see about it,' she said.

'You'll need some money behind your for furnishings for when you do get a place,' Sean said to Barney later. 'Any news on selling that house?'

Barney shook his head. 'Market's dead at the moment.' In actual fact, Barney had made no enquiries as to selling the house, for renting it suited him fine. Every month, the agent would send him a nice cheque, which he would cash, putting the money in the tin. His stash of money was severely depleted now, and the extra was always useful, but he knew better than to tell Sean that.

'I would see about it, if I were you,' Sean advised. 'If you were to contact the agent and tell him that you could use the money, he might try harder. Thank God you have the money from the boatyard, so you can make a start, at least.'

'There isn't a lot left from that sale,' Barney said. 'There were the fares and all over here.'

'Only yours. I paid for Maria,' Sean pointed out.

'Still and all, there were all sorts of expenses.'

Aye, like gambling debts and beer, Sean might have said, but he didn't. It frustrated Sean that he couldn't take Barney to task more. It upset him greatly to see his beloved niece so careworn and unhappy as she often appeared.

However, when he had suggested doing that a time or two. Martha discouraged him, remembering Maria's word the day after that first beating and the panic in her eyes. She didn't dare tell Sean that she was afraid that Barney might hit Maria. If he thought he had laid a hand on her, there would be no holding him and the consequences then did not bear thinking about. So she told him that if he were to upset Barney, she was sure Maria would bear the brunt of the man's ill humour.

She was pretty sure Barney did still hit Maria now and again, for she had seen marks on her face, although she was getting more skilful at covering them now. It haunted Martha that he might really hurt her if Sean was to go for him.

Sean was well aware of the surly, ill-tempered way Barney already spoke to his niece, which she just put up with. For her sake, he would often bite his tongue where Barney was concerned, though sometimes he felt less of a man doing so. However, after Barney's words about the boatyard money he decided to contact the agent in Derry himself and see what was what regarding the house. Maria and Barney couldn't move anywhere with no money.

The mood in the country was more optimistic at that time. The Family Allowance being paid out from 1946 of five shillings for second and subsequent children, was proving a boon, particularly for those with big families. The rationing of bread was lifted in 1948, and jam was also declared off ration. In July in London there was the first Olympic Games of peacetime but, more importantly, for the average man in the street was the arrival of the Health Service on 5 July.

It cheered everyone too when a baby boy called Charles was born on 14 November to Princess Elizabeth, who was heir to the throne. Maria was three months pregnant herself by then, and delighted about it, despite the fact that Therese would be only fifteen months old when the new baby was born.

'It will be hard work at first,' she said to Martha, when she expressed concern about it, 'but Sally is a great hand, you know, and often appears older than her years. Anyway, I am thrilled and sure, won't they all grow up together?'

The lady from the council visited the day after the royal prince's birth. Maria told her that she was pregnant and the woman noted it down in the file she had. 'You have two other children, I believe?' she said.

'Aye.' Maria said. 'Sally is three and Theresa nine months.'

'And is your husband is in full-time work?'

'Aye, at the Dunlop.'

All this was written down too, and then she enquired about Sean and Martha and the names and ages of their children.

'Is there a chance of a place?' Maria asked, as the woman was putting all the papers in her case.

'It's all based on a points system,' the woman said, 'but the fact that you have been on the list for nearly three years and will soon have three children, plus the fact that, as your husband is working, you will have no difficulty in paying the rent, will undoubtedly make a difference. Have you a preference for a particular area?'

Maria shook her head. 'I hardly know the city at all,' she said. 'But I wouldn't want to be that far from the Dunlop.'

'I'll bear it in mind,' the woman promised. 'You will be hearing from me in due course.'

When Sean heard of the woman's visit he told Barney to redouble his efforts with the agent in Derry. When he had been in touch with the man earlier in the year he'd been astounded to hear that Barney told him there was no rush to sell the property, and that he had been receiving a nice cheque every month from the people renting it. Sean knew where that money had been spent: what hadn't been tipped down Barney's neck had been laid on the card table. Sean had told the agent the situation had changed and the money from the sale of the house would soon be needed, but there had been no luck so far.

Then in early December, Barney had a letter from Ned, who made him an offer for the house. To get the boatyard up and running the way he liked it, he needed to be on the spot.

'It's just perfect,' Barney said, 'for the tenancy runs out in just over a fortnight.'

The transaction was completed in the New Year and this time, mindful of what had happened to the money from the boatyard, Sean insisted that Barney deposit it in the Municipal Bank.

It was early March before Barney and Maria were given the keys to a house in a road called Westmead Crescent, on the nearby Pype Hayes estate. It was on the corner and had a lawn in front of the bay window. On the other side of the path to the door were small trees and shrubs.

Barney turned the key in the front door and they stepped into a small hall with stairs facing them. Without a word, Barney mounted them and Maria followed him. Three doors opened off the small square landing. Two of the rooms were double sized and even the smallest room wasn't tiny.

'No bathroom,' Barney said.

'Must be downstairs,' Maria said. 'Shall we go and find it?'

It was off the fair-sized kitchen, though the toilet was outside, next to the back door. Looking through the kitchen window, Maria saw the large and well-kept garden, with fruit bushes at the very end, and she could imagine her two little girls and the third child, as yet unborn, playing there in safety. Maybe they could buy a swing if they had money enough.

'I like it,' she said. 'And with the rent at twelve and six a week, we can well afford it.'

'You will wear yourself out with all this gadding about shopping,' Martha said to Maria a week later. 'You are only two months from giving birth. Why don't you take it steadier and leave some of it until you've had the baby?'

Maria couldn't take the risk that there would be any money left then. It might melt away, like the money from the boatyard. Once they were on their own she knew she would have little say in anything. Here, with Sean and Martha taking an interest in everything, she knew Barney wouldn't risk drawing huge sums out of the bank.

By the time they were ready to move in, all the floors had lino on, though in the living room a carpet square almost covered it, leaving just the edges showing because Martha said it was the latest thing. An uncut moquette three-piece suite in medium brown was drawn up before the fireplace and a large table, with four dining chairs tucked under it, stood in the bay window.

She and Martha took frequent trips to the market for the pots, pans, crockery and cutlery, all utility, which was all there was available, and later to buy the material for the curtains and cushions, which Maria ran up on the sewing machine. It gave Maria a thrill of pride to see how fine the house looked. Martha too thought she had the place lovely and told her so.

It was Saturday and moving day. Barney had gone down to the house to await the arrival of the gas man, who would fit the new gas cooker and boiler, and Maria stripped the covers from their double bed, Sally's bed and the cot so that Sean could dismantle them. She was going down the stairs with the bedding in her arms to put in the scullery when the cot sheet slipped through her fingers. She made a grab for it but the sheet tangled around her legs, causing her to lose her balance. She tipped forward, screaming as she hurtled through the air, the clothes tumbling from her hands as she tried in vain to grab anything to break her fall.

She bumped and thudded from one step to the next until she landed with a thump at the bottom.

'Almighty God!' Sean cried as he thundered down the stairs at the same time as Martha came running up the passage.

'Are you all right?' Martha said, berating herself for saying something so stupid. Would anyone be all right after such a fall?

'Where are you hurt?' Sean said. 'Can you stand?'

Maria didn't answer but just lay stunned, aware she was aching everywhere.

'I think we should get you to bed and let the doctor take a look at you,' Martha said.

Maria opened her mouth to say she needed no doctor, but all that came out was a groan. As she struggled to her feet, helped by Sean and Martha, a dull pain began throbbing in her back. By the time

Barney and the doctor had been summoned, she was ensconced in Martha and Sean's bed. The pain in her back was joined by drawing pains across her abdomen. She wondered if history was repeating itself, for she knew that she was in labour and two months too early.

The doctor said there was no time to go to hospital and he would be back later. Martha sat with Maria all day, holding her hand and wiping her face, while Patsy took on the running of the house and looked after the children. Martha told Sean to take the boys to the match as usual – they could do nothing hanging about the house – but Sean was hesitant to leave and even the boys were reluctant at first.

Patsy agreed with her mother. 'What good will you do by staying?' she demanded.

'Nothing, I suppose,' Tony said. 'But she will be all right, won't she?'

'Course,' Patsy said, knowing Tony needed that assurance. 'Go on, it will probably all be over when you come back.'

Six agonising hours later, with the doctor in attendance, Maria expelled the baby from her body.

'Tell Barney he has his son,' she told Martha bitterly.

And he had. The child was small, perfectly formed and quite, quite dead.

Maria was so distraught by the death of the child the doctor gave her something to help her sleep. When she wakened from her drug-induced sleep on Sunday morning, she was, for a little while, disorientated. She was still in Sean and Martha's bed, so she presumed they had used hers and maybe Barney had spent the night on the settee, not wishing to disturb her.

The house was quiet and she got out of bed gingerly, but she was afraid to take a step because her head swam. The room spun around her in an alarming way and she lay back on the pillows. The alarm said it was a quarter to ten and she guessed they'd all gone to Mass. Barney didn't usually go so early, but if he had spent the night on the settee then there would be little chance of a lie-in.

Maybe, just maybe, he had gone willingly to church to pray for the soul of his infant son, who, according to the church's teaching, would never be given a place in heaven, because he hadn't been baptised. Instead he would be in Limbo forever. That knowledge caused Maria further heartache and she would have welcomed Barney coming to comfort her and talk about the child they had both lost.

However, it was Tony who came into the room first, with her breakfast after they had all returned from Mass. When Martha did come to see Maria, she was accompanied by the three little girls and she couldn't speak in front of them. Deirdre and Sally, picking up the atmosphere, had been very worried about Maria, while thirteen-month-old Theresa had just been fretful. All of them were glad to see Maria sitting up in the bed and looking normal.

Sean warned that no one was to say anything to Maria about Barney slamming out of the door the previous evening and not coming home; she had more than enough to put up with. So when Patsy took her a cup of tea after dinner and Maria asked where Barney was, Patsy said, 'Where is Barney usually this time on a Sunday?'

Maria felt a stab of disappointment. He'd gone to the pub, as if it was a normal day, as if she'd not given birth to a stillborn baby, and he'd gone too without even poking his head around the bedroom door and asking if she was all right.

But there was no sign of Barney that evening either. By the next day Martha said Maria should be told, for something could have happened to the man, so when she asked again where her husband was that evening, Martha said, 'No one has any idea where Barney is, Maria.'

'Does he know I gave birth to a son and the baby died?' Maria asked.

'Yes, he knows that.'

'Did he see the child before they took it away.'

Martha nodded dumbly. 'That's when he left,' she said at last. 'Sean has contacted the police.'

'They won't be interested,' Maria said. 'They take the view that if a man wants to disappear, then he can. Unless he has done anything wrong they won't be in any rush to find him.'

She remembered when she had given birth to Sally and Barney had done a disappearing act, but then he had a network of villains to help him, including his brother. This time there was none of that, and yet she wasn't concerned. 'Don't worry,' she told Martha. 'He won't have disappeared for good. He'll turn up.'

She was sickened by the whole thing. She had carried the child for seven months and was looking forward to the birth, hoping for Barney's sake it was a boy, but knowing she would love it whatever the sex. When the child was born dead an ache settled around her heart and she wept for the baby who'd had life wrenched from him before he had time to draw breath.

Maria was right: Barney turned up the following evening. His clothes were dishevelled and stained and he stunk to high heaven. He was so drunk he could barely stand. Sean was at a lost what area to tackle first, especially as he had no wish for the children to see more that they had to, and he was heartily glad the little girls had already gone to bed.

Much later, in bed, with Barney bedded down on the settee in the living room, Martha asked Sean, 'Did he give you any explanation of where he has been the past few days?'

'I didn't ask him for one,' Sean said. 'Do you think for one minute that he was capable of putting together a sensible sentence?'

'No,' Martha said, and gave a sigh. 'Poor Maria.'

'Aye,' said Sean with feeling. 'I echo that.'

Maria didn't even ask Barney to explain his absence. She knew why he had taken off and knew too if the fall had injured her inside, as it had her mother, so that she'd never bear another child, Barney would be unlikely to take that in a calm and rational manner. In a way, she didn't want to face that, but mourn for the baby her arms still ached to hold. In the end, though, she had to know. She plucked up courage to ask the doctor if she had damaged herself permanently.

'Why should you think that?' Dr Linden wanted to know.

'My mother did just what I did when she was expecting my brother,' Maria said, 'and she could never have another child after it.'

The doctor smiled. 'Don't worry, my dear,' he said. 'There have been great strides forward in medicine since then. Rest assured that there is no permanent damage, as far as I can tell, though I will know more at your post-natal check-up. If there is anything wrong then, I'm certain it will be able to be put right. I should say there is no reason, medically speaking, anyway, why you shouldn't go on to have a whole house full of children.'

CHAPTER TWENTY-ONE

Maria and Barney moved into their new house ten days later. Martha and Sean thought it much too soon. Maria was still weak and burdened by sadness, but Barney insisted. He was so angry about everything and nothing that Maria just went along with things for the sake of a quiet life – and not for herself alone; for sometimes the look Barney cast over his daughters was one of sheer dislike.

It didn't help that the girls were difficult. Sally had been excited about the house, but she hadn't followed through the realisation that once they moved into it, she would be separated from Deirdre. She protested long and hard, and was often whiny and hard to please. Theresa took the lead from her elder sister, cried often and was very uncooperative and began waking in the night and demanding attention. Maria was worn out with the pair of them.

She also found pleasing Barney hard work, and harder still the fact that he never spoke of the dead child. It was just as if it had never happened; that the wee child had never been. Nor did he say one word as to where he had been when he disappeared for three days.

'Haven't you asked him?' Martha said incredulously, calling down for a visit a few days after the move. 'God, I'd have had it in fine detail from Sean if ever he'd done such a thing. You have a right to demand an explanation of where he was that time and you should tell him so.'

Maria tried to imagine what would happen if she did and she shut her eyes for moment against the picture. 'I couldn't do that,' she said.

'Why not?'

'God, Martha, Barney would never stand it.'

Martha saw the fear-filled eyes and suddenly had to know. 'Maria, does Barney still hit you?'

Maria just stared at Martha, before saying in a flat, expressionless voice, 'I'm going to forget you even asked that question.'

'Maria . . .'

'No, Martha. We've spoken about this before,' Maria said. 'Barney isn't easy and I have never pretended he was. I try not to rock the boat and I put up with things other wives might not put up with. But, as my mother used to say, I've made my bed and now I must lie on it.'

Eventually life settled down. The little ones got used to the change and the only thing Maria had to worry about was making the money stretch. Almost as soon as they moved into the house, Barney cut the amount he gave Maria for housekeeping. She did complain over this, for it was a little over half what she'd had to manage on before, but it got her nowhere. Barney said it was he who sweated blood for it and he'd decide how to spend it, and if she couldn't manage it would be her look out.

Maria did get depressed over this at times. She was grateful for the five shillings Family Allowance that she was able to cash at the post office, but even with that added to the housekeeping, some weeks she couldn't even afford the rations she was allowed. She was heartily glad that bread was off ration because she could use it to fill Sally up, and herself too, glad that as yet Theresa didn't eat much. She always made sure that she had something to put before Barney when he came in each evening though; she could just imagine his temper if she hadn't.

After his tea, he would go out and Maria would breathe a sigh of relief when the door closed behind him. She knew there would be a respite until he returned, when he would usually stagger around the bedroom until he fell into bed beside her. Then she would often feel his groping hands pawing her body. He usually stank of sweat, stale beer and cigarettes, but she didn't say a word about it and would also suppress any sigh of annoyance. If she let him do what he wanted, they rubbed along peaceably enough most of the time.

Patsy passed her Higher School Certificate that summer, and was to start at Leicester Teacher Training College in September. Maria remembered when a golden future was held out to her and she hoped that nothing would happen to dim the shining light in Patsy's eyes. She kissed her and congratulated her warmly.

Once she was resident there, Maria wrote to her every week, along with the regular letters she wrote to Bella and Dora and the occasional one she wrote to Philomena, now steeped in domesticity, bringing up her sister's family.

She hardly seemed the same person who had coached Maria with such diligence, encouraging her to focus only on her future. But then was she the same person as the vibrant young girl who thought her future rosy and her life her own? It was circumstances that shaped people's lives, and a person often had no control over those.

Bella and Dora seemed much the same. When Maria got their replies, it was like them being in the room with her and that sometimes made her a wee bit homesick. They would tell her all the news and gossip from the village, especially of the boatyard, a great place of interest and speculation altogether. They said Ned was making a fine turnaround of the place and Maria felt pleased about that, for she had liked Ned.

Barney wrote to his brother regularly, but his visits to see Seamus had had to be curtailed somewhat, for now he had less money in his pocket. They paid more on rent than they had when they were lodging with Sean. There, the bills had been shared between them too. Added to that, Barney had lost the rental that used to be sent to him each month, so even after cutting Maria's housekeeping, he was still worse off. The money in the tin was all gone now and he knew soon he would have to draw some from the bank.

Maria wasn't aware of Barney's concerns. She had her own and the most pressing one was Christmas. By scrimping and scraping, virtually living on bread with a smear of margarine or dripping for weeks, and scouring the Rag Market while Martha minded the girls, she'd been able to buy some little things for them to open on Christmas morning. A colouring book and crayons for Sally, chalks and a slate board for Theresa, plus a book for Maria to read to them, a small bar of chocolate she had saved the sweet rations for and a orange each she had queued for hours to get, ensured the day would go with a swing for them at least.

After Mass, they were to spend the day with Sean and Martha. Barney hadn't wanted to, but for once Maria had dug her heels in and said they would think it strange if they didn't. There was no way she was sitting in with Barney all day – and it would be all day, for the pubs were closed until the evening and she could guess the mood he would be in because of it.

All in all, it had been a grand day, although Barney, looking decidedly the worse for wear, didn't make an appearance at the house until the dinner was being dished up. The children were as excited as any would be and Patsy, home for the holiday, regaled them with her life at the hostel and the tyrannical housekeeper in charge of the place.

'She's lost her calling,' Patsy said. 'She should have been a sergeant major in the army.'

Martha said nothing and tried to hide the smile. Despite Patsy's moans, her sympathies were with the woman trying to keep a watchful eye on a hostel full of young girls. It was little wonder her hair was as grey as Patsy said it was.

It had been an alien thing for her to understand that

Patsy would move out of the house and live elsewhere. In Martha's world, a girl stayed at home until she was married and then she was in her husband's keeping. She knew what girls together could get up to, and was glad the housekeeper let them away with so little if it meant she could rest easy in her bed at night.

In June 1950 another war began in a place called Korea and many of the British boys doing their national service were drafted in to fight. 'Where is bloody Korea anyway?' Martha said irritably one day when she was visiting Maria. 'I mean, what's it to us? Why put our boys at risk again?'

Maria knew what Martha was afraid of. Tony had turned fourteen in April and she didn't want him shipped overseas when he was eighteen to fight in some obscure country she'd never even heard of before. Maria understood her concern. In her opinion, Martha had lost more than enough family members. It was no good her saying the skirmish would be finished well before Tony would be old enough for national service because, as Martha said, the last war went on for six years.

Maria was pregnant again, the baby due in November and by then she would only have Theresa at home all day because Sally and Deirdre would be starting up at the abbey school in September. Both girls were fizzing with excitement about it.

'You can almost pity the teachers,' Maria said. 'For if there is any devilment about, you can bet ours will be in the thick of it.'

'What do you mean, in the thick of it?' Martha

said, with a wry smile. 'They will more likely be the instigators of it.'

'Aye,' Maria said and laughed. The girls were full of mischief, especially when they got together. What one didn't think of, the other would, and Theresa would trail after them, copying anything they did. But they were growing up fast and Maria was looking forward to another baby, although she couldn't help feeling a little apprehensive.

The two girls left their mothers without a tear that first day at school, and it was Theresa who cried all the way home because she had wanted to go with her sister. Once in the house, Maria lifted her from the pushchair and on to her knee.

'How could I lose the pair of you?' she asked the tearful child as she hugged her tight. 'Won't I need someone at home to help me with the new baby?'

Theresa stopped crying then, because that put a new complexion on everything. For so long she had been the baby and then the little one, allowed to play with the older girls as a favour just, pushed around by them, and they were not always terribly kind to her. This was something new.

'You will be the baby's big sister,' Maria said.

Big sister sounded good, Theresa thought, and her eyes opened wider as she asked, 'Will I?' She needed to be sure she had got this right.

'Of course.'

'Will Sally be a big sister too?'

'Aye,' Maria said. 'This baby is lucky and will have two big sisters, but you will be the one at home, the one that will show the baby how to do things.'

Theresa could see that and she nodded. 'I'll do that, Mammy. I'll help you all you like,' she said.

Maria gave her a kiss. 'Don't I know that?' she said. 'You'll be grand, so you will. So now, I want no more tears.'

And Theresa could see plainly that big sisters couldn't go around crying and carrying on. That was for babies.

'Wee Theresa has come into her own at last,' Maria told Martha two weeks later. 'She still misses Sally, but for so long she was overshadowed by her and your Deirdre too, and just gave in to whatever they wanted. Standing on her own two feet is good for her and I think she is more anxious for this child to be born than I am.'

'Have you everything booked?'

Maria nodded. 'I've contacted the midwife and I have to go to the doctor's regularly now too. It's a good job it's all free, I can tell you.'

Maria had never said what a struggle she found it to manage on the money Barney gave her, but Martha was no fool, and she had eyes in her head. Maria hadn't bothered registering to collect her rations from a shop nearer to her and continued to go to Erdington with Martha. Martha would often look askance at the small amount of food that Maria got and could guess why.

She knew Maria often went to jumble sales to get material to make things for the girls; even their winter coats were homemade that year. Often on a visit, Martha would sit and help Maria unpick things, or unravel woollies so that Maria could knit them up again. She did this without commenting on it and thought it a good job that Maria was so handy with the sewing machine and knitting needles.

Shoes were a headache, for there were few shoes at the jumble sales and any there looked as if they were held together with a wing and a prayer. Maria would go down the Rag Market and buy second-hand shoes for the girls. They were often shabby and not substantial enough for the weather, but they were all that Maria could afford.

Jack Samuel McPhearson was born on Friday, 3 November 1950. Maria hadn't told Barney she was in labour before he left for work that morning, so when, on his return, he was told he had the son he craved, he was ecstatic. He went in and gazed at him as he lay in the cradle. 'Took a couple of false starts, but you got there in the end,' he said to Maria, scooping the child from the cradle, as if he had been used to doing it every day of his life.

She could scarcely believe he could refer to his lovely little daughters in that way, but knew it would do no good to say anything. She was just glad the girls were out of the way and hadn't heard what he said. 'By God,' he said to Sean, who'd come down to see the child when the boys told him Maria had had the baby, 'I intend to wet the baby's head well tonight. Are you on, Sean?'

Martha was cross with Barney's suggestion. She'd been with Maria all day, for she'd taken to calling daily to see how she was when she'd had a fortnight to go. It was she that had fetched the midwife and taken care of Theresa, held Maria's hand when Theresa took her nap, and saw the baby born.

After Maria had been cleaned up and was having a well-earned rest, Martha had taken Theresa to collect the girls from school. It had already been arranged that Sally and Theresa should be stay at her house overnight, and as soon as Paul and Tony got home from school, Martha returned to stay with Maria until Barney would be home from work. Now, it appeared the man wouldn't be in the house a moment longer than necessary and she would hesitate to leave Maria on her own all evening.

She had no wish either for Sean to accompany Barney on what she knew would turn out to be a drunken spree, but she could hardly forbid Sean to go. That was a thing she had never done and she'd not shame him in that way. But she was annoyed, and Sean was fully aware of it, when she said, 'Before you go anywhere, you can give me a hand at home getting the little ones to bed – that is, after someone is sent out to fetch fish and chips for I have had no time to prepare us something to eat, though I've made a fish pie for Barney and Maria. Maria at least needs to build her strength up.'

Maria knew about the fish pie and her mouth watered at the smell of it cooking. But her purse didn't stretch to buying fish and she knew Martha would have paid for it herself. She was immensely grateful because she was starving.

'I'll be back when I get the little ones in bed,' Martha said.

'Ah no,' Maria said. 'There's no need. You've done enough.'

'I've done nothing much,' Martha said. 'And there is no way I am leaving you by yourself this evening at least.'

Maria said nothing more. She would value the company.

By the time Jack was approaching his first birthday, Barney was getting into deep water. For months, using the money from the bank, he had joined the big boys at the card schools where the stakes were high. He had lost heavily, gambled more to try to recoup the losses, and borrowed when the money ran out.

Now he was in debt and knew those fellows weren't the sort to wait for ever for their money. They were already murmuring what their heavies would do to him if he didn't pay up and quickly, but he hadn't a clue how he was going to do that.

He was drinking more than ever to blur the edges of the dilemma he was in, resenting even the pittance he gave Maria to manage on. This resentment often came out in a blow, but she was wise enough to say and do nothing to further enflame him, so the punch or hefty slap was all it was.

He was no nearer finding a solution in the New Year when, one January evening, as he left the factory, he spotted one of the organisers of the card school leaning against the wall by the bus stop. Sean also saw the man and knew from the look of him he was likely up to no good. He was concerned when the man called Barney over.

'What's he want?' Sean asked.

'Don't know,' Barney said. 'I had better see.'

'Don't get mixed up with his type,' Sean warned. 'Do you want me to wait for you?'

Barney would have liked to have someone at his

back, but he knew it was better for Sean to know nothing of the money he owed so he said, 'No, you go. The bus won't wait. I'll just see what he wants and then walk home.'

'You sure?'

'Aye,' Barney said, impatient now to get the man away. 'Martha will worry if you are late.'

And Maria won't? Sean wanted to say but didn't. In many ways Barney didn't appear like a married man at all and he certainly didn't play by any rules. Few that Sean knew went to the pub as often as Barney, and would have had the rough edge of their wives' tongues if they had tried it. As for the state he was often in when he left the pub, the consensus from most men was that their woman would be at them with a rolling pin if they were only half as bad.

'Your niece must be some sort of saint,' one of the men had said to Sean that very day.

'Aye, that or a doormat,' another replied, and though Sean had been angered enough by the comment to growl at the man to shut his mouth if he knew what was good for him, he had to admit privately that he had a point.

Now Sean watched Barney walk towards the man and knew from the way he greeted him that he knew full well who he was. He sighed as got on to the bus after Tony, who was working at the Dunlop factory as an apprentice cabinet maker. Sean wondered what Barney had got himself involved in now.

'All right,' said the man Barney knew only as MacKay. 'We need to talk. Is there a pub near at hand where we can be a bit private, like?'

'Aye, the Norton is no distance at all,' Barney said. 'It's my local now we're in Pype Hayes and there is a small room there that they call "the snug" that will be near empty this time of day.'

'Lead the way then.'

The landlord was just unlocking the door and he laughed when he saw Barney. 'God, you're starting early tonight, ain't yer? Missus come to her senses at last and thrown you out, has her?'

Barney grimaced. 'Very funny, George. Now, if you don't mind, we have got a bit of business to discuss and need somewhere quiet. Can we use the snug?'

The landlord shrugged. 'Use what you like and I'm sure you would like a drink to help the business along.'

Later, in the small room, with pints of beer in front of them, MacKay said, 'Let's get down to facts, McPhearson. Just how long do you expect us to wait until you pay us what you owe?'

'I haven't got it,' Barney said. 'I pay what I can.'

'You call that pay! Piddling little amounts that wouldn't keep me in fags.'

Barney took a large gulp of his drink, wiped his mouth with the back of his hand and said, 'I don't know what you want me to do.'

'Look,' MacKay said. 'I'm not playing games here. There are some very vicious men in our group that want to tear you limb from limb.' He leant forward and went on in a menacing whisper, 'It will be serious if they start on you. They don't mess about.'

Barney knew they didn't and he was scared – so scared he felt his limbs turn to water. He finished his pint, laid his empty glass on the table, turned to MacKay and said, 'So, what do I do?'

MacKay shook his head. 'Point is, I have been able to get them to lay off you for now, but I don't know how much longer I can do that, unless you have something to offer them.'

'Like what?'

'You have a little think,' MacKay said, getting to his feet and picking up the glasses, 'while I get us a refill.'

Barney thought, but there was nothing he could offer these men to stop them beating he to pulp, as far as he could see, and this is what he told MacKay when he sat down again at the table.

MacKay took a long drink and sat back almost leisurely in his chair before he said, 'Oh, I don't know so much.'

The whole thing had got to Barney and he was jumpy and nervous. 'Who's playing games now, MacKay?' he snarled. 'If you've got anything to say, then say it, for Christ's sake, and be done with it.'

'Let me remind you, you are in no position to throw your weight around,' MacKay snapped. 'How long have you been at Dunlop's?'

The question took Barney by surprise, but he answered readily enough. 'Six years.'

'Know your way about then?'

Barney shrugged. 'Well enough,' he said.

'You know where the storerooms are, the keys are kept?'

At last, Barney had a clue as to where all this was leading and he said, 'Most of them.'

'And how do you feel about lifting some of those tools?' MacKay asked. 'We'll tell you the type of things we need. It would make certain people very happy if you could do that. In fact, so happy would they be that they might not feel like bashing you any more. Do you reckon you could manage it?'

Barney nodded. He was filled with the same exhilaration that he had felt going on the raids with his brother. He knew how it was to be achieved. It would be a piece of cake. There was a men's toilet block right beside one of the main storerooms with the key to it on a hook, just inside the door of the reception place. It should be manned and the stuff signed out, but it hardly ever was, and if he was to crawl out of the window in the men's toilet then he would be hidden from the main body of the factory. He could be in that storeroom and the things lifted in no time, and no one would have seen him near the place.

'I'm your man,' Barney said extending his hand. 'Let's shake on it.'

Barney didn't know how he got home that night. He had no recollection of it and Maria had seldom seen him in such a state so early. She couldn't get him up the stairs and left him on the settee covered with a blanket.

CHAPTER TWENTY-TWO

In June 1952, Patsy graduated as a fully fledged teacher and returned home to live for a while, as she would be working in Paget Road School from September to do her probationary year. Martha was glad to have her daughter home for a little while, and Maria too was glad Patsy was close at hand. The school actually opened off Westmead Crescent.

Then a fortnight after Patsy's graduation, Sally and Deirdre made their First Holy Communion and Maria sewed them matching dresses. They looked angelic. Martha insisted on paying for everything, which she said was still a pittance to what she would have paid out if she had bought just the one dress. Maria was so grateful for the rosary and white missal that Dora and Bella sent to their goddaughter, as she could afford no Communion presents. Martha had bought a Box Brownie camera for the occasion and took many photographs of the day. She said Maria could send some to the two women as a sort of thank you and Maria knew that would delight them.

She was feeling happier as Jack's second birthday

approached, for though there was still Barney's drinking and gambling, and the pittance he gave her to manage on, there was the consolation of the children. Sally and Theresa were growing into lovely, kind and generous children, and Theresa would spend hours playing with her little brother. Jack loved both his sisters dearly, but then he was a sunny child who loved the whole world. A bundle of fun, he was a source of joy to them all.

Even Barney would take notice of the boy. It never extended to taking him to the park a time or two at the weekend, or even tucking him in bed at night, but he'd at least acknowledged he was there and would tell him they would go to the football together and, when he was old enough, he'd take him out and buy him a pint. It wasn't really what Maria would have him say to a child if she had had any sort of choice in it, but maybe it was better than ignoring him, as Barney still did with the girls.

Jack was far more confident than either of his sisters and loved being the centre of attention. Sean's family were particularly taken with him and laughed at many of the things he did.

'You have him ruined,' Maria told her uncle one day. 'The child is precocious.'

'Not at all,' Sean said. 'Sure isn't he just a wee boy enjoying life? Isn't it what we would wish for all our children?'

Of course it was. Jack would grow up one day and have plenty of cares and worries then, so she relaxed a bit more. Her daughters too were well loved by everyone except their father, and Maria often wished Barney would throw them some little morsel of affection. She had seen them looking quite wistful sometimes as they watched him with Jack, but she knew there was nothing she could do to ease that situation for them and in time they would have to learn to cope with Barney the way he was, as she had had to do.

It was the last Friday evening in October and Barney was feeling pleased with himself. In his haversack was another lot of tools for MacKay, and a football for Jack's birthday, which he had pinched from the shop. The line was going slow that night leaving the factory, and he shouted to a tall man beside him, who went by the name of Lanky, 'What's the hold-up? Can you see?'

Lanky had little trouble looking over the heads of the others, being six foot five in his stocking feet. 'Yeah, seems like they are checking everyone's bag as they leave,' he answered.

Barney felt his blood turn to ice and he had the urge to run, but where to? Anyway, with the body of men pressed to every side of him, there was no way he could go anywhere but forward. With every shuffle towards the gate, he felt the dread in him increase.

Maria had Barney's dinner almost ready and, with the fire on, heating the water in the tank behind it meant there was plenty of warm water without the need to boil a kettle. She told him this as he came in the kitchen door. He didn't answer, but this wasn't unusual. He threw something on the kitchen table in front of her.

'What's this?'

'What's it look like, you stupid bugger?' Barney snarled. 'My cards.'

'Your cards?' Maria repeated.

'Aye, my cards. Are you deaf, or some sort of imbecile?' Barney cried. 'I'll spell it out for you, shall I? See if it makes things any clearer. I've been sacked.'

'Oh, Barney! What on earth for?'

'Well,' Barney said, 'it could have something to do with the football I had in my bag for the young fellow's birthday that I neglected to pay for.' No need, he thought, to mention the tools that he had been pilfering for ten months.

'A football,' Maria repeated. 'They gave you the sack for stealing a football? I don't know why you stole it in the first place, but didn't you say you were sorry, offer to pay for it?'

'You really are some sort of half-wit, aren't you?' Barney scoffed. 'You think that would make any difference? They want their pound of flesh and caught me red-handed, so I got my marching orders and they said I should think myself lucky I am not on a charge too.'

'For stealing a football?'

'Aye. Now I am away for my wash and you have the dinner ready when I finish, for I am going out to get blind, stinking drunk.'

'But, Barney, shouldn't we talk about this? Decide what is to be done?'

'I've done all the talking I am going to do,' Barney said, wondering how he was going to tell MacKay that not only had he not got the tools on order, but that the source of getting more had dried up too.

Martha, knowing that Barney wasn't in the habit of staying at home in the evening and also knowing Maria would be distressed by the news he'd lost his job, went down that night.

'It was all over a football,' Maria told Martha, handing her a cup of tea.

'No it wasn't,' Martha said. Sean had said it was better Maria hear it from them rather than someone else.

'What do you mean?'

Martha sighed. 'Barney was hauled back to the office when the stuff was found, so he didn't get on the bus with Sean and Tony, and that's where they heard.'

'Heard what?'

'Heard that Barney has been stealing tools for months.'

'Tools!'

'Yeah, some of them are worth a pretty penny, so Sean says.'

'No doubt, but what would anyone want with a load of tools?' Maria asked. 'And where are they? Not here, for sure.'

'No, he sells them to a man down the Norton pub. That's where the fellow overheard the two of them talking and was telling Sean. Anyway, this time when he was caught, he had tools in the bag too.'

'He was lucky, wasn't he, that they are not pressing charges?' Maria said.

'I'll say,' Martha said. 'Point is, though, it will be hard for him to get anything else with that on his record and no reference.'

'What are we to do, Martha? How are we to manage?'

'Barney will have to go down the dole office and see about it,' Martha said. 'They will give you something because of the children and all. He'll have to wait until

Monday, of course. Have you enough to be going on with?'

'Martha, all I have in my purse this minute is one and thruppence, for Barney gave me nothing before he left,' Maria said. 'I'll have the Family Allowance on Tuesday, and all I can say is, thank God the Government raised it to eight shillings this year, so I'll have sixteen shillings from that, but I don't know how I'll find the five shillings for Monday to pay for Sally's school dinners.'

'You might not have to,' Martha said as she rooted in her bag. 'I think if your husband is unemployed you get free dinners – or something off them, at any rate. But take this for now.' She handed Maria a pound.

Maria shook her head. 'I can't take it from you, Martha.'

'You can't not,' Martha said. 'Think of the children. How can you feed them all weekend on one and thruppence? Unless, of course, you get more out of that bugger of a man you married.'

Maria knew Martha had a point. 'Okay,' she said, 'I see what you say and I'm grateful to you, but I'll not take a pound.'

'I have more than enough.'

'I don't care,' Maria said. 'Leave me some vestige of pride, for God's sake. It is all I have left and ten shillings is ample.'

'Are you sure?'

'Quite sure, Martha. My children aren't used to high-quality living and fancy fare,' Maria said sadly.

Maria was told at the school on Monday morning that Sally could have free school meals if she brought in the documentation to prove Barney had no employment. Then she went back home to rouse him, for he was sleeping off the excesses of the weekend. The punch he threw at her split her lip, but her efforts had the desired effect and the man was out of bed at last, though like a raging bull because of it. Maria kept herself and the children out of his way as much as possible and didn't really breathe easy until he was out of the house.

Later, she was to stare at him as if she couldn't believe her ears. 'Twenty-six shillings! Is that all?'

'That's it,' Barney said. 'And seven shillings extra for Sally.'

'What about Theresa and Jack?'

'The woman said you have Family Allowance for them. So we'll get thirty-three shillings a week and that's sixteen bob six pence for me and the same for you.'

'You must be joking, Barney. For God's sake, the rent is fifteen shillings, after that last rise.'

'You only need to pay the part of that when you are unemployed.'

'Even so, there's money for coal and for the gas and electric meters as well as food. I can't do it all on such little money.'

Barney gave a malicious grin. 'You'll have to, for you'll not get a penny piece more.'

And then, because she was worried and angry, she forgot to be cautious. 'Why should we all suffer because this situation is totally your own fault?' she shrieked at him. 'It wasn't just a ball you had in your bag when you were stopped and searched, but tools too, and it

412

wasn't the first time either. You think you are so bloody clever and yet half the factory knew all about it.'

The punch hit her between the eyes and she staggered against the wall, her nose spurting blood. The children began to scream.

Barney looked from Maria to the distressed children. 'Christ Almighty!' he exclaimed. 'A man would have to be mad to want any of this.' He snatched his jacket from the hook and went out. It was left to Maria to try to calm the children and staunch the blood from her nose, less upset by Barney's violence than she was about the realisation that she wouldn't have money to care for the children properly.

The sound of the children crying with hunger and cold tore Maria apart, but she couldn't make the money stretch, even though she was eating less than a sparrow herself. Often she hid from the rent man to buy food. Patsy would sometimes pop in after school before going home and she never went in empty-handed, for her mother had told her how little Maria bought each week at the shops.

'Fine welfare state this is,' Martha complained to Sean one night. 'I thought they were supposed to look after you from the cradle to the grave. They're not looking after Maria at all. If you saw what she buys to live on for a week, I tell you, Sean, ours would demolish it in one meal.'

'Well, the money is not to buy luxury food,' Sean said. 'But it should provide the basics. No child should have to go hungry.'

'But they are, and Maria looks ill. I popped in the

other day and the house was so cold, my breath was coming out in whispery vapour. Our Patsy says it's often like that. The point is, with rationing I can only do so much, and there is only so much she will take anyway. If she does ever agree to take any food from me, I think she gives it to the children.'

'You'd do the same,' Sean said. 'Any mother would.'

'I know, but—'

'You know, it might not be the Government at fault here at all,' Sean said. 'It all depends on how much Barney gives her out of his dole.'

'Ah, well, that's it, isn't it?' Martha said 'And she'd never tell us what he allows her. She has too much pride.'

Maria often felt as if she was on a treadmill and not going anywhere fast. Each week she would put two shillings out for the gas and the same for the electricity, try to put some aside for coal, and buy food with the rest. The rent was always the last consideration, so by Christmas she was seriously in arrears.

There would have been nothing at all in the children's stockings that year if it hadn't been for the kindness of Martha and Sean. Patsy bought for them too, and so did Tony, despite the fact that, as an apprentice his wages were small. Pooling the ration books together, with the generosity of Martha, ensured they all had plenty to eat and Maria sat at the end of the meal on Christmas Day and realised she felt full for the first time in weeks.

She barely saw Barney, she told Martha as they washed up, as he was out all day and at the pub all night. She preferred it that way. She didn't know where he went, didn't really care and she spoke to him as little as possible, glad he didn't seem to expect her to provide food for him too. He still demanded sex regularly, whatever state he would come home in, and sometimes she had to resist the urge to push him away because she knew what might happen if she did that.

Barney, in fact, had got himself a nice little earner. MacKay owned a bookie's and the night Barney had told him about the events at Dunlop's, he offered him the job of bookie's runner.

'The last geezer has just been sent down for three months,' he told Barney. 'So you've got to keep your eyes peeled for the rozzers, like, but the job's yours if you want it.'

Barney wanted it all right and the money was useful, especially as now he began to be hooked on horse racing as well as poker, where he could lose money just as effectively.

All through the cold days of January, February and even into March, Maria took Theresa and Jack out when they couldn't stand the cold in their house any longer, tucking them both in the pram to keep them warm. On very bleak or wet days, they would make for the library in Erdington, where it was warm and dry. Maria would read countless books to the children and for a little while they were able to forget their grumbling stomachs.

It was at the end of March that Patsy had an idea to put to Maria.

'Dressmaking?' Maria said doubtfully. 'Do you really think I could make money with it?'

'Course you could,' Patsy said confidently. 'Look at the great comments you got when people realised you had made the girls' Communion dresses.'

'Yes, but—'

'No buts. You'll not know until you try and, God knows, it is better than doing nothing.'

Maria had to admit that. It was just that when you were stuck in grinding poverty and constantly hungry, it was hard to think about anything other than the next meal, let alone get enthusiastic about anything.

'I mean,' Patsy went on, 'after September, you will only have Jack at home.'

'Aye,' Maria said. She could hardly wait for Theresa to join her sister. At school she would have a third of a pint of milk each day, as well as a hot cooked meal. Then the worry would slide off her a little.

Patsy's voice broke in on her thoughts. 'Anyway,' she said with a shy smile, 'I want you to keep in practice because I want you to design and make my wedding dress.'

'Your wedding dress!'

Patsy blushed as she said, 'His name is Andrew Forrester and he is a teacher, like me, only he teaches maths in King Edward's Grammar School in Aston. We were at college together, but didn't want to start anything serious then. Anyway, we met again at a conference and decided we liked each other as much as we ever had. Andrew had moved to Birmingham for this job and we starting seeing each other. Just last night he asked me to marry him. We are choosing the ring on Saturday.'

'Well, well you dark horse,' Maria said. 'All cut and

dried, it seems, and I have never caught even a glimpse of him.'

'I know,' Patsy said. 'It was all a bit sudden. Mom and Sean didn't really meet him to talk to till yesterday evening, though of course they have seen him when he has picked me up when we were going out.'

'Have you a wedding date set?'

'Not yet,' Patsy said. 'We're not in a desperate rush, and really a lot depends on the housing situation. I could hardly move into the flat Andrew rents with two other teachers.'

'Hardly,' Maria agreed.

'Enough about me now, Maria,' Patsy said. 'Are you going to give this dressmaking a go?'

Maria was undecided. Her self-esteem was at an all-time low. She felt she was a lousy wife and a lousy mother, and at that moment she didn't think she was a good dressmaker either – all right for the family, but not to sell to other people. She couldn't do it.

The light dimmed suddenly and Maria said, 'Hang on, I'll put some money in the meter.'

But there was no money. Her frantic fingers scrabbled on the shelf, and she was desperately telling herself the coins had been pushed to the back, or perhaps fallen out on the floor. They hadn't, however, and in the end she faced the realisation that the money was gone. She would give no prizes for guessing who had taken it. Now she faced a choice. She could either sink to the floor in abject misery and despair, and howl like an animal, which she longed to do, or she could square her shoulders and fight.

She took a deep breath, went back into the room

and said, 'OK, Patsy, what do we do about this and where on earth do I start?'

Martha, delighted that Maria was attempting to pull herself out of the mire, loaned her money to get her started, and minded Jack and Theresa while she went into the Bull Ring for the material. Adverts were put up in the newsagent's shops just down the road from Maria's, and the church hall at the abbey, and Patsy did a good job of passing the word around. Gradually the work came in. It was Communion dresses she was in demand for at first. Each one was unique as Maria would first ask what the mothers wanted and then do a few sketches before starting on the material. The trickle became a flood as other mothers saw and were often amazed by the finished articles.

Maria was happier than she could remember being in a long time. Turning raw material into something beautiful always soothed her; actually to be paid for it, so that she could put food on the table and buy coal for the fire, was wonderful. But she was careful. She hid the amount of food she bought, buying only so much a day. She never left money lying about again and carried her purse with her at all times. Barney knew nothing about it because the sewing was done in the bedroom and all sign of it tidied away by the evening, when he might be home for a few hours.

The first thing Maria did was to pay Martha back. The next was to pay off her rent arrears, so that by the time the new Queen Elizabeth was crowned in Westminster Abbey on 2 June, Maria was debt free. She felt it was a new era in her life too. She had felt her self-confidence seeping back, and Martha thought it was marvellous to see her cheerful smile again and hear her laughter. She mentioned it to her when she arrived to see the Coronation on the television set Sean has bought to mark the occasion and they were making tea for everyone.

'I do feel good,' Maria said. 'Wonderful, in fact. Can actually feel we have a future – me and the children, anyway. Oh, I know there is still Barney, but he is in so little these days I see him less than I would a lodger.'

'He stays long enough to get you pregnant on a fairly regular basis,' Martha commented drily.

'How do you know?' Maria said. 'I'm not showing yet.'

'I told you before there is a sort of bloom about you. How do you feel about it, anyway?'

'I'm delighted,' Maria said. 'I don't care how many children I have as long as I have the money to care for them properly, and now I have.'

There was a sudden roar from Sean. Martha said, 'Come on, it must be starting. We wouldn't want to miss anything. Can you manage that tray?'

The streets of London were gilded in gold and silver, bedecked with flowers and filled with cheering crowds of people lining the route the royal coach would take. Not even the unseasonable cold and drizzly rain could dampen their enthusiasm.

Watching them even stirred something in Maria, and she was able to feel a sense of pride in her adopted country, which was at that moment riding high. The Korean War, much to Martha's relief, was drawing to a close, Edmund Hillary had climbed Everest, the highest mountain in the world, just a day before, and now a new Elizabethan age was to be born. No wonder the nation was called *Great* Britain.

The young and very beautiful queen stepped into the abbey and the multitudinous noise of the crowds outside could still be heard. She had a diadem of precious stones on her head and a royal robe, which the commentator explained was of crimson velvet trimmed with gold lace. The long, heavy, exquisitely decorated train was carried by six maids of honour, all dressed in gowns of white and gold.

Then the robe and diadem were removed and the Queen stood alone, just clothed in a garment of plain linen to be anointed by the Archbishop, while music, said to be Handel's *Messiah*, swelled about the church. Elizabeth knelt for the blessing and to receive the bracelets of sincerity and vision before approaching the throne. When the heavy crown was taken from the altar and placed upon her head, a collective sigh went around all those watching in Martha's house.

The rest of the day was given up to merriment. Street parties had been organised, though the weather meant it took place in the abbey church hall. Even so, a fine time was had by all. Maria took her tired children home at a fairly decent hour, but she was told later the parties had gone on till the early hours.

Maria had to get back to work the next day. The First Communion day was in just over a fortnight and she had a couple of dresses to finish. But it had been quite lucrative and she wondered for a moment if she could afford Irish dancing lessons for Sally. She knew the child longed to be able to go. Deirdre had been going to the lessons on Saturday afternoon at the abbey church hall for over a year now, and she demonstrated what she had learnt the previous day on Sunday after Mass. The girls would practise all week. Deirdre had been disappointed that Sally couldn't join her, but Sally wasn't stupid and had accepted it without whining when Maria said she hadn't any spare money for dancing lessons.

Now there was, but Maria wouldn't tell her just yet. She knew there was bound to be a lull in the dress orders once the Communions were over, and she wanted to know, before there were dancing lessons to pay for, just how much work she would pick up on a day-to-day basis.

However, Maria picked up work all through the summer, although some of it was repairs – replacing broken zips or altering dresses. There was also better-paid work, like making outfits for weddings and special parties. Maria was very careful with the money she earned, knowing it could dry up at any time, and she hoarded it in a box she had hidden under the mattress.

Theresa joined her sister at the Abbey School in the autumn and Maria accepted the fact that now that Theresa wasn't at hand to watch and play with her little brother, any major sewing would have to wait until the evening. She was sure, however, she could manage to go on some time yet, for the baby wasn't due till the middle of December and she had money enough to last a few weeks without earning, until she was on her feet again.

* * *

Maria returned to the house one day in late November after leaving the children up at the school and was astounded to find the front door ajar. She normally went in the back way, but she pushed the front door open cautiously. Jack was clamouring to get out of his pushchair, so she unstrapped him and took him in her arms, putting her finger to her lips. Had someone broken in? But then why would they? She hadn't anything worth stealing.

It must be Barney, she decided, and she called out, but there was no answer. There was no one in the living room or the kitchen. Holding Jack's hand, she went up the stairs, laboriously because the baby lay heavily on her now.

There was no one in the bedroom either, but neither was there the sewing machine that had stood on the table by the bay window. Maria sank down on the bed. The bloody bastard had taken her sewing machine. By Christ, she'd not let him get away with it, not this time. That sewing machine made the difference to whether her children had enough to eat or not. She'd find out where the bloody selfish bugger had taken it and buy it back if she had to, she decided.

Barney had had a bad day. Solly at the pawnshop had given him bloody peanuts for the sodding sewing machine and he'd near bust a gut carrying it up the village. It was a ton weight and what he'd got for it went nowhere near paying off the debt at the bookie's. Even MacKay had got shirty, and he'd laugh if he tried to give him so little. The only thing to do, as far as Barney could see, was put it on another horse and try to increase it that way. There were races all afternoon. In that way he lost every penny piece he had.

He went to see MacKay that evening before the man sought him out. 'Take what I owe out of my wages,' he pleaded.

'You ain't got no wages,' MacKay told him. 'Not this week, anyroad. You've taken it already in advances and so far it would take nearly three weeks' wages to clear that debt.'

'I know . . .'

'You know nowt, mate,' MacKay said. 'Face it, you're just a loser. A piss artist. Get out of my sight!'

'You mean—'

'I mean you are sacked, fired, finished. I don't want to see you ever again.'

Barney stumbled from the man's office. He hadn't even the money for the bus fare and he set off to walk home. When he reached the Norton, he went inside.

'Give us a pint George and put it on the slate.'

George shook his head. 'Sorry, you already owe too much.'

'Just a bloody pint.'

'I'm running a business here, not a bleeding charity,' George said. 'Pay up or sling your hook.'

With no option but to leave, Barney stood outside the pub, undecided what to do. Jesus, how he needed a drink. The only way he could see of getting any money was from Maria. Oh, he knew she would moan, complain, cry and say she had none, but if she knew what was good for her she would make no fuss about it.

Maria had just put the children to bed and washed

up the dinner dishes when Barney came to the door. She was surprised to see him so early and comparatively sober, but she was ready for him.

Barely was he properly through the door, and before her courage could fail her, she said, 'What have you done with the sewing machine?'

'What you on about?'

'You know,' Maria spat out. 'You've taken that sewing machine. It had to be you.'

'Yeah, I needed the money. So what?'

'It belonged to me.'

'No, it bloody didn't. I paid for it,' Barney said. 'Anyway, it's no bleeding use and I needed the cash. And now I need more, so what you got in that purse?'

'What I have is already accounted for and you won't get a penny piece from me.'

'We'll see about that, you cocky bitch,' Barney said, making a grab for her.

Suddenly, something snapped in Maria. She saw in her mind's eye how it had been just a few months before, the half starving and shivering children crying with discomfort and pain she could do nothing to ease. Never ever, while there was breath in her body, would she go back to that situation.

Although her bulk made her clumsy, she flew at Barney, raking his face with her nails as she cried, 'Tell me what you've done with it, you bastard.'

Barney, taken unawares, staggered under the assault. Then he recovered himself. All the frustrations of the day were in the punches he powered into Maria's face. She tried to protect herself, but she groaned and cried out in panic as she felt her mouth fill up with blood.

A final punch knocked her to the floor and she instinctively curled in a ball and put her arms around her stomach protectively as Barney kicked at her viciously till even the moans and sighs had stopped and she lay still.

Patsy, coming down with Andrew to tell Maria they thought they had found a house they could afford, found her.

'Who in God's name . . . ?' began Andrew, shocked beyond measure, but Patsy had flown to her cousin's unconscious frame and, leaning over her gently, put the fingers against her neck and sighed with relief when she felt the pulse.

'Get an ambulance,' she told Andrew. 'There is a phone box on Wood Acre Road. I think that will be the nearest.'

'God this is awful,' Andrew said. 'I'll get an ambulance, don't worry, but who did this?'

Even while Patsy had tended her cousin, she had taken account of the room, the overturned chair, and the fact that Maria's bag lay open on the floor. The purse, stripped of money, lying beside it, told her plainly who had done it.

'It was Barney,' she said bitterly. 'Her husband. Now go for the ambulance, for pity's sake, and then get Mom and Sean. We'll have to take the kids up to our house, for I am not leaving them here and I want to go in the ambulance with Maria.'

Martha and Sean arrived minutes before the ambulance, and while Martha cried at the state of Maria, Sean was too shocked and angry to shed a tear and asked only if she was alive. He saw Maria and Patsy into the ambulance, helped wrap blankets around the children and carry them up to his house, and then he made for the door again.

'Where are you going?' Martha cried in alarm.

'Where do you think?' Sean said. 'I'm going to find him.'

'Ah, Sean, no,' Martha cried.

'Let him go,' Andrew said. 'No man should get away with what Maria's husband did to her. Sean will feel less of a man if he doesn't do this. If she was any relative of mine I would feel the same.'

However, he saw the rage bubbling in Sean and knew he could be piling up a heap of trouble for himself if he sought out Barney on his own. Maybe just now, while he was in this mood, Sean needed protecting from himself.

'If it makes you feel better I will go along with Sean,' he said.

Martha didn't argue any more. After all, Sean had good reason to beat the man to pulp. Poor dear Maria – and on her time too – but her first priority now was to settle the confused children.

CHAPTER TWENTY-THREE

The two men strode down Holly Lane, making for the Norton. Sean knew that if Barney had money at all he would make for a pub, and he had the change he had taken out of Maria's purse. George told them he'd seen Barney earlier in the evening and he wouldn't serve him until he had paid some off his slate.

'When you do find him, remind him he owes me two pound ten, will you?'

Sean pulled out his wallet and paid the man. 'God, Sean, you don't have to do this.'

'Aye, I do,' Sean said. He leant across the counter and said quietly, 'Between you and me, that brute has beaten Maria up tonight.'

'Ah God! Bad, like?'

'Bad enough,' Sean said. 'She's a right mess, unconscious and away to hospital. It's only just over two weeks till she is due to give birth. Me and Andrew here are out to find him. And when I do, he'll wish he'd never been born. I tell you, George, when I find the man, I'll bloody swing for him.'

'No one will blame you, mate,' George said. 'Give

him one for me while you are about it. You might try the Black Swan, down Aston way. I know he goes there to play cards sometimes.'

'Thanks, George.'

'Drink before you go? On the house, like?'

'No, thanks all the same, George,' Sean said. 'When I meet up with the man, I want to be stone-cold sober.'

They did find Barney at the Black Swan, hard at a game of poker. When Barney saw Sean he paled at the murderous look in his eyes. 'Get up,' he said through gritted teeth. 'You and I have business outside.'

Barney had no intention of going outside or anywhere else with Sean in that sort of mood. 'I'm busy,' he said brusquely.

'Like hell you are,' Sean said, jerking Barney to his feet.

'Hey, what's going on?' one of the others demanded. 'You nearly had the table upended then.'

Sean didn't even hear him. He was staring at Barney, who was shaking in fear.

'Tell him,' Barney said, appealing to the others desperately.

The men didn't know what was up. One of them said, 'We were in the middle of a game, so I don't know what you are about, but—'

'I am about beating this little shit here to pulp for the way he has left my niece this night,' Sean said.

The men looked uncomfortable and Andrew put in, 'This is family business, but he has put his wife in hospital tonight.'

Barney was blustering his innocence and pleading with his card partners not to let this happen. One of the men said, 'I hear all you say and it's bad right enough, but I never did hold with two against one.'

'I'll lay no hand on him,' Andrew said. 'This is between the two of them.'

'Take him then,' the man said. 'He was bloody losing anyway, and there is nothing I like better than a good fight.'

They grouped in a nearby alley and Barney was so scared, sweat was running in rivulets down his face. His mouth was suddenly dry and he had trouble swallowing. Someone held his coat, and Andrew took Sean's. They faced each other, circling slowly.

Sean was the older, but hardened by physical work, sober and angry, while Barney was semi-drunk and gone to fat with all the beer he had put away. Yet Sean knew it would be wrong to underestimate him: the man had bulk and youth on his side.

It was obvious from the first that this would not be a gentlemanly fight. Sean was out for blood and the fists he pummelled into Barney's face left that in no doubt. Barney had a few good punches that winded Sean and battered his face, but eventually, under a barrage of blows, Barney sank to his knees, too dazed even to attempt to protect himself. Sean continued to lay into him until he eventually lost consciousness and crumpled in a heap on the cobblestones.

Then Sean did something he'd never done before. He remembered how Maria had been and lifted his foot and powered the kick into Barney's stomach. Sean saw him shudder and moan, but he had no pity for him.

When he lifted his foot again, Andrew put a hand on his arm. 'Away now,' he said. 'He's had enough, Sean.'

Sean shook his head, trying to clear the black mist from his mind and the anger running white hot through his veins. He knew he had come near to killing Barney – had wanted to kill him and would have done so and not even felt sorry about it. This shocked him because never in his life had he wished to hurt another human being. Yet he still said, 'Enough? While there is breath in his body it's never enough. Scum like him don't deserve to live.'

'Come on, Sean,' Andrew coaxed. 'Let's go home now. It's over. Maybe someone had better call an ambulance.'

'I'll do it, mate,' one man offered. 'But don't worry, we'll say we know nowt about it and just that we found him like that.'

Patsy sat beside Maria's hospital bed, though Maria wasn't aware that she was there. Tears rained down the young girl's face as she looked at her cousin, her face swathed in bandages so that only her eyes were left uncovered. Why, she wondered, had everyone allowed this to happen? She and Martha had both known that Barney was regularly beating Maria up and yet neither had encouraged her to throw him out. Forget all that shit about marrying for better or worse. Nowhere in the wedding service did it say a man had the right to hit his wife, never mind render her senseless. Well, if she pulled through this, they must all make sure Barney was never let near her again.

Sean joined Patsy there. Though a distraught Martha had done what she could with his face, he still bore the marks of the fight: a black eye, busted nose and grazes on both cheeks. Patsy knew without asking how he'd got those marks. 'Dear God,' he breathed as he saw the state of his niece. 'How is she?'

Patsy fought to control her tears as she said, 'Bad enough. She is bruised nearly from head to toe and there are a number of ribs broken.' Her voice wobbled and she couldn't go on. Sean put his arm around her and eventually she was able to say, 'They are worried about internal damage too and will be taking her to the theatre tomorrow if she remains stable tonight.'

'What about the baby?'

Maria shook her head. 'It's alive at the moment and that's all they know. She might go into labour and she is so injured it could be dangerous if she did. The baby could be born alive, dead, or brain damaged.' She heard Sean's sharp intake of breath, and she leant closer against him, needing the comfort as she asked, 'What's going to happen next, Dad, if she pulls through this?'

Patsy had called Sean 'Dad' for the first time. In other circumstance, that would have delighted him, but it hardly registered then, and he said, 'What do you mean?'

'I mean, she can't go on the way she was,' Patsy said impatiently, 'living with that madman because she was once married to him.'

'No,' Sean agreed. 'Indeed she cannot. I am taking tomorrow off work and will go off to the Council to tell them the situation. All the locks will need to be changed on the house, for a start, and then I am off to the police station. A man at work was telling me there is some order that Maria can take out, when she is well enough, that will prevent Barney ever coming near her again. Mind you,' he added, 'there is no immediate rush about this. Barney will be going nowhere but a hospital bed for some time yet, I'm thinking.'

'I can see that you have been fighting.'

'Fighting?' repeated Sean. 'I near killed that man tonight and if it hadn't been for your Andrew I might have done.'

'Andrew?'

'Aye, he came along with me,' Sean said, then added, 'Don't look like that. He had no hand in anything. He never laid a finger on Sean and likely stopped me ending my life on the gallows.'

Patsy looked at the good, kind man she had loved for years and knew there would have been no justice in the world if he had suffered because he had rid the world of scum. She was heartily glad Andrew had been there and been able to stop him.

'He's a good man you have there,' Sean said. 'He's coming round tomorrow after school and helping me move Maria's things up to our house. Knows a mate with a van, apparently.'

'He's like you, Dad,' Patsy said. 'He will do a good turn for anyone. I think underneath I was looking for somebody like you. I did date a few creeps at college, but for marriage I had to go for gold.'

'As I did,' Sean said quietly.

'I know. Dad,' Patsy said, kissing Sean on the cheek. 'My dearest wish is to have a good and happy marriage like you have with Mom.'

Later that night, Maria gave birth to a baby boy. She had it by caesarean section, as they couldn't risk her giving birth naturally. First indications were that the baby was fine, though smaller than they would have liked. The doctor advised the family to have the child christened, just in case.

It seems dreadful to do this without his mother being there and without even giving her a say in the name chosen,' Martha said that night, when Sean and Pasty returned with the news.

'We can't afford to drag our heels over this,' Sean said. 'The hospital stressed urgency.'

'I know. It's just . . .'

'I know what she wanted the baby called anyway,' Patsy said. 'Martin Patrick if it was a boy.'

'That's it then,' Sean said, and gave a sudden yawn. 'I'll see the priest in the morning.'

'It is morning,' Martha said, because the time stood at two o'clock.

'Aye,' Sean said. 'I'll give the poor bugger a few hours' rest. To tell you the truth, I'll need it myself. I'm bushed.'

'Wait a minute,' Martha said. 'Don't we have to decide on godparents? It can't really be us again, being godparents already to Theresa.'

'And me and Tony to Jack,' Patsy said. 'There's always Andrew, though.'

Andrew was delighted to be asked. As there was no one they could think off to be godmother, Martha decided to do the honours again, for the baby's sake. The next morning, the little group assembled in the hospital chapel to name the small, protesting baby Martin Patrick McPhearson.

*　　*　　*

Maria opened her eyes five days later and wished she hadn't bothered. As soon as she was conscious, she was aware of pain everywhere. For a minute or two she was disorientated and then the memories came flooding back. She knew why she was in hospital, but how she had got there she didn't know. There had been a baby inside her, and she felt it that had gone, though she couldn't be sure. Her hands were heavily bandaged, and so was her body in parts, it seemed. Her face felt stiff, strange, and the tips of her fingers protruding from the bandages felt binding there too.

A nurse, catching sight of the slight movement, approached the bed and beamed approval at her. 'Doctor will be glad to see that you are awake at last,' she said.

'I hurt,' Maria said, the pain causing her to gasp. 'Everywhere I hurt.'

'The drugs trolley will be along shortly and we can give you something for that,' the nurse said. 'Now I'll just tell Doctor—'

'No, wait,' Maria cried. 'What happened to my baby?'

The nurse smiled. 'You had a little boy,' she said. 'He was baptised as a precaution, but he is a little darling and we have him in the nursery now.'

The words spun in Maria's brain. 'You mean he is alive.'

'He's very much alive' the nurse said with a laugh, 'and letting us know it. He's a little fighter. You can see him later if the doctor thinks you fit enough. Your people were here and named him Martin Patrick.'

She was away then to fetch the doctor. Maria tried

to imagine a tenacious little baby surviving such a beating. She longed to hold him in her arms and feel him suckling against her.

However, she was allowed to do nothing but gaze at him. She was saddened to find that for the first five days of the baby's life, she hadn't even known of his existence.

'Sure, you'll have a lifetime to get to know him,' the nurse said, when she spoke of this. 'Now you must rest and heal yourself quickly, so you can take the baby home and care for him.'

The doctor stressed rest too. 'You have a number of broken ribs,' he told her. 'However, far more worrying was the damage to your spleen, one of your kidneys and your liver. Now, we have done a small operation to repair the spleen, but we have left the kidney for the moment, to see what time will do. A damaged liver, providing the damage is not extensive, will heal itself.'

'So how long will I be in hospital?'

'It's impossible to be accurate about these things, my dear, but a few weeks yet.'

Maria didn't care how long she was in hospital, for she felt protected there. Sean had told her he'd had the locks changed on the house and about her lodging an injunction against Barney, forbidding him to come near her. As if waving a piece of paper would stop Barney doing anything he wanted to do, she thought. If he couldn't open the door, he would kick it down. No, she was better in hospital and, much as she missed her children, she dreaded the time when she would leave.

'She's scared stiff, and little wonder,' Sean said to

Andrew, after the locks had been changed. 'Someone should go and see Barney, warn him off. It can't be me, for even now I would be tempted to put my hands around his scraggy neck, and squeeze hard.'

'I'll do it,' Andrew offered. 'He needs to know the house is out of bounds to him or he might just turn up there. For our own sake too, we ought to know how he is and if he is going to make a formal complaint or something like that.'

'He wouldn't do that, would he?'

'He might well,' Andrew said. 'He's just the type. But let's cross that bridge as and when we come to it.'

Barney came to, twenty-four hours after he had been brought into the hospital, to find a policeman sitting beside his bed. The policeman explained about the attack. The memory of Sean and what he had done came flooding back. Everywhere ached and throbbed. Hatred for Sean festered inside Barney and he wanted to make a complaint, tell the copper. To see the man hauled off to gaol would give him the greatest pleasure in the world.

But then he remembered what he had done to Maria. He couldn't remember all of the attack, for it had been done in a blinding rage, but he could remember enough. He might end up the loser again if he made waves, so he told the copper he was jumped as he left the pub. It was dark and he didn't see his assailant.

He left hospital a week later, on Friday, 4 December. Because he was not allowed home, the police got him a bed in a hostel. The place reeked of unwashed bodies, vomit, wee and a hint of meths. It was peopled by down-and-outs, whom Barney thought were the dregs of society, and the mattress of the bed he was given to sleep on was so flee-ridden he was kept up all night scratching.

The first thing he did next morning was see the governor of the place and say he didn't belong there. For God's sake, he had a nice comfortable home and a wife to warm his bed. True, she'd gone all prissy on him just lately because he had smacked her about a bit, but he was sure when he had a talk to her she would see where her duty lay.

The governor glared at him. 'You injured your wife so badly that she is still in hospital, as far as I am aware,' he said. 'If you attempt to see her or even approach the house, then you will find yourself in prison. If you feel you don't belong here, then prove it. Go out and get yourself a job. With a bit of luck the council might rent you out a flat or you will be able to rent one privately. That is the only option open to you.'

Over a week later, Barney thought he was going mad. Because the hostel wasn't considered a proper address, he had to call for his dole daily and most of it he had to give in for his lodgings. It was worse than bleeding prison anyway, the sodding place. One time, he'd spent most of his dole, arrived back drunk and they wouldn't let him in. Another time he tried to come in late and they said all the beds were full. Two nights out in the freezing cold nearly did for him.

And if he didn't have a drink soon, he felt he would go crazy. So far he had refused the meths a couple of tramps had offered him. One of them had said, 'In a day or so you won't be so choosy.' By God he was right, because by the end of that first week he would have drunk anything. What he wouldn't give for a bottle of poteen now. That brought Ireland to mind. He thought of the last letter his brother had sent him. He'd written that they were thinking of an early release for him on account of his good behaviour. Funny, he'd never have thought 'good behaviour' and Seamus would ever be mentioned in the same sentence. Barney could write to him, but Seamus couldn't write back because he had no address. Maybe Barney should just go over and see him? Surely to God he would find some place to hang out once he got there.

But to go to Ireland he needed money. You needed money for any damned thing. He wandered down to the Bull Ring. He'd had the watery porridge and toast at the hostel but that had been a few hours before. He couldn't afford to spend what he had left on food because he needed a drink so badly. The Bull Ring was the place for pinching off the barrows, especially on a Saturday when the place was always so full. While the costers were plying their trade up at the front and had queues forming, they couldn't keep an eye on the back of the stall as well.

And suddenly, there just in front of him, was a woman with her bag open and her purse almost poking out of it. In a split second, it was transferred to Barney's pocket. Then he was pushing his way through the crowds and out on to High Street before he opened the purse.

'Twenty-two pound, six and four pence,' he breathed.

He put the lot into his pocket, threw the purse in the nearest waste-paper bin and stood a moment, deciding where to go.

He needed to go to the house and find out if Seamus had written him another letter for, not knowing of the latest developments, that was where he would write. Anyway, he needed clothes. He only had those he stood up in, and even he could smell the pong coming off him. Surely to God he had a right to get his clothes, whatever order Maria had to keep him away.

First, though, he badly needed a drink. He went into a pub on Corporation Street. He had a great many drinks and some hours later he staggered out. The short winter's day was almost at an end and it was very dusky by the time he got to Steelhouse Lane to catch the bus home.

However, in his drunken state, he got the bus to Erdington, instead of Pype Hayes. He got off at the village. Darkness had fallen now, but this suited Barney's purpose, which was to get into the house unseen. He set off to walk.

Most people at the church knew about Maria being away in the hospital to have the baby and Martha looking after all the children. One Sunday after Mass, a woman gave her some tickets to see the afternoon showing of the pantomime *Puss in Boots* at the Repertory Theatre in the town on the following Saturday afternoon.

'Cheer the babbies up,' she said. 'And my girl works there and gets some tickets for nowt, like.'

Martha thanked her warmly, delighted to have them,

and only sorry Deirdre couldn't come with them. She had her dancing class on Saturday afternoons and, as she was in a doing a solo in the Christmas concert, she couldn't afford to miss a lesson. As Sean and the boys would be off to the match, Patsy, who wanted to visit the library anyway, arranged to pick Deirdre up from her class and bring her home. Martha didn't want her returning to an empty house and Patsy didn't mind. She was at a loose end anyway, as Andrew was refereeing a school football match.

So when, that Saturday, Deirdre emerged from the hall, shrugging herself into her coat, her cheeks glowing crimson from the exertion, Patsy was waiting for her. Deirdre was glad she was there because it was pitch-black. As they walked, and Deirdre prattled on about the dancing, this girl and that, and what they had done or said, Patsy let her mind wander to her wedding day, which was set for late August, when hopefully the weather would be sunny, warm and dry.

They were walking down Orchard Road. At the end of it was a crossroads, where to the right was the village, while Arthur Road was to the left.

Barney was at the crossroads. He heard them coming, stepped back behind a hedge and waited until they were nearly level with him.

'Well, well,' he said, suddenly appearing. 'Look who's here.'

Patsy looked at him and in the glow of the street-lamp, she could see that his eyes were red-rimmed and glazed, his skin coarsened by drink and there was a smell coming off him like rancid cheese. She was repelled by the thought she had ever found this man in any way attractive. She wanted to smack him across the face, or spit at him, but she knew that if she was to complain about Barney, Sean could go after him again and then anything could happen.

'Keep away from him at all costs,' Martha had said. 'But if you do meet up and if you have to speak, be polite for God's sake. And whatever he says to you, keep quiet about, even if it's offensive – in fact, especially if it is offensive. If you care about Sean at all, the least he hears about Barney the better.'

So, mindful of her mother's words, Patsy said, 'Hello, Barney,' and felt Deirdre's hand slip inside her own.

Barney noticed this and bent to Deirdre's level.

She smelt the putrid stench of him and saw the brown stubs of teeth in his mouth that stunk of stale beer and cigarettes as he said, 'What's up with you? Cat got your tongue?'

'No.'

'That's good then. You frightened of me?'

Deirdre had never felt so scared, but her daddy said you should always stand up to bullies and so she willed her voice not to shake as she said, 'No. No, I ain't.'

'Bet you are . . .' Barney began.

'Leave her alone, Barney,' Patsy said sharply.

Barney ignored Patsy as if she hadn't spoken. 'You should be scared. God, I eat little girls like you for breakfast.'

'No you don't,' Deirdre said scornfully.

That's enough,' Patsy tried again. 'Come on, Deirdre, we have to go home.'

Barney's hand shot out and fastened around Deirdre's

arms so tightly that she cried out with the pain of it.

'Leave go of me,' she yelled, trying to wrench it away, but the grip didn't slacken.

'Let her alone, for pity's sake,' Patsy protested.

Deirdre remembered that Sally said her mommy said that when their daddy was going to hit her. 'Does he hit her, your daddy?' Deirdre had asked, appalled.

'Yes he does,' Sally had said fiercely. 'Mommy never says. She always says she walked into something to explain the marks on her face and that, but I hear him. I hate my daddy, I do, and I'm frightened of him too. I just wish he'd go away somewhere and not come back.'

Deirdre had been quite shocked. She couldn't think of a time when she might not love her daddy, but then her daddy was nothing like Sally's. Now, suddenly, she was sick of it all. She was sick of Barney going around hurting and frightening people and just getting away with it.

Barney gave her arm a sudden twist and Deirdre bit her lip to stop the gasp of pain escaping, because she decided she was going to stand up to this man, however scared she felt inside.

'Do you want to know what I do to bold wee girls who don't do what they're told?'

'No, I bloody well don't.' Deirdre yelled straight into Barney's face. 'In fact, I don't want to listen to anything you say. I hate you. Everyone hates you and I wish you would just drop dead.' And then, before Patsy could do a thing about it, she hit Barney full in the face with the flat of her hand. The surprise caused him to loosen his hold slightly, and she jerked and was free.

'Don't you dare lay a hand on her,' Patsy cried suddenly, catching hold of Barney's arm, raised to retaliate with his fist balled. She knew she couldn't hold Barney for long, and to Deirdre she cried, 'Run, for Christ's sake.'

Deirdre ran like the wind, streaking along Arthur Road, expecting any minute to hear feet pounding after her. She ran up Holly Lane and into Grange Road, where she had to stop, out of breath. She took the precaution of hiding behind a hedge of one of the large, imposing houses there until she had stopped gasping. Still there was no sign of pursuit. She risked a cautious look out and saw Barney walking down Holly Lane, almost dragging Patsy behind him.

Deirdre chewed her thumbnail and wondered what to do. There was nowhere for her to run to escape a Barney intent on finding her. Patsy had the key to their house, which was the first place he would look for her, and Maria was still in the hospital. Anyway, where was he taking Patsy? What if he hurt her – killed her even – and she, Deirdre, had just run away and hid? She knew she had to follow them and she set out stealthily.

Deirdre soon knew where they were making for: Nock's Brickworks on Holly Lane. It had been worked for years and, as they had dug out the clay, a deep quarry had formed behind. Now the place didn't even warrant a watchman. It was deserted most of the time, the buildings fast becoming derelict. The children were forbidden to go near it, both because of the depth of the quarry and also because it had quicksand at its base, so of course it drew them all, but especially the boys, like a magnet.

Deirdre had just been the once, six months before with Paul, when she threatened to tell on him if he didn't take her, so using the guise that they were going to the library, they left the house together one Saturday morning. It was as easy as pie to get in, because the fencing had fallen into the same disrepair over the years as the buildings. Paul said in broad daylight it was best to cut down the side, so that you wouldn't be seen going into the place by people in the houses on the other side of Holly Lane. 'Once we are in, there is a mound of earth that hides us from the road,' Paul said. 'The only place you can be seen then is at the edge of the quarry.'

Deirdre soon saw that down the side large areas of the buckled fencing had been pushed in, leaving mangled shards of rusty metal sticking up, which she was careful to step over. The ground was littered with half-bricks, broken slates, splintered glass and, here and there, lumps of wood and all of it covered in muck and mud.

Deirdre was glad she had come for a look and could see the draw for boys – once over the mound it was a grand place to build dens and all – but she knew she wouldn't be a regular visitor. Now she was this far, though, she did want to look in the quarry. She cautiously approached the edge of it and looked down into that deep, deep pit.

'How did they get down?' she asked.

'Same way we do, I suppose,' Paul said nonchalantly.

'You never go down there?' Deirdre asked, appalled.

'Course we do,' Paul said, pointing. 'Look you can see where the clay has been cut to make steps that go all the way down. It's quite safe. We go down on our bottoms. I'll take you, if you like.'

'But, the quicksand . . .'

'Oh, we keep well away from that,' Paul said, pointing again. 'See, that's the quicksand there. It's a deeper orangey colour.'

The thought of it made Deirdre shiver. 'There's an awful lot of it.'

'A fair bit,' Paul admitted. 'Like I say, we keep well away and hang about on the other side. Do you want to go down?'

Deirdre didn't know if she would have gone or not, for at that moment a man came out of his house, shouting at them and shaking his fist.

'Come on.' Paul said, catching her hand. 'This lot aren't above calling the police.' And they hurried out of the place, leaping over the piles of debris. Deirdre had never been back.

But now that was where Barney was taking Patsy and she was going to follow him and find out exactly what he intended to do with her, though her insides trembled with fear.

CHAPTER TWENTY-FOUR

When Patsy had stopped Barney's balled fist hitting Deirdre, he had given a malicious smile as he watched the frightened little figure fleeing and then said to Patsy. 'Let the little shit go, for now. Anyway, you and I have some unfinished business.'

'I don't think so,' Patsy said coldly.

'Oh, yes we do,' Barney said. 'For nearly a year you teased and tormented me, promising me everything and giving me bugger all. And me, like a bloody fool, put up with it. I told myself that you were young, but now you are no longer young and it is pay-back time.'

'No.'

'No? What do you mean, no?' Barney said, a sadistic smile playing around his lips. 'I am not asking you.'

'I'll scream if you touch me.'

The punch took Patsy completely be surprise. She staggered under the power of it and before she could recover herself, one arm was clasped tightly around her mouth. With the other arm encircling her, Barney began dragging her down the road.

Patsy's heart was pounding against her ribs, her mind

full of fear. She was unaware of the stealthy footsteps behind them, but Barney heard them and knew who they belonged to because in the glare of the streetlight he had spotted Deirdre peeping out from Grange Road. Let her follow, he thought savagely. It'll be her turn soon. That was the only way he knew to take revenge on Sean. But for now he intended to teach the teasing and tormenting Patsy a lesson she wouldn't forget in a hurry.

As they neared the brickworks, Deirdre felt her stomach tighten in dread. However unnerving the brickworks were in daylight, she knew they would be twenty times worse in the dark. The darkness did mean, though, that Deirdre could follow Barney and Patsy through the fence. She got as close to them as she could, and ducked down behind a pile of bricks.

She saw Barney hurl Patsy savagely to the ground and she knew how uncomfortable Patsy would be, lying amongst all that rubble. Patsy, though, was barely aware of the bricks digging into her back, or the slime she lay on, for she was petrified by fear. This man intended, at the very least, to violate her and there was little she could do about it.

Even knowing it was futile, through her tears she pleaded with him. 'Please don't do this, Barney. Please let me go now. Please, please,' she begged, clawing at his arm. 'I'll not say a word about it, not to anyone.'

Barney shook her off as if she was a troublesome fly, and continued pulling her clothes off. 'Shut up you little bitch,' he snarled. 'You're a prick teaser. D'you know that? I've waited long enough for you and you might even enjoy it if you let yourself.' With that, he threw himself on top of her.

Oh God! Deirdre knew now what they were doing. Her and Sally had discovered a couple doing the same thing in Pype Hayes Park just the previous summer when they were looking for a good place to hide in a game of hide and seek. They'd been so scared then and had run home without stopping, never giving a thought to the children who might be seeking them. They had told no one what they had seen. So she knew Barney was . . . oh, God, it was disgusting.

She heard Patsy give a sudden shriek and then begin to cry. Deirdre felt sick and knew that she shouldn't be watching this, but she couldn't seem to tear her eyes away from the man powering into Patsy with pig-like grunting noises, while Patsy herself sobbed in anguish, despair and shame.

And then it was over. Barney gave an exultant cry and was still, but continued to lie on top of Patsy as he said, 'That was bleeding marvellous. I didn't know you were a fucking virgin. Jesus, it's a long time since I've had one of those.'

Patsy felt sick to the core of her. Everywhere hurt and she knew she'd be a mass of bruises, but the greatest pain by far was the throbbing one between her legs where she could feel stickiness. Her innards felt as if they were on fire.

Deirdre couldn't take any more. She got to her feet, too disturbed to be cautious, and stumbled over a pile of bricks she hadn't noticed were there. Barney jumped to his feet and peered into the darkness. At first, he saw nothing, but he heard vague scrabbling noises. And then Deirdre reached the road and Barney caught a glimpse of her running up Holly Lane, illuminated for a second by a streetlamp. He smiled. He would definitely deal with her later.

Patsy took the opportunity to sit up and begin replacing her discarded clothes, hard enough in the dark. She felt dirty, degraded and mortified by shame for what she had allowed this brute of a man to do to her, and would hate for anyone to think she had gone with him willingly. So, struggling to her feet, she asked in a scared and shaky voice, 'What was it? Did you hear something?'

'Thought I did,' Barney said. 'But it was just a couple of cats.' He heard Patsy sigh in relief. 'Right then, I'm off,' he said. 'You all right?'

'Course I'm not all right,' Patsy snapped. 'I'll never be all right again, you bloody moronic pervert.'

Barney laughed. 'Don't be so sodding dramatic,' he told her scornfully. 'You'll get over it, and I don't have to say that, if you know what's good for you, it had better remain our secret?'

No he didn't. Patsy knew she would keep quiet, not because of what Barney would do to her if she told, but because of the consequences to others if she let on. Sean would seek him out and kill him. Last time he said Andrew had saved him from the gallows; this time there would be no man living who could stop him. He would kill Barney and hang for it. This time Andrew might not want to stop him – in fact he might want to help him if he had heard what Barney had done.

How could she risk losing the two men she loved most in all the world because of Barney McPhearson? She couldn't, and so she would say nothing. But she still felt immense sorrow and regret for Andrew who'd had his right to be her first lover snatched from him, and she didn't know yet if she could look him in the face, let alone marry him. She felt soiled, defiled.

She sank to her knees, put her hands over her eyes and began to sob as the enormity of what had happened that bleak December evening hit her.

The next thing she was aware of was Deirdre's arms around her shoulders. Deirdre hadn't run far up Holly Lane because she hadn't known if that was all Barney was going to do to Patsy. She had secreted herself behind a hedge in a garden opposite the brickworks and waited. A few minutes later, she saw Barney stride down past her towards his house. She had crept back and found Patsy on her knees, crying as if her heart was broken.

'Don't, Patsy. Please don't,' Deirdre begged. 'Let's go home. When Daddy comes home from the match, we'll tell him and—'

'No,' Patsy said, jerked into awareness. 'Dad must never know about this, Deirdre. Promise me now.'

'But why?' All Deirdre's young life she had been convinced nothing bad would ever happen to her because her father would see that it wouldn't, and would be there to fix anything always.

Oh God, how Patsy hated to tell all to Deirdre. She was so young. But if she was to let something slip . . . Patsy couldn't risk it. There was too much at stake.

'Listen,' she said. 'You don't know all this and normally you wouldn't have to know either, but this is so important. Maria isn't in hospital just because of the baby, as we told all of you. The truth is that Barney beat her up so severely that she was extremely ill and really could have died. Dad went looking for Barney that night and it was only Andrew that stopped him killing the man. If Barney had pressed charges, then Dad would have got into trouble, but Barney didn't, probably because of what he had done to Maria. But if I was to tell Dad about this, well, I wouldn't like to think what he would do, or what Andrew might do to Barney because of it. We might want Barney out of the way permanently – I know I do – but if Dad or Andrew had any hand in putting him in that position then they could hang.'

It was too dark to see Deirdre's face, but Patsy heard the sharp intake of breath and could feel the shock waves running through her. She regretted the fact that she had had to tell a child such sordid things, but she needed her to realise how important it was that she said nothing.

'And now,' said Patsy, getting to her feet, 'if we are to keep this secret, as we must, we have to get home quickly, before everyone is back and sees the state of me.'

She took hold of her sister's hand and they began to pick their way over the rubble.

Fortunately, no one had returned home before them, though when Patsy glanced at the clock she knew that Sean and the boys could be in any time. She ran a bath and it wasn't until she'd reached the bathroom that she had the chance to look at herself properly. The face that looked back at her, with eyes that were panic-riddled, was pasty white and furrowed with strain lines, one cheek and the side of her nose already sporting a nice bruise she would have to hide with make up.

As for her clothes, her winter coat was ripped and filthy and she doubted it would ever recover. Her jumper and skirt too were ruined, and her stockings were in tatters.

As she pulled off the soiled and torn clothes to give them to Deirdre to hide at the bottom of her wardrobe, the young girl caught sight of Patsy's bruised back. Scratches and gashes ran from between her shoulder blades to her buttocks, and there was dried blood at the top of her scratched and discoloured legs.

She felt so sorry for Patsy, but she knew nothing she could say would make any difference. She took the offending clothes away and hid them well before sorting out clean things for her.

Patsy didn't think she would ever get the stink of Barney out of her nostrils, and she scrubbed at her body ruthlessly as the tears flowed once more. She wondered if she would ever feel really clean again. In the end, Deirdre took hold of her hands. 'Enough now, Patsy,' she said. 'Let me bathe your back with the flannel.'

Patsy nodded. Gentle as Deirdre was, she couldn't help wincing. When Patsy eventually heaved herself from the water, Deirdre dried her back, patting it delicately with a soft towel before rubbing salve on. 'Does it feel any easier at all?' she asked.

Patsy sighed and wiped her eyes. There were to be no more tears, she decided, for they were no earthly use. 'If I'm honest, not a lot,' she said, struggling to dress. 'Everything aches and throbs and stings, and my back feels as if it is stiffening up.'

'It's not fair that Barney should get away scot-free

with what he did to you,' Deirdre said. Then, as Patsy went to speak, she said. 'I know we can't say anything and I shan't, but it *isn't* fair, is it?'

Patsy shook her head. 'No, Deirdre, it's anything but fair.' And she put her arms around her young sister.

'Where do you think he is now?' Deirdre asked with a shudder.

'I asked Sean where he would go when he came out of the hospital and he said into some hostel place near the centre of town, because he isn't allowed to go home.'

'So what was he doing out here?'

'Well, there are buses, and I don't suppose they are kept prisoner.'

'Pity they aren't.'

'I agree,' Patsy said. 'And while it is good to talk sometimes, rehashing it all now is just stirring up bad memories, so I am going to try to put it out of my mind and I think you should do the same.'

'I'll try,' Deirdre promised.

However, another worry was pressing on Patsy's mind and not one that she thought she could share with Deirdre – or anyone else, for that matter. What if that disgusting pervert had made her pregnant? She wouldn't be able to keep that secret for long, and how would Andrew react to know that she was pregnant with another man's child?

Patsy knew she wouldn't rest easy until she'd had her period.

Both Patsy and Deirdre would have been even more worried if they had known that Barney was just down the road from them, at the house in Westmead Crescent.

He didn't walk boldly up to the door. He knew about the injunction thing that Maria was supposed to have, and he didn't want any of the neighbours sending for the police before he had a chance to make Maria see that the whole thing was crazy. She had trapped him into a marriage, but he had stood by her in all good faith. Before the priest and more than half the village she had married him for better or worse, richer or poorer, and had also promised to obey him, so what the hell was she playing at? He'd soon make her see how ludicrous the whole thing was. He'd rip that bloody injunction into a million pieces, just see if he didn't.

But first he had to get into the house undetected and he knew full well how to do that. Behind the houses in Westmead Crescent there was a social club and a sports field. The entrance was just round the corner in Woodacre Road. There was a fence surrounding it, but many of the posts had been bent, over the years, to provide access when the gates were closed. That evening, however, the gates stood open and Barney went through them, skirting the clubhouse where he could hear the sound of merriment and loud voices.

Thanks to the lighting surrounding the clubhouse, he was easily able to see where he was. All the gardens ran straight up to the chain-link fence and then, as a sort of screen, the sports field had privet hedges set at intervals along the boundary. Barney slipped through one of the gaps in the privet. And then he was standing at the top of his garden, wondering why the whole place seemed to be in darkness.

He pulled at the link fence, surprised that it wasn't

cemented in anywhere, or even sunken into the ground very far. It was easy to pull it up and make a sizeable hole he could scrabble through. He would need to keep a weather eye open for was the groundsman, though, if he tried this route in daylight.

Once he had cleared the fence, he would be at the top of his garden and protected from view by the mature gooseberry and blackcurrant bushes. The only place anyone could catch sight of him was as he skirted the lawn, though there was little danger at that time of night.

Barney couldn't believe that his key didn't fit the back door. Maria had changed the locks, he thought. The crafty sod. Just wait till he got his hands on her. Not that it mattered. The kitchen window had never fitted properly and he had asked Maria more than once to see about it, for the wind whistled through it shocking at times. However, Maria had never done so, and now he was glad. By inserting the blade of his penknife in the gap and wiggling it about, he was able to force the opening wide enough to get the penknife right in, then push up the catch, open the window and climb inside.

He knew straight away that the house was empty. He didn't turn on any light at first, not wishing to advertise the fact that he was there until he had seen Maria, but used the torch he had knocked from the windowsill as he climbed in. In the living room someone had drawn across the bay window the thick velour curtain that Maria used to draw in the winter to make the room cosier. Barney knew then he could turn on the light because no light penetrated through that curtain. He surveyed the room. There was a light film of dust over everything, but everywhere else was tidy and the grate cleared. Upstairs the children's beds and cot had disappeared from the rooms, their cupboards were empty and a lot of bedding had disappeared from their bed.

He recalled what the governor had said in the hostel. Could it be the poor cow was still in hospital? He shrugged. Wherever she was, it suited his plans, for the house was a far more comfortable place to stay than the bloody hostel. He would stay there as long as he had to, come and go the same way as he had that night, and no one would ever know.

'D'you think there is something wrong with Deirdre?' Martha asked Sean the following Wednesday morning.

'She's quiet certainly,' Sean said. 'But maybe she's just tired. It is coming up to the end of term.'

'Maybe,' Martha said. 'And, of course, she's doing a solo in the concert. I know she is excited and everything, but it would be natural to be a little nervous.'

'Have you asked her if there is anything bothering her?'

'Oh, yes. She says nothing, of course.'

'What does Patsy say?' Sean said. 'Aren't the two of them always as thick as thieves?'

Martha frowned. 'Normally,' she said. 'But there is something up with her too. Course, that could be something to do with her and Andrew. She has been sharp with him a few times and I heard them having a real spat the other day.'

Sean groaned. 'I hope whatever it is she's soon over it before Christmas. I suppose he is still coming to us?'

'As far as I know,' Martha said. 'And travelling to his parents the day after Boxing Day. I hope it is nothing serous between them. They're probably tired too. It's been a long term and, from what they both say, I don't think teaching is an easy job.'

Sean chuckled. 'Oh, no, indeed not.'

'I'm glad that Maria is coming out of hospital at the weekend.' Martha said. 'With the Christmas holidays beginning on Friday, it would be difficult to find a minute to visit her. Anyway, she has been away from the little ones long enough.'

Sean agreed, but added, 'She has, and it was kind of you to say she must come to us, but I don't want you taking on too much yourself and becoming ill.'

'Am I likely to?' Martha said. 'I am as strong a horse. You've always said so.'

'Even horses need a rest now and then.'

'Sean stop fussing,' Martha chided. 'How could I let Maria go back just now? She is scared stiff still, and little wonder. Anyway, she is still very weak. Remember the hospital weren't that keen on her coming out yet until I said she could stay with me, and she is certainly not strong enough to look after three active children and a new baby on her own. By the New Year she will be stronger. Once the girls are back at school she'll only have the new baby and Jack all day, and he is a grand little chap.'

'He is that,' Sean said, for the little boy always had a smile on his face. He was naturally very funny, and Sean knew he would miss him when they returned to Pype Hayes. He knew too Martha spoke the truth. Maria was nowhere near better yet. Her nerves were so bad, often her hands shook uncontrollably, and even her speech was sometimes hesitant. So, despite his concern for Martha, he'd be glad to have Maria there for a bit so they could all keep their eyes on her and check that she wasn't overtaxing herself.

'Now are you sure that you will be all right coming home on your own after the extra dance practice?' Martha asked, as she tucked the scarf around Deirdre's neck a little later. 'It will be black night, and it won't take me a minute to fetch you.'

Oh, how Deirdre longed to fall against her mother and say yes, she did want collecting, because since that business with Barney the previous Saturday she was petrified of the dark. But she had just won the battle with her mother to allow her and Sally to come home from school by themselves, and in Sally's case take Theresa too, and she didn't want to miss out on her new-found independence. She knew as well that her mother has her hands full enough as it was.

Added to that, most of the dancers were much older than she, and many who were passed over for a solo spot were jealous of Deirdre. If she asked her mother to collect her, she was sure they would make fun of her afterwards. And so she said, 'No, I'm fine. Anyway, Grainne O'Farrell lives in Orchard Road and we will walk down together.'

'If you are sure?'

'I'm sure.'

'You are happy about this solo spot, aren't you?' Martha asked. 'You're not getting in a state and worrying about it, are you?'

'No. Why?'

'You seem . . . I don't know, different somehow.'

Deirdre could have said anyone would have been different after the events of the previous Saturday, but she could say none of this.

Nor could Patsy, who was also trying to cope with a frustrated and confused fiancé. She was embarrassed with Andrew, feeling, however inadvertently, that she had betrayed him and so wasn't keen to kiss him or show him how much she loved him. She also hurt too much and too extensively to allow Andrew to hold her tight, or even drape a heavy arm over her shoulder, and so she would push him away and hold his hand instead.

Andrew and Patsy had been controlled in their love-making, wanting their wedding night to be something special, and sometimes it had been hard to be that strong. Andrew, then, could be forgiven, when their engagement was open knowledge and the wedding date set, for thinking they might enjoy greater intimacy, not less. However, whenever he tried to press Patsy, she would say primly that you didn't know what it might lead to. It was so unlike her and he was bloody sick of it and even began to wonder if she had gone off him entirely.

Patsy saw Andrew's hurt and bewilderment and her heart bled for him, but she could do nothing to ease his pain.

On Tuesday morning Barney came down the stairs to find a letter from Seamus to say he was being released on Wednesday, 13 January, and could Barney be there?

Of course he could, and sod the lot of them here; it would be just him and Seamus again. He only wished he could pay Sean back properly before he went.

The following day, he'd lifted a bulging purse from a bag in the Bull Ring, with a packet in it. He'd taken it to the Lyndhust pub close to the top of Holly Lane, where he'd heard there was poker being played. There he had trebled the money in his pocket and he celebrated with gusto. Staggering out at afternoon closing time, he had bought and eaten fish and chips, and was on his way home to sleep off the beer and the food till the pubs should open again, when he saw two girls coming towards him. God, he thought, Deirdre was being handed to him like a gift from the Almighty, the icing on the cake, as far as he was concerned.

He melted into the shadows, the girls passed without noticing him and he slipped into step behind them. Barely had Deirdre bid good night to Grainne and the door closed behind her, when she sensed someone was following her closely. She turned cautiously and slowly, and came face to face with Barney, crouched down so that his face was inches from hers.

'Hello, Deirdre.'

'What do you want?'

'Tch, tch. Where's your manners? I only gave you a greeting, that's all.'

Deirdre was so scared she was shaking inside, but she couldn't stop the words tumbling from her mouth. 'Well, don't greet me. I don't want you to and . . . and . . . I . . . I don't have to have manners with you, 'cos you're horrible and disgusting.'

Barney laughed. 'You'd better be careful. I chastise

naughty little girls,' he said, and added menacingly, 'You'd better watch out I don't come for you one of these dark nights.'

'Leave me alone!' Deirdre shrieked. 'If you don't I will scream my head off.'

'No need,' Barney said nonchalantly. 'I'll leave you well alone . . . for now at least.'

And he was gone, melting into the darkness. Deirdre felt light-headed with relief. Her legs trembled so much, she wondered if they would give way before she reached home. Two or three times she turned swiftly, sure she had heard footsteps behind her, but she saw nothing. She was so exhausted by fear when she reached home she wasn't sure she could mount the steps, and when eventually she reached the safety of her house, she burst into tears. But she knew she couldn't say why.

Sean declared all these extra dancing lessons were too much for her, especially coming, as they did, at the very end of term. She was exhausted, that was all. No wonder she was tearful. He didn't know if he shouldn't have a word with Deirdre's dancing teacher. No way did Deirdre want that, and Martha knew how Deirdre felt by the expression in her eyes.

'Come on, Sean,' Martha said. 'This is the last time she will have to do this. On Friday they break up for two weeks and so it won't be so bad for her, and you know the concert is the day after Boxing Day. I think it would be wrong to complain at this late date.'

'Aye, maybe you are right,' Sean conceded. 'It's just that I hate to see our wee girl so worn out.'

'And so do I,' Martha said. 'But with a good night's sleep she'll be as right as rain, you'll see.'

Deirdre hoped she would. She did feel totally exhausted, but once she reached her bed, she tossed and turned. When she fall into a fitful sleep, she was jerked out of it by an horrific nightmare, her screams loud enough to wake the dead. She shared a room with Sally and Teresa.

Later, when Deirdre had been comforted and all was quiet again, Sally said, 'Crikey! You really put the willies up me then. What the hell did you dream about?'

'Can't remember,' Deirdre said. But she did. She remembered everything to the last little detail.

Barney was waiting for her again on Saturday, and repeated what he had said to her the previous Wednesday, but by the next week he contented himself with a wave. She went home fearfully, expecting any minute to feel a hand on her shoulder, or worse, and she became jumpy and nervous.

Maria often looked at Deirdre and wondered what was the matter with the child. She had frequent nightmares, looked scared to death most of the time, and was often so locked in on herself, she didn't hear if she was spoken to.

Patsy too was behaving strangely. She was almost withdrawn and would never sit with the family, but instead escape to her room or go for long solitary walks. Maria felt really sorry for Andrew the way Patsy treated him the time or two she had seen them together.

However, she hadn't time to worry about it overmuch for her own children had missed her sorely and, now she was out of hospital, vied to have the lion's share of her attention. Then there was baby Martin to care for too – not that Maria got much of a look in there, with Sally and Theresa both trying to mother him. Normally, Deirdre would have been the same, but she was too bound up in misery and fear even to notice the baby. Sally couldn't understand her and was annoyed that she took little notice of her baby brother.

'Ain't he lovely?' she said one day, as she leant over the crib, watching him suck on his fingers.

Deirdre had been in a dream, wondering how Barney seemed to know all about the dancing classes, and hadn't heard what Sally had said. 'What?'

'I said ain't our Martin lovely?'

'Yeah, I suppose.'

'What's up with you?'

'Nothing.'

'There flipping well is. You're all posh and stuck up 'cos you're in that concert thing.'

'No, I'm not.'

'Yes, you are.'

'Girls,' Martha chided. 'Come on now. You rarely fight. What is all this about?'

'Ask her,' Deirdre snapped. 'It's all her fault, anyway.' And she burst into tears and went flying upstairs.

Sally looked at her mother fearfully. 'It weren't my fault, Mom,' she said. 'I never done owt.'

'It's all right, Sally,' Martha said. 'Deirdre is just overwrought at the moment. I'll go up to her in a minute. Tell you what though,' she went on to Maria, 'I will be glad when this blasted concert is over and we get our daughter back the way she was.'

*   *   *

463

It was the worst Christmas Maria could ever remember having in that house. Patsy and Andrew were so stiff with each other it was embarrassing, and Deirdre was jumpy and inclined to burst into tears for the slightest thing. She took no interest in anything, not even the wonderful doll's house that Santa had brought, and Martha chided her for her lack of appreciation and said some children would be more grateful for half as much.

Maria knew it wasn't just lack of appreciation, but something else, and she thought Martha should take Deirdre to the doctor's if she didn't pick up after the New Year. Her own girls, she had to admit, were nearly as bad. Both of them were whiny and hard to please too.

Sally and Theresa's bad humour was all explained the next morning when Maria went to rouse them and found them both sweating profusely and covered in spots.

Maria asked Tony to fetch the doctor. 'Where?' Tony said. 'He'll hardly be at the surgery on Boxing Day.'

'No,' Maria agreed. 'But he just lives on Grange Road, only a step away for there was a note of his address and phone number in the surgery if you needed him out of hours,' Martha said. 'And I wrote it on an old envelope and it's behind the clock on the mantelpiece.'

'Measles,' Dr Linden declared. 'No surprise. There was a proper epidemic at the school just before the end of term. Probably go around the house.'

'I've had it,' Martha said, 'and so have Patsy and the boys. Deirdre hasn't, though, and then there is Jack too.'

464

'What about the baby, Doctor?' Maria asked.

'He will be protected by your antibodies until he is about six months old,' the doctor said. 'Have you had the measles yourself?'

'I don't know,' Maria said. 'I can't remember having them.'

'No, I don't think you ever did,' Sean said.

'Well, if you haven't, it is highly unlikely that you will escape this time,' the doctor told her cheerfully.

Deirdre suddenly wished she'd catch the measles too. The joy had gone out of the concert for her now. She would have given it all up, even the coveted solo spot, to be able to stay at home, which was the only place now where she felt safe.

CHAPTER TWENTY-FIVE

The concert was over and Deirdre had been so proud of her own performance. It was obvious others had been too, for her hand was pumped up and down and she was hugged by many powdery ladies who smelt of lavender.

In the end Sean, Tony and Paul were the only ones who could go. Patsy had left that morning, with Andrew, to visit his parents. She was very sorry that she would be missing Deirdre's debut, but the visit had been decided before she knew the date of the concert. Andrew had tried to change it to arrive the following day, but his mother had been very stiff about it. Apparently they had arranged a party for that night.

'I have to go,' Patsy had told Deirdre miserably. 'Things between myself and Andrew are dicey enough at the moment. I really can't risk alienating his parents too.'

Deirdre had been bitterly disappointed, but could see that neither Patsy nor Andrew had much choice in the matter.

Then, that very morning, just an hour or so after

Andrew and Patsy had left, Maria had complained of feeling unwell. She did look decidedly flushed and Martha insisted she get into bed. Again, Tony was sent out for the doctor.

'Measles, as I more or less expected, and a bad attack too,' the doctor said. 'These childhood illnesses can be the very devil in an adult. She will need careful nursing. Treatment the same as the others, but keep the room well darkened.'

Martha knew she would have her hands full. As well as her own family, she would have to cope with a boisterous three-year-old, a new baby and three sick people. The bed Sally and Theresa occupied was moved into Maria's room to make it easier to see to all the invalids together, and Jack and the baby moved out. Martha was bitterly disappointed that she wouldn't see her daughter dance, but she insisted that Sean, Tony and Paul go, for the child had to have some family members in the audience.

Sean and the boys were immensely proud of Deirdre and told her so. Sean hugged his daughter with tears of pure happiness in his eyes. 'Now collect up your things, pet, and say your goodbyes for we have to be off.'

But the adrenalin was still coursing through Deirdre's veins and she didn't want to be dragged home just like that. She wanted to wear the beautiful dress that Maria had made her, and bask in the glory a little longer, to talk it over with fellow dancers. Before he had left the house, however, Sean had seen the lines of exhaustion on Martha's face and he told her he would be back as soon as ever he could. Now it was already after nine.

'But there is a party arranged, Dad,' Deirdre said.

'Oh, I don't think you can stay to that,' Sean said.

The dancing teacher, Norah Bellingham, came across to them at that moment, heard the exchange, and said, 'Oh, but surely Deirdre must stay. She is the star of the night.'

'I know and it can't be helped but it's getting her home, d'you see?' Sean said. 'I don't want her walking home alone, and yet half of the house is down with measles.'

Tony felt sorry for Deirdre. 'I could fetch her, Dad,' he said.

'I thought you were away to a party of your own?'

'Well, yes, I am, but—'

'You wouldn't know what time to come for her anyway,' the dancing teacher said. 'Look, could she stay a little longer if I guarantee to get her home safely?'

Sean hesitated. He'd really have liked to take Deirdre with him so she could sit and drink her bedtime cocoa, and tell her mother all about the night. However, he saw plainly that the child wanted to stay.

The boys saw it too. 'Go on, Dad. Don't be mean,' Tony said.

'Yeah,' Paul put in. 'Let her go to the flipping party. I bet all the others are going, and you'll make her look stupid if she can't.'

'And it isn't as if she hasn't earned it,' Tony put it.

'All right,' Sean said, holding up his hands. He smiled wryly at Mrs Bellingham. 'It seems I am outvoted, but you will see that she gets home all right?

'You have my word,' the teacher said. 'Don't worry, she will be quite safe.'

There was someone in the shadows who watched Sean and the two boys leave. He had known all about her dancing classes and the date of the concert because one of his drinking partners at the Cross Keys had a daughter at the class too, though she was much older than Deirdre. He'd told him about the party afterwards too, but as Deirdre was so young and neither Sean nor Martha liked the wind to blow on her, he didn't know if she'd be allowed to go to that. But he saw she had, and he slunk back to the pub to sink another few pints before it was time to return to the hall.

Barney had been back there only a few minutes when the door to the hall opened and a woman appeared with Deirdre beside her, both dressed for outdoors. He heard the woman say, 'Now, I'll just take you home first and then come back and help them clear up.'

So, thought Barney, Sean is not coming back for her. He was surprised but it suited him very well and he stepped forward. The teacher missed the look on Deirdre's face as he approached. She had seen Barney at Mass and knew he was related to Sean and Martha. No one had complained to her of his drinking, gambling and violence.

So the teacher smiled at Barney as he said, 'I was passing and heard what you said. It would be no bother for me to walk home with Deirdre.'

No, Deirdre's mind screamed, but if she was to say she wouldn't go home with Barney what reason could she give? Not the true one certainly, and she couldn't think of any other plausible explanation. Already the teacher was saying it was good of him. Mrs Bellingham smelt the beer on Barney's breath, but thought that didn't indicate a problem. Truth to tell, she had had more than a drop herself that night and now she was worn out. She had been on the go and on tenterhooks about the concert all day, and yet the room had to be put to rights before she could leave. If Barney could take Deirdre home it would help her a great deal. After all, no harm could come to her; the man was a relation. Yet still she said, 'If you are sure, for I gave my word to the child's father.'

Barney could still turn the charm on when he wanted. He smiled at Mrs Bellingham and assured her it would be no trouble, 'Sure, she's my niece. Don't I love her like one of my own, and anyway, aren't I near passing the door?'

I'll run away, Deirdre thought as they turned from the hall. She did try, but Barney's arm shot out and grabbed her, his fingers digging into her upper arm with such a vicelike grip she could feel it even through her coat.

'Let go of me,' she cried, trying to twist out of his grasp but his grip tightened still further so that she cried out with the pain of it. 'Please leave me alone, Barney,' she said gasped.

'When I am good and ready,' Barney said grimly. He was walking at such a pace, Deirdre could barely keep up, and often she was dragged to her feet just by her arm. Each time it was agonising, and she knew there was no possibility of escaping him.

Barney could afford to be reckless. He didn't care any more about Sean, about any of them, because in two days' time he was going back to Ireland. He had the train and boat booked and until then he would lie low. If Sean came looking for him, he would never find him. Once in Dublin he'd be safe. He had dreamt of getting even with Sean before he left, and now the means of doing that so effectively was in his grasp. It was his last chance.

Deirdre began to beg, 'Please let me go, Barney. Please.' She was transfixed by terror. She wanted to scream and shriek out this abject fear, and only her father's face floating before her stopped her. Tears of helplessness ran down her face and she didn't even try to wipe them away. It didn't matter, nothing did any more. She knew Barney was heading for the brick-works and she knew he intended to hurt her at the very least.

Deirdre felt the corroded, fractured fencing of the brickworks sear down both her legs as Barney dragged her over it and into the velvet darkness. 'Let me go,' she cried in panic. 'You must let me go. You must see this is wrong . . .'

She might as well not have spoken, for Barney made no response other than to throw her to the hard, frozen ground, as he had Patsy. She lay stunned for a second or two, feeling as if every bone in her body had been loosened. She had a terrific pain in her head when she had hit it with force, and she felt the bricks and rubble digging into her back, her bottom and tops of her legs. Her whole body began to quake.

Without any sort of warning, Barney landed on top of her, his weight almost crushing her and his poisonous breath full in her face as he said, 'First I'll give you a little taste of what your sister had and then I just might throw you into the quarry and let the quicksand close over you.'

He couldn't see her eyes, but it didn't matter. He could feel her fear, could even smell it, it was so intense, and he smiled.

This can't be happening to me, Deirdre thought, and she sobbed out through chattering teeth, 'Please don't do this, Barney. Let me go. Oh, please, please . . .'

But though she pleaded, she had little faith that it would change anything. She remembered Patsy begging Barney in the same way. As he fumbled with her clothes, she lay as though paralysed by fear and imagined that when Barney had done dirty unspeakable things to her, he would throw her away as if she was of no more account than a stone. She imagined herself hurtling through the air to land bruised and broken on the ground below, and the quicksand clawing and sucking at her, dragging her down, filling her noise and mouth.

She couldn't stand it. She *wouldn't* stand it. Even knowing it was useless, she began to struggle frantically and beat at Barney with her fists until he smacked her across the face so hard she cried out in pain, tasting blood in her mouth. 'That's for the one you gave me,' he said. 'Now lie still, you shameless little whore.'

Bile filled Deirdre's mouth and then her scrabbling fingers felt a half-brick. Not knowing if it would do any good, she lifted it and hit out. Barney was unprepared for the clout on the side of his head, which dazed him for a split second. 'You little bastard. I'll . . .'

He didn't finish the sentence. Deirdre, frantic now – for she knew if she allowed Barney to recover from this, it would be the worse for her – lashed out again. She heard the crack as the brick connected with his head and she followed it with another thump.

Barney, groggy and disorientated, felt blood seeping down his cheek. He knew he had to get to his feet, but as he tried, Deirdre struck out again. This time the brick struck his forehead, right between the eyes. Barney, in a semi-kneeling position, his arms folded in front of him to protect his face, began to sway. The next smack caused him to fall across Deirdre with a groan.

Using all her strength, Deirdre rolled Barney off. When she felt him twitch and heard him moan slightly, she really laid into him. She knew she had to kill him. It wouldn't be enough to injure him, for then he would come after her. She lashed out, battering him over and over, as if a kind of madness had taken her over, until she was panting with the exertion of it. She felt sweat dampen her armpits and trickle down her back. By then, every sound and every movement from Barney had ceased.

She flung the brick away from her harder that she had ever thrown anything in her life – as if she couldn't bear to be in contact with it any more and wanted it to be as far away from her as possible. Then suddenly overcome with nausea, she vomited into the mud. She wiped her hands, sticky with blood, on a bit of scrubby grass she'd felt as she bent over to be sick. She fastened up her clothes with hands that shook, and though she had an urgent need to get away from Barney's inert body, it was hard to hurry across that rubble-strewn ground in the pitch-black.

Though she knew Barney lay still on the ground, any minute she expected to feel his hand on her collar, dragging her back, and tears once more began to rain down her cheeks.

He was dead, she told herself. Surely she had killed him, and she was not the tiniest bit sorry. Barney could never terrorise or bully anyone any more. Now she could tell her father everything and he wouldn't get into any trouble.

And then the horror of what she had done began to kick in. She had killed a man, taken a life, and they hanged murderers. She couldn't go home, but she had nowhere else to go, and she just walked aimlessly, in despair, wondering what on earth she was going to do about the heinous crime she had committed.

Eventually, despite her thick coat, the cold, mixed with shock, caused her teeth to chatter and her head to swim. When she felt herself lurching from one side of the pavement to the other she knew she had to make for home; there was nothing else she could think to do. She had almost reached the gate when a fog of blackness descended all around her and she collapsed in a heap on the pavement.

Sean had not long returned from the town, for when he and Paul had returned to the house after the concert, it was to find that Maria had worsened, and Sean had been concerned enough to go again for the doctor. He too had been worried and had left a prescription to be made up immediately. The only all night chemist was Boots, in the town, and Sean had gone straight off.

When he returned he had expected Deirdre in the

house, maybe even in bed, for it had been turned half-past eleven, but on finding she wasn't home he decided to fetch her himself. He tripped over her unconscious form just outside the gate. He gave a cry of alarm and, picking her up in his arms, he carried her into the house, shouting for Martha.

'Almighty God, what's happened to her?' Martha cried.

'That is exactly what I want to know,' Sean said grimly. 'That woman gave me her word that she would bring Deirdre home safely. God, she will have some explaining to do when I catch up with her.'

'That will have to wait,' Martha said impatiently. 'Leave her on the bed, fill two hot water bottles and send our Paul for the doctor. Poor man, he's hardly away from this door this evening.'

Deirdre didn't stir as Martha took off her things, puzzled by the mud and fifth on the back of her coat and thoroughly upset by the rips in her black stockings and the deep score lines all the way down her legs. Sean had laid her on her back, and Martha didn't attempt to move her, but just eased the top clothes from under her, leaving her petticoats on and so didn't see the bruises and grazes on her back. But she did see the vivid, vicious bruise on her arm and the other one on her face.

The doctor examined her gently and was perplexed. 'She has had a fall, at the very least, I should say, for she has a nasty bump on the back of her head, but I am pleased to say there is no evidence of sexual interference.'

Martha hadn't been aware that she had been holding

her breath, but now it escaped in a sigh of relief and Sean's did the same. 'Thank God for that,' he said. 'But what do you think happened to her?'

'It's hard to say accurately,' the doctor said. 'I think I must take a look at her back.'

Sean helped lift her over very gently and, though Deirdre's eyes remained shut, she gave a small moan. The doctor pulled up her petticoats and vest, and he whistled when he saw Deirdre's back and buttocks covered with grazes, bruises and weals.

'I would say she has had a very bad fall,' he said.

'She was only supposed to walk from the abbey hall home,' Sean said. 'So how could she fall? You don't think she was attacked?'

'She could have been, but there is no evidence of an attack, as such.'

'That woman Bellingham gave me her word she would bring her home safe, that's what I can't get over,' Sean said. 'First thing tomorrow I am paying her a visit and see what she has to say about it.'

'I understand that,' the doctor said. 'I'd feel the same – any parent would – and maybe this woman can shed some light on this whole episode. Of course, Deirdre will probably be able to answer these questions for you when she does wake up.'

'When d'you think that will be, Doctor?' Martha asked. 'It's terrible to see her lying there so still.'

'She moaned when we lifted her over so I'm sure it is just a light coma,' the doctor said reassuringly. 'But, of course, any head injury can be tricky and she will need absolute peace and quiet when she does wake up.'

'I'll see she gets it, Doctor.'

'I'm sure you will,' the doctor said. 'And let's hope she is not incubating measles, for that is a complication we can do without.' He looked from Maria to Sean. 'You two are surely having a time of it. Did you get the medication for Maria, Sean?'

'Aye, Doctor. I went to Boots in the town and had it made up straight away. Martha gave her a dose before she settled down for the night and she said her chest and all was easier. Maybe you'll see that yourself.'

'More than likely,' the doctor said. 'But I'll not disturb her now. I will see them all in the morning when I come to check on Deirdre.'

Deirdre's eyes flickered open and she slowly turned her head from side to side. Then, with her troubled eyes full of confusion, she said, 'How did I get here?'

Sean, who'd taken the day off work till he was sure Deirdre was all right and he'd seen Mrs Bellingham, had been sitting with her while Martha got breakfast for the others and was delighted to see her eyes open at last. He approached the bed and said gently, 'We thought you might be able to tell us that.'

'What do you mean?'

'What do you remember of last night?'

Deirdre thought, her brow furrowed in concentration. 'I remember the concert,' she said at last slowly. 'And I remember the party afterwards and standing in the doorway, and the teacher saying she was going to take me home and then . . . then nothing till I woke up here.'

'Are you sure there is nothing more you can tell me?'

Deirdre shook her head. 'It's just like a big black hole.'

'Don't press her,' Martha warned, when Sean went downstairs with the news. 'You know what the doctor said. We'll get to the bottom of it in time, and I must say I am glad that she has woken up at last. I'll go up in a minute to see if she will have a bit of breakfast and you best be off to see that teacher, and if she can tell you any more.'

'Aye,' Sean said.

Less than ten minutes later he was pounding on the woman's door.

'You won't get any joy there,' said the next-door neighbour, hearing the commotion. 'Her's away to her sister's for the New Year, like. Left real early this morning.'

Sean sighed in frustration. 'I don't suppose you have an address?'

The woman shook her head. 'All I know is, her lives Bournville way. Lovely out there, by all accounts.'

There was no alternative for Sean but to return home. He felt utterly miserable and helpless, and hoped in time Deirdre would be able to clear up the mystery of how she came to be lying unconscious in the street outside the house.

Knowing the heavy load Martha had, Sean took the next day off too. That afternoon, when Deirdre had still been able to tell them nothing, he said, 'Maybe we should go to the police and let them handle it.'

'And tell them what exactly?' Martha said. 'The doctor really doesn't seem to think any other person was involved, so there is no crime being committed.

Perhaps we should be patient and listen to what Mrs Bellingham has to say when she comes home.'

'Anything might have happened to Deirdre,' Sean snapped. 'What if I hadn't gone out when I did, for example?'

Martha put her hand over his. 'Darling, I know how worried you are,' she said soothingly. 'If I tell the truth, I am myself, but thank God nothing worse happened to her. I am sure when she is recovered properly her memory and all will return. The point is, Deirdre might get upset if we come down all heavy before even talking to Mrs Bellingham, and that is the last thing we want. Let's wait a wee while longer.'

Sean sighed. 'It's the not being able to do anything that gets to you,' he said. 'And I can't afford to lose time like this. I will really have to go back tomorrow, though I'll be officially off again on Friday, with it being New Year's Day. How will you cope with all this on your own?'

'I'll be fine,' Martha assured him. 'Anyway, Patsy is coming home.'

'Is she?' Sean said. 'But I thought she was intending to stay to see the New Year in with Andrew's parents?'

'She was,' Martha said. 'It wasn't anything to do with me, but Paul and Tony discussed it and thought Patsy would like to know about Maria coming down with measles and this latest incident with Deirdre. Paul apparently knew Andrew's parents' phone number and he rang them from a public phone box and the upshot of it all was that Patsy is coming back as soon as the trains allow.'

'A phone is a very handy thing to have in a house,'

Sean said. 'I've thought it this long while. Maybe in the spring I'll see about us having one in.'

'Oh, Sean. That would be wonderful.'

'Wouldn't it?' Sean said. 'Look how useful it has been in this instance, and I can go to work easier in my mind, knowing Patsy will be here to lend you a hand.'

However, Patsy hadn't returned by the evening and, with the meal over, Martha sat feeding the baby, with Sean, as he was wont to do, reading snippets out of the paper, when there was a knock at the door.

'That will be Patsy,' Martha said. 'I bet she can't find her key again.'

Tony was out on a date, Paul in his room and Sean in his stocking feet, so Martha passed him the baby and almost ran down the hall to open the door, knowing she'd be immensely glad of Patsy's help.

But it wasn't Patsy and Andrew. It was two policemen. She knew that from the badges they showed her, though there were in plain clothes and they asked to speak to a Mr Sean Tierney.

By the time Patsy did make it home, just over an hour later, Martha was still crying. She thought she'd never stop. Paul thought so too, and though he had been weepy himself he'd never felt so inadequate. He had tried putting his arms around his mother and made her more than one cup of tea, but she continued to cry and when little Martin joined it, Paul saw from the bottle on the mantelpiece that the child had been only half fed.

At least, he thought, that was something he could

do. So he fed the baby the rest of the bottle and even changed his nappy for the first time, very grateful it was merely wet. He had just put the drowsy baby into the pram where he slept until Martha would take him to bed, as she had since Maria took sick, when he heard the key in the lock. He ran to meet his sister, so thankful she was there at last.

'God, I'm glad you're here,' he said. 'Come and see if you can do something with Mom. She's cried for hours.'

Patsy had got a very garbled message from Paul about Deirdre, for the boy knew little more anyway, and now she grabbed his arm, 'Why is she crying? Has something happened to Deirdre?'

'Not Deirdre,' Paul said. 'It's Dad. The police have arrested him.'

He wasn't arrested, but he was helping with their inquiries into the murder of Barney McPhearson, which had happened the previous evening. Patsy, even though the news about Sean was worrying, felt a lightening in her heart, knowing that Barney was dead

'Where was his body found? she asked.

'Nocks Brickworks,' Martha said. 'There's some waste ground this side of the quarry and it was there.'

Patsy felt as if justice had been done. The bloody great pervert had met his match at last. Every time she remembered what he had done to her, her skin would crawl and she often would push Andrew away when, during any intimacy, it would all come flooding back to her. God, she would have killed the man herself, given the slightest opportunity, and not felt a whit sorry about it.

As for this business with her stepfather, she was sure that it would soon be cleared up. 'What did they want with Dad anyway?' she asked. 'They can't really think he had anything to do with this.'

However, Martha's reply thoroughly disturbed Patsy. 'Many heard Sean threaten what he would do to Barney. He said he'd swing for him more than once.'

'That's just something you say in the heat of the moment,' Patsy said. 'Surely, Mom, you don't think—'

'Of course I don't,' Martha snapped. 'What do you take me for? Sean has given me his word he had nothing to do with it and that is good enough for me, but what I think or believe doesn't matter a jot to the police. The point is, though I know there was little love lost between Sean and Barney, if he was going to attack the man, he wouldn't do it this way.'

'What do you mean?'

'This was a frenzied attack,' Martha said. 'Those were the exact words the policeman used. Someone had smashed Barney's skull in, they think with a brick or something very similar, and not just the once, but many times. Sean would hit no man with a brick, he'd just use his hands and Sean told them that himself, for all the good it did.'

CHAPTER TWENTY-SIX

By the night of 29 December, the police had witnesses that Sean had attacked Barney before and in fact had had to be restrained from finishing him off then. Most of the men from the Black Swan, who had been privy to the fight, had come forward once the victim had been identified and his name printed in the *Evening Mail*, as it had been that evening.

They'd said nothing earlier, for a fight was just a fight, but murder was another matter and not something they wanted to get into trouble about for withholding information, or some such. So they overcame the usual reticence they had towards the police and told them what they had heard and seen.

Some of them told what Sean had done reluctantly, even said maybe the man had cause and that he seemed a decent sort of bloke. But the police ignored that. They had a man in the frame that had committed the murder that would wrap it up nicely. As the inspector said, the nicest man in the world could turn killer, given the right motive and the opportunity.

Sean had certainly had the opportunity. By his own

admission, he had left the house and gone into the town for medicine. The police suggested he'd come across Barney McPhearson on his journey there or back and decided to finish what he'd started. He denied it, of course, but then he would, wouldn't he? They gathered further evidence against him.

George from the Norton pub and some of the regulars were also questioned, and his workmates at the Dunlop who, when prompted, spoke of Sean's hatred for Barney for the way he treated his wife and the money he gambled and drank away that meant his wife and children often went without.

Some of the men from the Black Swan had spoken of the young fellow with Sean Tierney that night, a well-set-up, finely dressed young man, who told them it was family business, as if they were related in some way. So when Andrew went to the police station on the morning of the thirtieth, when Sean hadn't returned home and they had had no news, he found himself hauled in for questioning too. He noted the way the questions were loaded and knew they had already decided on Sean's guilt and he left the police station later with a heavy heart. He knew just how bleak the situation looked for him.

He wasn't even surprised therefore when Sean was charged with the murder of Barney McPhearson on 31 December, yet shock waves reverberated around the rest of the family. Patsy, though bowed down with sorrow and worry herself, thought Maria ought to be told before she found out some other way.

As Maria now shared her bedroom with Sally and Theresa, Patsy carried the two girls down the stairs first and tucked them both up on the settee before the fire, so that they could sit with Martha for *Watch with Mother* while Patsy broke the news to Maria.

The tears Maria shed, though, were for her uncle, for whom she felt immensely sorry. The knowledge that her husband was dead evoked only a feeling of relief in her and she didn't care how wicked that was. Patsy told her that Sean had given her his word that he had had no hand in Barney's death.

'I wouldn't have cared if he had,' she said, 'except for the way it would rebound on him, of course. I would have said the person who did it had done us, the whole God damned world, a favour, and the only pity is that Uncle Sean has been picked up for it.'

Patsy and Andrew had told the boys together, but neither wanted to share that news with the younger children and decided to leave things as they were for the moment. Martha just told them that Sean had had to go away for a few days to do a special job for Dunlop's.

'Without even saying goodbye?' Deirdre asked, incredulously.

'He was in a rush,' Martha said.

Deirdre looked at he mother's white face. It looked sort of sad, and her eyes were swollen to mere slits. 'You've been crying,' she said accusingly. 'Why you been crying? Are you mad with Daddy for going away?'

Martha was holding herself together with difficulty. 'I haven't been crying.' she told her young daughter. 'I have a bit of a cold.'

'No you haven't.' Deirdre stated flatly. 'You've been crying.'

'Oh, stop this, Deirdre,' Martha snapped. 'I have a cold and that is the end of it.'

Deirdre was quiet. She was hurt and confused by her mother's reaction, and even more certain she was being fobbed off and not being told the whole truth. But she also know she would get nothing out of her mother just then and she decided she would bide her time.

Martha and Patsy found it very hard trying to stay even moderately cheerful in front of the younger children when they felt so burdened with sadness. That night, when they heard the church bells peal out the old year and ring in the new, and the sounds of revelry in the adjoining houses and even the streets, it was like a mockery to those locked in misery in the house.

But it did show them that life would go on all around them. Martha knew that, now the papers had got hold of the story, it would be common knowledge very soon. They'd even had reporters come to the house that day asking questions and she'd seen photographers lingering around the gate. She realised she wouldn't be able to shield the children much longer. Deirdre, Sally and Theresa, at least, would have to be told a modicum of the truth before all the sordid details were thrown at them across the playground when they were well enough to return to school.

On Sunday morning Martha was upset to be shunned at Mass by people whom she counted as friends, and it didn't really help that Father Clancy sought her out afterwards and asked if the Church could do anything to help her. There was nothing anyone could do and that was the very devil of it. Martha knew many would believe there was no smoke without fire and she hoped fervently that the people on the jury, who would decide Sean's fate, were more open-minded.

Even the boys were suffering. Martha knew. She had seen tear trails on Paul's cheeks and the boy often looked incredibly sad. Tony had lost his impudence and ready smile, and often seemed far away from them all, as if he was sunken inside himself. He had admitted to Paul that some of the other lads and men had been giving him a hard time at work about his stepfather's arrest, but warned him not to tell their mother.

'She can't really do anything about it and, anyroad, she has enough on her plate without worrying about me,' he said.

Paul, who had clearly seen the burden that his mother carried, couldn't have agreed more. He thought he would probably be subjected to some of the same when school opened on the seventh of January and he too would keep quiet about it in front of his mother.

Martha often wondered what they would have done without Andrew. He had made all the enquiries and dealings with the solicitor he'd engaged to represent Sean, and began to make the arrangements for Barney's funeral, when his body should be released, which was taking a little time as there'd have to be a post mortem. He'd even contacted Mountjoy Prison, so that Seamus could be informed of his brother's death, and was always willing to step in and throw together a quick lunch or wash the pots.

Sally and Theresa were not fit enough to go back to school when it reopened after the holidays and Martha had no intention of sending Deirdre on her own. Anyway, she wasn't right yet and still had no recollection of that night, though Martha and even Patsy had quizzed her about it on more than one occasion. Patsy, intrigued by the whole thing, had even gone up to see Mrs Bellingham on Tuesday, two days before the schools were due to reopened. But there was no response to her knock and the lady next door said she hadn't returned yet.

Deirdre herself would have liked to have gone back to school, because being at home left her too much time to think, probing and poking that black hole in her life as if it were a loose tooth.

When Paul came home from school that first afternoon with a black eye, a nose that had definitely been bleeding and the mark of the cane across both hands, Martha knew he had been fighting. Though he said he didn't want to talk about it, she didn't have to be a genius to work out what it was over.

'I must tell the children tonight,' she said to Patsy as they washed the dishes together. 'The more I put it off, the worse it is.'

'Do you want me to come in with you?'

'Would you?' Martha said gratefully. 'You're not seeing Andrew?'

'Not tonight,' Patsy said. 'He has a staff meeting, and when it's over, the usual pattern is to carry it on in the pub, so tonight I am all yours.'

So, a little later, with Jack and Martin settled, Paul at his homework and Tony also in his room, knowing what was afoot and wanting to be out of the way, Martha told Deirdre she wanted to see her and would she come into the room that Sally and Theresa shared with their mother as it had a fire lit in there.

Deirdre knew that this was it. Her mother was now going to tell her the truth, clarify what it was that was making her so touchy and bad-tempered, and maybe also tell them what manner of place her father was in that he hadn't sent them a letter yet. Sally and Theresa were almost fully recovered. Maria, though, still looked very pale and also had a hacking cough that shook her whole frame.

'Sit down, Deirdre,' Martha said. 'This won't take long.'

There was only one chair in the room, which Martha took, and so Deirdre climbed on to the edge of the bed that already housed Sally and Theresa, and Patsy perched on Maria's. They waited.

For days, Martha had rehearsed this, wondering if there was any way that she could soften this blow. But she couldn't think of one and she decided now to pitch straight in and cope with the fallout later. She gave a nervous cough and she saw Patsy's sympathetic eyes on her as she said, 'You know I told you Sean was away working?' She looked straight at Deirdre, who nodded. 'Well,' Martha went on, 'that was a little lie, I'm afraid.'

'I knew it,' Deirdre said, almost triumphantly. 'I knew you weren't telling us the truth. Where is he really then?'

She was totally unprepared for the answer, or for the sadness in Martha's face or the break in her voice as she said, 'Your father, Deirdre is . . . he . . . he is in prison.'

Deirdre jerked as if she has been shot. She stared at her mother for a moment, her mouth agape. She noted her mother's distress, her eyes glistening with tears, and the shocked faces of Sally and Theresa. Then her eyes found Patsy's. Patsy knew Deirdre would be hurt and confused. They were the only ones to know how hard they had tried to save Sean from this dreadful fate.

Deirdre thought her mother must have made a mistake. 'Don't be stupid,' she shouted. 'This isn't true. It can't be true. What would anyone put Dad in prison for?'

Martha went over to the bed and sat beside her daughter, her arm around her and went on, 'Maria's husband, Barney, is dead. He has been murdered by someone and they think that someone is your daddy.'

Deirdre again stared at Patsy, her eyes wild. Was it all for nothing, that secrecy?

While she was coming to terms with this, Sally turned to her mother and asked. 'Is this true?'

'I'm afraid so,' Maria said. 'Your daddy is dead. Come up here to me. The two girls scrambled off their bed and on to their mother's, where she settled them either side of her. Deirdre saw the only expression on Sally's face was one of relief and she remembered her telling her fiercely how she hated her father. Someone else obviously hated him too, but not her father, because he had no need to. He didn't know what Barney had done.

'Daddy can't have killed Barney,' she burst out. 'There weren't no reason to. We never told him on purpose.'

490

'Never told him what?' Martha asked.

'You tell,' Deirdre said to Patsy. 'It was you it happened to.'

Patsy felt uncomfortable saying what she had to in front of the children but there was no point keeping anything a secret now. In the end, she sat down beside her mother and looked her full in the face as she said, 'Barney attacked me. He dragged me down to that waste place by the quarry where his body was found and assaulted me.'

Martha knew by her daughter's eyes what manner of assault it was. Sadness and anger almost overpowered her and, though she still kept hold of Deirdre, she put her other arm around Patsy as the tears flowed.

'And we never said,' Deirdre cried. 'Neither of us in case . . . in case Daddy went after Barney and got into trouble. See, there weren't no reason for him to hurt Barney 'cos he d'ain't know nothing about that.'

Maria, almost reeling from these fresh revelations, felt a terrible dread filling her body, because there was only one way that Deirdre could know so much about it. 'Where were you when this was going on?' she asked.

'Watching from behind a wall,' Deirdre said. Then turning to her mother, she told her, 'It was the day you went to the pantomime with the others. Patsy came to pick me up from dancing and on the way home we saw Barney. Patsy told me to run and I did a bit at first, you know, but then I followed them because I thought Barney might hurt her or summat.'

She looked at Patsy, ran her tongue over her lips nervously and went on, 'I never even told you this, 'cos you said it don't do no good to keep talking about it and that, but Barney used to lie in wait for me after dancing lessons and say horrible things to me, just like he did after the concert.'

There was complete silence in the room. Maria, Patsy and Martha were all staring at Deirdre and she herself was wondering where those words had come from. She concentrated on the black cloud that seemed to have lodged in her mind for so long and it was as if a window had appeared in it and the window was enlarging, expanding, pushing away the blackness to reveal swirling grey mist with unformed images behind it.

She tried to make some sense of it, and very suddenly all the memories the black cloud had blocked began to seep through. As it all came back to her, she began to shake uncontrollably and she gave a sudden blood-curdling scream and then another and another. Overcome by nausea, she ran for the bathroom with a hand covering her mouth.

It was Patsy who followed her and held back her hair as she vomited over and over, and who later wiped her face with a cloth. She knew dreadful things had happened to her sister, things she needed to talk about, but maybe not before Sally and little Theresa. She picked her up in her arms, as if she was half the age she was, and Deirdre was glad of it. Her legs felt very strange and she was weakened from being sick, so she held on tight and buried her face in Patsy's shoulder.

Patsy took Deirdre down to the living room, and there she sat in the big armchair, Deirdre still in her arms, and the child at last gave in to the tears threatening to engulf her. So much had happened to her and Patsy, and now her father. She cried about it all – cried as if she never intended to stop. Patsy just held on to her tight until the paroxysm of grief abated somewhat. Then she urged, 'Tell me, Deirdre. This is too big a burden to keep to yourself.'

Martha came into the room then, helping Maria, who was out of bed for the first time but insistent on knowing it all. 'He was my husband, Martha,' she said as they made their laboured way down the stairs. 'I will fret more if I just lie here and try to pretend this does not affect me in the slightest. If you want to know the truth, I feel somewhat responsible, and really nothing you can say will change that attitude. I need to know what my bastard of a husband did to a little girl the same age as his own daughter.'

And when she did, when Deirdre told what had happened to her and what she had done in response to it, Maria felt laden down with guilt and shame. She lowered her head, unable to meet anyone's eyes as Deirdre said, 'I killed Barney, not Dad. I know that now. He said that he would do to me what he had done to Patsy and then throw me into the quicksand in the quarry. I was struggling and that, and then I found a half-brick and hit him with it, and just kept on hitting him till I was sure he was dead.'

'Dear Almighty God,' Martha said. 'For these dreadful things to happen to the two of you . . .'

'We couldn't tell you,' Deirdre said. 'We couldn't tell no one in case Dad killed Barney, or at least hurt him bad, and then I killed him after all.' She suddenly began to shake and said in hushed tones, 'I'm dead scared now. I don't think I've ever been scared like this. Will I get locked up for years for that, or . . . or even hang?'

'Neither,' Patsy said. 'You were a child and he was a man and you hit him with a brick to defend yourself. I think it was very brave of you and, by God, I wish I had thought of the same thing. If I had been as resourceful, such a thing would never have happened to you. And you were right, you had to make sure that he was dead. If you had just left him injured, in time he would have come after you again.' Remembering then that she was talking about Maria's husband, she said to her, 'Sorry, Maria. This is probably really painful for you.'

'It is,' Maria said grimly. 'And I'll tell you what is painful: the fact that I brought this man into your home, Martha, and that he did so much damage in your family.'

'You weren't to know how he would turn out,' Martha said, though she was still shaken. 'You have nothing to blame yourself for.'

The two policemen were very nice to Deirdre, as if they knew how terrified she was. They didn't look like policemen at all, for they were dressed in ordinary clothes, but in a way that made it worse, as if she was telling her tale to a couple of strangers who'd walked in off the street. The room she was shown into was bare except for a table in the centre of it with two chairs arranged either side of it. They even pulled the chair out for her as if she was a grown up and she sat beside her mother and faced them across the table. Then one of them said, 'Now we have already spoken to your sister and we would like you to tell us in your own words and in your own time what happened to you.'

It was hard – the hardest thing Deirdre had ever

done – to describe the things Barney had done. One of the policemen listened intently, sometimes stopping her to ask a question, or to go back over something, especially when she got to the incident in the brickworks where she killed Barney. The other man said very little, but made notes all the time she was speaking.

At last it was over. Deirdre sat back in the chair with a sigh, suddenly aware of how weary she was. The first man smiled at her and said, 'Good girl, Deirdre. Now my colleague here has made lots of notes and he has to have to have them typed up so you can sign them before you go home. What about if I ask your sister to join you and rustle up some tea, and I'm sure we can find a few biscuits?'

Deirdre was sorry to learn that Sean could not come home with them, when they were ready to leave, but the man explained that Sean wasn't being kept there and certain formalities had to be adhered to before he could be released. He promised to see that these were done as speedily as possible.

In the middle of that night, Patsy was woken with stomach pains and for a moment or two she lay in bed, not quite sure what had woken her. Then she felt it again, that drawing pain beginning in her back and going around to the front, and she knew what it was, and she smiled, got out of bed and went to the bathroom. She was glad she had confided in no one, for the pregnancy she had dreaded had turned out to be a false alarm after all, and no one need know anything about it. She knew she had to tell Andrew about the rape, however, for the time for secrecy was well gone.

When, the following morning, she told Andrew, he was shocked – so shocked he couldn't speak for a moment. He remembered how Patsy had appeared to change and how she would push him away and snap and snarl at him for little or nothing. Now he understood why she had behaved that way. Certainly the man didn't deserve to live, he thought, for not only did he rape Patsy, he also abused, frightened and he was sure would have gone on to violate a young girl.

'Say something, Andrew,' Patsy pleaded. 'Surely you can see that I couldn't have married you with such a secret on my soul.'

Andrew's response had been to take her in his arms and declare that it made no difference to his love for her. If she could have seen inside Andrew's mind, though, she would have seen how hard it had been for him to say those words. When Patsy had told him, he had felt cheated for a moment or two. He had imagined their wedding night as a journey of discovery, as they explored each other's bodies, finding out how to please each other, and then on to true fulfilment. The first time for both of them, a coming-together in love, and now some filthy pervert had robbed him of that; some other man had touched Patsy in the most intimate and private of places.

Then he realised that Patsy had been robbed too. 'That's why you used to push me away, isn't it?'

Patsy nodded. 'I felt dirty and defiled, and not really worthy of your love.'

Andrew felt humbled by such honesty and ashamed of himself for his earlier thoughts. 'Ah, Patsy,' he said. 'My lovely, beautiful, darling girl, you mustn't ever again feel this way. I love you with my heart and soul and nothing you have told me today will change that in any way.'

Patsy might have doubted the man's words, but not the ardent kiss that he placed upon her lips, full of love and longing that she responded to so eagerly, thankful that she hadn't lost the love and respect of this man, as she had feared she might.

It was about eleven o'clock the following morning when Martha opened the door to an agitated Norah Bellingham.

'I only got back yesterday,' she said. 'I caught a touch of flu at my sister's and I had to stay on a few days. Then, this morning I heard the news about Sean and had to come and tell you that I don't believe a word of it, not one word.'

'Thank you, Mrs Bellingham,' Martha said. 'The thing is—'

'I was wondering if I should go to the police,' Mrs Bellingham asked. 'The point is that Barney McPhearson was supposed to be attacked the night of the concert, and it was that night he offered to take young Deirdre home. I mean, would it help or hinder if I was to tell them?'

Martha was about to say it would make no difference, when she stopped herself. The police had said that as far as they were concerned Deirdre had no case to answer and her name could never be mentioned in connection with Barney's death because she was too young. But still, what Norah Bellingham could tell them could at least point to the first part of Deirdre's story being accurate and so she advised the woman to go ahead.

She didn't tell her anything else. It wouldn't help either Patsy or Deirdre for people to know what had happened to them and they would keep it within the family. She could barely wait for Sean to return home where he belonged. That would be better than Christmas. She needed his strong arms to enfold her and help her cope with it all.

Maria was anxious to return home, especially with Sean's imminent release. She felt that she had encroached on his family's kindness long enough. She was anxious too to get back to her dressmaking. Money wasn't a problem in the short term, for Andrew had looked into it and told her she would get thirty-seven shillings a week for thirteen weeks, plus the seven shillings for Sally and twenty-four shillings a week Family Allowance for the others. But after the thirteen weeks her money would be reduced to the same as Barney had got. Despite the fact she no longer had to share this meagre amount with a selfish and uncaring bastard of a man, it still wouldn't be a fortune.

'It isn't as if I have anything to fear any more,' she told Martha.

'I know that,' Martha said, 'but you are no way well enough yet, in my opinion. Besides, January is the very devil of a time to move and the house has not being lived in for months, remember. It might even be damp. Certainly your bed will have to be aired. Come on, Maria, be sensible. You don't want to make yourself worse, and what if the children were to get some sort of relapse? None of you is totally out of the wood yet.'

'I know that. It's just, with Sean—'

'D'you think he would like to think he was chasing you away?' Martha said. 'God, he'd be more likely to go for me for allowing you to back before either you or the house was fit.'

Maria smiled, for she knew Martha had a point. 'All right, what do you suggest?'

'Leave it at least another week,' Martha said. 'Let me give the place a good clean, air it thoroughly and warm it up a bit. And you build your strength up. The girls will be back at school by then, so you'll only have Jack and the baby to deal with. It would be better all round.'

Maria agreed to this, but in the end it was Patsy and Andrew who went down the next day, which was a Saturday, armed with cleaning materials and cloths, saying that Martha had plenty to do already and it would do them no harm to lend a hand.

They knew straight away that Barney had been living in the house and he'd made a mess of the whole place. The injunction had obviously made little difference to him and had the man still lived, they knew he could have continued to abuse Maria for years.

Not two hours after Patsy and Andrew had gone, Sean came home in a police car. It soon became apparent that initially Martha would have to help him cope, rather than the other way around. The policeman who had interviewed both Patsy and Deirdre had been to see him. He'd not only told Sean what had happened to them both, but left him a copy of their statements to look over. Maria, Martha and Sean sat on at the dinner table long after the children had left it, Maria feeding the baby.

Sean said, 'Those statements made harrowing reading. They would for any father. I felt as if it ate right into the core of my manhood that I had been unable to protect my daughters from this madman.'

'I can see that,' Martha said. 'I have a theory as to why the two were attacked. It might have something to do with Barney getting even because he couldn't beat you in a straight fight.'

'I wouldn't have just killed him, if I had known the half of it.' Sean said savagely. 'I would have torn him apart limb from limb.'

'And might be hanging from a noose this very minute,' Maria said with asperity. 'What then would it achieve and how would it help any of us?'

'It's just that—'

'No, Sean,' Martha said. 'Don't you see that this unbridled violence towards Barney was the very thing that stilled the girls' tongues.'

'Aye, of course I do,' Sean said. 'D'you think I don't know that? D'you think I don't torture myself with the thought that if Patsy had been able to confide in me, knowing I would leave it to the police, what happened to Deirdre might not have done?'

'And what then?' Maria put in 'You know as well as I that if Barney had been allowed to live, none of us would have been safe.'

She looked at her uncle with pain-filled eyes, and went on, 'I love Deirdre as much as I love my own, and not in a million years would I have had this thing happen to her. Christ, no wonder the child could remember nothing. Such a burden could have turned her brain for ever. Thank God that didn't happened. Yet nothing will be achieved by wishing things had been different. I feel guilt and shame too, but it is something we have to deal with, or Barney will have scored a victory over us all.'

Sean knew Maria was right.

She continued, 'And Deirdre isn't over this yet. I think it will take time. There is something still bothering her. I mean, she was thrilled you had come home, Sean, so delighted, but even then there was some worry lurking behind her eyes.'

'Come on, Maria,' Martha said. 'When you think what she has gone through, is that any wonder?'

'No, of course it isn't,' Maria said. 'But maybe someone should talk to her. I mean, I know you want to keep this to yourselves and I can see why, but Deirdre might need professional help to deal with this.'

However, no one did anything then, because Patsy and Andrew came in.

'Oh, Dad, I am so pleased to see you,' Patsy said, hugging him. Andrew then shook his hand warmly.

'Now tell us whatever else it is that you are clearly bursting to tell us,' Martha said. 'And I'll make us all another pot of tea. Oh, isn't it marvellous to be able to say that and not be wondering if the ration will stretch?'

Maria knew exactly what Martha meant. Rationing had been a headache for them all. Butter, cheese, cooking fats, margarine and meat were still rationed, but the Government had promised that these too would be off ration by the end of the year. She smiled at Martha and said, 'I'll give you a hand.'

'Not yet, Maria,' Patsy said. 'You need to hear this. You see, we think Barney has been living in the house. We found a docket for some money from the dole office, so we know it was him. He'd left dirty plates stacked in the kitchen and cups all over the place, together with the nub ends of cigarettes and beer cans and bottles. The bed had definitely been slept in and the grate was a disgrace. In fact the whole place needed a damned good clean and it took us ages.'

'I am very grateful to you,' Maria said, but her insides quailed at the thought that, despite any injunction, Barney had seemingly come and gone at will. She didn't know how he had got in the first time and didn't really care. The point was he had. If she had returned she was sure he would have murdered her.

'Oh, that's not all,' Patsy said, withdrawing some letters from her bag. 'These are from Seamus. He is being released on the thirteenth of January and Barney fully expected to be there with him, for we found a train ticket and a ticket for the boat.'

Maria scanned the letters and, turning concerned eyes on Sean said, 'What are we to do, Sean? He will be out on Wednesday and he'll make a beeline for here.'

'He can't come here,' Martha said vehemently, catching the gist of the conversation as she came in with the tea.

'And it would really disturb Deirdre, meeting the brother of the man she killed,' Patsy said. 'She's bad enough as it is, and to tell you the truth, I'm not mad keen on seeing him either.'

'Don't fret,' Sean said. 'None of you has to meet him. I will got to Dublin and be waiting for him when he comes out of the gaol.'

'You! You can't,' Martha said, not wanting Sean anywhere near the brother of the man who had raped his stepdaughter and had very nearly done the same to Deirdre. 'You can't just take off like that. What about your job?'

'I have some holidays owing to me,' Sean said. Then, because he knew what Martha was really fretting about, he went on, 'Don't worry, I'll not lay a hand on him. From what I have seen of the man, I haven't taken a liking to him, but whatever we think of Barney, Seamus will have been affected in some way by his death. Whether the man has changed, or whether he hasn't, I will not hold him responsible for the actions of his brother. This is done only to make life easier for the rest of you.'

Martha didn't want to tell Deirdre where her father was bound for, but Patsy insisted. 'There isn't any lie you could tell her that she could believe, and that would worry her more,' she said. 'Let's have no more secrecy. I know Deirdre is only young, but after what happened to her . . .'

'She'll be upset.'

'I'd expect her to be, but we will be here to reassure her and hold her when she cries. God, sometimes I think she hasn't done enough of that. She is coiled up inside like a spring.'

And Deirdre was upset. After Sean left, she lay on her bed sobbing. Patsy crept upstairs to comfort her a little later. Deirdre had stopped crying, but still lay full stretch, her head buried in her folded arms.

Patsy spoke to her back. 'Dad had to do this, you know,' she said. 'If he hadn't, then Barney's brother would have probably come here. That would be worse, wouldn't it?' There was no response and so she said again louder, 'Well, wouldn't it?'

'I suppose,' Deirdre said.

'Don't you see that this is almost the end?' Patsy said. 'Dad has to see Barney's brother to discuss how he wants the funeral organised. He's next of kin, but he hasn't been able to do anything before because he was in prison.'

'Huh. He's not a very good man either then.'

'I suppose not,' Patsy conceded. 'He was a thief, and while that is bad enough there is no suggestion that he would be up to doing the things Barney did. We can't hold him responsible. I mean, what if I did something wrong and people said you were just as bad because you were my sister? That wouldn't be very fair.'

'No, it wouldn't,' Deirdre said, raising her head a little as Patsy sat beside her on the bed.

'It'll all be over soon and Barney will be buried six foot under, and he will never be able to harm any of us again. Tell you what, me and you will dance a jig on his grave. I'm sure you can teach me the steps.'

There was a tremulous smile on Deirdre's face as she said, 'I don't think I would have a hope of teaching you. Dad says you have two left feet.' And then she sat up and put her arms around her sister. 'Thanks, Patsy,' she said, and now it was Patsy's eyes that were damp.

CHAPTER TWENTY-SEVEN

Maria was back in her own house by the time the letter came from Sean a few days later. She went to Martha's to discuss it after delivering the girls at school.

'I got a letter from Sean this morning,' Martha said as she put the kettle on. 'Did you?'

Maria laid the snuffling baby against her shoulder and nodded. 'Seamus wants his brother buried in Ireland.'

'Who's Seamus?' Jack piped up, and Maria raised her eyes to the ceiling. 'Little pitchers have big ears,' she said.

'I know what that means,' Jack cried. 'Paul told me. It means—'

'Jack,' Martha said quickly, 'would you like to play with Paul's train set?'

Jack knew it would be laid out on a board in the boys' room, and he had never been allowed to play with it on his own before.

'By myself?'

'Well, you are getting a big boy now,' Martha said. 'I'm sure you won't damage it.'

Jack considered. He knew he was being got rid of,

but then a train set was still a train set. 'OK,' he said. 'Can I have a biscuit and a drink, to take up?'

'Jack, that is rude,' Maria said sharply. 'You mustn't ask for things.'

'Well, Auntie Martha won't know unless I tell her.'

Before Maria could reply to this, Martha came from the kitchen with a mug and a couple of biscuits on the plate, trying in vain to hide her smile. 'Here,' she said handing it to him.

'Thanks, Auntie Martha. Can I go now?'

'Yes, go, for heaven's sake,' Maria said.

Not until they heard his feet scampering up the stairs did Martha say, 'Won't that cost a lot of money?'

'Well, I suppose, but Seamus will bear the cost of it,' Maria said. 'Sean said he seems to have unlimited funds. Illegally earned, no doubt.'

'Does that matter any more?' Martha said. 'At least then the man will be out of all our lives for good. There will not be even be a grave to remind us of how evil he was. And if his guard of honour at his funeral is made up of thieves, vagabonds and various other scoundrels, isn't that a fitting finish for him in the end?'

'Ah, yes, it is indeed,' Maria said.

Sean stayed on to attend the Requiem Mass Seamus had arranged, which was five days after he had arrived in Dublin. As the drinks flowed, Seamus, who had undoubtedly been shocked and upset by his brother's death, started asking questions about the police finding out who had killed his brother.

'There was no love lost between you two,' he had snarled at Sean.

'No, and I'll not pretend there was,' Sean said. 'The

police thought the same at one time and I was in for questioning, until they found out it wasn't me.'

'Then who was it?' Seamus demanded. He grasped the lapels of Sean's suit jacket and was almost spitting into his face as he went on, 'I want them found and punished.'

Sean pushed him away. 'Well, you will not find them by trying to intimidate me. You don't know the manner of man your brother had become. If I were you, I would let sleeping dogs lie.'

'What are you on about?'

Sean sighed. 'Barney was heavily into gambling and he owed money left, right and centre. But there were other things about him – things so bad that, had he not been killed, he would likely have spent years behind bars. There is nothing now to be gained by raking all this up again.'

'So what you are saying is, there were any number of people who'd have wanted Barney dead?'

'That's what I'm saying.'

'And if I was to go on about getting justice for my brother, things might come to light that were better left covered.'

'That's it exactly.'

'Did he accept that?' Maria asked, when her uncle recounted this on his return.

'He did.' Sean said. 'He seemed to know what I was intimating. Maybe he wouldn't have left it there, but shortly after that conversation, he was too drunk to say anything much. Most of the people there were the same, and I could see that very soon there would be trouble. Some of them were fairly spoiling for a fight, so I left and made for Dun Laoghaire where I hung about until the boat was ready to sail.'

'I am really grateful to you,' Maria said.

'I am the only one who could have gone,' Sean said. 'There is no way I wanted you to get involved. Now you can put all this behind you and look forward.'

Maria was now able to do just that. The sewing machine was back in place. The pawn ticket had been found in the pocket of one of Barney's jackets that Maria was packing up to get rid of. Her uncle insisted on redeeming it for her, and now business was thriving once more.

Her life was now free from menace or fear, and she looked forward to a rosy future where she would see her children grow and blossom. Only Deirdre seemed unable to shake off her despondency, and that in turn affected Sally.

Nothing had been told to Sally about Deirdre's ordeal, only that Deirdre had been upset by what had happened to Patsy. But Sally thought her daft to carry on the way she was over it, because Patsy was all right now. Even before they returned home Sally had thought Deirdre a little strange, but after they began school again, Deirdre's strangeness had got worse, especially when her dad went to Ireland for some funeral. Even when he came back she was little improved.

'She ain't no fun any more,' Sally complained to Maria. 'Even in the playground and that. She never wants to play anything. She just moons about by herself. She don't want no one, not even me.'

Maria knew that would be hard for her daughter,

for she and Deirdre had always been as thick as thieves. 'So who do you play with now?'

'I didn't have any one at first and then this new girl started and she d'ain't know anyone. Miss asked me if I could keep an eye on her, like, and show her what to do and that.'

'Is she nice?'

'Yeah, dead nice,' Sally said. 'She comes from Aston. Deirdre would like her too if she would just let herself.'

'Aston is where Martha came from originally.'

'I know, Uncle Sean told me. I said that to Deirdre and she just looked at me as if I was talking double Dutch or summat. Anyway, it's a real shame for this girl, Shirley, 'cos her mom died three years ago.'

'That is sad,' Maria said. 'Has she got a daddy?'

'Oh, yeah,' Sally said, and her voice was wistful as she went on, 'She loves her dad. She is always talking about him.'

'Do you wish you still had your daddy?'

Sally gave a shudder. 'No fear. Not the one we had, anyway. I was scared of him, and he mustn't have thought much of me or our Theresa because the only time he spoke to us was to shout. If I had another daddy, I'd want one like Uncle Sean.'

'My daddy was very like him,' Maria said with a smile at the memory. 'When I was a little girl, growing up, I thought the sun shone out of him. The day was always brighter for me when he came through the door. I am just so sorry that you haven't got such a memory.'

''S all right,' Sally said. 'Least I have got a mom, not like Shirley.'

'Yes, and I am glad that you are being kind to her. But don't give up on Deirdre altogether.'

'You don't know what she is like, Mom.' Sally complained. 'She is a dead loss.'

'We must be a little patient,' Maria said.

However, she hadn't seen any improvement in Deirdre at all since she had remembered what had happened that terrible night. In fact, if anything, she was getting worse as each week passed. Little wonder Sally was frustrated by her behaviour. Maybe she should have a word with Patsy. She seemed to get through to Deirdre better than anyone else.

Patsy had been worried about her sister for some time, and when Maria voiced her concerns, she decided to take action. The following Saturday was a bright but brisk day in early April and Patsy took her sister to Erdington village and into Gardner's Milk Bar, where she had a cup of tea and Deirdre a milkshake.

'What is it, Deirdre?' Patsy asked as they sat down. 'Don't say "nothing", for it's obvious that something is worrying the life out of you. And now I have a good look at you, you have bags under your eyes. Aren't you sleeping?'

Deirdre shook her head, her voice little above a whisper. 'I'm scared to, in case I have a nightmare.'

'Do you get them often?'

Deirdre nodded. 'Nearly every time I close my eyes.'

'What do you see? What Barney did to you?'

Deirdre shuddered. 'That first,' she said. 'And then what I did to him and then me in hell. 'Cos that will be where I'm going, won't it? 'Cos I did the worst sin of all. I killed someone.'

'Yes, to stop him killing you,' Patsy said. 'That was self-defence. That's different.'

Deirdre shook her head. 'Our teachers are always going on about the thought being as bad as the deed, and I wanted to kill Barney. I hit him over and over, and all the time I wanted him dead.'

Patsy saw this fear that Deirdre had was a deep-rooted and her words of reassurance were not getting through. She had no authority to say everything would be all right. 'Drink up your milkshake,' she said, 'and we'll go along to the abbey and have a word with one of the priests.'

'I can't!' Deirdre cried, aghast.

'Yes, you can,' Patsy said firmly. 'Not in the confessional, just the church, and I will be right beside you.' And then, as Deirdre still hesitated, she said, 'Come on, this is one way to settle this once and for all. Don't you want that?'

With a brief nod, Deirdre drained her drink and got to her feet.

Once at the abbey, Patsy asked if they could have a private word with Father Clancy. He took them into the sacristy. He had been aware, of course, that Sean had been released without charge, but knew no more than that. When Patsy told her tale and that of her young sister, he was shocked to the core. With Patsy beside her, Deirdre felt confident enough to put in little snippets herself.

Father Clancy saw the suffering on Deirdre's face. He took one of her small hands in his and looked deeply into her eyes 'You, Deirdre, you are not the sinner here and you must reproach yourself no more.

As I see it, no other course of action was open to you and the Good Lord will understand that.'

Deirdre felt as if a heavy weight had dropped from between her shoulders. She smiled as she got to her feet. 'Thank you, Father.'

'Our Deirdre is almost back to the way she was and she has even returned to her dancing, thank God,' Martha was able to report to Maria a few days later.

Maria knew that Deirdre was all for never going near the hall again and she had spoken to her about it. 'If you let Barney stop you doing something you enjoy, and that you are good at, then he will have won,' she'd said. 'And you should never let a bullying pervert win.'

Deirdre could see how right that was and she had returned to the class, but she wasn't as confident as she had been. Maria saw this and felt for the child.

'Well, I want my two to start as well,' she'd said. 'And certainly at the beginning I will take and fetch them each Saturday. I can easily use the time up taking a dander around the village and doing a bit of shopping.'

'Yes, and I might come with you a time or two,' Martha said, and so it was established.

Patsy and Andrew's wedding day turned out fine and warm, and the sun shone from a cornflower-blue sky with just the odd fluffy cloud wafting across now and then. Martha held baby Martin as Maria arranged Patsy's dress in the porch after she emerged from the car.

She was breathtakingly lovely, Maria thought. She kissed her lightly on the cheek and told her so.

'The dress helps,' Patsy said. 'And this minute I would love to give you a big hug in thanks.'

'What, and crush all my hard work?' Maria said in mock indignation.

'I wouldn't dare,' Patsy said, with a smile. 'That's why I must use words, but thank you, Maria, from the bottom of my heart. It is the most beautiful dress I could ever have had.'

Maria's face flamed with embarrassment and there was a sudden lump in her throat that made her voice husky as she said, 'Be happy, Patsy. That is all the thanks I need.'

She was glad to see the second car pull up, for she had become dangerously near to tears, and she busied herself arranging the girls' dresses of lilac satin, and pulling Jack's dicky bow straight at the neck of his silk shirt, smoothing his plum-coloured velvet pageboy suit, and attempting to slick down his hair as she gave them all last-minute instructions.

And then the strains of the Wedding March could be heard. Maria retrieved the baby from Martha and slipped into place in the pew as Patsy pulled the veil over her face and, with her arm in Sean's, began the slow walk down the aisle.

The girls were beautiful, and it was odd to see Jack looking so angelic, his face without his usual impish grin as he concentrated very hard on not treading on the bride's train. But the star of the day was Patsy. True happiness shone out of her with such radiance that it almost hurt to look. As Patsy neared Andrew, standing resolute beside his best friend, he turned and saw his bride approaching. Maria felt an actual pang in her heart at the expression on his face. No man but one had looked at her in such a way and that man she had lost. Maybe such love only comes once in a lifetime.

Martha had made the three-tiered cake, so glad the rationing had ended and that eggs and dried fruit were a little more plentiful.

'Do you remember my cake?' she said wistfully as she gazed at her creation at the reception.

Maria hoisted the baby up in her arms and nodded. From a distance, it had looked similar to Patsy's and close up you saw that the bottom two tiers were of cardboard, because there hadn't been the ingredients available for any more than the smallest tier.

'So many things were a headache then,' Martha said. 'This cake was a delight to make.'

'And I'm sure will taste delicious,' Maria said. 'You are a terrific cook.'

Martha laughed. 'Is this the complimentary club, for if it is I will have to say, you are a first-rate designer and dressmaker. Patsy's dress is a masterpiece. I think it is a bloody shame you were never able to take up that course in Dublin all those years ago.'

Maria made a face. 'Water under the bridge,' she said. 'I always think regret is a wasted emotion, and really there was no other option open to me at the time. The worst mistake I ever made was in marrying Barney, and that was brought home quite forcibly today.'

'What do you mean?'

'All this is important,' she said, her one free hand sweeping around the room. 'It's grand to wear a beautiful dress and all, but there is nothing tops the love that sparked between those two young people today, a love that will sustain them over the years and help them cope with all that life throws at people. I never felt at one like that with Barney.'

Martha knew that full well, but before she could say anything, Maria seemed to give herself a mental shake. 'But this is a wedding, not a wake. Doom and gloom are strictly forbidden. I will see if his lordship here will take a nap in the pram in the foyer and then I can circulate with the best of them.'

There were a great many people invited to the wedding – Andrew's family, of course, and flatmates, special friends and some people from the church. But there were people not invited who might have got invitations at one time. They were those so quick to believe that Sean was guilty of Barney's death that they snubbed the family quite openly, often crossing the road to avoid them.

When Sean was released without charge, these folk were some of the first to say they always knew he was innocent of any crime, for wasn't he a fine, well-respected man. Martha despised them, and though she was polite if they spoke to her, it was an icy politeness. She made it plain she would never seek or welcome their friendship and Maria didn't blame her one bit.

All in all, though, the reception was quite enjoyable. Eventually Martin, though he protested at first, as a matter of form, did agree to give in and, with a huge sigh, curled on his side in the pram, his thumb in his mouth. Maria's sigh was equally heartfelt and she went back into the hall as her small son's eyes fluttered shut.

She was introduced to Andrew's parents and his two

younger brothers, whom she found to be very pleasant, and she warmed to them greatly as they told her how delightful her children were – her beautiful daughters and such a dear little boy. Jack, she saw, was stealing the show. He looked adorable and, because he was naturally extrovert, he was playing to an audience he instinctively sensed would find him amusing.

'That lad will go far,' Sean said suddenly, appearing by her side. 'He has the ability to read reaction at his tender age.'

'You don't think I should stop him, tell him to behave?'

'You might as well tell the sun to stop shining,' Sean said with a grin. 'And why would you do that anyway? No one is offended. Relax. Enjoy yourself and let the children be.'

After that, the day was just wonderful and Maria enjoyed herself as she couldn't remember doing in a long time. Many complimented her on the dresses when they had found out she had made them, particularly Patsy's, which was described as a work of art.

There was a lull in the late afternoon while the debris from the meal was cleared away and the room rearranged for the dancing that evening. Deirdre had asked about this one day as she watched her mother and Patsy write out the invitations.

'Why are some people coming to the day and night, and others only coming for the night?'

'The day time is for close friends and family, mainly,' Patsy said. 'The evening is for other friends, work colleagues, people like that.'

'So could I invite friends if I liked?'

Patsy laughed. 'How many friends? I'm not having the whole class.'

Deirdre looked indignant. 'As if I would invite them all,' she said scornfully. 'Half of them are boys anyway, and horrid.'

'Well, who then?'

'Just Shirley and her sister, Anna.'

'Shirley? Isn't she that new friend of yours?'

'Yeah, mine and Sally's. They're nice and, anyway, I feel sorry for them. Go on, Patsy, say I can ask them?'

'All right.' Patsy said. 'I dare say it will do no harm to invite them over for the evening.'

Maria wasn't staying for the evening do. She was going home with Jack and Martin. Sean and Martha were taking Sally and Theresa home with their own, and topping and tailing them for the night with Deirdre. Maria waited only until she had seen Patsy and Andrew drive off in the car that Andrew's friends had decorated well for him, with all variety of things tied to the back, before getting herself and the children ready to leave.

Tony was to take her home, though she protested that there was no need, and she was in the hall as Shirley and Anna came in. She caught a glimpse of the man she presumed to be the girls' father standing outside.

'Good evening,' she said automatically, but didn't look at him, as she was in the act of lifting Jack up onto the pram. She remembered that the man had no wife waiting for at home so, as she settled Jack, she went on, 'You can go in too, you know. No one will mind.'

The man didn't answer for a moment or two. Then: 'Maria,' he said tentatively. 'Maria, is that really you?'

Maria felt as if someone had punched her in the stomach. She turned slowly and knew she was staring at a man she never thought she would ever see again. He looked older. Lines of strain were on his face, though his beautiful eyes were just the same, and these were fastened on her.

She said, almost questioningly, as if she couldn't quite believe it, 'Greg? Greg Hopkins?'

'God Almighty, Maria,' Greg said. 'This is marvellous, wonderful. Can we talk or do you hate me still?'

'I never hated you,' Maria said. 'Believe me. I was full of hurt and disappointment, but never hate.'

'Then, can we talk?'

Maria was flustered and didn't really know how to react, but one thing she was sure of was that she didn't want this man just to walk out of her life again. But she had the children to attend to. 'I . . . I must get the children home,' she said.

'Where's home?'

'We live on the Pype Hayes estate.'

'That's quite a hike from here.'

'No, it's all right,' Maria said. 'It's a fine warm evening and I'm not going alone. Tony is coming with me. He's Uncle Sean's stepson. You mind my Uncle Sean?' At Greg's nod she went on, 'He married a widow and she had three children. They live in Arthur Road.'

Maria was aware she was gabbling and told herself to stop. Greg was smiling the smile she knew so well, which sparkled in his eyes too, just as if he was aware of her discomfort.

'See,' he said, putting his hand over hers on the pram handle, 'there is so much I need to catch up on.

518

Can I walk down with you? I'd like you to fill me in on what has happened to you since that terrible day when I caused you so much anguish that my parents effectively cut me off from the family.'

'Do you still not speak?' Maria said, surprised 'One of your sisters told me you had become estranged from your parents after we split up, but I never imagined it would go on this long.'

Greg gave a rueful smile. 'That is one of the things I'll tell you about if you'll let me.'

Tony came out of the hall then, flustered and with the stain of scarlet lips on his cheek. 'Sorry, Maria,' he said. 'A girl grabbed me for a dance and wouldn't take no for an answer.'

'Did you want to say no?'

Tony gave a grin. 'Not really.'

'Then go on back to her,' Maria said, and as Tony lifted his hand in protest she said, 'Tell Sean I have met an old friend, someone I used to know in Moville, and he will walk home with me.'

'You sure?'

'I'm positive,' Maria said, and added with a smile, 'Go on. Get in there before she starts dancing with someone else.'

'Thank you,' Greg said.

'It's all right,' Maria said, manoeuvring the pram outside. 'Like I said to Tony, we are old friends.' But she thought to herself, few old friends would set my heart thumping in this uncomfortable way.

'More than mere friends surely, Maria?' Greg said, glancing at her as they walked away from the hall.

'Aye, maybe, but for a short time only.' Maria said.

'And it was many years ago,' and she quickened her pace.

Greg couldn't think of a reply to that and in the silence between them he glanced at her again. She didn't seem to have aged a day. Her hair was still as vibrant, her eyes seemed greener than ever and they were shining. She seemed full of vitality and happiness, but he saw that she wore a ring, so he knew he couldn't take any relationship further than friendship. Maria had been right to check him.

The silence between them might have got uncomfortable, for neither of them felt they could break it, if it hadn't been for Jack. Although he was tired and was glad to be sitting up on the pram, he had been playing to the gallery for most of the day and wasn't used to being ignored. He smiled at Greg and said, 'My name's Jack. What's yours?'

Greg looked at the child, in his crumpled and stained pageboy's outfit, his dicky bow somewhere under his ear, his knees grubby and his unruly hair no longer even semi tamed, and he said with a smile, 'My name is Greg, and you look as if you have had a good time.'

'I have,' Jack said, and added proudly, 'I ate mountains of cake and stuff. No one seemed to mind.'

'I shall mind, young man, if you are sick tonight,' Maria said sharply.

Jack ignored that and addressed himself to Greg again. 'Have you got any little boys?'

'No, I'm afraid I haven't,' Greg said. He glanced in the pram, but Martin was fast asleep, and so he asked, 'Is your baby a boy or a girl?'

'A boy,' Jack said. 'He's called Martin and he ain't

no good for playing with yet. He's too little and he cries a lot. Mommy says he'll get better. I got two sisters too.' Here he stopped and made a face, before conceding, 'They're OK, but they keep trying to push me round and tell me what to do and that.'

Greg laughed out loud. 'I bet they are on a losing wicket with you.'

'You're not kidding,' Maria said under her breath as Jack burst out, 'What does a losing wicket mean?'

'It doesn't matter,' Maria said.

'Uncle Sean said it's good to ask questions,' Jack said. 'It's how people learn, he says.'

Maria sighed. 'Uncle Sean doesn't have to put up with you all day and every day. Give Greg a rest or he will begin to wish he had never asked to walk home with us.'

'No, Maria,' Greg said. 'I would never do that.'

'See, he don't care,' Jack said.

'OK,' Maria said. 'Maybe Greg doesn't mind, but I do. Be quiet, for pity's sake, and give us a bit of peace.'

Jack was a bright boy and he knew when his mother spoke in a certain way, it was best to do as she said. He contented himself with swinging his legs, a look of injured indignation on his face that caused Greg to bite his bottom lip to prevent a smile that he thought Maria probably wouldn't approve of.

Maria sighed in relief as they turned in Woodacre Road. 'Not long now.'

'You should have let me push the pram,' Greg said. 'It must be heavy with the two of them.'

'No, really,' Maria said. 'And it is all downhill. I'm

521

just jiggered. I've been on the go all day and I need a chance to put my feet up and get certain people to bed.'

'She means me,' Jack said to Greg knowingly. 'Mommy always says things like that when she means me.'

'Jack, I'm warning you.'

'I'm just telling Greg . . .'

'Well, don't. He doesn't want to hear you,' Maria said, and went on before Jack could leap in with anything else, 'You lived in Aston before, didn't you, Greg?'

'Yeah, all through the war we did,' Greg said. 'Nancy lived with her parents till I was demobbed, and Aston took a pasting. At times, I was more worried about Nancy and Anna than myself.'

'I know,' Maria said. 'I wasn't here through those times, but Martha, the widow Uncle Sean married, had her family near wiped out.'

'I can well believe it.'

'Where do you live now?'

'Holly Lane,' Greg said. 'The top end, near the convent.'

'They are big houses there,' Maria said surprised. 'Expensive too. Won the pools, have you?'

'Not quite,' Greg told her with a smile. 'Like I say, Nancy lived with her parents. She saved and so did I, and with my gratuity after my demob, we were able to rustle up enough for a deposit on a small house. Nancy wanted to stay in the same area. Her father was a bruiser of a man and a bully into the bargain. I tell you, no one shed a tear when he dropped dead just a year after we moved out, but Nancy was real close to her mother. She was all right, the mother, although quite timid at times – I should imagine the husband made her that way – and frail-looking, like Nancy herself. She never really got over losing her son at Dunkirk, though she took pleasure in Anna, and then Shirley, of course.' He smiled and went on, 'Nancy chose their names. A bit fanciful for my tastes because Anna is really Annabel, and Shirley, as you might imagine, was called for Shirley Temple.'

'Ssh,' Maria warned in a whisper. 'With the slightest encouragement, the boyo here will give you a tuneless rendering of "The Good Ship Lollipop". Anyway, we're here, thank God,' she said, pushing the pram up the path and fumbling in the bag hanging from the pram handle for the key. 'You'll come in for a cup of tea at least?' she said to Greg as she opened the door, not knowing whether it was sensible to invite him in, but going to do it anyway.

'Will it be all right?' Greg said. 'Your husband won't mind?

Maria wondered why Sally hadn't said she hadn't a daddy when Shirley had told them of her own mother's demise, but then neither Sally, Deirdre nor even wee Theresa ever mentioned Barney's name unless they were forced to. In a way, it was as if the man had never existed for them. So Maria said, 'I shouldn't think it will bother him in the slightest. He died last December.'

'Oh, my dear,' Greg said, 'I am sorry.'

'Don't be,' Maria said. 'If I am honest, I was relieved. You'll know him from Moville. I married Barney McPhearson.'

Greg was surprised. He wouldn't have thought Barney Maria's type at all. 'I did know him,' he said. 'Not well, although we were the same school year.'

'You missed nothing not knowing him better,' Maria said slightly bitterly, but she didn't elaborate further because Jack was listening intently. 'So will you come in now?' she said manoeuvring the pram up the step.

'If it won't put you out.'

'Not in the slightest,' Maria said. 'Though I will have to get Jack to bed and make up a bottle for Martin to give to him when he wakes.'

'I ain't tired,' Jack said,

'Jack,' Maria snapped, lifting him from the pram, 'I'm not even going to discuss this. Get into the bathroom. You'll have to do with a lick and a promise tonight.'

'Maybe I should go,' Greg said. 'You said you were tired.'

'I'd welcome adult company,' Maria said. 'And one thing we could always do was talk, wasn't it? Anyway, you'll be the worst daddy in the world if you go up for the girls too soon.'

'Oh, don't I know that well enough,' Greg said, with a rueful grin. 'And I would be glad to stay if you are sure.'

Later, with Jack in bed, they sat with a cup of tea and some of the wedding cake Martha had pressed on Maria as she was leaving.

Maria asked gently, 'How did your wife die, Greg?'

'She had a tumour, on her lungs,' Greg told her. 'They said she must have had it for years and, thinking back, she never really picked up after Shirley's birth and was often short of breath. She never complained, though. She always said she was fine and she was determined to have another child, a son for me, though I told her not to fret, that I was happy enough with the girls. She was determined, though, and she became pregnant when Shirley was three. She miscarried when she was about five months gone, and when they had her in the hospital, they found the tumour. They told me there and then that they could do nothing and that I was not to tell Nancy.'

He looked at Maria and went on, 'She knew, though; she was no fool and even then, all she worried about was me. Poor Nancy. I always felt guilty about her, for she loved me so much and I could never love her the same way. For a while, I didn't know what to do. I was truly saddened to lose her, for she had been a good wife and a first-rate mother. The children, of course, were distraught. Everything in the house, the area, reminded them of their mother and they felt truly bereft when Nancy's mother died less than six months after her daughter. I think she just lost all reason for living.

'I decided to move right away, though of course these things take time,' Greg said. 'But eventually I sold our house and the much larger house that had been Nancy's family home. With the money I put a hefty deposit on the house in Holly Lane and bought part shares in a garage on the Bristol Road.'

'You have done well for yourself,' Maria said. 'I am sorry about Nancy, although of course I never knew her.'

'Didn't you resent her?'

Maria thought back to the time when she had found herself pregnant and unmarried, and the despair she had felt when Barney had seemed reluctant to marry her at first. She said, 'No, I never did, and if Anna was your child, you had to stand by her. What else was poor Nancy to do?'

'You are very understanding.'

'As I said before, it was years ago.'

'And what of you?' Greg said. 'You have had my life story, now I'd like yours.'

'There's not much to say,' Maria said. 'Barney was a bully of a man, and worse. I don't want to go into it, but I am happier without him.'

'You have to get over these things and go on anyway, if you have children,' Greg said. 'I suppose you found the same.'

Maria nodded and then, in an attempt to lighten the atmosphere and to prevent Greg asking probing questions about Barney, she said, 'And I think this fixation many have about having boys is madness. They are, in my opinion, very overrated. I mean, look at the performance Jack gave this evening.'

Greg laughed. 'He is a sharp boy, all right.'

'Aye, so sharp he'll cut himself one of these days,' Maria said grimly. 'I'd prefer to call him precocious. The child isn't four years old yet and I'm sure I don't know where he gets some of the expressions he comes out with, though, of course, he mimics his older sisters. Then Sean's two stepsons and Sean himself think he is terrific and encourage him. The girls are nothing like him. In fact Sally often gets embarrassed by her young brother.'

'Oh, I'd say she will survive,' Greg said. 'Phil and Billy used to embarrass the life out of me at times.'

Maria heard the wistful note in Greg's voice and said, 'Do you miss the family, Greg?'

Greg shrugged. 'Not so much now. You can get used to anything if you have to.'

'Didn't you think of contacting them when Nancy died?' she asked.

Greg shook his head. 'No. To be frank, I didn't think of anything much at first and then . . . how could I take two young girls still grieving for their mother to visit people who hadn't accepted her when she was alive?'

'Yes, I see that.'

'I suppose I was cross too,' Greg admitted. 'I had to put my own grieving on hold anyway to cope with my mother-in-law who took sick almost as soon as Nancy's funeral was over, and there were the girls fretting and missing their mother terribly, yet I still had to go to work to ensure we kept a roof over our heads. I had little time or energy for anything else.'

'Oh, I do see that so clearly,' Maria said. 'For me it was totally different. My marriage generally was not a happy time for me. Let's leave it there and talk about more pleasant things.'

They reminisced about the times they could remember in Moville. Maria remembered other things, like some of the gestures that Greg used and expressions, the little smiles that crinkled up his eyes and the way his laughter would ring out. With each jolt of memory, she would feel her heart thud against her ribs, and it was as if she had butterflies in her stomach. She felt like a love-sick

527

teenager, and when their hands accidentally touched, she didn't imagine the tremor that ran through her whole body. She saw by Greg's face he had felt the same.

'Maria . . .' Greg began.

But Maria was confused and not ready for anything more that friendship with Greg for the moment. She didn't want him to say anything to spoil that yet, and so she cut across him, 'Goodness, is that the time?'

Greg took the hint and got to his feet. 'I can't remember when I have enjoyed myself more,' he said. 'It's good to talk over old times. Can I come again?'

Maria was glad the baby had begun to stir and she was able to turn her flushed face away from Greg to attend to him. She forced herself to speak calmly as she said, 'Of course. I am always glad to see an old friend.'

She missed the expression on Greg's face at her words as she was lifting Martin out of the pram, but later, as she fed the baby the bottle, she wanted to hug herself in delight at the prospect of seeing Greg again.

CHAPTER TWENTY-EIGHT

Greg called to see Maria the following Saturday, just after lunch, and had Shirley and Anna with him. They were a little shy and reticent with Maria, though they were different again with Sally, quite prepared to tolerate Theresa, were amused by Jack and enchanted with little Martin. Maria dispensed cordial and biscuits, and she and Greg took their tea at the kitchen table with the door open, so that they could keep an eye on the children in the garden.

'Sorry I can't ask you to stay,' she told Greg. 'But the girls have Irish dancing lessons on Saturday afternoon.'

'Irish dancing lessons,' Greg said. 'Mine might like something like that. Where is it?'

'The church hall at the abbey.'

'And it carries on through the holidays?'

'Through the summer, it does,' Maria said. 'The teacher, Mrs Bellingham, says she has to start all over again with some of them if they have a lay-off of seven weeks or more, and then she hardly has the time to whip them into shape for the shows they have at

Christmas. Deirdre goes too, and she is a cracking little dancer.'

'Could I come along with you today and see if my daughters would like it?' Greg asked.

'Of course,' Maria said. 'I usually take a turn around Erdington while they are there, and then I am on hand to bring them back. Martha usually comes with me, but she has something on today and, to be honest, I would value the company.'

Anna and Shirley liked the look of the dancing and agreed to stay and watch. Then they could start the following week when they had the regulation plimsolls with them. 'The Irish costume dresses look lovely, don't they?' Greg said, as Maria turned the pram towards the village. 'I bet they are a price, though.'

'You only need them for a show or competition,' Maria said. 'And the mothers are good about selling them on. I mean, it isn't as if they are worn out, but I get a lot of the new orders.'

'You?'

'Don't sound so surprised,' Maria said with a laugh. 'You knew that I had won that scholarship to the Grafton Academy before Daddy had his accident and I had to have talent to win that. It was Patsy suggested I use it, and to tell you the truth, it changed my life and that of the children too, because, you see, Barney was a drinker and a gambler. The dressmaking at least ensured that the children had enough to eat.'

It was said in such a matter-of-fact way, and yet Greg, watching her eyes, could guess how she had suffered. He wished he could hold Maria in his arms and tell her the bad times were over, but he had thrown away any right to do that, and Maria was nowhere near ready for such a declaration. He faced the fact that she might never be. He might have hurt her so badly that she wouldn't be able ever to trust him totally again, and if that was the case he would have to accept it. Just to look at her set his heart racing. He thought her so beautiful, but now hers was a mature beauty, and he knew he loved her as much as he ever had.

Maria wasn't aware of what was in Greg's mind. She thought only how pleasant it was to be with him and how good he was with the children. Already Jack and he were the best of friends, and when the child's legs got tired, rather that put him up on the pram, Greg swung him up on his shoulders. Jack squealed in excitement, and little Martin laughed and clapped his hands.

When they dropped Deirdre home that day, Maria took the opportunity to introduce Greg to Martha and Sean. Sean remembered Greg slightly and told Martha later of the boy who had asked Maria to marry him and then had left her in the lurch and married another.

'It fair broke her heart at the time,' he said.

'Why did he do that?' Martha asked.

Sean shook his head. 'I never did get to the bottom of why he just upped and left the way he did. Maybe he just didn't love her in that way.'

Martha smiled. 'Maybe he didn't, but he sure does now.'

'What do you mean?'

'I mean the man is besotted by our Maria,' Martha said. 'He can barely keep his eyes off her. She is unaware of it so far, anyway, and while I wouldn't push her into anything, I think I will find something to occupy me every Saturday afternoon and let them have a bit of time to themselves.'

Sean chuckled and shook his head. 'You women,' he said. 'You're terrible schemers.'

'I want Maria's happiness. Don't you?'

'You know I do, more than anything,' Sean said. 'And I don't want her to go through life alone. She's only a young woman yet.'

'So, let's give them the chance,' Martha said.

When Martha said the following week she had something she had to do on Saturday afternoon, Maria was glad, though she hid it well. She had so enjoyed the time she had had with Greg the previous week. As before, after leaving the girls at their dancing class, they strolled up the High Street, looking at this and that.

In the market, Maria was stocking up with reels of cotton, buttons, lace and other sundry items. When the children got bored, Greg wheeled the pram around and they went to see what they could get at the sweet counter, returning with a couple of bags of cakes, and sweets for everyone. Maria chided him for spoiling them.

'Come on,' Greg said. 'It's just a few little treats, so take the frown from between your eyes, Maria Foley.'

'Huh. It's a long time since I have been called that.'

'You will always be Maria Foley to me,' Greg said softly. And then, because the urge to hold her in his arms threatened to overpower him, which might alarm Maria, he said briskly, 'D'you fancy going to the Milk Bar? I could just murder a cup of coffee.'

As Greg left her at the house that day, he said, 'Maria, can I see you tomorrow?'

'Tomorrow?'

'The truth is, I hate Sundays,' Greg said. 'It's such a family time.'

Maria knew exactly what Greg meant. She was often lonely on Sundays herself, and yet would hesitate to land at Sean and Martha's door every week, feeling they needed time on their own sometimes. So she said. 'Yes, all right, Greg.'

'We could go to Sutton Park, if the weather's as pleasant as it is today.'

Sutton Park was a massive place that Maria had never been to, though it wasn't that far away. It had vast areas of woodland, and others of meadows, with streams running through them, feeding the five large lakes. It could be reached either by the Midland Red bus that ran along the Birmingham Road at the top of Holly Lane, or the little diesel train from the station at Wylde Green, just a little further along the Birmingham Road. Maria hadn't felt she could manage such an outing with four children to see to on her own, but with another pair of hands, it could be achieved. 'Oh, Greg that would be wonderful,' she cried. 'Can we go on the train? The children would love that.'

'Well, I thought we might take the car.'

'You have a car!'

'I have part shares in a garage,' Greg reminded her. 'So, yes, I have a car.'

'Jack will be beside himself,' Maria said. 'But will you get us all in?'

'I think so,' Greg said. 'The car is like a shooting brake. It means there is no boot, just a space at the back. It was bought that way so that I can transport tools if I have to, without getting oil or dirt on the seats, but with a blanket down it could accommodate a fair few.'

And it could, of course. Maria held Martin on her knee, the three older girls on the back seat, and Theresa and Jack sat on cushions at the very rear.

That was the beginning of a wonderful period in Maria's life and she was happier and more content than she could remember feeling for years. She lived for the weekends. Sometimes, if the weather was wet or cold, Martin and Jack would be left with Martha while Greg and Maria took the dancing troupe to Erdington, and then had time for themselves alone.

Often they would stay on into the evening at Sean and Martha's house on Saturday after they delivered Deirdre home. Greg met all the family, including Patsy and Andrew, who called in one Saturday evening while they were there. It was primarily for Patsy to inspect the man that her mother had said was besotted with Maria. She wanted to ensure herself that he was good enough for her cousin, whom she thought had had life hard enough. She wanted her happiness too and was impressed by Greg.

'Maria is as keen as he is,' she said, when they had left.

'D'you think so?'

'I know so,' Patsy said definitely. 'It's in her eyes when she looks at him, in her whole demeanour, but she isn't aware of it herself. She isn't allowing herself to feel anything for the man but friendship.'

Patsy was so right, for friendship and companionship with Greg was all that Maria would permit herself to feel. She tried to ignore the times when her heart beat faster as she looked him, and the times she yearned to be enfolded in his arms and feel his lips on hers. There were other things she longed for too, which she refused to acknowledge in the day, but they invaded her dreams at night. When she woke and remembered them, she often flamed with embarrassment.

Greg never touched her, because he was afraid to – afraid that if he felt her body close to his he might forget himself and do something to frighten or upset her. So he didn't hold her hand, or drape an arm about her shoulder. Sometimes she would have liked him to, but she would never ask him. Thinking he didn't feel that way about her, she hammered down any feelings like that.

They went somewhere every Sunday. Sutton Park was a firm favourite and so were the Lickey Hills, which were the other side of the town. Anna and Shirley got over their reticence with Maria, and all the children got on well together. If the weather was too wet or cold and blustery for outdoors, the family would go to the cinema, occasionally the theatre, or sometimes for a drive into the country, stopping at a country pub or a traditional teashop for a meal before coming home.

Time and again, Greg wanted to tell Maria how he felt, but his courage would fail him, terrified, if he spoke of his feelings for her, that he risked losing the friendship they shared.

They were to have Christmas together at Greg's house, as it was larger than Maria's, and then they were invited to have tea with Martha and Sean. Greg decided that on Christmas Day he was going to tell Maria of his feelings for her, and ask how she felt about him. Not knowing one way or the other was eating the heart out of him.

First, though, the day belonged to the children. When they all piled into Greg's house, it was to find Santa had made a special delivery while they had been away at Mass. A new bicycle was waiting for each child. Anna's was almost full size. She was twelve now, and teetering on the verge of womanhood, a slender and very beautiful child. Maria was sure her mother would have been proud of her. Sally and Shirley, now nine years old, had matching bikes but Sally's was bright blue and Shirley's bright mauve. Theresa had a little blue fairy cycle, and Jack a big red and silver three-wheeler with a large bread basket on the back. Even Martin had a tricycle.

'I couldn't leave him out,' Greg said to Maria, as the two of them washed and dried the breakfast dishes. 'I know he can't use it much yet, but in no time he will be scooting it along with his feet, I bet.'

'Never mind that,' Maria said. 'While the younger children at least might believe that these things were from Santa, I know they were not. You had no right to spend so much money.'

'I had every right,' Greg said. 'It was my money and this was how I wanted to spend it.'

'Not on my children. Greg, it's not right.'

'Is that so?' Greg said. 'You best go out into the garden and tell the children, who are almost speechless with pleasure, that Santa has made a mistake and the bikes are not for them at all.'

'You know I can't do that,' Maria said. 'It's just—'

'Just that you are so stiff-necked with pride,' Greg said, throwing down the tea cloth and drawing Maria into his arms for the first time since they had met up again, causing her to gasp with pleasure. 'I would like to do more for your children, if you would let me,' he said. 'I don't know how you feel about me, Maria, and maybe I have no right to ask you, but I must tell you that, just as I said that awful day in the boatyard, my heart belonged to you. Well, it still does, and I love you more, if anything, than I did then. Even poor Nancy knew she could never have the whole of me, that my heart belonged to another, though she never complained or asked who you were.'

Maria was both shocked and delighted by Greg's revelation. She felt herself sag against him with a sigh, her head against his shoulder, suddenly realising how right it seemed.

'Can I hope that you feel something for me?' Greg asked tentatively. 'Other than friendship, I mean, nice as that is.'

'Yes, Greg,' Maria said. 'I feel a great deal for you, but I had no idea about you. You gave me no hint that you felt this way.'

'I was afraid of being shown the door, of not being allowed to see you at all,' Greg said. 'I mean, you did go on about us being friends from the moment we met again, and I didn't really know if you had changed your mind. Over the weeks and months my feelings for you have grown stronger and stronger. I knew I had to tell you today and take the risk.'

'There is no risk, darling,' Maria said, admitting at last what her heart had been telling her for months, 'for I love you too with all my heart and soul.'

'Would you . . . ?' Greg began tentatively. 'Maybe this is too soon for you – I know your husband has not been dead that long – but would you consider becoming my wife?'

Maria didn't even have to think. Almost since she had met up with Greg, she had fantasised about just such a proposal, never dreaming it would happen, trying to come to terms with the fact that she would never be anything more than a good friend to Greg.

Now those suppressed feelings had surfaced, and the effect on Maria was such an overwhelming rush of love for this man that she caught up his hand, her eyes radiant with happiness, and said, 'Yes, I will marry you. I would be honoured to marry you and I would marry you tomorrow if we could manage it.'

'Oh, my darling girl,' Greg said, drawing her close.

Their lips met gently at first and then with greater intensity. In the end it was Greg who broke off first. He was breathless and his voice was husky as he said, as he withdrew a ring box from his pocket, 'Then this, darling, is yours.'

Maria recognised the box and she opened it to see the sparkling diamond ring that Greg had given her before.

'This is the one I sent back to your parents.'

'Yes, I know. They sent it on to me, no note, nothing, just the ring.'

'Didn't you want to give it to Nancy?'

'No,' Greg said. 'I had given it to the one I loved, the one I knew I would always love. Nancy wanted no engagement ring, anyway. There was only one ring she wanted and that was a wedding ring. I carried that engagement ring all through the war like a talisman. If ever I lost sight of the reason for the brutality and the carnage, the ring would remind me of you, and people like you all over the world, who we were fighting to protect.'

Maria had seldom worn the engagement ring Barney had given her once he had confessed the stone in it was a real emerald and she had realised how he had paid for it. From that moment, the joy had gone out of wearing it and she'd had left it on the chest in the bedroom. One day she had noticed it had disappeared and she presumed that it had been pawned, but she hadn't asked because she didn't really care what happened to it. Greg's ring, however, bought with money honestly earned and given with love, was very special to her. She knew she would be proud to wear it and she slipped it on her finger.

The kiss was wonderful and would have gone on for a lot longer if they hadn't been interrupted by Theresa, asking if one of them would help her ride her new bike because she kept falling off it.

The children were told about the engagement as they all tucked in to a huge Christmas dinner.

'Does that mean you intend to get married eventually?' Anna said.

'Yes.' Greg said. 'Does that bother you?'

'No, but . . .' she looked across at Maria, 'I couldn't call you Mother or Mom or anything.'

Maria remembered that Patsy had been the same with Sean – certainly at first, at least – though she now called him 'Dad' with ease and she realised that Anna would have more memories of her own mother than her younger sister and might feel it would be disloyal to call another the same. She smiled across at her, seeing the girl's discomfort. 'I understand that perfectly,' she said. 'Maria will be just fine,' and she saw relief flood Anna's face.

Jack had been digesting the news. He hadn't understood about engagements, but he understood what Anna had said and he burst out, 'Does that mean you will be my daddy?'

'When we get married, yes, I will be your daddy,' Greg told him.

'Oh, boy!'

Everyone laughed at the expression on Jack's face. 'I take it you approve?'

Jack nodded vigorously. 'And can I call you "Dad"?'

'If you want to,' Greg said. 'I'd like that. What about you girls?' he asked

Sally sneaked a look at Greg and said impishly, 'I once told you, Mom, that if ever I had another dad, I would like one like Uncle Sean. I suppose you're better than nothing.'

'You cheeky young whippersnapper!' Greg said in mock indignation. 'I might just tell Santa you don't deserve that bike after all.'

There was howl of protest, and when it died down

Sally said, 'I'd like to call you "Dad" too, if you don't mind. I didn't care for my own dad very much.'

'Nor did I,' Theresa said. 'I agree with Sally.'

'What about you, Shirley?' Maria asked gently, for the child hadn't spoken, but her large expressive eyes looked troubled, as if she was thinking hard about things.

Eventually she said, 'Sometimes I can barely remember what Mommy looked like, but I spent ages talking to her when she was ill in bed and I think she would have liked you, Maria. I don't think she would mind either if I called you Mommy.'

Shirley's words brought tears dampening Maria's eyes, but she blinked them away. It was Christmas Day, not the time for weeping and wailing. She felt only happiness and contentment lay ahead. So she smiled at them all grouped around the table, her own big, happy family and her darling Greg at the head of it, and she raised her glass. 'Happy Christmas, everyone.'

They left for Sean and Martha's as soon after dinner as they could, for the winter day was very short. The children riding their bikes, to find Santa had brought Deirdre a bike too, in vivid green. All the family were thrilled and delighted at Greg and Maria's news too, and admired the ring.

Sean saw that Martha would like to have a little time alone with Maria and so he said, 'These bikes need a proper test. How about if you all go for a ride to Pype Hayes Park?'

There was a chorus of agreement to this plan and only Theresa was the slightest bit hesitant. 'I'm not so good at it yet,' she said. 'I need someone to hold the saddle for me.'

'Don't worry your head about that,' Greg said. 'Sean and I are going too, and I'll hold the saddle for you gladly. You know, to get better at anything, it is best to get lots of practice in.'

As it was Christmas Day, the parlour was in use and a bright fire burned merrily in the grate as Maria, Martin in her arms, stood at the window and watched the children and two men leave in a fever of excitement.

'Penny for them,' Maria said, coming in with a tray of tea and Christmas cake.

'They're not worth a penny,' Maria said, giving Martin a kiss as she put him down on the floor. She watched him take a few tottering steps before dropping to all fours again and settling himself with the collection of toys Martha had sorted out for him to play with. 'You don't think it too soon, do you? I mean, Barney hasn't been dead a full year yet.'

Maria looked at her astounded. 'I can't believe I heard you said that,' she said. 'I would think this family is well aware of the day that Barney died and I would like to know why you think that he needs one minute of your consideration.'

'Won't people think it odd?'

'Who gives a tinker's cuss what anyone thinks. No one knows the type of man Barney was, nor the life he gave you,' Martha said. 'Tell me, Maria, what do you really think of Greg?'

'Oh God, Martha, I love him with every part of me, and so much I ache. I can scarcely believe I met up with him again and both of us are free. We haven't told the children about the time we were engaged and due to be married before, for it might be upsetting for Anna and Shirley, though, of course, we did say we knew one another in Moville.'

'What happened before to stop you getting married?' Martha asked. 'Sean said he never knew the reason, but Greg doesn't seem the unreliable type.'

'He isn't,' Maria said. 'Greg wasn't even going to speak of love or commitment of any sort until I was done at the Academy, and hopefully the war over. Daddy's accident changed all that and Greg told me how he felt, how he had felt about me for some time. Before this, though, he had had some dalliances with other girls and one of those was Anna and Shirley's mother. He had made her pregnant, but he was unaware of it. He had to marry her. What choice had he? You know the life she would have had if he hadn't? Greg told me the father was a bully and that he had beaten her black and blue before she would admit he was the father. You see why we can't tell the girls any of this yet. It would reflect so badly on their mother.'

'You're right, of course,' Martha said. 'I would so hate for one of mine to think badly of me. Maybe they'll never need to know.'

'Well, we'll cross that bridge when we come to it. Just now I am so grateful that Greg and I have another chance. I can hardly believe it.'

'Your trouble,' said Martha, 'is that you never expect happiness to last.'

'You know,' Maria said, 'I really think you are right. It seemed to me that every time I really longed for something to happen, something else would get in the way to stop it. I am almost afraid to be happy, or get excited about anything.'

'Listen, Maria.' Martha covered her hands with her own. 'This time you have nothing on God's earth to worry about. You and Greg will go on to have a long and happy future together.'

Maria sighed. 'Of course we will,' she said. 'I am just being silly.'

That night Maria and the children were all staying at Greg's. Boxing Day was a Sunday, so there would be Mass again in the morning and Greg had a pantomime booked for the afternoon. There was plenty of room. Greg's house was very large, with five bedrooms on the first floor and two further bedrooms on the second. That night, Greg showed Maria to the room he had prepared for her. 'Is it all right?' he asked anxiously, as Maria said nothing.

'It's lovely,' Maria said. 'And such a pity it won't be used.'

'What do you mean?'

'Oh, Greg,' Maria said, laying her hand on his arm. 'What do you think I mean? We have waited long enough, Greg. Years, in fact.'

'Oh God, I never dreamt, wouldn't let myself hope . . . Oh, darling, I love you so,' Greg said. He held her in his arms and the kiss left her longing for more. She wondered what had come over her, for never had she done such a forward thing before, but she felt as if a furnace was burning inside her and she so longed for fulfilment with Greg, she could wait no longer.

Greg took her hand and led her down the passage

to his room. Once they were inside it, he sat her on the bed, turned her to face him and looked into those green eyes that had haunted him since the day he had left her. 'You are sure about this?' he said.

'I have never been more sure about anything in my life,' Maria replied, and began slowly and seductively to unfasten her blouse. Greg watched, mesmerised, as she shrugged her blouse off and undid her brassiere so that her breasts were exposed.

Even in their earlier courtship, Greg had never touched any part of Maria inside her clothes, but now she took his hands and cupped them around each breast and she felt no hint of shame. Now he took each breast in his hand. An explosion was happening inside Maria. She was in a frenzy of desire, and she began to tear the clothes from Greg and herself in a passion. Neither of them could wait, they were both fully aroused, and though their lovemaking was as rapturous as Maria had known it would be, it was over in minutes. Then however, Greg began again, awaking Maria's passions, but slowly this time.

He kissed her lips, her throat, her neck and her breasts while his hands stroked, fondled, caressed and teased. Maria's breath was coming in short gasps and, greatly daring, and to please Greg, she reached out and touched him. When she felt his throbbing member and held it in her hand, she thought she would die in an agony of lust for this man if he didn't satisfy her, and soon.

'Quickly,' she begged, but Greg gave the low laugh she so loved.

'Not yet,' he said. 'Have patience.'

He began kissing her again, this time over her

stomach while his hands slid between her legs. Maria gave a long moan and let her fingers trail all over his body. When she felt she really couldn't stand any more, when she was almost crying in despair, Greg entered her and she groaned in ecstasy.

Afterwards, as Maria lay in bed, listening to Greg's easy breathing, she told herself there had not been word written to describe the lovemaking they had enjoyed that night. And that is what it was – lovemaking, not just sex. This was different entirely from the sex she had endured and sometimes enjoyed with Barney. This time, she'd given herself freely and completely to a man whose one desire in life was to please her and not himself. She felt deliciously warmed by his love and almost healed of fear and uncertainty. She was definitely not afraid of the future any more. She kissed Greg gently on the lips, curled herself around him and fell into a deep and blissful sleep.

CHAPTER TWENTY-NINE

Had Maria been able at that moment to look across the Irish Sea to Dublin, she wouldn't have been so complacent. As the anniversary of Barney's death approached, Seamus was furious that he had allowed himself to be fobbed off by what that Sean of a one had said to him about his brother's murder.

He must have been in a state of shock just to have accepted it the way he had. He couldn't just leave it there. As one of the gang said, if it had been his brother, he'd not rest until he would find out who was responsible.

His solicitor had got all the Birmingham newspapers running the story at the time, but Seamus had been too upset even to look at them. But he had packed them carefully when he left prison and now he spread them out in the bedroom of his mate's house where he was staying.

He read everything there was to read about it and then folded the papers and put them away. He knew who had killed his brother and that was Maria. It said in the paper she had been in hospital having a baby, so she had not been able to do the deed herself, but he just knew she had been behind it. She had been the ruination of Barney, from the day that he had been duped into marriage with her, and he was gong to make her pay for killing his brother.

He arrived in Birmingham on Wednesday, 5 January and found lodgings in Erdington. He discovered first where Maria lived and saw Nocks Brickworks, where his brother's body had been found, a little way away. He actually went in there for a look, but he didn't go far, for it was dusk and he could see little. He thought justice would be done properly if he could have killed Maria there.

But, no matter, the important thing was to murder the bitch as she had had his brother murdered. He kept a watch on the house and was further incensed to find that she had another man in her life. Jesus, he thought, she hasn't wasted any time. But then, he thought, maybe he was the reason Barney was killed; maybe Maria had been carrying on with him all along. Then, he thought, Christ, I bet he was the one who beat Barney to death.

Well, neither of them would get away with it. Withdrawing the knife he'd equipped himself with from its sheath, he rans his finger along the blade, but gently for it was razor sharp. They'll both get carved up and that would be just revenge for them both.

He knew he had to bide his time; he wouldn't take on the two of them together, even armed with a knife. There seemed lots of children too and he wanted them well out of the way, or they'd start screaming and could alert people.

*　　*　　*

It was hard to arrange a night out with so many children to see to, but Greg wanted to take Maria out to celebrate their engagement and *South Pacific* was showing at the Alex.

'Look,' said Patsy, when Maria mentioned the problem. 'Mom doesn't mind having all the girls stay with her after dancing, and Andrew and I will come and mind the boys for you. You do deserve a night out.'

'You don't mind?'

'No, of course not. Why should I?'

And so it was arranged.

That Saturday, when Seamus had been in Birmingham for three days, he watched Maria arrive home from Erdington alone. Greg, who had been at work that morning, had stopped at his house for a bath and change of clothes before calling for her in the car.

Maria was so excited and she wanted to get the boys to bed early and take a leisurely bath. The fire had been on all day so the water would be lovely and hot. She had made herself a new dress in dark blue velvet and she was dying to try it on and see what it looked like.

Unfortunately, the two boys were totally uncooperative that night and Maria began to wonder if she would even have time for a bath at all by the time they were settled. Eventually, all was quiet and she glanced at the clock. Less than half an hour till Patsy and Andrew get here, she thought, and Greg will be arriving before that. God, I could have killed those boys tonight, playing me up like that.

All thought of a leisurely bath fled and she knew it would have to be a quick scrub, which was all she usually had time for. She went into the bathroom and turned on the taps. Outside, Seamus watched the house fall silent. He waited ten minutes to be sure and then began moving stealthily. He knew there was a back way in, for he had had a good look around one day after he had seen Maria leave.

Maria had left the gate unbolted and the back door unlocked. Seamus was in the kitchen in minutes and stood listening. He heard the sounds of washing and Maria humming one of the songs from her homeland and he licked his lips malevolently. It must be a bathroom and the stupid cow was having a bath. Better and better, he thought, and he withdrew the knife and moved forward.

'We will be ridiculously early,' Andrew complained, as they neared the house.

'Yes I know,' Patsy said, 'Maria won't mind; she might be pleased. All I know is, on the fairly rare occasions that Sean and Martha went out, Deirdre always played up. It's like they sense it, or something, and if either or both of those boys are giving Maria a hard time then she'll welcome an extra pair of hands.'

They pulled up outside the house and as they had a key, they let themselves in the front door. 'All quiet on the Western Front,' Andrew whispered, his finger to his lips.

'Seems so,' Patsy agreed, and then they heard the scream, the sort of scream that turns the blood in the veins to iced water. They both sprang towards the sound.

Maria had been transfixed by terror when she saw Seamus with the knife paused to strike. However, that scream was the only sound she was able to make, for now he had her head back held fast by her hair, her throat exposed as he told her that he was going to slit it from ear to ear and watch her life blood drain away into the bathwater.

And then Andrew, followed by Patsy was in the door. Seamus took one look at them both and with a violent shove that sent Andrew falling backwards into the water, he was off. Andrew struggled out and went after the man. Patsy had her hands full with Maria, who was gibbering and yelping with terror, her whole body trembling and twitching. Patsy put her arms around her, helping her from the bath and covering her with a towel.

Greg was just about to ring the doorbell when the door opened and the man stood before him. 'Stop him!' Andrew cried, and automatically, Greg put his arm out. He had not see the knife but felt it power into his stomach. He gave a gasp, sank to his knees and crumpled unconscious to the floor.

Andrew hesitated when he saw what had happened to Greg, but he knew he had to catch this madman before he struck again. Maria, coming in that moment, supported by Patsy, seeing Greg lying still on the floor, gave a cry and flung herself on top of him.

'Call an ambulance and the police,' Andrew said to Patsy. 'I'm off after the bastard.'

'Leave it to the police, Andrew. The man has a knife,' Patsy pleaded, trying to lift Maria from Greg as she began to keen and rock backwards and forwards in distress, seemingly unaware that the towel had fallen from her and that she was totally naked. But Andrew was gone out into the night.

'What's wrong with me, Patsy?' Maria cried. 'I must be jinxed and if I have lost this man for the second time, I will not want to live, for the pain will be too great.'

Patsy laid her head on Greg's chest and when she heard the steady beat of the heart she nearly sobbed with relief, though she was worried by the crimson stain that had spread over his coat and begun to drip on to the floor. 'He's alive, Maria. Greg's alive,' she told her.

Alive! It barely penetrated her brain and Patsy went on, almost brutally, for she could see her cousin was in deep shock, 'If we want him to stay that way, we need to phone for an ambulance. Have any of your neighbours got the phone in?'

'Next door,' Maria said, jerking her thumb. But first Patsy went to the bathroom and fetched Maria's clothes, which she had laid ready.

'Get dressed!' she told her. 'You're shivering like a bloody leaf.' As she stepped over Greg's inert figure to reach the door, she heard the children, alerted by the noise, begin to grumble upstairs.

For a minute or two Andrew was undecided what to do, for he didn't know where the man had gone. The night was as dark as pitch, except for the pools of light from the streetlamps. Suddenly, at the turn in the road, he saw a flash of the man in one of those pools and he was off after him.

Seamus was making for the brickworks, certain he could find somewhere there to hide away. He didn't fancy tackling Andrew and he knew the darkness would make finding him nigh impossible.

Andrew hesitated when he got to the fence, not sure whether to follow the man in there or not. Though he had no idea who the man was, he had the idea he was more used to dark, sinister places than he was himself, and he knew he would be in further danger, following him in there.

Maybe it would be better to wait for the police at the entrance. But then, Patsy wouldn't know where to direct the police and there was probably another way out of the quarry that he might know of. He was a madman of the first order certainly, and a very dangerous one. He needed to be apprehended and quickly. He pulled the buckled fencing aside and stepped over it to the frozen and muddy debris-ridden ground beyond.

A man in Holly Lane, just setting out for a pint, saw the furtive man run up the road and caught the glint of a knife in his hand as he passed under the street-light, before he disappeared down the side of the brick-works with another man behind in hot pursuit. He went back into his house, very glad they had had the phone installed.

'Something's up,' he told his wife. 'And I think we should phone the police.'

A police car followed the ambulance into Westmead Crescent. Maria was more concerned with Greg and the ambulance men trying to staunch the blood before they took him away, but the police needed details about the attack. She didn't want to talk in front of the children either, particularly Jack, who was already distressed enough. While Patsy had been next door phoning, Maria had been struggling into her clothes so that she could go with Greg to the hospital. Jack had got fed up shouting and nobody coming, so he'd climbed out of his bed and went downstairs He saw Greg lying bleeding on the floor and screamed. 'What's happened?' he said, eyes like saucers standing out in his head.

'He's had an accident.'

'What sort of accident? He's bleeding everywhere.'

'I know. The ambulance is on its way,' Maria said, very glad to see Patsy and the neighbour coming in the door. Patsy first bounded up the stairs to rescue a frightened and also very angry baby, whose wails had reached a tremendous level when his brother too had left the room, and she came down with Martin in her arms.

'I can say nothing in front of the children,' she told the officer firmly. 'Surely you can see that.'

'They can come home with me,' the neighbour said, lifting Martin from Patsy's arms. 'What do you say to chocolate biscuits and cocoa?'

Jack's eyes widened. They didn't often have chocolate biscuits – chocolate anything for that matter – and he would be glad to be away from that room where there were strange people with serious faces and Greg lying bleeding. He took the hand the neighbour offered him as he said, 'Can I have two biscuits?'

'Yes, if you are a good boy,' the neighbour answered and as Jack was led down the path through the open door, they all heard him say, 'If I am very, very good, can I have three?

'Now,' the policeman said, notebook at the ready. 'Can you tell me anything about the attacker? Description, anything distinctive?'

'I can do better than that, officer, I can show you a photograph of him from my wedding day,' Maria said wearily. 'It is from years ago, but in the brief glimpse I had of him he has hardly changed. A more up-to-date photograph I should imagine would be given by Mountjoy Prison in Dublin. He was resident there till last year. He is my brother-in-law and his name is Seamus McPhearson.'

Both the policeman and Patsy were astounded by what Maria said, but before they could speak, another policeman was at the door.

'Call on the blower, sir,' the young constable said. 'Two men acting suspiciously, one with a knife, have been seen entering the Nocks Brickworks site.'

'Two men?' the officer queried.

'One of those will probably be my husband,' Patsy said. 'He took off after the attacker.'

'That, madam, was a very foolish thing to do.'

'I did try to tell him that,' Patsy said. 'I couldn't physically stop him and I did have my hands full, as it were.'

'Right,' the officer said. 'We'll send in the dogs and large flashlights and flush him out. Set it up, will you, and stress that it is urgent?'

'Right, sir,' the younger policeman said, and went out to the car to radio in.

The ambulance men had done all they could for Greg and were preparing to leave. 'Your questions must wait now,' Maria told the police. 'I am going to the hospital with my fiancé.'

'I can give you a lot of the details and we were on the scene within minutes.' Patsy said. 'And now I know who the man was, I know a lot of the background too, though I have never set eyes on him before.'

As Patsy was answering the policeman's questions, and Maria was holding Greg's hand as the ambulance sped through the night to the Accident Hospital, Andrew was feeling it had been a bad mistake to follow the man into this black and dismal hole. He hadn't a hope in hell of finding anyone in this place, but the man might just see him first and he had a knife. What a bloody fool he had been.

Every nerve ending was twitching as he moved cautiously forwards, and it was hard on that junk-filled ground to be as quiet as he would have liked. Though he stopped often to listen, he couldn't hear another sound except the odd drone of a car driving down Holly Lane.

He should go back, call the police and let them deal with it. But where was back? He was totally disorientated by such blackness and realised he might easily have wandered around in circles and would never find the way out till there was more light. It was a worrying thought. He wouldn't give much for his chances if he had to spend a night there. As it was, he was shivering like a leaf and his teeth were chattering, for the bath water had soaked through all his clothes to his skin.

Seamus was, in fact, not far from him, effectively hidden by the darkness, wondering if he should just slip past Andrew and go back to his digs. He could be packed and on the boat home in the morning. Pity he hadn't been able to mark that conniving bitch, but still, he did for the man who had killed his brother.

He sat and waited for Andrew to go further in and the minutes ticked by, but Seamus was used to waiting quietly in the dark. He was almost ready to make a dash for it when he heard the police siren and decided to wait until it had passed. But the police car didn't pass. Instead, it pulled up by the fence. This was followed by another one and a police van. Suddenly powerful searchlights were playing over everything.

Andrew saw the man almost beside him with the incriminating and bloodied knife still in his hand. 'There he is!'

He was spotlit in the powerful beam and he looked scared to death. Dogs were the only thing that Seamus was afraid of and he could hear them the growling and snarling, desperate to be off their leashes.

He threw the knife from him, then took off towards the quarry, running, stumbling and staggering, over the littered ground and tripping and lurching over tussocks of grass, hidden by the darkness.

'Look out!' Andrew called. The police also called out a warning, but Seamus was past hearing anything anyone might say. He knew the dogs were free, for behind him he could hear their baying, and the search-light was keeping him in view so that the dogs could locate him. He would never outrun them.

He was in a panic, dreading to feel the dogs' hot breath on his neck, their teeth around his arm or leg, dragging him to the floor. He ran faster still. He didn't know the deep pit was there, but even when the policeman called out another warning he was too fearful to hear it.

Andrew saw it in the beam of the flashlight, and

then, with a horrendous and terrifying scream, the man disappeared.

Patsy and Andrew found Maria sitting in a corridor at the Accident Hospital, crying. With a dread feeling in her heart, Patsy ran forward and Maria turned at the sound. She was buried in a sorrow so deep, little could touch her.

'Maria,' Patsy cried. 'What is it? Is Greg . . . ?'

'They think that Greg will live this time,' Maria said. 'But that hardly matters for I cannot marry him, I know that now. We must part.'

'What nonsense is this, Maria?'

'Not nonsense, Patsy,' Maria said, grasping her hand. 'You must understand that man came for me tonight. He had no argument with Greg – he got it because of me – and he won't give up ever. He will hurt everyone associated with me.'

'The man's dead,' Andrew said, but his words didn't register with Maria.

She said, 'How could I live with myself if Greg was to be killed outright next time and what if Seamus was to harm his children?'

Patsy sat beside Maria and took hold of both her hands. 'Listen to me, dear, dear Maria,' she said. 'Seamus McPhearson will never terrorise you or anyone else again. The man is dead.'

'Dead!' Maria repeated. 'Really and truly dead? You have seen the dead body?'

'Not quite.'

'Then I don't believe it.'

'Maria, listen, please,' Andrew pleaded. 'The police

caught up with him in the brickworks. I was there too and saw it all. When they released the dogs he took off. He didn't know about the quarry and by the time he saw it, it was too late. If the fall didn't kill him then the quicksand did, for by the time the police got down there, there was no trace of him. They say he will probably never be found.

'Don't you see what this means?' Patsy said, giving Maria's arm a little shake. 'You are free of the McPhearsons for ever.'

'You don't know how good that sounds.'

'I can guess,' Patsy said with a smile.

'And you can become Mrs Hopkins as soon as Greg is well enough.'

'Yes,' Maria said. She felt as if she was floating on air, truly free now. Despite Sean telling her he had advised Seamus not to dig too deep to find Barney's killer, and that he'd seemed to accept it, she knew Seamus didn't work that way. While he had lived she had always thought there was unfinished business between them, now it was at an end. She couldn't even feel sorry that his death had been such a brutal one, for had Patsy and Andrew been a minute later she would be dead now, and he wouldn't have lost a minute's sleep over it either.

'Come on,' she said suddenly. 'I need to see the children, reassure them, and I cannot see Greg again until tomorrow.'

'They will be glad to see you,' Patsy said. 'Mom was having a bit of a time with them all when we left.'

'Lead on, then,' Maria said. She left the hospital filled with elation.

* * *

The next afternoon, when Maria saw Greg lying back in the stark hospital bed, his face as white as the pillow he lay against, one arm attached to monitors of some kind, she felt tears prickle her eyes. And then he turned and saw her in the doorway, and his smile lit up his entire face. 'God, how I have longed to see you,' he said. 'Don't be crying. Come and sit the other side where I can put my arm around you and tell you how much you mean to me.'

'Oh, Greg,' Maria cried. 'I am so pleased to see you looking so well. I really thought he had killed you.'

'Can't keep a good man down,' Greg said with a grin.

'Do you know who it was attacked you?' Maria asked.

'Yeah, the police were in this morning and told me. I never knew Barney's brother really, he being so much older, and then my dad always told me to steer clear of him because, he had been told, he was a bit of a bad lot.' He winced suddenly and went on, 'I have evidence of my own on that score now, of course.'

'Well, the man's dead and gone now, and can never hurt me or anyone belonging to me ever again.'

'So, we can get on with arranging our marriage. No need for us to hang about, Easter is a nice time of the year.'

'But, Greg, I'll hardly have the dress and bridesmaid outfits ready for then.'

'Oh,' Greg said with a wry smile, 'shall we postpone it for a year or two then?'

'You dare,' Maria said in mock severity. 'If I have to work till midnight every night I will be ready for

Easter, never fear. But one thing I insist on and that is to tell your parents about our marriage. They were always good to me.'

Greg's face was like a mask, something she had never seen before, and he said, 'How do you explain to my two daughters that my parents couldn't stand their mother?'

'Greg,' Maria protested, 'do you think I would ever do such a thing? I'll not let them know it had anything to do with Nancy. Trust me in this.'

Greg's face relaxed. 'Of course I trust you,' he said, 'and you must do as you see fit.'

On Greg's insistence, Maria moved into his house, for, with his girls, they would be too squashed in their own. That evening, with Martin in bed, Maria told the children about the wedding in April.

'There are lots of people to invite to a wedding and some of them you may never have seen before. I mean, Anna and Shirley, did you know that you have grandparents in Moville?'

'No,' Anna said.

'Why haven't we seen them before?' Shirley asked.

'They had some silly fight with your daddy and probably said things they regretted later – you know how it is when you are angry. We've all done that, haven't we?'

'Yeah,' Anna said, 'but we make it up later.'

'And probably they would have, too, but the war got in the way and your daddy had to go away and fight. The row might have been about him joining up. He didn't have to because Ireland wasn't in the last war.'

'Doesn't he know what it was about?'

'No. After all these years he can't remember how it began, but he says it was probably over something silly,' Maria told them 'But because he wasn't able to go and sort it out, it grew and grew in importance and neither side wanted to back down.'

Both girls nodded solemnly. They could see how that could be.

'Anyway, this is a new start for us all and your daddy thinks it is time to try and make amends, and he has asked me to invite them to the wedding.'

'Have we got grandparents we can invite?' Jack asked.

'No, Jack.'

'Why not?'

'That's just how it is,' Maria said.

'It's not fair,'

'Jack!'

'Never mind,' Shirley said. 'When your mom marries our dad, we'll all be brothers and sisters and so you will be able to share our grandparents.'

'All of us?'

'Course.'

'Oh, that is all right then,' Jack said. Maria smiled to herself. Jack could be an aggravating child at times. But at others, he could lighten the tone as he had then. She had wondered if Nancy had ever let slip to her daughters, Anna especially, that Greg's parents had resented her, but she couldn't have done that, for Anna's surprise that she had grandparents in Ireland had been genuine.

That night Maria composed a very careful letter to Greg's parents and hoped that the breach between them might be healed.

Greg was in hospital a fortnight and so he was still there when the reply came from his parents. Maria guessed who it was from. She noted the Moville postmark, yet didn't recognise the handwriting and so, though it was addressed to her, she took it to the hospital that afternoon unopened.

Greg was ridiculously nervous about opening it, but he needn't have worried. His mother wrote that many times she and Greg's father had regretted the angry and unforgiving words said when they were both in a state of shock. They had often wished them unsaid and didn't know how to heal the breach, for they had no address once Greg had left the training camp, and after the war no idea at all where he had gone.

They went on to say that they deplored the years spent apart, would not miss his wedding for a fortune, and were looking forward to meeting his daughters.

'How stiff-necked I have been,' Greg said, as he folded up the letter. Maria noticed with compassion and sympathy that his eyes were glitteringly bright. 'I should have written to them, apologised, because I did hurt and disappoint them, especially my mother, very much.'

'You weren't to know how they might be feeling.'

'It wouldn't have taken much to find out.' Greg said. 'Nancy wanted me to do that too, you know. She said people say things in the heat of the moment that they don't mean and for the girls' sakes now and again she would ask me to contact them. I wish I had. I feel they have missed out as well as the girls.'

'Don't worry about your parents missing out,' Maria said with a laugh. 'They might just get more than they are bargaining for.'

'How come?'

'Well, according to Jack, it isn't fair that your children have got secret grandparents just come to light and he hasn't. Your Shirley told him that when we are married and all one family, they will be his grandparents as well. And I will say if anyone can break any stiffness that might be there in the first few meetings with your parents, it will be my first-born son.'

'I couldn't agree more,' said Greg with a smile. He kissed her on the lips, but gently because of the delicate state of his ribs. 'Oh God,' he said, 'I can't wait to be out of here and back home with you.'

'I feel the same,' Maria said. 'It's less of a home without you in it. The children are missing you quite dreadfully – and not just yours either.'

'Let's have less of my children and yours, Mrs Hopkins-to-be,' he said in mock severity. 'Soon they will just be ours. I hope you understand that.'

'Certainly I do, Mr Hopkins,' Maria said with a grin. 'Ooh, and I love it when you are being masterful.'

'You wait until I leave this place,' Greg said with a licentious leer, 'and you will soon see how masterful I can be.'

He kissed her again gently and Maria felt her innards tighten in delicious anticipation of her future together with this man that she loved so very much.

There was hardly a dry eye in the abbey on 16 April. Maria, in a gown of apricot satin, was attended by five beautiful bridesmaids in dresses of pale blue, and Patsy in a costume to match Maria, as maid of honour. 'To keep us all in order,' Sally said knowledgeably.

Jack had refused point-blank to be a pageboy. Eight months on from Patsy's wedding, he declared it a babyish thing to do. Greg said he shouldn't be forced and had taken him out and bought him a new suit of clothes, a shirt and the shiniest black shoes imaginable. He looked as smart as paint, and Martin, in a sailor suit, was just adorable.

But just as important as the clothes were the people who had come to wish the couple well: Joanne from Derry, and Dora and Bella, brought all the way in Ned Richards' car. According to their letters, Ned was turning Moville around, and people said it was lovely to see the boats bobbing about in Greencastle Harbour again. Just as important were Greg's parents and two sisters, the rift between them and Greg healed at last. Greg's parents, desperate to get to know their granddaughters, were all staying in Greg's house for a few days to give Martha and Sean a hand with the children, as Greg was taking Maria away for a week's honeymoon.

Maria would have been happy with a caravan in Wales, for she had been nowhere, but Greg had pooh-poohed that idea. 'I thought the South of France,' he said. 'In fact, I have already booked the hotel.'

Maria had given a squeal of delight and thrown her arms around the man's neck. 'Oh, Greg, what can I say?'

'The only words I want to hear, Maria, are that you love me and will continue to love me till the breath leaves your body.'

'That is such an easy promise to make,' Maria said, 'except that I think I will love you more with every passing year.'

'And I you, you darling desirable, beautiful woman,' Greg said. When their lips met, Maria's moan was one of pure, unadulterated desire.

She thought of this, walking down the aisle on Sean's arm, Patsy and the children falling in behind her. As she drew close to the altar, Greg turned to look at her with such love mirrored on his face that she felt her own heart stop beating for a moment or two. Sean relinquished her arm and she gave her bouquet to Patsy and stood beside her beloved for the priest to bind them together until death should part them. She knew she loved Greg as she had never loved any other and never would love any other, and she also knew that their love would never fade, but just grow stronger.